LEGACY OF LEATHER AND LACE

Hell's Handlers MC 2nd Generation
Book 1

Lilly Atlas

ISBN: 978-1-946068-58-3

To Sam.

One decade down on this insane writing journey. Thank you for supporting, encouraging, and helping me every step of the way. <3

Beth grew up in the morally gray world of the Hell's Handlers Motorcycle Club. Daughter of a legacy, surrounded by overprotective alpha bikers and fierce women who never backed down, she's spent her whole life trying to prove she's more than an MC princess. Smart, stubborn, and desperate to carve out her own identity, she left home determined to stand on her own. But independence comes at a price, and by the time she admits needing her family isn't weakness, she's trapped in a nightmare relationship that shatters her confidence and breaks something deep inside.

Saint knows what true darkness looks like. Raised in a militant cult, he learned early how to protect the vulnerable and fight with everything he has for the people he loves. As the second oldest of many siblings, responsibility is etched into his bones. So when he finds Beth in danger, he doesn't hesitate; he pulls her out and becomes the one steady place in her crumbling world. And somewhere between watching over her and trying to keep his distance, the attraction he swore he'd never feel ignites.

She's younger. She's his president's daughter. She already left the club once.
Wanting her isn't just reckless, it's dangerous.

As one of her father's men, Saint is off-limits. Crossing that line could cost him everything, including the family he's chosen. Beth refuses to be the reason Saint loses the brotherhood that saved him. But some connections are too strong to deny, and some temptations refuse to be ignored.

When enemies surface with Beth in their crosshairs, the biker who promised to stay away becomes the only man capable of burning the world down to keep her safe. And Beth, tired of being protected, tired of being told who she can be and who she can love, finally chooses her own life and her own man.

Table of Contents

Prologue

Beth stared at the face in the mirror—the barely recognizable face with desolate eyes, wet with tears, and six raised welts in the shape of a man's palm and fingers.

The skin burned, with heat spreading out from the handprint like a brand. Her throat felt too tight to draw in air, and her chest too small to hold it. A tear slid off her jaw and hit the porcelain sink, then another, and she watched it like she was witnessing someone else fall apart. Someone else trying to process their bruised face and crumbling emotions.

Shame hit her hard as it always did, rushing over her in a wave of embarrassment that heated her skin to unbearable levels and made her want to disappear off the face of the planet. If she could crawl out of her own body and into someone else's, she would.

She could still see sixteen-year-old Beth rolling her eyes so hard they nearly got stuck, arms crossed over her chest as Maverick and Zach flanked a nervous boy named Tyler on her parents' front porch. Tyler had come to pick her up for a movie, just a movie, and they'd made him stand there for ten whole minutes answering questions about his grades, his car's safety rating, and whether he understood that Beth had approximately forty uncles who owned shovels and knew how to dig holes. She'd called them ridiculous. Dramatic. Embarrassing. She'd told her dad if they kept this up, they were going to scare off every guy in town, and Copper had just smiled and said, "Good."

That Beth, the one who'd stomped her foot and told Maverick he was being a psycho, felt like a stranger now. A girl from a movie she'd watched once and barely remembered. That Beth had no idea how lucky she was to have men who cared enough to be psychos, and who would never in a million years leave a handprint on a woman's face.

All she wanted was to crawl, maybe sprint, back into their comforting embraces. To let her big, crazy, outlaw family wrap her up, shield her from her mistakes, and erase the last year like it was nothing more than a bad dream.

But she lived in reality.

Going home meant admitting something she was too ashamed to acknowledge, even to herself, for more than a few seconds at a time. Saying the words out loud would make this real, and she was barely holding it together as it was.

Some nights, the humiliation of her situation was so thick she choked on it as she lay there rigid and silent, listening for every change in Jason's breathing, every hitch in his snore that might mean he was waking up. The sour smell of beer on his breath drifted across the pillow, mixing with the Irish Spring soap he used every night in the shower. She used to love that scent, but now it made her stomach turn. Now it meant danger.

She'd huddle into the fetal position as close to the edge of the bed as possible without falling off, her shoulder aching, her hip going numb against the mattress. She never rolled over, never adjusted, no matter how badly her body screamed for relief. Movement might brush against him. Movement might wake him.

Hitting the floor would wake him.

Jason didn't like to be woken in the middle of the night.

She'd made that mistake exactly one time. Her ribs still ached when she thought too hard about it.

Worse than failing the men who'd shown her exactly what a good man should be was the way she'd let down the women. If the guys had been incredible, the women she'd spent her childhood worshiping had been perfect, and they were still perfect. Each one had overcome tremendous odds and found happiness with the MC and in their relationships, including her mother.

Her mom, Shell, was the most incredible woman Beth had ever met, no exaggeration.

When her mom was only a teenager, a man named Rusty raped her, resulting in her pregnancy with Beth. As if that wasn't traumatic enough, Rusty, may he rot in hell, had been Copper's brother. Copper, the man Shell had loved since before she knew what romantic love was. Her mom had spent years suffering in silence with a deep, unrequited love for a man she'd feared would never love her back if he discovered the truth.

Luckily, she'd been wrong. Copper was the best man *ever* to walk the planet. He fell hard for both Shell and Beth, marrying her mother and becoming the best father a girl could have asked for. Another person Beth had taken for granted. He was her father in every way that mattered. Beth couldn't say her parents' journey to each other had been an easy road, but they'd made it and had been joined at the hip for more than fifteen years. Never once, not even for a second, had Copper treated Beth as anything other than his daughter, full stop.

Throughout her life, Beth had witnessed not only healthy, enviable relationships but also people who maintained their individuality while being part of a tremendously close pairing. Everyone she'd grown up with was complete 'couple goals.'

Why on earth had she turned her back and walked away from it all as though better existed somewhere in the world and she could find it? Was it young, dumb hubris, or did she have something fundamentally wrong inside her?

She wasn't happy with her life and hadn't been for a long time. The realization sat heavy in her chest, like a stone she couldn't cough up.

"Yo, B, where the fuck's the beer I bought last night?"

Right in the fridge, where you watched me put it yesterday, you piece of shit.

Her shoulders slumped, and her skin paled in the mirror. Even expecting it, the sound of his voice still made her muscles clench, and her hands tremble. She gripped the edge of the sink to still them. As much as she might want to, she'd never sass Jason out loud. Not unless she wanted a night of screaming, berating, and possibly another handprint on her cheek. Though when he hit her, the fighting typically ended. A few times, she'd been tempted to goad him into getting physical to stop the screaming.

Wow, that's the saddest thought you've ever had.

This was what her life had become.

She'd need a mountain of therapy to undo the twisted mess this relationship had caused to her psyche. Of course, she'd have to attend therapy first, and that meant admitting out loud that she had a serious problem. That she was the kind of woman who stayed.

For the past week, a statistic she'd stumbled across in some magazine at the dentist's office had been eating her alive. On average, women went back to their abusers seven times before finally leaving for good.

Seven times.

She'd done the math on herself more times than she could

count. Had she already 'left' when she'd slept at Megan's for three days after Jason shoved her into the wall? Did it count as leaving if she'd only thought about it, *really, seriously thought about it,* while he was at work? How many of her seven had she already used up?

And what kind of person needed seven tries to save her own life?

Yet there she stood, rubbing the tears away and rushing out of the bathroom to appease a man who didn't act like he gave a shit about her. A man who'd humiliated her, fucked with her mind, and hit her more than once.

"They're in the refrigerator. I'll grab one for you, Jase," she called, forcing brightness into her voice as she hustled into the kitchen and found him standing in front of the open refrigerator, scowling.

"Right here." She slipped under his thick arm and grabbed a bottle of his favorite beer from the top shelf of the refrigerator. How he couldn't find anything would always remain a mystery, but one she'd never asked him to solve. Asking why, even about something small, could be the wrong move on the wrong day.

Back at home, she could and would have teased the hell out of her dad's MC brothers if they'd been unable to find something practically staring them in the face, which, to be fair, would probably happen. The difference was that they'd shrug off her teasing and join her in laughing. Those guys had always been able to laugh at themselves. It was a quality she'd never fully appreciated until Jason.

Around the club members, she didn't have to measure her words or tiptoe around a volatile temper. She didn't have to catalog tone, expression, and the number of beers someone consumed and run it through some twisted internal safety calculator before she opened her mouth. And if they ever saw her acting like a timid mouse around a boyfriend, well, the boyfriend wouldn't be breathing for long, and that wasn't a hyperbole.

"Don't fucking hide my shit next time," he grumbled as he snatched the bottle from her hand.

Or, you know… you could open your damn eyes.

She clamped down on her tongue as she nodded. Her throat ached from all the words she swallowed each day.

Jase twisted off the top, then took a long drink that had more than half the bottle disappearing. Looked like tonight would be a multi-drink night, and her nerves fluttered. Drunk Jason could go either way, sleepy and lazy or mean and destructive.

"Grant and Benny are on their way over. We're gonna play some GTA. I'm hungry. Make us some of those spicy cheese fuckers we like."

"Jalapeño poppers?" she asked, even though she knew exactly what he meant.

He snapped and pointed at her with a grin she used to find sexy. "That's it."

Oh, of course. Let me drop everything and deep-fry appetizers for you and your mouth-breathing buddies while you shoot hookers in a video game. Would you like me to fan you with a palm leaf while I'm at it? Rub your feet? Maybe I should crawl on all fours and bark on command.

"Sure." The word tasted like ash. Hopefully, she had all the ingredients, so she wouldn't have to run to the store and make him wait for his snack.

He didn't like to wait.

He didn't like *so many things.*

He really was a good-looking guy, with deep blue eyes, light brown hair, and a muscular physique that women drooled over. On his most recent barber trip, he'd cut his hair shorter than she preferred. Jase liked his hair buzzed, whereas it had been longer when they'd met. Back then, in the beginning of their relationship, she'd loved running her fingers through the soft strands. Back when, for a short time, he'd made her feel special and safe. When he'd told her she was pretty, intelligent, and precisely what he wanted in a girlfriend.

How stupid she'd been to fall for his lip service.

As she turned to preheat the oven, Jase caught her arm and spun her back to face him with a rough tug. Her pulse spiked. The movement was so fast her brain didn't have time to catch up.

"Everything okay?" she asked, staring up at him. He had eight inches on the five-foot-three stature she'd inherited from her mom. For one second, she thought she might get a kind word. A thank you for retrieving the beer and cooking for his dickhead friends. Maybe it was nice to know she wasn't so completely jaded that she automatically expected something hateful to fall from his lips, but thinking positively only made the reality of his cutting comments sting more.

"Cover that shit up."

She blinked. "What?"

He huffed and rolled his eyes, giving her a none-too-gentle shake. "Your face. Go put some goddamn makeup on. Fuck's sake, Beth, you tryna make me look bad in front of my friends?"

Her stomach soured as her hand went to her cheek, fingers brushing the tender spot his palm had already found once today. "What? N-no, of course not. I didn't have anywhere to go today, so I didn't bother with makeup. And I had no idea the guys were coming over. I'm s-sorry."

She'd forever hate the way her voice wavered. She used to be the girl who flipped off Gator when he teased her about a bad haircut and told him his beard looked like a ferret had died on his face. The girl who'd once called Screw an 'overprotective Neanderthal' to his face and made everyone at the table laugh, including him.

Where had that girl gone?

Jason shoved her away with a grunt of disgust. "Well, get moving. They'll be here soon, and I'm fucking hungry."

As she skittered past him, he cracked her on the ass with an open palm. It hurt, and she bit her lip to keep from yelping, though she couldn't hide the way her body reacted. Her muscles automatically tensed for another hit.

This wasn't a playful light ass smack or a lead-in to a consensual sexy spanking, but a warning.

Stay in line tonight or else.

She gritted her teeth and forced herself not to snap at him. He wouldn't appreciate it if she fired back or flipped him off like she wanted.

And there it was.

She'd become conditioned to act and react as *he* wanted. Trained, like one of the dogs she groomed at work.

And she *hated* it.

She *hated* him.

She *hated* living like this.

She *hated* herself.

But most of all, she *hated* that she'd walked away from something good because she'd been too young and stupid to recognize it. She'd had everything, including love, safety, people who would die for her, and she'd thrown it away like it wasn't enough. Like she deserved better. Like better even existed.

And look what she'd found instead.

The average woman went back to her abuser seven times before leaving.

Seven times.

She could break the cycle. She could come in below the average. She could tell him to fuck off and walk out of the apartment forever. She could make everyone she knew proud and dig into the strength she'd always thought she possessed.

She could…

Go *home*.

For one second, she let herself imagine it. Her hand on the front door. The click of the lock. The night air on her face as she walked to her car in her pajamas with nothing but her keys and her phone. Driving until Jason was a speck in her rearview mirror. Driving until she couldn't smell Irish Spring anymore.

So why did she walk back into the bathroom and retrieve her makeup bag?

Why did she feel paralyzed by her own life?

Why, with her heart pounding and palms sweating, did staying feel easier than leaving?

Maybe because leaving meant admitting she'd failed. Maybe because starting over felt like climbing a mountain with broken legs. Maybe because some sick, twisted part of her still hoped tomorrow would be different, and that the Jason she'd fallen for would come back, and this version would disappear like a bad dream.

Or maybe she was just tired.

So goddamn tired.

Chapter One

"So, did y'all fuck?"

Saint tore his gaze from the prospect polishing chrome on his motorcycle and found Gator plopping his wild ass on the opposite bench of the picnic table outside their clubhouse.

The crazy fucker had his signature red bandana tied around his head like a headband. Dirty blond hair in desperate need of a trim poked out in every direction above and below the fabric, like he'd lost a fight with a leaf blower. Sticking with his classic style, he wore a white beater under his cut and the ridiculous cut-off jean shorts they'd teased him about since he'd prospected three years ago. Gator loved nothing more than showing off the missing chunk of his thigh and the jagged scar left by a hungry alligator on his family's Florida wildlife farm.

He propped his scarred leg up on the bench like it was a trophy. "You got that post-sex glow, brother. I can see it from here. Shoulda worn my damn sunglasses."

Crazy fucker.

Saint raised an eyebrow at his smirking brother, who threw his head back and laughed his loud, infectious laugh that always got at least one other person chuckling, whether they wanted to or not.

"Oh yeah, you fucked her," Gator declared, pointing at Saint with the neck of his beer.

Saint had not, in fact, fucked her or anyone last night. "She was a sorority girl wearing a pink skirt made of fucking sparkly feathers."

Still snickering, Gator shook his head. "And? You don't like the skirt, you rip it off before you fuck her. Problem solved. The feathers float away, and you concentrate on the important shit like getting your dick wet."

Her skirt had been the least of Saint's issues. Sure, she'd been hot and obviously down to fuck, but she'd been as high maintenance as they came, wearing shoes that cost over eight hundred dollars according to her equally prissy friend. She'd pouted when she found out they didn't have chilled champagne stocked behind the bar at the clubhouse or any champagne, for that matter. His dick didn't get hard for prissy anymore. When he'd been younger and less discriminating, he wouldn't turn down a fuck from any pussy, no matter how high maintenance, but he'd learned to be a little choosy in his early thirties. Prissy women tended to be stage-five clingers who never left and cleaned out his wallet.

"Sorority girls aren't my type," he said.

Gator's face screwed up in exaggerated confusion. "She got a pussy?"

Saint shrugged. "Assume so. Didn't ask. Was too blinded by the glitter."

Gator slapped the table. "Brother, you don't ask the pussy questions, you just appreciate it."

Rev, the newest prospect, finished polishing Saint's bike and moved on to the next and most important. At fifty-something, Copper was as formidable an MC president as he'd always been. The man's Harley was a beast, all gleaming chrome and matte black, and every brother knew better than to breathe too hard near it.

"Careful with that one," Gator called to the skinny kid. "Fuck it up, and Prez will shove the whole bike up yer ass."

The prospect's eyes widened, and he froze an inch away from touching Copper's bike with a microfiber cloth. "Really?"

That set Gator off in a fit of laughter. "You'll see. As they say, fuck around and find out, little buddy."

The poor kid's face turned a sickly shade of green. Saint could have jumped in and rescued him, but he kept his mouth shut. Prospects got hazed, that's just how the game was played. Many prospects had been tortured before Rev and lived to tell the tale, including him and Gator. Some of those prospects had been fantastic, and some had been absolute shit, but Copper had yet to shove his bike up someone's ass despite threatening them all.

"Not seeing the problem here, brother," Gator said, turning back to Saint. "She has a pussy, she should be your type."

"Sorry, I've got standards, man."

Grunting, Gator shook his head. "All standards will get you is blue balls and a tired right hand."

Maybe. But they'd also keep Saint from ending up with a girlfriend he didn't want who demanded he buy her next feather skirt. "And having none will get you burning piss."

"Eh, nothing a little pill won't fix right up." Gator winked.

"Classy."

"That's me, baby. All class." He swallowed a mouthful of beer, then belched so loud the prospect glanced over again. "The ladies love it."

Saint snorted. "Sure, they do. Nothing gets the panties wet like acid reflux and a diseased dick."

Before Gator could issue another snarky comeback, the clubhouse door swung open, and Copper and Thunder,

Saint's brother-in-law, strode out carrying a bucket with ice and a bunch of frosty beers.

The easy chatter dipped for half a second. Nothing obvious, nothing stiff, but the subtle shift always happened when their president stepped up to his men—respect without fear, loyalty without question.

"Hey, boys, mind if we crash your party?" Copper asked as he lifted the bucket. "We brought gifts."

As if they could or would say no to their president.

Saint didn't have a death wish. "Of course," he said, sliding over to make room for Thunder.

Copper settled his giant body next to Gator, making the bench groan under his substantial weight. Even nearing sixty, the man was muscular as hell, all thick shoulders and corded forearms covered in ink. He carried his power with ease, like he'd been born wearing the patch and running the circus.

Gator scooted a fraction of an inch away. "Careful, Prez. This bench collapses, I'm blaming your old ass, not mine."

Copper snorted. "You blame me, you better be ready to run laps around the clubhouse until those chicken legs fall off."

"Joke's on you," Gator said, lifting his scarred thigh. "One's already halfway gone."

Thunder chuckled as he sat, reaching immediately for a frosty beer. Copper set the bucket in the middle of the table. "Help yourself, gentlemen."

Saint grabbed his first of the day while Gator went in for a refill, humming some off-key country song as he fished around in the ice.

"Fuck," Thunder said after drinking a long pull from his beer. "Been a day."

"You ain't shittin'," Copper said as he popped the top off his bottle.

Saint recognized the tone and casual words, but the muscle in Copper's jaw flexed. The past few years had been smooth sailing as far as rivalries or problems with other clubs. The Hell's Handlers owned the Smoky Mountains, and anyone who was anyone knew it. Other clubs respected them and didn't fuck around in their area.

Until recently.

Over the last three weeks, they'd spotted bikers in cuts no one recognized riding around town, setting off alarm bells in their president's head. Saint didn't like it. This was his family, and the idea of anyone fucking with them brought out his murderous side.

He'd grown up protecting his siblings at all costs, taking the belt when his little brother was too exhausted to keep up in the fields, drawing the elders' attention to himself so it didn't land on the younger ones. Makenna claimed his protective streak for those he loved was a trauma response or some shit like that. Good for her for getting all healed in therapy, but he was fine, living his life, ready to fuck up anyone who side-eyed his family. The philosophy served him well as he worked with Zach and one day hoped to take on the role of club enforcer.

"Think they're gonna be a problem?" he asked.

Thunder grunted. "Too early to tell."

"But you don't like it?" Saint pushed.

"I don't fucking like it," Copper agreed. The quiet certainty in his voice held more weight than a shout ever would.

Copper understood the need to keep his family safe at all costs. Hell, he'd built an empire around that need.

"And I really don't fucking like them being sneaky about it," Copper added.

"What do you mean?" Gator asked, beer at his lips and interest sharpening his usually joking expression.

"He means we've seen three separate riders with the same cuts, but no one seems to know who they are or where they're holing up," Thunder said. "If you don't have anything to hide, you don't bother hiding." He set down his beer and shrugged. "And they're hiding."

Shit, it did sound shady. "Need help tailing them?" Saint asked. His knuckles itched for the weight of brass and a good confrontation.

Copper nodded. "Probably. Execs are gonna meet tomorrow to come up with a plan, and I'll fill in the whole club at church."

"Got it." Saint resisted the urge to crack his knuckles. Been a while since he'd roughed up anyone. He could use the release.

Shit, maybe Gator was right, and I should have fucked the feather-skirt woman last night.

Gator rubbed his hands together as a slightly psychotic grin curved up his lips on one side. His sharp blue eyes lit with an eager gleam that Saint had seen one too many times. It usually led to an uncomfortable conversation with the local police. Luckily, they'd had the chief in their pocket for the past decade, though rumor had it he'd be retiring soon.

"Been too long since I've kicked a motherfucker's ass," Gator said. "My joints are starting to squeak."

"Pretty sure that's all the cheap beer in your system," Thunder muttered.

Before anyone could respond, the purr of an engine had their attention shifting to the lot where Shell was parking the monstrosity of an SUV Copper insisted she drive.

"Shit," Copper muttered, glancing at his watch. When he looked back up, concern radiated from his green-eyed gaze, undercutting the gruff word.

The beer in Saint's gut immediately soured. Growing up in a compound where wrong answers got you locked in a shed overnight had honed his ability to sniff out trouble. He couldn't help it. His older sister, Makenna, and he spent their entire childhoods looking out for the younger ones, even if he didn't pull it off with as much grace as Mak. The club was his extended family and just as important as his blood, and he wouldn't stand for anyone fucking with them.

Shell climbed out of the car and strode toward them with her bottom lip tucked between her teeth. She wore short denim shorts and a body-hugging tank top. Copper had hit the jackpot with his ol' lady, and every man in the club knew it. She was as sweet and loving as she was gorgeous, but she took no shit and would kick any man who crossed her square in the balls. Only a formidable woman could bring a man like Copper to his knees, and Shell had been running circles around their president for a decade and a half.

"Hey, baby," Copper said as she strode up to the table. His whole face softened in a way Saint had only ever seen when the prez looked at Shell or Beth, their daughter. He slid an arm around her waist and kissed her as though he'd been at sea for a year rather than having met her for lunch three hours ago.

Gator let out a low whistle. "Get a room, Boomers," he muttered under his breath, but the fondness in his tone matched Saint's feelings about the first couple of the HHMC.

Saint didn't bother to look away. Overt displays of affection were part of everyday life around the club, especially with the OG members who were all wifed up and disgustingly happy. If they didn't want him to stare, they'd do it behind a closed door.

When Copper finally allowed his wife to breathe, her cheeks were flushed and her eyes glossy, but still sad.

"What's wrong?" Copper asked immediately. No teasing, no delay, just straight to it.

Shell sat on the small free space on the bench next to her ol' man and directly across from Saint. As soon as her ass hit the seat, Copper tucked her close with a possessive arm around her shoulders, his fingers absently rubbing circles on her upper arm like he could soothe her before she even spoke.

"Beth missed our call…*again*." Shell leaned heavily on her ol' man as she spoke.

As the words left her mouth, Copper's face darkened, worry morphing into anger with a force Saint could practically feel radiating across the table. "Fuck. Third week in a row, right?"

Shell nodded.

Saint wanted details. The urge to pry rode him hard. Beth might not be his blood, but she was club family—princess of the whole damn kingdom—and every man at that table knew what that meant. As he debated the wisdom of opening his mouth, Gator, the nosy fucker, took the decision out of his hands.

"What's up, Prez? Need me to talk some sense into Beth's independent ass?"

Copper's expression turned so thunderous that Saint had to work to keep from shuddering. The man whacked the back of Gator's head.

"You get within a hundred feet of my daughter's ass, and I'll peel your skin like a fucking grape."

"Ow!" Gator's eyes bugged, but he still grinned. "Hey now, I meant like a brother. A very respectful, not-trying-to-die kind of brother."

"But you said ass and Beth in the same sentence. Foolish, my man," Thunder said, snickering.

"My bad." Gator lifted his arms in surrender, but his smirk did nothing to make the submission believable.

Saint shot him a look that, with any luck, said, *Keep your trap shut*, but the way Gator continued to smirk didn't give him hope.

"Everything okay?" Thunder asked Copper as he threw his bottle cap at Gator, who tried to smack it away but failed. It bounced off his forehead and onto the table with a clink.

Shell sighed. "I have a standing weekly phone call with Beth. This is the third week in a row she's missed it. The first two times, she texted with a flimsy excuse, but this time, she's ignoring my texts too. She never ignores my texts." Her voice wobbled on the last word. She lifted her chin and stared up at her ol' man. "Something's wrong, Cop. I can feel it."

Copper's arm tightened around her shoulders. His jaw flexed hard enough to crack a tooth, but his hand stayed gentle, fingers still stroking her shoulder.

Saint frowned right along with him. He didn't know Beth well. When Makenna and Thunder had gotten together, he'd been a damaged teenager not interested in hanging around the clubhouse. By the time he'd gotten his shit together and decided to prospect in his late twenties, Beth had been off with her friends more than at the clubhouse, and at some point, she'd moved out of state. She was a good deal younger than him, so their paths rarely crossed.

But he did know the entire club loved her to pieces, and it was common knowledge that Copper would murder any member who glanced his daughter's way with anything more than brotherly affection.

The last time Saint ran into her was Christmas, when she'd come to visit for the holiday. He'd walked into the clubhouse kitchen for coffee and found Beth laughing at something Screw said with her head thrown back and that strawberry blonde hair catching the light. She'd turned and smiled at him, a friendly smile, nothing more, and his whole chest had gone tight.

He'd made himself scarce after that. Because damn, the woman was gorgeous and exactly his type. Short, cute, sweet, and sexy as hell. The sass she'd come by honestly sealed the deal.

God, he loved a woman with reddish blonde hair. His dick liked it, too, which was why he'd stayed away rather than pop a boner in her father's presence. Copper would have sniffed out his lust, ripped off his dick, and fed it to Screw's new pittie puppy. Better to avoid the temptation and potential trauma altogether.

Copper didn't respond right away. He stroked his ginger-colored beard with one hand while toying with the ends of Shell's blonde hair with the other. When thinking, he often fell silent, a trait Saint had learned Copper hadn't always possessed. Rumor had it, once upon a time, Copper's temper had rivaled the most volatile of bikers, but he'd gotten smarter and more controlled as the years passed. Plus, the ladies in his life had mellowed him, or so the stories went.

"Maybe her boyfriend is causing shit," Gator said before tipping his beer back for a chain of swallows.

Copper stiffened as rigid as a statue. A very angry, very large, very deadly biker statue carved from marble and icy to the touch. "The fuck did you just say?"

Holy shit. That tone alone could freeze a man to death.

Gator's eyes widened. "Um…" He lowered the bottle, then swallowed once more as his gaze darted between the rest of them.

"Sorry, brother, you stepped on a landmine." Thunder raised his hands in surrender. "Nothing I can do for you."

"That dude. The fucking poser guy. I don't remember his name," Gator muttered.

"Speak fucking English, Gator," Copper said in a low rumble that made the hair on Saint's neck rise to attention.

Gator scoffed. "Come on, you guys know who I'm talking about. We met the fucker on that trip to Arizona last year when we stayed the night near Beth on the way. Back me up, Saint. You remember him, right?"

Saint shrugged. "Sorry, brother. I wasn't on that trip." Now he wished he had been, but Zach had needed his help back home with some businessman who owed the club a large chunk of money. Gambling debts came calling every time.

"Douchebag, wannabe biker guy? Rode something that looked like a goddamn kiddie bike." Gator rolled his eyes. "Come on, you two ain't old enough to have memory loss."

"Him?" Copper's eyes bugged as he turned to Shell. "She's still seeing that shit stain?"

"I..." Shell shook her head, frowning. "She hasn't mentioned him in ages. I thought they broke up. He was... a bit of a jackass."

Saint chuckled under his breath. Shell was the best, always ready to call a man a jackass and then make him dinner if he looked hungry. Though from the sound of it, this guy wouldn't be invited to sit at their table any time soon.

"Nah, pretty sure they're still a thing," Gator said.

"Wait..." Copper's gaze swung back to him. "How the fuck do you know?"

Gator paused with his beer halfway to his mouth. His face lost all its color, and his mouth opened and closed without a sound, like one of the fish he spent much of his free time catching.

Saint couldn't hold back his laugh. It came out strangled as he failed to hide it behind a cough. Thankfully, Thunder laughed out loud, covering his blunder. Poor Gator would be lucky to come out of this alive and with all his organs intact.

"We're, uh, friends," Gator said. "Me and Beth."

"Friends?"

Oh shit. Gator was seconds from losing another chunk of his body, and Copper's bite would be a hundred times worse than an alligator's. Saint bit his lip to hold back another laugh as he imagined Copper chasing Gator around the clubhouse while snapping at the idiot's heels.

Once again, Thunder didn't bother to hold back his laughter.

"Uh..." Gator squirmed beneath Copper's glare.

"Copper, leave the poor guy alone. You put the fear of God into your men. No one will ever look at Beth as more than a friend." Shell narrowed her eyes at her ol' man, but the smile gave her away. "Poor girl," she muttered.

"Excuse me?"

Saint swore Copper's jaw hit the table as he stared down at Shell.

"You want your daughter with one of these fuckups?"

She shrugged without shame. "What? There are some very nice perks to being with one of you guys."

"Michelle Gallagher, I am going to pretend you didn't say that. We're talking about our innocent child here."

Shell snorted. "Of course, dear." She patted Copper's arm in the most patronizing way possible. "I'll be sure to send her some Barbie dolls for her next birthday."

Saint was pretty sure Copper growled as he turned his attention back to Gator. "Not necessary, as long as this one remembers to keep his eyes, hands, and any other body part to himself."

Gator raised his hands near his ears. "Wouldn't dream of it, Prez. Got nothing but respect for you and your daughter. And I like my dick attached to my body," he muttered under his breath, earning himself a nod of approval from Copper. "I don't do nothing but talk to her every so often."

"Let's get back on track," Shell cut in, the voice of reason as always. Worry still pinched the corners of her eyes despite the back-and-forth teasing. "What should we do about this, Cop? Do you think this guy is keeping her from calling us? Because that is a huge red flag."

"Simple," Copper replied. "We take some guys, ride out there, and kill the motherfucker."

Thunder slapped a hand on the table hard enough to rattle the bottles. "Sounds good to me, brother. I can be ready to roll out tomorrow morning."

Shell held up a hand as she straightened away from Copper. "Hold up, Rambo. How do you think she's going to react if ten of you guys show up at her door, guns blazing? You know how stubborn she is about her independence and her reluctance to let the club meddle in her life. She's likely to dig her heels in and tell us everything is fine. And we don't even know if there is a problem with the boyfriend. This could be something completely unrelated."

Thunder let out a frustrated groan. "Ugh, why you gotta be so reasonable, Shell? Always ruining our fun."

She smiled at him as she shrugged. "I know my daughter."

Almost mindlessly, as though touching her was automatic, Copper's hand slid up to the back of her neck, thumb rubbing slow circles. "So what do you think we should do, babe? We can't let this go. My gut is screaming just like yours." He kissed Shell's temple as she sagged before their eyes, all that strength folding in for a moment.

"I don't know."

For the rest of his life, which might be much shorter than he'd planned, Saint would wonder what possessed him to open his mouth right then. Something in Shell's worried face, maybe. Or the memory of strawberry blonde hair catching the light in the clubhouse kitchen. Or maybe just the itch under his skin that said something was wrong, and he needed to be the one to fix it.

"I can ride out to Texas," he said.

All eyes fell on him, making him feel like a lab specimen.

Shit. He didn't often have the full focused attention of the club's president on him, and Copper's dark expression nearly had him shitting himself. Respect didn't cancel out the fact that Copper could end him six different ways with a pool cue.

"Um…"

"What do you mean?" Shell asked, setting a hand on Copper's thigh before her ol' man could shoot down the idea.

Saint shrugged. "My repo schedule is light this week with just a couple of small jobs I can push. Find some club-related reason for me to be out there, and I'll go. Whenever any one of us is out there, Beth always feeds us. I'll show up unannounced and act all embarrassed when I realize you didn't let her know I'd be in town. This way, she can't hide the scumbag away if he's still in the picture."

And he could be the one to break the guy's teeth if necessary. It had been too long since he'd felt the sting of his fist connecting with a cheekbone. Too many people repaid their loans on time lately.

"Oh, Saint, you're so sweet to offer, but I don't know." Shell glanced up at Copper with a contemplative expression. "What do you think?"

"You get even a hint of a feeling that this guy is the problem, you'll tell me?" Copper asked, eyes drilling into him.

Saint nodded. "Of course. Full transparency, no matter what I find." He didn't have a death wish.

"And you'll make it clear to him he's no longer welcome around my daughter?"

"Copper…" Shell shook her head. They still didn't know if the boyfriend was the problem, though Saint was on Copper's side here. He'd put money on the guy being the issue.

"In the most painful way possible," Saint promised.

"Men," Shell muttered under her breath with a huff, but she didn't object to his promise. Worry still shadowed her eyes, but there was a spark of relief surfacing.

"All right." Copper held out a closed fist. "You sort this shit for us, and I'll owe you big time."

"Nah, happy to do it. You're my family." Saint tapped his knuckles with his president's as Thunder patted him on the back in a heavy, approving thump.

"Stop by the house in the morning. We'll feed you a good meal before you hit the road," Thunder said. Respect sat under his casual tone. Saint didn't miss it.

"Thanks, man. I'll do that." Saint hadn't popped by his sister's house in a week, and if he went much longer, she'd track his ass down and whop him upside the head. Not only did two of his siblings still live there, but he also had a passel of nieces and nephews to hang with.

"All right." Copper stood, taking Shell with him as naturally as breathing. "We're outta here. See you guys later."

"Where are you off to?" Thunder called as Shell and Copper strode away hand in hand, like there wasn't a damn thing in the world they couldn't handle together.

"Going to fuck my wife. That okay with you?" Copper shouted over his shoulder, making the prospect polishing his bike drop the rag.

"Huh, good idea." Thunder hopped to his feet. "Mak's home this afternoon. Think I'm gonna go fuck my wife as well. Too bad you guys don't have a wife who wants your dick all the time. It's fucking awesome."

"Oh, fuck off," Gator said as Saint cringed. Old as they were, it never got easier hearing Thunder brag about his sex life with Saint's sister. "I don't need a goddamn wife," Gator muttered as Thunder jogged off, chuckling. "I get all the pussy I want, and it's not the same damn one day after day, right, brother?"

Saint shook his head as he snorted. "I'm sure as hell not shacking up with anyone anytime soon."

The mere thought of it had him shuddering. Settling down meant handing someone the power to wreck him. Every relationship he'd witnessed as a child had been nothing more than a horrendous abuse of power and authority by men who ruled with manipulation and fists, and women who had no choice but to submit. He'd had enough of that for one lifetime.

"See, you agree with me."

As much as Saint would have loved to sit around and shoot the shit with his batshit crazy club brother for the next few hours, he stood with his empty beer bottle. "I'm gonna knock off."

Gator nodded and clinked his bottle against Saint's. "Later, brother. Hey, I don't need to tell you to hit me up if you run across any trouble, right?"

"Of course not."

The man might be off his rocker, but if Saint needed him, Gator would be halfway there before he even accepted the call for help. That was the kind of crazy Saint trusted.

"Have a good trip and say hi to Beth for me."

Yeah, he wasn't doing that. Not with the way Copper had reacted to the news of their friendship.

Keep dreaming, Gator.

The crazy fucker laughed his ass off, then shouted something to the prospect about a smudge on Copper's bike.

Shaking his head at Gator's antics, Saint strode toward his motorcycle shining in the afternoon sun.

He had some packing to do and a club princess to check on.

Chapter Two

Look at that. Rylee had been right. The lipstick color complemented Beth's skin tone perfectly.

She smiled at her reflection as she swiped a clear gloss over her rosy bottom lip. It had been a hot minute since she'd worn anything more than a cover-up and mascara. Why waste money on expensive makeup, not to mention time and energy, when she worked at a pet grooming boutique and ended up covered in fur and sometimes unmentionable animal fluids daily?

Going out in a cute sundress with a full face of makeup and curled hair was a welcome change, sending a low buzz of excitement through her veins. Yesterday, her friend, the salon owner, Rylee, turned twenty-seven, and her friends had planned a happy hour party in her honor for tonight.

Beth had met most of Rylee's core friend group multiple times when they'd popped by the shop, and they'd insisted she join them for the birthday celebration. Jason already had plans to game with his friends—*shocker*—so why wouldn't she go? She hadn't been out in ages and couldn't wait to laugh, have a few drinks no one expected her to serve, and eat food she wasn't expected to prepare.

Jason's friends hung out at their apartment all the time. *All. The. Damn. Time*. Not a Friday or Saturday night went by that Grant, Benny, and a few other losers didn't have their lazy asses parked on her couch. They, along with Jason, sucked back beers and ate half her paycheck in snacks every weekend.

When she told Jason about the party invitation a few days ago, she'd been sure he'd tell her to blow it off as he typically did. And of course, she'd have listened to avoid an ugly blow-up. But something went right that day when he'd responded with, "I don't give a shit."

Worked for her. He could veg out and game all night while she got dolled up, ate delicious Mexican food, and downed a few spicy margaritas with friends.

Satisfied her makeup looked great, she fished through her closet for the strappy sandals she'd purchased on clearance last fall and had yet to wear. As soon as they were in place with her freshly painted toenails peeking out, she practically bounced out of the bedroom.

For once, excitement felt bigger than the dread that had become her constant companion—the tight knot in her stomach that never fully loosened, the way she held her breath every time she heard his key in the door.

As she reached the front hall and grabbed her purse, the door swung open. Jason stumbled through, making a racket. He bounced off the doorframe, then staggered into the apartment, missing the table as he tried to deposit his keys. They fell to the tile floor with a jarring clatter.

Jason managed a salvage yard owned by his uncle and often knocked off early on Fridays to grab a few beers at a nearby dive bar. It annoyed her to no end how he came home drunk by five in the evening nearly every Friday, but tonight, even his inebriated state couldn't fully deter her good mood.

"Hey, Jase," she said as she twirled around, arms

outstretched. "What do you think?"

She beamed as she waited for an assessment of her outfit. When they'd first got together nearly a year and a half ago, she'd loved dressing up for him. Jason would always tell her she looked beautiful. He'd had no shortage of compliments and praise, making her feel special and desired. As time went on, those words faded, and eventually, ugly, berating remarks took their place.

Tonight, her confidence was higher than usual, and she couldn't wait to wow him with her dolled-up look.

He paused, halfway bent to retrieve his keys, and stared at her.

Her grin grew.

Speechless, she'd take it.

Then his eyes narrowed, and his expression turned to stone.

The air in the apartment seemed to thin.

Beth's stomach plummeted to her feet. "Never mind," she said quickly as she dropped her arms to her sides. "I'm just being silly."

"What the fuck?" he said, voice low, menacing, and slightly slurred.

A warning.

"Um… I…"

He straightened to his full height, then strode toward her with heavy, booted steps that had her backing up on instinct. Every thud against the tile reverberated through the quiet apartment.

"What is this shit?" he shouted, grabbing the thin strap of her sundress as he reached her. The pop of threads snapping combined with his aggressive approach had her jolting like she'd caught a live wire. "Benny and Grant will be here in five fucking minutes, and you're prancing around half naked."

Stale, beer-laden breath exploded across her face as he invaded her space.

"You hoping one of them will notice? You gonna try to fuck one of my friends right in front of me in my own goddamn apartment?"

Her jaw dropped. "What?" *Never in a million years.* She shook her head so hard the room spun. "No. God, Jase, how can you even say that to me?"

Words tumbled out at a rapid clip, fear pushing them faster than she could think. "I'm not even going to be here. It's Rylee's birthday party. Remember? I mentioned it to you the other day. I told you her friends were having a little party for her at La Rosa Roja."

The slap came so fast and so suddenly that shock overrode the pain. Her head snapped to the side, and the copper taste of blood flooded her mouth. She froze, blinking twice before the sting made itself known, blooming across her cheek in a fiery blaze of pain and humiliation.

Her ears rang.

Her chest constricted as a sob lodged in her throat.

"You telling me you're going out looking like this? Dressed like a fucking slut?"

"N-no." She could feel the side of her face swelling, and a trickle of blood running from her lip where his palm had smashed it into her teeth. "I-it's just a sundress."

Wrong thing to say.

He slapped her again. This time, she felt the agony on impact and couldn't keep from crying out.

"Just a sundress?" Jason shouted again, grabbing her strap. This time, he yanked, severing the material in half. "Look how fucking easy it is to rip this shit off you."

He grabbed her upper arms and shoved her against the nearest wall so hard her head hit with a loud thunk. Bright spots exploded behind her eyes.

"There's only one reason you wear a dress like this, and it's to get men fucking hard. You fucking around behind my back, whore?"

"No. *No!*"

This had escalated so fast and gotten so out of control that she could barely process the bombardment of shouting, pain, and fear. Her brain scrambled to keep up, throwing thoughts like lifelines she couldn't catch. "I just… I just wanted to look nice. For the party. That's all."

Her voice shook.

Her hands shook.

Everything shook.

Wrong thing to say, again.

He lifted his hand, and she flinched with a whimper. "Please don't hit me again." A choked sob left her as his palm slammed into the wall next to her head instead, close enough she could feel the rush of air against her ear.

"Shut the fuck up and don't even think about telling me what to do right now. No woman of mine is going to go out looking like a damn streetwalker."

Her heart raced, and she trembled against the wall as she shook her head. "N-no. Of course not. I won't go. I'm so sorry. I-I don't know what I was thinking."

She pleaded with her eyes, staring up into his menacing, stormy gaze.

You're doing it again. You're giving him complete control over you.

He grunted. "Jesus, you're a dumb bitch."

The pain of those words sliced deeper than his slap ever could.

As his words registered, shame as she'd never known washed over her.

She'd given this man *exactly* what he wanted—power over her. There she was, cowering, apologizing, and promising to give in to his demands when she hadn't done a single thing wrong. Not a single thing to warrant this treatment.

She'd never been so low, and she hated herself for allowing it.

A small flame of defiance, the one she'd had her entire life but had snuffed out since meeting Jason, flared to life, deep in her gut, a tiny spark under a tidal wave of alarm. She was tired, so tired of stamping down her own wants, needs, and personality.

"S-stop it."

He leaned in until their noses touched. "What the fuck did you say?"

Dark eyes she'd once thought she loved hovered an inch from hers, full of fury and hate. *True hate.*

Why was he here? Why did he stay with her, a woman he so obviously loathed? Jason was an attractive man, or at least she had thought so at first. His behavior and personality made it difficult for her to appreciate his physical appeal as she once had, but women came on to him all the time. He could easily find someone else. So why did he stay here, making her life miserable?

Why do you let him?

She dug deep, taking a breath. Enough was enough. "I said *stop*." She squared her shoulders and stared him straight in his untrustworthy eyes. "Take your hands off me, Jase. I'm not dumb. I said I won't go to the party. B-back off."

Her voice might have trembled, but the words hit home. This was the first time since early in their relationship that she'd talked back to him, and even as her insides quivered, pride filled her chest for half a heartbeat.

"Oh-ho." He let out a bone-chilling, sinister sound. "Little kitty dresses like a slut and suddenly thinks she has the claws of a jungle cat."

He grabbed her throat and shook her against the wall.

The attack knocked the air from her lungs.

"I'll put my hands wherever the fuck I want to," he shouted as spittle hit her face, and she gagged and choked. "Wanna know why?"

Pressure built in her head until it felt like it would explode right off her neck. His hand squeezed until she feared her windpipe would collapse in his fierce grip.

She gasped and coughed, clawing at his hand in a futile effort to draw in a breath. Her nails scraped his skin, finding no give. Panic exploded full force now, a roaring in her ears that drowned out everything else.

She tried everything she could think of, thrashing, kicking, scratching, but nothing broke his death grip.

Her vision began to blur as a rushing sound in her ears made it impossible to hear, and rivers of tears streamed down her cheeks.

Her mother's face flashed through her mind with the way she smiled when Beth came home for Christmas, the way she always smelled like vanilla and home. Her father's voice, low and steady, telling her she could always come back. *Always*.

She'd never see them again. Never hug her mom. Never hear her dad call her baby girl.

This is it. He's really going to—

Then, as suddenly as it started, the brutal pressure on her throat vanished.

Her legs sagged, but her chest spasmed as she sucked in air as quickly as possible. She coughed and gagged as the air rushed into her abused throat, each breath like swallowing glass.

"I asked you a fucking question," Jason screamed in her tear-stained face. He grabbed her hair in a punishing hold, tilting her face up and stretching her aching throat, which he still held, but not to the point she couldn't breathe.

She had no idea what he'd asked her, but she knew she

needed to say something if she wanted any hair left on her scalp. "Y-yes," she croaked. *God, let that be the answer he was looking for.*

"Because I fucking own you," he whispered in her ear, making a chill run down her spine. His lips brushed her ear, intimate and vile. "I'm the one who puts up with your shit so I can put my hands wherever the fuck I want, whenever I fucking want to. Get me?"

"Y-yes," she rasped. She tried to nod, but he had her head wrenched back, and her chin tilted up too high.

"That's better," he said. "Now get on your fucking knees. You owe me a damn apology."

No.

She wanted to scream it in his face, but the only way to make the agony end was to give him what he wanted.

Survival over pride.

Every time.

Hopefully, she could keep from puking all over his dick.

As he pushed down to bring her to her knees, a loud bang reverberated through the apartment, rattling the wall behind her.

The door. Someone had opened the door.

One second later, a man in dark jeans and a biker cut ripped Jason off her and flung him across the apartment with a roar.

The sudden freedom was another jolt to her traumatized system, which she could barely process. Her legs buckled. If it hadn't been for the wall behind her, she'd have crumpled to the floor.

As soon as Jason hit the floor, the biker pounced, landing punch after punch on her boyfriend in a way she'd secretly hoped someone would do for ages.

A flash of a back patch she'd know anywhere caught her eye.

This was one of her father's men.

Shit was about to get really bad, really fast.

Deadly bad.

"Stop," she tried to scream, but her rough voice barely made it above a whisper. The last thing they needed was a nosy neighbor calling the cops.

Her legs shook, then her knees gave out, and she slid down the wall. When her ass hit the floor, a fresh round of tears exploded from her eyes, and a sob welled up from the deepest part of her.

"Stop," she tried again, this time with slightly more strength. If one of her father's men ended up in jail for killing Jason while saving her, she'd never forgive herself. "Please," she choked out. "He's not worth it."

The fighting stopped.

From his spot, crouched over her boyfriend's limp body, a dark head swiveled her way, and eyes she hadn't seen in a long time met her gaze.

Lee.

She'd had the hugest crush on him during her teen years when he'd had no idea she existed, and rightfully so. She'd been way too young for anyone in her father's club at that time. But that hadn't stopped her from watching him whenever he was around. The way he moved with controlled, deliberate steps, like he was always aware of everything in the room. The rare rumble of his laugh that made her teenage heart flip. The time he'd caught her staring and winked, sending her scurrying to her room with flaming cheeks.

But she'd been an adult for years now, and the object of her teenage affection was in her apartment, seeing her at her lowest.

It was a humiliation she had no way to prepare for, yet at the same time, the second their gazes collided, she felt safe for the first time in more than a year.

Chapter Three

Nothing beats a long road trip on the back of his motorcycle. Extended days of sun on his skin, wind in his face, and gorgeous scenery as far as the eye could see. Sure, it meant a sore back, exhaustion, and the occasional wicked sunburn, but the time to clear his head and enjoy the rumble of his bike for endless stretches of road couldn't be topped. Out on the highway, shit made sense. Throttle, clutch, brake. Move or die.

This trip, he got lucky, barely hitting any traffic and only encountering picture-perfect weather the entire ride, so when he rolled across the town lines into Terrell, Texas, near six in the evening of his second day traveling, he was in a damn good mood.

He was also hungry as hell.

Beth would be surprised to see him for sure, and maybe a little suspicious of his motives, but it wasn't uncommon for his brothers to pop into town and pay her a visit. The club had a close personal and working relationship with an MC out in Arizona, and someone was always making the cross-country trip to visit or conduct business.

GPS guided him straight to Beth's small apartment

complex, which consisted of two three-level buildings and a packed parking lot. He pulled his bike into a spot marked *Prospective Tenants Only*, right outside the leasing office. Since it was a Sunday evening, the office was closed. No one should fuck with his bike after hours, and if they did, well, he'd happily send them to the emergency room without a twinge of remorse. No one touched his motorcycle without an engraved invitation, and he rarely issued those.

Before he dismounted, he did a quick recheck of the address Copper had texted him. Beth lived in apartment 2C. Simple enough.

His stomach growled loud enough to alert the entire complex to his arrival. Maybe he could convince Beth to go out for Tex-Mex once she got over the shock of his unannounced and uninvited visit.

Sorry, not sorry.

Especially if his trip helped clear the worry from Copper and Shell's eyes.

As he climbed the outdoor staircase leading to the second floor, a loud thud had his well-honed danger senses prickling.

Most people would assume a tenant was rearranging furniture, but Saint had kicked enough asses to recognize the sound of a body being slammed against a wall.

A sharp, feminine cry, followed by a shouted, "*No*!" came floating down the stairwell, clear as day.

Shit.

His gut tensed for one second before his reflexes kicked in. He sprinted up the stairs two at a time, arriving on the second floor in time to hear a terrified sob coming from the apartment to his right.

Apartment 2C.

Protective instincts he worked hard to keep from spiraling out of control thundered to life inside him, shredding through his earlier good mood like paper. He didn't think twice. The part of him that belonged to the Hell's Handlers—the enforcer-in-training, the patched brother, the ruthless bastard when necessary—took over.

He charged through the door like a raging bull. The wood banged against the wall, then rebounded, slamming into his shoulder, but he barely felt the impact. His entire attention narrowed to the large man with one hand around Beth's throat and the other fisted in her hair, craning her neck up at an unnatural angle.

The soon-to-be-dead man.

Beth's face was mottled red, eyes wide with panic, and lips parted as she fought for air. Bruises darkened the soft skin of her neck. Her bare feet scrabbled uselessly against the floor.

A roar ripped from Saint's chest, raw and primal. He lunged, latching onto the asshole's T-shirt and ripping him off Beth with one brutal yank.

The choked, strangled sound Beth made when the pressure vanished would haunt him for a long damn time.

Without a thought for what he might damage in the guy or Beth's apartment, Saint flung him across the room, where he crashed into a coffee table and crumbled to the floor with a satisfying cry. Wood splintered, and something glass shattered, but all Saint could hear was his own pulse pounding in his ears.

Fury boiled his blood, scorching hot and uncontrollable.

How fucking dare you touch one of ours?

He pounced before the prick had the chance to rise, planting his knee on the guy's chest to keep him on the ground. "Who the fuck do you think you are? What the hell gives you the right to put your hands on her?" he shouted at the stunned and furious man.

"Who am I?" the piece of shit spat, wheezing beneath the pressure on his diaphragm. "I'm her fucking man. Who the fuck are you?"

Fuck that.

Saint spent enough time busting kneecaps with Zach over the years to learn how to put the fear of God in men with just one look, and this guy didn't disappoint, paling beneath Saint's deadly glare.

His lips curled in a sinister smirk as he leaned down and whispered, "I'm the man who's gonna make you wish you'd learned the right way to treat your woman."

The guy's face contorted in anger. "Fuck y—"

Saint plowed his fist into the asshole's face with a rewarding crunch.

White-hot satisfaction exploded across his knuckles.

The man howled and thrashed beneath his weight but was no match for the firestorm of fury coursing through Saint's veins. Over and over, he rammed his fist into that smug face until the eyes swelled and a red river ran from the nose. His other hand fisted in the guy's shirt, anchoring him as Saint turned his features into unrecognizable meat.

Time and space disappeared until nothing remained but the desire to inflict pain on this motherfucker who dared touch their club's princess with anything but care. Every scream from his childhood, every bruise he'd suffered, every protective instinct he had for his loved ones poured into each punch.

In the back of his mind, he heard the faintest shout, but couldn't pull himself out of his rage haze. His heart pounded, his breath came in harsh grunts, and his world shrank to bloody knuckles and the satisfying give of bone.

After a few moments, Beth's boyfriend went limp beneath him, but the lack of struggle wasn't enough. Saint wanted to bathe in his blood for what he'd done to her.

This was nothing compared to what Copper would demand he do to the piece of shit.

He tensed with his fist cocked back for another blow.

There it was again, the low cry that penetrated deeper into his brain this time.

Beth.

Jesus Christ. Beth.

His body froze, hovering over her boyfriend's still form. He hadn't even checked on her. What kind of asshole was he?

Breathe.

His inner voice, the part of his brain that kept him sane and taught him to compartmentalize years of childhood trauma, whispered in his ear. So he listened. Who was he to ignore the instinct that had helped him survive brutal beatings, psychological warfare, and working twelve-hour days as a small child?

He inhaled, drawing in the pine-laden scent of Beth's apartment, tinged with her fear and the coppery tang of blood. His hand throbbed, knuckles already swelling, but the pain helped. After holding his breath for a brief second, he blew out slowly, then repeated the action.

Whether the deep breathing had a calming effect or the sound of Beth's quiet sobs overrode his anger didn't matter. The result was the same.

Still crouched over his prey, he turned his head and met the green-eyed gaze of his president's beloved daughter.

The utter despair in her eyes punched him in the gut ten times harder than he'd hit the piece of shit on the floor. Her dress, a short, flowy purple number, had a torn strap dangling. Her gorgeous strawberry hair, which she'd clearly spent time curling, was mussed and tangled from her boyfriend's rough grip. Makeup she'd applied at some point ran from her eyes, streaking across her flushed cheeks and emphasizing the trauma she'd just endured.

Individually, each of those was enough to earn the boyfriend a solid beating, but when he added the bruises on her throat and the swelling on her cheek, the bastard would be lucky to survive the night.

Even traumatized and tear-streaked, she was stunning. The observation felt wrong, but his brain noted it anyway.

Shit, he'd made a mistake volunteering to be the one to check on her.

But none of that mattered now.

He rose with slow, sure movements, designed to keep from scaring her. She'd just been assaulted, then witnessed him perform a spectacular act of violence. Most likely, she wouldn't be too keen to have another large man in her space. As softly as he could manage in size twelve boots, he crossed the distance between them and kneeled before her.

Now that he was close, she averted her gaze, staring at her updrawn knees. Her shoulders shook with silent tremors.

"Are you hurt?" he whispered.

She shook her head immediately, a jerky, automatic denial.

Yeah, he didn't buy that. She might not be hurt enough to need medical attention, but her throat had to be raw and her face throbbing. As soon as he got her out of there, he'd make damn sure to get some ice on her cheek.

"May I touch you?"

She tensed, muscles going tight as guitar strings.

"Just to check your neck and your face," he added, keeping his voice low.

This time, he got a nod and a raspy, "Yes."

As he lifted his hand, both their gazes locked on his torn and bloody knuckles. "Shit," he whispered. "Sorry."

"Are you okay?" she croaked.

He grunted. "Don't even feel it. Too much adrenaline. My fingers are clean. Promise I won't get that bastard's blood on you."

Gently as he could, he lifted her chin with one fingertip. There it was again, that punch to his solar plexus when their gazes collided. Those eyes had always been bright, sassy, full of mischief. Seeing them washed out with fear made something vicious curl in his chest.

Conflicting violence and tenderness warred inside him. A huge part of him wanted to go back over to Jason and finish the job—rip him from limb to limb, make him beg for his life, only to snuff it out. But another impulse, softer and more dangerous, wanted to gather Beth in his arms and promise he'd never let her experience a moment of sadness again.

And beneath both of those lurked something he shoved down but knew would be harder to ignore once she recovered her sass and sparkle. He wanted her, plain and simple. That desire could easily land him in the same position as her boyfriend, beaten and bloodied, except Copper would be the one dealing the blows.

As gently as possible, he tilted her chin side to side, inspecting her cheek and neck. Despite how hard he tried, he couldn't keep the scowl off his face as he stared at her discolored skin. A small trail of blood ran from her lower lip, but that seemed to be the worst of the damage aside from bruising. Before he could stop himself, he traced his finger up the line of her neck, over the worst of the marks, barely skimming her soft skin.

Beth shivered as a tiny gasp escaped, but she didn't protest.

"This ends *now*," he said, forcing himself to release her and sit back on his heels before he did something foolish. "You're safe, and that piece of shit will *never* touch you again."

"Jason," she said, voice rough. "His name is Jason."

"I don't give a shit what his name is, though I guess someone will need it for his obituary."

That had her snapping into action. She dropped her knees and lunged forward, grabbing his arm. "No, Lee, you can't. Please, you've done enough to him."

He growled like a junkyard dog. "I haven't begun to make him pay."

She didn't seem aware of how tightly she gripped his arm, and he tried not to enjoy the feel of her fingers denting his skin. Beneath her hold, his Hell's Handlers brand burned like it had the night Copper had held the white-hot iron to his skin.

Fitting.

Copper would also be the one to flay it from his body if Saint didn't do right by his daughter.

She shook her head. "Please. You said it was over, so let it be over."

Clearly, she'd been away from the MC for too long. "Babe, you forget who you grew up with? You think Copper is gonna let this shit slide? That douchebag, Jason, or whoever the fuck, will be lucky if your father doesn't kill him, then resurrect him so he can kill him again."

"Don't tell him."

The idea was so absurd he couldn't help but laugh, sharp and humorless. "Christ, Beth, are you crazy? Who do you think sent me here?"

Her jade eyes bored into his, pleading. "This is my life, Lee. Mine. I love my parents, but I'm an adult, and they don't get to know if I don't want them to know."

Fuck. Saint was a goddamn sap because he already knew he'd regret what he was about to do, but would still do it. The look on her face wrecked him. Fear and shame tangled together into a woman who'd just had every ounce of control ripped from her, now begging to keep the one thing she had left, the choice of who found out.

He sighed and glanced at Jason, sprawled on the floor, before turning back to her. "Why do you want to protect that piece of shit?"

"I'm not." She shook her head, jostling his arm with her

movements. "I'm trying to protect you. And my dad. I don't want his blood on your hands."

"Too late," he said, showing her his knuckles once again.

"You know what I mean, Lee."

His heavy sigh heaved his entire upper half. "Beth… you know who we are."

She sniffed as she squeezed his arm tighter. "Not at my expense. Please, Lee. I don't want you to have to do this because of me. It's not worth it."

Of course, it was worth it. If not to protect the ones they loved, why did they do any of it? The loans, the threats, and the beatings were all to keep the club safe, fed, and standing. That was the code.

Fuck.

"Three conditions," he said finally.

"Okay…"

He held up a finger. "One, you don't see that fucker again. *Ever*."

A shudder ran through her, visible from hair to toes. "I never want to."

He nodded as he lifted a second finger. "Two, you come back to Tennessee with me."

Her eyes widened. "For good?"

Yes. The word sat heavily on his tongue. "For now, to start."

"And the third?"

The one she'd have the hardest time accepting. "You tell your parents eventually. Not today or tomorrow, but when you're ready. It's not a secret that can be kept forever."

Her gaze drifted to Jason, and Saint clenched his teeth against the urge to snap at her not to even look at the shitbag. Her defeated sigh had him close to wavering, but fuck that. There was no way he'd leave her in this town alone with this jackass still breathing.

"All right. Okay. I…I can do that."

"Good." He climbed to his feet and extended a hand for her. "You get cleaned up and pack while I take out the trash," he said, pointing to Jason, who groaned and began to stir. His fingers flexed, wanting another round.

She narrowed her eyes at him, but as she let him help her to her feet, he swore she muttered something about damn bossy bikers. He'd take her fire and sass any day over the traumatized state she'd been in when he arrived, though he had a feeling her road would be rocky over the next few weeks.

As soon as she was on her feet and steady, he released her hand. "Good?"

"Um, yeah." She nodded, glancing around the apartment with a lost expression. "Just… processing. Are we going to head back tonight?"

Much as he loved riding, his ass had sat on his bike enough for one day. "Nah, I've been riding too fucking long. I'll get us a room for the night, and we can head out in the morning."

Beth gnawed her lower lip as a troubled cloud crossed her face. He was sure she didn't love the idea of being in close quarters with him, a man she barely knew, but two rooms were out of the question. She'd have her own bed and could erect a damn electric fence between them if it made her feel safer, but she wouldn't be out of his sight. Not with this asshole still breathing, a decision he prayed he wouldn't come to regret.

"Okay, I shouldn't need more than thirty minutes or so," she said.

"Take your time, babe. I'll chat with my man, Jason."

She opened her mouth as though to warn him not to hurt Jason again, then shut it with a nod. "Okay."

Then she lifted her gaze to his, and something twisted low

in his gut, something he had no business feeling right now. He dug his fingernail into his palm to redirect the sensation.

She didn't seem to realize her effect on him, and he needed to keep it that way. Some lines didn't get crossed, and Copper's daughter was one of them.

After a final frown at Jason, Beth turned for her room, then stopped before stepping away from him. "Lee?" she said as she spun back.

He raised an eyebrow.

"Thank you. If you hadn't shown up when you did…"

The vulnerability in her voice stabbed his heart. His jaw ticked. Despite giving Beth his word, it would take every ounce of strength he had not to break Jason's neck the second she walked into her room.

"Babe…"

"I know." She shook her head. "I shouldn't think that way. You're here. I'm safe, and I'm actually excited to go to Tennessee. It's been way too long. Just… thank you. I know I'm asking something huge of you, keeping this from Copper."

"Well, maybe just put in a good word for me if your dad ever decides to murder me," he said.

Her lips twitched. "I can do that. Thank you, Lee."

"Saint."

He couldn't handle hearing his given name falling from that sexy mouth. It made him imagine her saying it for other reasons, in different positions, in a much breathier, pleading tone, and that way lay death.

His literal death.

Her nose wrinkled, and his damn dick twitched. *Why did she have to be so damn attractive?* "Saint?"

"No one has called me Lee in years."

"Yeah, but… Saint?"

He shrugged as he winked, needing the lightness as much

as she did. "I guess it was opposite day when Thunder gave me the name, seeing as how I'm nowhere near sainthood."

Beth's face lit up as she laughed for the first time since he'd set foot in her apartment.

He bit off a groan before she could hear it.

It was going to be a long few days back to Tennessee.

Chapter Four

In the span of half an hour, Beth's entire life flipped upside down.

When she should have been at Rylee's birthday party, sipping a margarita and stuffing her face with guacamole, she was standing in a motel room with fresh bruises, a bloodied ex-boyfriend out there somewhere, nursing wounds from a severe beating, and a growly biker setting her bag on the bed farthest from the door.

Panic hovered at the edges of her psyche, waiting for the one second she wasn't consciously working to keep it at bay. As soon as something distracted her from that goal, the anxiety would slip in, and she'd have a full-blown meltdown in front of Lee—*Saint*.

That would be fun.

The motel was exactly what she expected from a cheap roadside stop just off the highway. The room boasted an ugly, geometric-patterned rug in murky colors, faded mauve bedspreads over two full-sized beds, and art on the walls that had probably come in bulk from a bargain bin. It wasn't glamorous, but it was clean enough and, more importantly, discreet. No one here knew her name. No one cared.

Before leaving her apartment, she'd shut herself in the bathroom and stood under the delicious warm spray until the hot water ran out, watching rivulets of water swirl down the drain and telling herself she was washing Jason's touch off her skin. When she'd finally emerged with her damp hair hanging around her shoulders and her face scrubbed completely free of makeup, Jason was gone. Saint had done God knew what with her ex, and he refused to tell her. All he'd said was that he'd kept his promise and didn't kill 'the motherfucker.'

Without foundation, without mascara, without lipstick, wearing only the bruises Jason left, she felt raw, exposed, and weirdly clean and filthy at the same time.

A thick taupe curtain hung in one corner of the large window, giving a stark view of the drab parking lot, but not for long. Saint yanked the curtain shut after depositing her duffel on what she assumed would be her bed for the night. As he blocked the window, the natural light disappeared, leaving the room lit only by a dim nightstand lamp and a soft overhead light that made everything feel smaller and closer.

Too close.

They were going to sleep in the same room. She trusted Saint more than she'd trusted anyone in longer than she wanted to admit, but the idea of being in such close quarters with a large man made the back of her neck prickle. For too long, she'd lived in fight-or-flight mode. Her body hadn't caught up yet to the fact that Saint wasn't Jason.

He pulled his phone from his pocket and tapped out a few messages while she tried to figure out what to do next. Her brain bounced around in a hundred directions. Jason on the floor, the anticipated joy on her mom's face when she returned to Tennessee, Copper's rage when he inevitably found out about Jason, the feel of Saint's fingertips coasting over her sore neck.

Do not go there, Beth.

With a sigh, because she seemed to do that every few seconds now, she watched Saint on his phone. Was he contacting her father? Did Copper know Saint would be starting back for Tennessee in the morning with her in tow? Saint had promised he wouldn't spill her secrets, but they hadn't discussed what exactly he'd say to her dad or the club in general.

"Beth?"

She blinked and found the object of her thoughts standing very close, too close, scowling.

"Shit," she yelped with her heart nearly leaping out of her chest as she jumped away on instinct, raising her hands as though to ward off a punch.

"Fuck. I'm sorry." He lifted his hands and stepped back, softening his posture, but his expression remained serious. "I didn't mean to scare you. I asked a few times if you were hungry, and you didn't answer."

"Oh." *He'd spoken to her?* Her spine relaxed, but her heart still thumped way too fast, and her insides tumbled around like clothes in a dryer. The surge of anxiety morphed into a hot wave of shame. This man had literally rescued her, and she was acting as though he'd attack her at any moment. "Don't apologize. I'm the one who's sorry. I didn't hear you. Must've been lost in my mind."

He nodded. "Understandable. I'll make sure I don't approach you unless you're aware."

"I'm not afraid of you." God, now she sounded like a petulant child.

He tilted his head and stared at her. She could practically hear his thoughts loud and clear in the room.

Who are you trying to convince, yourself or me?

"Didn't say you were, but I wouldn't blame you, babe. A man's been hurting you for a while, and I'm a big man. You saw me beat the fuck outta someone tonight, and now I got in your space without your permission. It was my bad. Won't happen again."

Her stomach sank. *Was this her life now?* Would she flinch every time a large man came near her? If so, she'd never be able to step foot in the clubhouse she considered a second home. Every damn man she knew was huge, aggressive, and loud.

"But—"

"No buts. It's on me, and I'll be more careful." He smiled as he let his arms drop to his sides. "Now, I could really use some tacos. Please tell me you know the best taco place in all of Texas."

None of the men in her father's club would hurt her, or any woman, for that matter.

They'd die before hurting her.

She'd remind herself of that a hundred times a day if she needed to because she refused to let herself be afraid of her family. A cold knot in her gut whispered it might be a long time before she stopped jumping at shadows, but she was stubborn enough to deny it for now.

Beth forced a smile as she nodded. "As a matter of fact, I do." Tacos she could handle, and it would give her something to focus on besides the shitty state of her life.

Thirty minutes later, Saint dragged the small, round table from the corner of the room to between the beds, where they loaded it down with enough Tex-Mex to feed the entire MC.

He looked slightly ridiculous sitting at the small table, like a kid trying to eat at their doll's table. His cramped legs didn't seem to bother him. He rubbed his hands together as he studied the food with a gleeful smile before grabbing a few items.

"Dig in," he said, before chomping half a taco in one bite. His eyes rolled upward as he groaned. "Damn, woman, you know good food."

He took another bite. This time, the sauce lingered on his lips, but not for long. He swiped it away with a quick lick she couldn't help but stare at.

Note to self, Saint likes to eat. And you can stop staring at his mouth anytime now.

Now that some of the utter shock of the day was settling from sharp and jarring to a dull disbelief, she was able to really look at him, and, *God,* was there a lot of him to look at. He was big, muscular, and one of the hottest men she'd ever seen.

Most of what she remembered of him from when she'd spent her younger years around the club was a surly, volatile guy in his twenties who drove Thunder and Makenna crazy for a few years while finding himself and his place in life.

She could relate.

Back then, he'd been tall and gangly, all elbows and attitude that had fascinated her. Now, he'd filled out into this rock-solid, powerful man full of tattoos and capability. She couldn't put her finger on it, but something about his demeanor gave off the impression that he could handle anything that came his way with ease. There was a quiet confidence about him that she admired. Saint wouldn't be the loud, center-of-attention guy at a party, but he'd be the one to call when shit hit the fan.

That realization gave her a sense of security she hadn't felt in a long time and hadn't even realized was missing until tonight.

Not missing. Stolen. Jason stole it piece by piece while you watched.

Like the frog slowly boiling in the pot, her life had reached the point of unbearable, and she only recognized it now that this man had helped her escape.

Seriously, when had Saint developed all those muscles? Riding behind him, with her arms around his waist on the way to the motel, had been eye-opening and distracting in ways she didn't have the bandwidth to think about.

Not that she was in any position to do something about it, but two solid days of clinging to him on the back of a bike would be its own brand of torture. Maybe it was a good thing she wasn't in the headspace to think about anything more than appreciating his good looks. Her dad would flip his shit if he knew she was attracted to one of his MC guys. From the moment her hormones started surging, he'd drilled into her brain how she was not to so much as look at the men in his club.

"You gonna stare at me all night, or you gonna eat something?"

Her face burned as she jumped.

Busted.

She grabbed the closest thing, which happened to be a rolled taco smothered in cheese, sour cream, and guac. *Yum.* "Yes, of course."

What the hell is wrong with you? Caught lost in thought twice in less than an hour.

She needed to get her head in the game.

"Okay, because if I'm so hot it's too distracting, I can put a pillowcase over my head or some shit." He winked before taking a long sip from his super-sized soda, large enough to induce diabetes.

"Funny," she said, even as the butterflies in her stomach agreed with his description of himself. "You seem to think very highly of yourself. Sounds to me like you might need a bigger helmet."

"I do have a big… head," he said with another wink.

That had her sputtering out an unladylike half snort, half laugh. She did not remember Saint being open and funny, but the fact that he could make her laugh despite all that had happened today felt incredible.

"Wow. I see you have the sense of humor of a thirteen-year-old."

He grunted. "Eat your dinner, brat."

So, she did. They chatted a little. He filled her in on some shenanigans from home, and she talked about her job at the pet grooming salon, but most of the meal was quiet. Saint seemed to realize she had a lot to process and let her do so without his two cents, which she greatly appreciated.

As she listened to him describe the clubhouse, the mountains, and Copper snarling about some new bikers in the area, a strange swell of emotion rose in her chest. She missed home, missed the noise and laughter, her mom's hugs, and her dad's gruff affection. Excitement tugged at her. She was really going back, and she was more than ready.

Right on top of it sat fear. Fear of the questions. Fear of their judgment when they eventually learned what she'd allowed to happen. Fear that she wasn't the Beth they remembered anymore, but a beaten-down version they'd no longer be proud of.

By the time they finished eating, her energy had bottomed out, and an all-consuming heaviness settled over her. Whether she was tired or just ready to turn her brain off didn't matter. She wanted nothing more than to crawl under the scratchy covers and pass out.

Would Saint care if she turned in early? Jason always got mad when she went to bed before him, claiming it meant she didn't want to be around him. He was a night owl, whereas she preferred mornings, and more than one fight had begun over her inability to stay up as late as he did.

You say you love me, Beth. If you really loved me, you'd want to spend some fucking time with me.

Ugh, she hated that statement because it always preceded a horrible mood and either a lengthy silent treatment or Jason's screaming. Opposite ends of the reaction spectrum, but equally awful.

"You wanna tell me what's on your mind?" Saint asked after a long stretch of silence.

"Huh?" Her cheeks heated. This guy would think she was the biggest space cadet if she kept zoning out.

"You look like you got something to say. What's up?"

"Oh…well, I was just thinking that I'm, uh, pretty tired."

He tilted his head and studied her with those dark, intense eyes. Her face warmed. Being the focus of such robust scrutiny was unnerving. "I imagine you would be pretty fucking whipped. Today was shit for you."

A harsh laugh burst from her gut. "Yeah, you could say that," she said as she touched her bruised neck without thinking.

His eyes narrowed as his gaze darkened. "All right, you ready to call it a day then?"

"Oh." She blinked. "Only if you are. I don't want to mess with your plans any more than I already have. I'm good to stay up as long as you want."

Grunting, Saint began to clear the table. "Babe, in case you haven't figured it out yet, you are my plan. I came here to make sure you're okay and find out why you're ghosting your mom. But even if I wasn't here for that, if you're tired, you sleep." He shrugged. "Simple as that."

"Are you sure?" God, she hated the meek insecurity in her voice.

He paused in his task to give her his full attention. "Seeing as how we're gonna be spending a lot of time together over the next two days, I'm gonna tell you a little something about me. I'm nothing like that weak, pathetic fucker you were dating. I don't need to beat on or scream at a woman to feel like a goddamn man."

His eyes burned, nostrils flaring as he spoke with ferocity

and heart. Beth's breath caught.

He tapped a hand on his chest. "You need something, you tell me, and you'll get it. I piss you off, tell me. I'm being a dick, tell me. I will not lay a hand on you in anger now or ever. I saw way too much of that shit growing up, and it fucking sickens me. You can get mad, freak out, break down, or annoy the fuck outta me, and you will remain safe. I am not that man. Get me?"

Her eyes widened as she nodded. The words sank beneath her skin, piercing her core, but they didn't magically erase the tension in her muscles. It was going to take time. More than a day, more than a road trip. For the first time, she understood that on a bone-deep level. "I got you," she whispered.

He nodded once. "Good. Now, I'm gonna take a quick shower to wash the road off me, and you get comfy." His lips quirked. "Or as comfy as you can be in this shit-ass motel."

Smiling, she glanced around. "What? You too good for smoke-stained yellow walls? Didn't know the club had gotten so bougie since I've been gone."

Saint snorted. "You really are a brat, aren't you?"

She just grinned.

After rolling his eyes, he set their takeout bag, now full of trash, in the center of the table, then pushed it back in the corner of the room. "I'll be quiet, promise." He stopped in front of her on his way to the bathroom. "Sleep well, Beth."

He stood close enough that she could feel the warmth wafting off him and smell the familiar and comforting leather scent of his cut. But there was an added layer that had her fighting not to squirm. His cologne mixed with the leather gave him an erotic and intoxicating aroma she could have inhaled all day.

"Um, thanks. You too. I mean, have a good shower or… whatever."

Oh my God, kill me now.

Saint winked, then grabbed his duffel and headed into the bathroom as she sat there stewing in her own awkwardness.

The snick of the locking door shot her into action. She dug through her bag, then scrambled to get changed into her sleep clothes before he could walk back out. Hopefully, he'd take a while, and she'd be long asleep before he emerged.

As soon as she had her T-shirt and sleep shorts on, she dove beneath the covers. Screw brushing her teeth. She had excellent dental hygiene. Missing one night wouldn't kill her. All she wanted was to sleep and wake to a brand-new day.

But her body and mind had other ideas. Despite extreme exhaustion, she lay in the bed, eyes wide open, staring into the darkened hotel room. All of a sudden, she became intensely aware of the fact that Saint was showering on the other side of the wall at her back.

Naked.

With warm water running over all that tattooed skin.

With a groan, she flopped to her back. "Go. To. Sleep," she whispered.

Her brief pep talk didn't work. She rolled onto her side again, with her back to the wall, which did nothing to help. All of her senses went on high alert, listening for every sound, inhaling to catch the scent of his body wash through the door, and trying to see out the back of her head and through a wall into the shower.

After a few moments, the shower shut off. Beth sucked in a breath, keeping it in her lungs as she strained to hear what was happening. Was he shaving? Brushing his teeth? Staring at himself in the mirror?

No more than sixty seconds passed before the door opened and steam floated into the room. Saint killed the light immediately, then strode into the room.

She froze.

Did he think she was asleep?

Should she pretend to be?

By now, her vision had adjusted to the dark, and she zeroed in on his form as he strode across the room to his empty bed.

Holy shit.

He was bare-chested, muscles and tattoos on full display, with nothing but shorts riding low on his hips. Muscles rippled up his stomach, and his hairless chest looked firm and lickable. Every inch of him screamed power, heat, and trouble she had no business wanting.

She squeezed her eyes shut, but it was too late. The image burned itself into her memory. It would be all she saw every time she closed her eyes for the foreseeable future. An untouchable torture she'd have to endure all night long while she breathed slowly and evenly, wishing to be asleep.

At least it was a hundred times better than the memory of Jason's hand around her throat.

Chapter Five

"Yeah, Prez, I expect we'll pull into town early this evening."

Saint leaned against the cement wall outside their motel room. The early morning sun warmed his face and boded well for another good day of traveling weather.

"Why don't you come straight to the clubhouse. Shell and I will be here all day," Copper said.

Saint rolled a small rock back and forth beneath his boot as his suspicions rose. Straight to the clubhouse, huh? "Uh, Prez, Shell isn't planning some big welcome home thing for Beth, is she?"

Copper grunted. "Nah. She wanted to, but I managed to talk her out of it. Figured y'all would be tired from the trip and whatever the fuck else you're not telling me. Wasn't sure Beth would be up for it."

Yeah, that sounded like Copper. Grumbling and suspicious but not pushing, *yet*.

Saint still didn't know Beth all too well. Most of their time had been spent in peaceful riding, and even when they'd been in the motel rooms, Beth had stayed quiet for the most part, processing the shift in her life. They'd chatted, but mostly surface level, and mostly him filling her in on the tea back at home. He hadn't tried to force her to open up, mostly because he hated when someone did that shit to him. What she needed was time, and he was happy to be a silent supporter if that was what she needed or to fill the silence with clubhouse gossip.

A rowdy party with all the attention on her didn't seem like it would go over too well, given her current introspective state.

"Yeah, good call," Saint said. "I think she'll need some time to adjust to being back home and might not be ready for a big party."

His stomach twisted. Copper wasn't a fool. He'd played along when Beth called yesterday, telling him she was overworked and under-rested and that was why she'd been off lately, but he sure as hell didn't buy it. A man didn't run a group of outlaw bikers for two decades without developing a Grade-A bullshit detector. Still, Saint had made her a promise and wouldn't break it unless absolutely necessary.

"Fine," Copper said with a rumbled sigh. "Keep your secrets. I appreciate you heading out there and convincing my daughter to come home more than fucking anything, which is why I'm not pushing you on this."

"I get that."

"But if I find out you're keeping shit from me that I need to know…"

Fuck. He didn't need to finish the sentence to make the Hell's Handlers brand on Saint's forearm tingle. The patch meant more to him than anything, but the thought of his family, his place in the club, and the risk of jeopardizing those relationships was like a knife to the gut.

Yet there he was hiding something he knew Copper would want to know.

Beth's bruises weren't as spectacular as they'd been that first night, but she'd need a good deal of makeup or a goddamn turtleneck in the middle of the summer to hide them from her father's savvy gaze.

Or her mother's.

Hell, sometimes Shell scared him more than Copper. His president might be lethal as fuck, but Shell handled the big guy with the ease of a knife gliding through melted butter.

"I hear you loud and clear," he said. Once Copper found out how Jason had abused Beth, and he would find out, Saint was fucked.

"All right. Just making sure. Back to tonight, we are doing a barbecue, but it's super casual, typical weekend shit with no focus on Beth."

Saint nodded as though Copper could see him. "Yeah, that should work."

The motel door opened, and Beth popped her freshly washed and dried head out. "That my dad?"

Saint nodded, then passed her the phone when she held out her hand.

She stepped outside, and his eyes nearly fell out of their sockets. Dressed in baggy jeans and a tiny fucking tank top that hugged her like a second skin and left enough skin on display to be nearly obscene, she looked like temptation wrapped in sin.

He had to press his tongue to the roof of his mouth to keep from trying to lick her. How the fuck was he supposed to survive a whole day on his bike knowing the body pressed against his back was a few severed threads away from being naked?

"Dad, Saint is being a perfect gentleman, so you can stop threatening him," she said into the phone, utterly oblivious to the growing problem in his jeans.

Why did she have to be so damn sexy?

If she'd been any other woman in any other circumstances, he'd have backed her into that motel room and fucked her until they were both too exhausted to ride a few hundred miles on a motorcycle. Instead, he'd get to feel those full tits on his back all day while he fought to keep his blood circulating through his entire body.

Wonderful.

"Dad, I'm fine. I swear it." Beth rolled her eyes as she tried to soothe her overprotective father.

If Beth was fine, then Saint was a damn teddy bear, but he kept his mouth shut. Beth was an adult. She didn't deserve him telling her what to do, especially not two days after escaping a violent and controlling relationship.

"Yeah, okay," she said. "A Tennessee barbecue at the clubhouse sounds great. Been too long since I've had Mav's famous ribs. Yeah… okay… I will. You need Saint again? Okay, then we'll see you tonight. Love you too. Bye."

She ended the call, then handed his phone back. As he grabbed it, their hands brushed, and electricity shot up his arm, raising the hairs. Beth sucked in a breath, then lifted her gaze to his. For one second, they stood frozen, locked in a heated stare-off until his phone chimed, breaking the spell.

Beth stepped back, clearing her throat. "Ready to go when you are."

Saint nodded. "I'll get our shit loaded on the bike, and we'll take off."

Four hours later, he was in hell. *Complete and utter hell.*

He took an exit to refill his gas tank and give them both an opportunity to stretch their legs, but mainly to preserve his sanity. Most of yesterday, Beth had sat straight behind him with her hands on his waist, enjoying the scenery. Today, she'd decided to try her hand at becoming a sadistic tormentor.

At his insistence, she'd thrown a leather jacket over her skimpy top, but kept it open and leaned fully into his back. She was a small woman, short and on the thinner side, but by no means a twig like so many women these days. She had a softness to her that melted against him and made his eyes roll back in his head. Her ass and tits were the things of men's fantasies, and feeling her nestled against his back all day while her thighs cradled his hips was a cruel and unusual punishment.

He'd battled a raging boner for most of the ride.

He wanted to fuck, and he wanted to fuck Beth, but his dick needed to get the message that it would never happen. Instead of sticking around for the barbecue, maybe he'd head to a local bar and find some willing woman to work off his sexual energy.

If he were smart, he'd go straight home and make up for days of missed work. He had a stack of recovery orders waiting on his desk back home. Deadbeat car owners didn't repo themselves, and he'd already lost a week's pay on this trip, not that he'd change a thing.

As soon as he pulled up alongside the gas pump, Beth hopped off, grinning. "I'm gonna hit the bathroom and grab some snacks. I'm in the mood for something sweet. Want anything?"

You. Naked and spread-eagled in my bed. Nothing would be sweeter than the taste of you.

"Just grab me a Diet Dr. Pepper, if you don't mind." He pulled a twenty out of his wallet and held it out to her.

Beth rolled her eyes. "It's a soda, Saint. I can cover it."

He raised an eyebrow but didn't put his money away. After a fifteen-second stare down, Beth huffed and snatched the bill from his hand, muttering something about stubborn bikers as she strode toward the convenience store. The way her ass moved in those damn jeans should be illegal.

"Fuck," he muttered as he stared up at the sky. No lightning bolt came down to smite him or solve his problem, so he turned to the pump and got to work filling the tank.

By the time the meter stopped, Beth was back and munching on a Twizzler. Her plump lips looked obscene wrapped around the red candy, and his cock twitched with jealousy.

Three hours. Just three more hours. You can do this.

"I'm gonna hit the bathroom," he said, glancing over his shoulder. They were at a busy travel station that seemed safe enough, but the thought of leaving Beth out there alone didn't sit well with him.

"Don't even think about it." She narrowed her eyes and pointed at him with a Twizzler. "I'm a big girl, and I can wait here all by my big-girl self while you piss, Saint. I'm not following you inside and standing outside the bathroom like a child."

"Babe, you don't know—"

"Don't you babe me. I've lived with you, alpha bikers, my entire life. I know how you operate. No one is going to kidnap me in broad daylight with a dozen vacationing families all around." She waved him away. "Go. Pee. I'll stand right here like a good girl. Promise."

"I'm starting to think you are the furthest thing from a good girl," he muttered, which earned him a sassy smirk.

Yeah, she was trouble, and once she was fully back to her old self and moving past her relationship with Jason, the entire club was fucked.

He stepped close until he loomed over her, but made sure she had plenty of room to escape if she felt uncomfortable. Her eyes widened, and she sucked in a breath as she arched her back to peer up at him, but nothing in her posture read as fear.

"Your sweet ass better be right here when I get back," he said. "Don't move even one inch from this spot."

"Um… yeah… I'm not going… I'll be here." Her cheeks flushed an appealing shade of pink as she sputtered.

"Good." He winked, then headed off to the building, not trying to hide his smirk. Pretty sure he won that round.

He hit the bathroom, then bought some ChapStick because the combination of wind and sun was murder on his lips. Walking out of the convenience store, he drew the gaze of more than one customer. Some gave him a wide berth, while others stared, and one busty woman with over-processed hair licked her lips and winked. She probably hoped he'd take her around the side of the building for a quick fuck, which he'd very much love, but not with her.

The one he wanted had better be standing next to his bike, munching Twizzlers like she was auditioning for porn.

He was used to all manner of reactions from people when they saw his cut. Most steered clear, assuming an outlaw biker would fly into a homicidal rage if anyone got too close. Civilians wildly misunderstood their one-percenter culture. But then there were fender bunnies like the bleached blonde eyeing him like her next snack. None of it fazed him anymore.

The store's automatic door slid open, revealing Beth right where he'd left her, only she wasn't alone.

His spine stiffened instantly, and his hand went to his pocket, where he always kept a switchblade. He preferred a gun, but traveling across multiple state lines with one often invited unwanted attention from the local cops.

Beth stood at the front tire of his motorcycle, posture rigid and uncomfortable. She held her leather jacket closed, hiding the skin she'd freely allowed him to see, while some douchebag leered at her from the opposite side of the bike. The guy's stance screamed gym bro with a puffed-up chest, spray-tanned muscles, and hair styled within an inch of its life.

He said something Saint couldn't hear, but it made Beth frown as she tugged the jacket tighter, and that was *e-fucking-*

nough for him.

Saint's blood zinged with the same thrill that surged through him when he got to fuck someone up for screwing over his club. The same delicious sense of homegrown justice he'd experienced pummeling the fuck out of Beth's piece-of-shit ex.

He reached his bike in time to hear the gym bro with his Instagram-muscle and shampoo-commercial hair say, "Promise I'll be the best lay you've ever had."

"Yeah?" Saint said, voice soft and deadly calm. "That's a pretty bold claim, my man."

Both heads snapped his way.

Beth's eyes widened with relief and embarrassment. She shifted closer to the bike, almost using it as a shield. Gym Bro's gaze flicked down to Saint's cut, lingered on the patch, then popped back up to his face with forced bravado.

"Just talking to the lady, man," the guy said. "Didn't know she belonged to anybody." His eyes slid over Beth again, slower this time. "Though maybe she wants to belong to someone else."

Saint's jaw flexed.

Wrong-fucking-answer.

He stepped in close, closing the space between them in two easy strides. "That right?" He had at least four inches on Gym Bro, but the guy had more bulk. Still, Saint would bet his bike the guy had no idea how to use those muscles in a fight.

And he'd never risk his bike.

Beth opened her mouth. "Saint, it's fine. I—"

"No, it's not," he said without looking at her. His gaze stayed locked on the guy who stared up at him with unwarranted arrogance. "When a woman's got her arms crossed and a frown on her face, it means walk the fuck away. You too stupid to figure that out?"

Gym Bro scoffed. "She's playing games." He lifted his

hands in mock innocence. "You ladies gotta stop fucking with us. How are we supposed to know you don't want it?" His gaze dipped to Beth's chest again, and he smirked. "Though, sweetheart, you're sending some real mixed signals with that slutty top."

Beth flinched and hugged her jacket tighter.

Something in Saint snapped.

He slung an arm around the guy's shoulders in what looked, from a distance, like an easy, bro gesture. "Walk with me a sec," he said, steering him a few steps away from Beth and the bike, turning their backs to the parking lot.

The man chuckled nervously. "Uh, what the fuck, dude? I don't swing this way."

Saint's fingers slipped his switchblade from his pocket, flicking it open with a quiet snick he knew would carry just enough to be heard by Gym Bro. He pressed the cold metal tip into the soft spot between the guy's ribs, right through his thin T-shirt. Not hard enough to pierce skin, but enough to let him feel the pressure and know how quickly his fate could change.

The man went stock-still. "Whoa. Hey… easy, man. What the hell?"

"Here's the thing," Saint murmured, voice low enough that only the two of them could hear. He smiled as if they were sharing a joke. "That woman over there?" He tilted his head toward Beth. "She's not just some random chick at a gas station. She's family. Part of the Hell's Handlers Motorcycle Club."

Saint increased the pressure a fraction.

The guy sucked in a sharp breath and lost any last hint of bravado.

"And I'm what we like to call an enforcer-in-training," Saint continued. "Means when people make my family uncomfortable, I fix the problem. *Permanently*."

"Hey, man, I didn't touch her," the guy whispered. Sweat beaded at his hairline, and his legs began to shake. "Jesus Christ, I was just talking to her." His pitch rose until he was nearly whining.

"Oh, I heard you talking." Saint's smile widened. "Promises, right? *'Best she's ever had.'* You talk to all women like that?"

"N-no." The guy flinched as Saint shifted the blade the tiniest bit. "Look, I'll fucking back off. I get it."

"See, now we're getting along," Saint said, squeezing the guy's shoulder so hard he winced. "Here's what's gonna happen. You're gonna apologize to her, not to me, and then you're gonna climb in that shiny little Prius your daddy bought you, and get the hell out of here. You will not look back. You will not circle back. You will not suddenly realize you left your emotional support energy drink at this gas station. You will not, for the rest of your miserable life, approach a woman who looks like she'd rather be anywhere else. You get me?"

The guy nodded quickly. "Yeah. Yeah, I get you." He nodded so fast that he looked like one of those dolls with the wobbly head. This guy better not piss himself.

"Because if I see your face near her again," Saint went on, tone still conversational, "I'm gonna take this little knife…" he pressed in just enough to make the guy grunt, "… and carve a reminder into your side. Something simple. Maybe the word *'no,'* so you don't forget it."

A strangled whimper escaped Gym Bro's throat.

"Am I clear?"

"Yes," he wheezed. "C-clear."

"Good man."

Saint flipped the blade closed and slid it back into his pocket in one smooth motion, then slapped the guy's back as if they'd just finished discussing sports. He turned him around by the shoulders and shoved him back toward Beth.

The guy swallowed hard. "Uh…sorry, ma'am," he mumbled in her direction. "Didn't mean to make you uncomfortable."

Beth's brows rose, but she gave a short nod. "Okay." Her voice was cool and controlled, despite the flush in her cheeks.

Saint could tell she'd have liked to eviscerate the guy verbally, but she kept her thoughts to herself.

Gym Bro backed away fast, then broke into a near sprint toward a shiny black car at a neighboring pump. He didn't look back.

Saint watched until the car pulled out of the station and merged onto the highway. Only then did he turn back to Beth.

She let out a breath. "You know…" she said, "… I was doing okay handling it."

He grunted. "You were uncomfortable. Your face was, at least."

She huffed. "He was a creep, yeah. But he was just spouting off bullshit. Doesn't mean he needs to get stabbed in a truck stop gas station."

"Didn't stab him," Saint said with a shrug. "Thought about it, sure, but I have self-control."

Despite herself, Beth's lips twitched. "You always travel with a knife?"

"Just a little one," he said. "Barely counts."

She stared at him for a long beat, then shook her head. "You bikers are insane."

"We prefer effective." He studied her, noting the way her shoulders were slowly relaxing now that the guy was gone. "For the record, you never owe a dude politeness when he makes you uncomfortable. You never owe a smile. You never owe a conversation. You sure as fuck don't owe him your time or your body."

Her throat worked as she swallowed and then nodded. "I know."

"Yeah," he said softly. "But sometimes knowing and feeling aren't the same thing."

Her gaze flicked to his, surprise and something like gratitude in her eyes. "You're getting *real* wise in your old age, Saint."

He snorted. "Fuck off. I'm not old."

"You gotta be what, like close to forty?" she said around a Twizzler, then smiled, for real this time.

"Come on, brat," he said, jerking his chin toward the bike. "We've got a few more hours till home. And I'm thirty-fucking-three. Nowhere near forty."

She giggled, then grew serious.

Home.

The word settled between them like a living thing.

Beth's fingers drifted unconsciously to the faint bruises along her throat. In the harsh daylight, they'd faded from angry purple to sickly yellow-green, but they were still visible. She glanced at the convenience store windows, where faint reflections showed her makeup-free face and loose hair.

"Gonna try to cover them up at the next stop?" he asked gently.

"Probably," she said. "I don't want… *them* to see this. Not right away."

He nodded. He got it. Shame had a way of making you want to hide the evidence, even when you weren't the one who'd done anything wrong.

"Helmet on," he said instead. "Let's roll."

The last stretch of the ride flew by, and crawled at the same time.

Beth leaned against him, quiet, as the scenery shifted from a flat mid-west sprawl to rolling hills and, eventually, the familiar rise of the Smoky Mountains. The air grew cooler, the ground grew greener. The smells changed too—less hot asphalt and exhaust, more pine and damp earth.

Tennessee.

Home turf.

For Saint, it meant club, family, and responsibilities. For Beth, it hopefully represented safety, love, and healing, but she feared it also meant facing hard truths.

He felt the tension humming through her body the closer they got. Every time he slowed for a town or a light, her fingers flexed slightly at his waist, like she was bracing for impact.

They stopped once more at a small station on the outskirts of town so Beth could duck into the bathroom. When she returned, her makeup was heavy on her throat and cheeks. She looped a scarf loosely around her neck despite the warm weather. It wouldn't fool Copper or Shell for long, if at all, but he didn't call her on it.

He'd already sealed his fate by keeping information from his president.

By the time the familiar road to the clubhouse appeared, Saint's chest felt tight. He rode in slowly with gravel crunching under his tires and the low rumble of his bike carrying over the quiet of the late afternoon.

The compound was its usual controlled chaos with bikes parked in a line, a few brothers milling about, smoke curling from the grill out back, and the faint thump of music coming from inside the clubhouse.

Out front, at one of the heavy wooden picnic tables that had seen more than their fair share of beer, laughter, and threats, sat Copper and Shell.

Copper's massive frame was kicked back on the bench, one forearm resting on the table, a bottle of beer in hand. Shell sat tucked into his side, their shoulders touching, her legs crossed, her blonde hair up in a messy knot.

They both looked up at the sound of Saint's bike.

His stomach gave a slow, uneasy roll.

He cut the engine. The sudden silence rang in his ears louder than the screech of skidding tires. Beth's arms loosened from around his waist, hesitating for a fraction of a second before she pulled away.

She slid off the bike, boots hitting the gravel, and lifted her helmet with shaking hands. Her scarf shifted, and Saint watched Copper's gaze zero in on that tiny movement like a laser sight.

For half a heartbeat, no one moved.

Then Copper set his beer down with deliberate care and rose to his full, imposing height. Beth let out a small squeak and then ran to her father at full speed. She threw herself into his massive arms, burrowing her face into his chest.

Beside him, a few tears escaped Shell's eyes. Her gaze met Saint's, and she smiled. *Thank you,* she mouthed.

He nodded.

He'd done his job.

Beth was home.

There wasn't any reason for him to stick around and torture himself staring at her all night.

Beth glanced over her father's shoulder and caught his eye. Something passed between them—gratitude, maybe, or the weight of shared secrets. Like her mother, she mouthed *thank you,* and he gave her a small nod.

Copper's gaze found his next, sharp and knowing. Saint held it, gave his president a respectful chin lift, then climbed back on his bike. Time to find someone to fuck so he could stop fantasizing about his president's gorgeous daughter.

Chapter Six

I'm home.

When Beth launched herself at her father, he caught her with ease, as he did when she was a small child. His strong arms closed around her in the familiar and comforting hug she hadn't realized how much she'd missed. He smelled of leather and sandalwood with a hint of the tobacco he still thought Shell didn't know he indulged in occasionally.

She knew. Of course, she knew. The man couldn't hide anything from his ol' lady.

For one moment, everything in the world made sense. The stress, fear, and pain stayed back in Texas as Copper's embrace transported her back to a time when life was simple, when her father's hug could cure every manner of ail and heartache.

" 'Bout time you came home to us." His deep, gruff voice wrapped around her like a warm blanket, chasing away the chill that had settled in her heart months ago.

"I'm sorry," she whispered against his massive chest. "Sorry I've stayed away so long."

He grunted. "You're here now. That's all that matters."

If only it were that simple.

"Enough! Stop hogging her. I'm the one who pushed her out of my body after hours and hours of painful labor," Shell said, swatting Copper's thick arms. "It's my turn."

Copper kissed the top of her head as he chuckled. "Can't help it if I give better hugs." The second he released her, Shell grabbed hold and yanked her into an equally strong embrace.

"Can't argue with that," she said as she hugged her daughter. "Nothing better than being in your dad's arms."

Beth held her mom just as tightly, inhaling the sweet scent of the vanilla lotion Shell had worn for as long as she could remember.

"Especially when I'm naked."

Beth barked out a laugh. "God, Mom, I've been home for three seconds. Do I really need to hear that shit already?"

They both burst out laughing as Copper muttered something about dragging Shell to his office. Growing up around the club, Beth learned about the birds, bees, and entire animal kingdom at an early age. PDA was commonplace, as was raunchy humor, swearing, and innuendos. She'd never censored herself around her parents, and they didn't hide much from her either.

"God, I missed you, my baby girl," Shell whispered.

Tears sprang to Beth's eyes. "Missed you too, Mom. I'm sorry it's been so long."

Clearing her throat, Shell pulled back but kept her hands on Beth's shoulders. "None of that. You're here now. We're not going to waste time on apologies." She smiled, then ran her hands over Beth's hair, ending by cupping Beth's cheeks. "I'd almost forgotten how b-beautiful you are." She blinked rapidly as though fighting tears.

Beth rolled her eyes as she fought to flinch from her mom's hand on her sore cheek. Makeup did a fantastic job of concealing the redness, but it still stung when touched. "Mom, you're ridiculous," she said as she pulled her face back.

"You must be starving," Shell said as Copper slung an arm across her mom's shoulders, pulling her tightly against him, probably to save Beth from more of her motherly fussing.

"We got a shit ton of food cooking out back."

"I can smell it. I'm starved." She turned, wanting to share a look with Saint, maybe thank him properly now that they'd arrived, but the space behind her was empty, and his bike was gone. "Oh. Where…" What the hell? Maybe he'd wandered past her while she'd been distracted by her parents. But where was his bike?

"Come on." Copper pulled her to his other side, steering her and Shell toward the side of the clubhouse. "I'm fucking starved."

"Yeah." Beth glanced around, frowning as she let Copper guide her to where the rest of the club milled around, eating and drinking without Saint anywhere in sight. He couldn't have vanished, so where the hell did he run off to?

"Oh, my fucking God, she really is here!" Maverick let out a whoop and charged her way from where he'd been hanging out with Zach at the grill. As a kid, he'd been her favorite 'uncle.' Covered from head to toe in tattoos, he'd been like a walking coloring book. Mav was loud, wild, inappropriate, and never-ending fun. He used to let her color over his tattoos with her markers, making them all various shades of pink and purple. Hours of her childhood consisted of redecorating his colorful arms and legs.

He plowed into her, whipping her off her feet into a twirl that had her laughing.

"Shit," he said, panting. "That was easier when you were seven, and I was in my thirties."

"Careful, old man, you don't want to throw your back out. You won't be able to do all those dirty things to Stephanie that you two freaks get up to."

Mav threw back his head and laughed. "Shit, Cop, she really was raised by a feral bunch of bikers, wasn't she?" He ruffled her hair like she was still a kid.

"Hey." She swatted his hands. "Go bother someone else."

"Good to have you back, kiddo."

Kiddo.

They all used to call her that. As much as she'd hated it during her teen years, hearing the familiar nickname again nearly brought her to tears.

The next few hours followed a similar pattern. Beth managed to shovel a few bites into her mouth between hugs, hellos, and introductions. Everyone wanted to reminisce and welcome her home, which she appreciated.

But after two hours, she needed a break. Her back ached from days on a motorcycle, her cheeks ached from smiling, and the damn scarf around her neck was soaked with sweat, but couldn't be removed because of the fucking bruises.

Thankfully, no one seemed to have noticed the bruising, and the club appeared to buy her flimsy I've-been-too-stressed-and-busy excuse for her distance. After a lengthy chat with her mom, Izzy, Toni, and Stephanie, the women who'd played the most pivotal role in her upbringing, she'd needed a break. They'd rambled on about how proud they were of her, how they admired her independence and drive, and how happy she should be with the woman she's become.

If they only knew.

Every word they spoke stabbed into her façade, carving a chunk out of the bullshit story she'd sold them. Every compliment and gush made her feel like the worst kind of fraud. What would they think if they knew the truth? If they knew she'd let a man hurt her? That she'd stayed with a man who belittled, humiliated, and hurt her?

They'd be devastated.

All of a sudden, she couldn't tolerate another second of the conversation.

"Excuse me," she blurted as she shot to her feet.

Four sets of startled eyes stared up at her from where the ladies sat at the picnic table.

"You okay, sweetie?" Shell asked.

"Yeah, of course. I'm just gonna grab a drink and…" She glanced around. *Come on, somewhere there had to be an excuse.* Gator sat alone, removed from the group, frowning at his phone. "Um, grab and drink and say hi to Gator. I haven't had a chance to chat with him."

"Okay, sweetie. I'm glad you're having fun." Shell squeezed her hand and grinned the same smile she'd been giving Beth all night—part adoration, part excitement, and all love.

"Do not let that man talk himself into your panties, missy," Stephanie said as she shook her finger and glared in Beth's direction. "He is a menace."

Laughing, Beth lifted her hands in surrender. "Don't worry about that. That man is way too insane for me." And that was the truth. As much as she loved Gator and as good friends as they'd become over the last few years, he was too unpredictable and wild for her, not to mention she had no interest in putting him in Copper's murderous crosshairs.

After refilling her cup at the keg and a second for Gator, she wandered to where he sat alone in an Adirondak chair, removed from the rest of the group. Two other chairs, one on either side of him, remained empty. He stared down at his phone with a very un-Gator-like scowl.

"Mind if I join you?"

Gator's head popped up. As soon as he laid eyes on her, his expression morphed into one of happiness. He set his phone face down on the armrest and grinned the smile that had charmed many, many brave women over the years. "If one of those beers is for me, then you better sit that sweet ass down."

Instantly, her mood lifted. Gator had that effect. His personality was so out there that she could do nothing but smile in his wacky presence. "It sure is."

"Well then, cop a squat, princess," he said, patting the chair on his right.

"You better not start in on that princess shit," she said as she handed him his Solo cup of beer and took a seat. "You know I hate that."

Grinning like the devil he was, he shrugged. "But you're the club princess. It's straight-up facts."

Beth glared at him. "Unless you want me to bite your other leg, you will *not* call me princess."

He snorted, then sipped his beer. "Fine, be like that."

The sun had set, and darkness wrapped around the clubhouse and the surrounding area. Screw lit a bonfire a while ago. It roared about twenty feet away from where she and Gator sat, chasing away the slight nighttime chill. A few of the kids roasted marshmallows, stuffing them between crackers and chocolate to make a delicious, gooey treat. Some of the guys flirted with their guests while others chatted in groups, drinking and laughing.

Beth couldn't help but smile as she watched the antics unfolding.

This was home.

They sat in silence for a while, each lost in their own thoughts. He might be off his rocker, but Gator could read people in a way most couldn't. Without words, he seemed to realize she needed some time to process. Of course, he couldn't keep his trap shut for too long.

"So, saw you getting grilled by the ol' lady brigade."

"Not grilled, just… told how amazing I am. It was super uncomfortable."

He chuckled. "Aww, p-cess, they just love you."

She arched an eyebrow as she stared at his mischievous smirk. "P-cess? Seriously?"

"What? You said no princess, and I think it's got a nice ring to it." His eyes sparkled with a whole lot of trouble.

"Fuck you."

Gator let out a loud laugh. "Damn, it's good to have you home, p-cess."

It was good to be home, even if she had a mountain of issues to get over. And she'd let the p-cess slide for now. As annoying as it was, having people call her silly nicknames made her feel loved in a way she hadn't in a long time. And stupid as it might be, p-cess was still better than full-on princess. *God, she hated that prissy nickname.*

Beth cleared her throat as she traced a line of condensation running down her cup. "Hey, uh… I haven't seen Saint since we got here." Hopefully, that sounded as nonchalant as it did in her head.

Gator gave her a knowing look over the rim of his cup. "That is a road you do *not* want to travel down, p-cess."

"What? There's no road. The guy dragged my ass all the way here from Texas, then disappeared." She shrugged. "I just wanna say thanks and make sure he's good. It was a long ride."

"Mm-hmm, I'm sure it was."

"Gator…" She tried glaring a hole through his stupid, smirking face, but it only made him grin bigger.

"Copper will take him apart piece by painful piece."

"Stop! You're making shit up. Nothing happened, and nothing will happen." She threw her hands up. "I don't even want anything to happen. I'm just asking a friendly question."

"Okay, so you won't give a shit when I tell you he took off to get his dick sucked?"

Air whooshed out of her as though someone punched her

stomach with a meaty fist. She swallowed. Her saliva tasted disgusting as it slid down to her roiling stomach. "No. Of course not. Why would I care?"

"Whatever you say, p-cess," he said with another of those wicked smirks. This time, she was tempted to slap it off his face.

"That's right, I do say."

Could she sound any more like a sullen teenager?

"Can we please talk about something else? This conversation is absurd."

"Sure. Wanna talk about those bruises you're hiding and why you're lying to everyone about your boyfriend being an abusive piece of shit."

Beth froze with her Solo cup halfway to her mouth. "W-what?" She laughed the best she could, but it sounded fake as Gator's last hookup's breasts. "What are you talking about?"

He gave her a glacial look that made her reach for the scarf on instinct.

"P-cess, I grew up in the backwater swamps of Louisiana, tried and true hillbilly shit. Trust me when I tell you I can spot an abused woman from a mile away. You're jumpy, you're hanging closer to the women, you're wearing a fucking scarf in the goddamn summer, and you're wearing more makeup than I've ever seen you wear."

"I'm not an abused woman," she snapped, glaring at him. What the hell did he know? *Nothing.* He knew nothing of her life or her situation. "I just found myself in a... bad situation."

Wow, convincing, Beth.

Gator's face softened, and he opened his mouth to speak. God, that look was worse than before.

"Do not pity me, Gator. Don't you fucking dare."

"Hey..." He reached over and took the cup from her, setting it down on the ground before taking her hands in his.

"I don't pity you, Beth. I'm sorry for what happened to you, and I'll happily feed the pieces of his body to my alligators, but I do not pity you. I'm not that stupid."

Her lips quirked. "He's not dead," she said as she pulled her hands from his grasp and picked up her beer.

"You fucking kidding me? Saint let him live?" His eyes widened, and he shook his head. "Find that fucking hard to believe. That motherfucker does not stand for that shit."

"He… well, he fucked my boy… ex-boyfriend up, that's for sure. But I made him stop before it went too far."

Gator whistled. "Didn't think anyone had that kinda power. You don't know Saint well, hon. He hides behind his chill exterior, but there is some serious rage simmering under the hood. That man is possessive as fuck and will go apeshit on anyone threatening his family."

"Huh." Hundreds of questions filled her mind, but it didn't feel right pumping Gator for information about Saint. The man hadn't pressured her to talk when she wasn't ready. Sussing out his story behind his back felt like an invasion of privacy he didn't deserve. Maybe one day, she and Saint would have a friendship where he could open up to her.

"I'm guessing Daddy Prez doesn't know about this."

"Why do you say that?"

Gator snorted. "Uh, because my ass is in this seat drinking a beer and chatting with you instead of heading to Texas with the entire club for an execution."

"Oh…" Beth glanced down at her hand in her lap. The nails were a mess. She didn't bother with fancy tips or designs since her hands were in water and dog fur all day, but she typically kept them neat and short. A few were chipped and jagged now, probably from struggling with Jason.

"P-cess, you know it's fucking wrong to ask Saint to keep something this big from your old man, right? From his president. That kinda shit's considered a betrayal and will get the patch stripped from his back."

Her heart sank so low that it might be lying on the floor. "I know," she whispered, picking at the ragged edge of a chipped nail. "I know I was wrong to ask him not to say anything. I just…" The tip of her nose tingled in a way that indicated tears would soon follow. "Shit," she whispered, shifting her gaze to the starry sky to keep them from falling. "Is that why Saint didn't stay? Is he worried Copper will be able to tell? Or is he pissed at me for asking him to keep it a secret?"

"Nope," Gator said, popping the p with an exaggerated pooch of his lips. "Told you, he went to get his dick sucked."

"Right." Why did that make her feel worse? It shouldn't matter what Saint did or with whom. They'd hung out for a few days while he did a pity job and rescued her from her abusive boyfriend. The least the guy deserved was a night out and a hookup. How selfish was she to assume he'd want to hang around her pitiful ass for another night? Hell, for all she knew, he had a steady girlfriend who'd been missing him over the past few days.

"You're hot, p-cess."

She wrinkled her nose. "What?" Was there something more than alcohol in his cup? "What the hell are you talking about, and what's it got to do with anything?"

Gator laughed long and loud. "Saint just spent two days with a sexy woman on the back of his bike, wrapped around him like a damn octopus. Then he had to sleep with the same sexy woman five feet away in a different bed. A woman he couldn't touch if she were the last damn broad on earth. The poor bastard needs some fucking relief. What man wouldn't? He might have the name, but trust me, he ain't that kinda saint. None of us are."

"That's ridiculous," she mumbled, but her face flamed to

incendiary levels as she digested Gator's words.

There was no way a gorgeous man like Saint found anything about her attractive over the past two days. She was an emotional and physical mess. Gator had to be wrong. Most likely, Saint hated the idea of keeping secrets from her father and was happy to be rid of her after two days glued to her side.

Of course, the man wanted a break, and he deserved one.

If the thought of him with some random woman bothered her, that was her own problem to get over.

"This a party for two, or is there room for one more?"

"Lindsey!" Beth flew out of her chair and threw herself at her friend, whom she hadn't seen in far too long.

"I am so mad at you," Lindsey mumbled as her words became muffled by Beth's hair.

"I know, I'm a horrible friend. Please don't hate me. I'll do better." Adopted by Toni and Zach at thirteen, Lindsey had faced serious challenges in her early years. She was about eight years older than Beth, who'd idolized her 'older cousin' growing up. In her late teens, Lindsey went from someone she followed around like an adoring puppy to her closest friend. Today, she was another person Beth alienated herself from, thanks to Jason. All she could hope now was that Lindsey didn't hold a grudge.

"Never. I love you too much." Lindsey released her and sat in the free chair on Gator's other side. "So," she said, narrowing her shrew eyes in Beth's direction. She pointed toward her own neck, indicating the scarf. "Wanna tell me the real story and not this bullshit about being too busy with work to keep in touch?"

Shit. Why did everyone have to be so perceptive?

Chapter Seven

The tinkle of the diner's bells was as familiar to Saint as his phone's ringtone. Not a week went by, hell, not more than two days passed before he was grabbing food or a coffee at Toni's Diner. Once a biker-free establishment owned by Zach's in-laws, who hated the MC, his ol' lady opened the place to all when she took over, and it was practically a second clubhouse.

"Hey, Saint," Lindsay called out as she restocked juice glasses behind the counter. "The other guys are here, usual table." A few years ago, Lindsey took over as manager of the diner, letting her adoptive mother, Toni, step back from day-to-day operations in her role as owner. "Mel will be over with coffee and to take your order in a second."

"Thanks, hon," he said as he strode straight to the farthest booth against the window. The same table the club's leadership sat at, as far back as he could recall. Sure enough, Copper, Maverick, and Rocket sat sipping coffee and talking.

Rocket took over as VP of the club almost fifteen years ago when Viper had been killed. Saint never met Viper, but the club had mourned his loss for years. As far as he was concerned, Rocket made a great VP. The guy was steady, thought before he acted, and had a mind for planning and organizing.

"Hey, Saint, thanks for meeting with us on short notice."

"No problem." As though he could refuse a call to sit down with the club's top officers. "How's Beth settling in?" The cushioned bench whooshed beneath him as he sat next to Zach and across from Rocket and Copper.

The president's expression darkened. "She's… okay. Not our usual spitfire. Why? Anything you want to tell me?"

Shit, why the hell had he brought her up?

Because you can't stop thinking about her and how you left her fucking ex alive when he deserved a pine box six feet under.

He'd dropped her at the clubhouse five days ago with every intention of finding some mindless relief. Instead, he'd ridden straight home, downed half a bottle of Jack, and passed out for fourteen hours.

So much for getting her out of his system.

"Cop, leave him alone," Maverick said, rolling his eyes. "He did his job and brought her home. She'll talk when she's ready."

Did that mean they suspected something more brewed beneath the surface of Beth's excuses? Maybe, but they probably weren't thinking her boyfriend fucking beat her. No way would Copper sit there calm and not murder someone if he did.

Saint shifted as though he could wriggle away from the discomfort while clearing his throat. "Pretty sure she'd cut my balls off if I tried to speak for her."

That had Copper cracking a grin. "True. My daughter knows how to take men down a few pegs. If there's one thing I taught her, it's not to put up with bullshit from assholes."

Christ, he was going to flip his shit when he found out the truth.

"Right." Saint ran a hand through his hair.

"Hey there, Saint, these handsome devils said you were

coming. What can I get going for you?"

Saved by the waitress. Thank God.

"Hey, Mel. Cinnamon roll waffles for me," he said to their beaming waitress. She, like the other staff at the diner, wore a light blue T-shirt with the diner's logo and a denim skirt. Her long, curly hair was tied back at the nape of her neck.

"You got it, sweetie. I'll put a rush on it, so your meal comes out with the rest." She placed her hand on his shoulder, letting it linger as she focused on the rest of the table. "Anyone need a coffee refill?"

"We're good, Mel. Thanks," Copper said with a nod.

Melody took it for the dismissal that Copper meant it to be. "Sounds good. I'll be back with your food in a few minutes."

As she turned away, she let her fingertips trail down Saint's arm.

"Someone's hungry," Maverick said, eyes gleaming.

"Of course I'm fucking hungry. It's ten, and I haven't eaten."

Rocket snorted. "Not what he meant."

Grinning like the idiot he was, Maverick laughed. "Yeah, I'm talking about Mel. That girl is starving, and I don't mean for fucking waffles. She's more interested in the sausage." He waggled his eyebrows. "Your sausage, to be specific."

"Your sense of humor froze when you turned fourteen," Rocket muttered.

Mav shrugged, completely unrepentant. To know and love Maverick was to accept his constant innuendo and out-there personality. God knew how his ol' lady, Stephanie, put up with him for so many years.

"You hit that?" Mav asked.

"Nah, not my type."

"What?" Mav glanced over his shoulder at the counter. "She's fucking cute. Got a great ass, good tits, and clearly wants you. Plus, she's always so sweet. What the fuck's not to like?"

"It's the sweet thing," Rocket said as he sipped his coffee. "Saint doesn't do sweet. He's too fucked up for sweet."

"What the hell?" He lifted his hands and scoffed. "Fuck's sake, I'm sitting right here, and I can speak for my fucking self, thank you."

"Okay, why are you passing up on readily available pussy?"

Well, shit. Melody hit on him every damn time he came into the diner during her shift. She frequently showed up at club parties as well, dressed like a snack, and gave clear signs of her interest. And he'd never gone for it for one particular reason.

"She's too fucking sweet," he mumbled, making two of the three men at the table laugh.

"Told ya." Rocket's expression never changed.

"You don't gotta keep her. Have some fun and move on." Rumor had it, before he met his ol' lady, Mav was the king womanizer of the MC. Saint had never witnessed it since it happened before his time. All he'd ever seen was the man so obsessed with his woman that he barely gave her a moment of peace.

"A sweet girl will give him sweet fun. Maybe he wants nasty fun."

A slow grin broke curved Mav's lips. "That true, Saint? You prefer a bad girl who's gonna let you do all sorts of nasty shit to her?"

Saint groaned and stared up at the fluorescent lights. No way was he admitting Rocket hit the nail on the head.

"You know, sometimes those sweet girls are closet freaks. The freakiest."

"All right, can we cut the shit?" Copper broke in. "Give the guy a break. He can pick his own women to fuck. "Long as he stays away from Beth, I don't give a shit who he fucks or how."

Awesome. Did that mean he shouldn't mention the dirty thoughts he'd had about Beth in the shower that morning? Or how he'd stroked himself raw imagining her in there with him, moaning and begging for his cock?

Probably not.

"No worries there, Prez," he said as his stomach turned over. "Pretty sure none of us are stupid enough to go there."

Copper grunted.

"All right, I'll get serious," Mav said as Melody walked back over with a loaded tray giving off scents of cinnamon and maple.

She deposited the food with quick efficiency and no flirtation this time, reading the change of tone at the table. "Enjoy, gentlemen. Flag me down if you need anything else."

"Thanks, hon." Mav wasted no time slathering his omelet in hot sauce. "So what've you got for us, Cop?" As soon as the question left his lips, he shoveled in an enormous bite of food in his mouth.

Copper shifted to pull his phone from his pocket. After a few swipes and taps, he laid it, screen up, in the center of the table. "Jigsaw took this last night."

Rocket must have already viewed the photos because he didn't lean in the way Mav and Saint did.

"Shit," Mav muttered as he swiped through the photos of a man wearing a biker cut distributing drugs to various buyers behind a dumpster. "Fentanyl?"

"That's my guess."

"Fuck. Last thing we need is an active dealer right here in town."

"Yeah."

Saint risked a glance at Copper, who wore a fierce scowl. "Where were these taken?"

"Behind that payday loan place on Wilkshire. He spotted

the rider on the highway when he was with Izzy in her car. They tailed him until he set up shop. Said he sold to about five people before they had to leave so Iz could get to work on time."

"Mav, zoom in so I can see their rockers." Mav separated his fingers, narrowing in on a back view of the biker's cut. "What's that say, Devil's something. Dominion?"

"That's what it looks like to me too," Mav added. He'd abandoned his food and frowned at the phone, entirely focused on the task at hand.

"Yeah, that's what I came up with. I did a cursory search on them. Not much info. Think they're based out of Memphis."

"Hmm." Mav stroked his chin, one of the few places on his body not covered in ink. "I'll head to the office and do a deeper dive when we leave." He owned a security company that specialized in PI work, camera installation, and the like. If information on these guys existed, Maverick would find it.

"I might know someone who could clue us in to who these guys are."

Copper raised an eyebrow. "Yeah?"

Nodding, Saint sat back against the booth and picked up his knife and fork. If he didn't start eating, his food would go cold, and nothing sucked more than a piping hot breakfast gone cold. "Yeah, you all know how I was when Mak and I first escaped the cult. I was an angry fucking kid. I fell in with a shit crowd for a while. Thunder and Mak basically slapped me upside my head, set me right, and helped me get legit work too. Started me repossessing cars, which turned out to be a perfect fit for someone who didn't mind confrontation and knew how to disappear fast. But I still know a few people from back then. I'm thinking of one guy in particular who probably shouldn't be alive right now. No way would a new supplier fly under his radar."

"Think you can get in touch with him today?"

"Probably. As long as he's not face down in a ditch somewhere."

"All right. Good. Mav, you get on the computer. Saint, you get with your friend. Hopefully, we can dig up enough dirt to have something to use as leverage to drive them out of town before shit turns violent or people start dropping dead from Fent ODs."

"Yeah, we don't need that shit. Next thing we know, we'll have Feds coming out of our asses. I do not want DEA agents crawling all over our mountains."

"Ugh." Mav rested his head back on the bench, staring up. "That always starts a chain reaction. DEA, then ATF, and fucking FBI. Christ, do I hate the fucking FBI." He scrubbed a hand down his face as he sighed.

Once upon a time, Stephanie worked for the FBI. After a series of screwed-up events, including Stephanie and Maverick being taken hostage together, the FBI sent her in to infiltrate the MC. Instead, she fell in love with Mav and almost ended up in a cell alongside the rest of the club. The FBI hung her out to dry, and she walked away without looking back. To say Mav carried a bitter grudge would be the understatement of the century.

"Let's not jump the gun." Rocket set his fork down as he looked at Mav. "For all we know, these guys are low-level dealers who'll leave town without a problem. Wait to freak out until we have to."

"Yeah." Mav sighed. "You're right." He rolled his shoulders, then went back to his food. "That shit gets me riled."

Made sense. Saint couldn't imagine being married. He couldn't even imagine being in a serious relationship. Most of the time, he assumed he was too intense to commit to someone else. He'd go off the fucking rails every time someone looked at his partner sideways, let alone threatened them. There'd be a pile of bodies in his wake, casualties of his possessive and distrustful nature. What woman would put up with that?

Though he came by most of his issues through nurture rather than nature, growing up powerless to shield his siblings from major abuse turned him into a feral animal when it came to the security and happiness of those he loved.

They dug into their food, eating in silence for a few moments. Melody came by to refill their cups, and Saint made sure to keep his gaze on his plate and avoid engaging with her. He liked the woman but had no plans to lead her on or indulge her flirting. She'd ramped it up lately, and sooner or later, he'd have to have a conversation he dreaded.

As he swiped the last bite of his waffles through a puddle of syrup, Copper's phone rang.

"Sorry, guys, it's Shell." In all the time he'd known Copper, Saint had never seen him ignore a call from his ol' lady. Prez made it clear his wife and daughter came first. Some would consider that a weakness, but Saint admired the hell out of it.

"Hey, baby," Copper said as he held the phone to his ear. "Hold on. Slow down." His expression turned to stone, and his shoulders went rigid. He gripped the phone so hard his fingers blanched. "What?"

That one word, said with such cold lethality, had a shiver running down Saint's spine. Instantly on full alert, he shoved his plate away and focused on every detail he could ascertain from Copper's body language and words. Mav and Rocket also picked up on the change in mood, abandoning their meals and focusing entirely on Copper.

"Baby, breathe," Copper said. After a short pause, he continued. "I just need to know two things right now. Is she safe, and is she hurt?"

She? Who the fuck were they talking about? One of the ol'

ladies?

Shell spoke for a few seconds, and while Saint understood why Copper wouldn't put a call like this on speaker phone, his insides screamed for more information.

"We'll be there in ten minutes. Tell her she did good, baby. God, I fucking love you too."

As Copper lowered the phone, his dangerous gaze met Saint's. His enforcer skills would be needed. He could feel that in his bones before Copper even spoke.

"One of these fucks approached Beth."

Oh fuck. Ice slithered down Saint's spine.

"Shell's bringing her to the clubhouse now."

He shot out of the booth so fast that a rush of wind sent a pile of napkins skittering to the floor, not that he cared. After tossing a twenty on the table for his meal and tip, he beelined to his bike. His brothers could dine on his exhaust before they caught up. He wasn't waiting.

Every protective instinct he'd ever had screamed at him to get to her. *Now.*

Someone was going to die today.

Chapter Eight

"Come in," Beth said to the soft knock on her door. It'd be her mother. They were the only two at home. Copper had club business, and her siblings in their late teens were out and about living their lives.

Cassie, who'd become her surrogate grandmother after moving in when Beth was a child, went on a six-month cruise with a band of wild senior ladies. Beth wouldn't see her for quite a while.

Sure enough, Shell opened the door and stepped into the room Beth had slept in since she was a child. It no longer had posters of her favorite shows or fairy lights, but Shell insisted it would always be Beth's room, no matter where she lived or how long she stayed away.

"Hey, honey, what are you up to?"

"Just reading." Beth set her e-reader on the armrest of the plush recliner her parents bought sometime after she moved out. "I like this chair here. It's a good addition."

"Thanks." Shell must have recently finished a workout. She wore running shorts and a black sports bra with her blonde hair pulled up in a high ponytail. "So..." she said as she walked into the room in her socked feet and sat on the side of the queen-size bed near Beth.

This chat had been brewing. Frankly, Beth was impressed by how long her mother held out before coming in for the what-the-fuck conversation.

Sighing, Beth righted the recliner and then curled her legs beneath her. "I know." She glanced out the large window into her parents' vast backyard before focusing back on her mom. "I've been home for five days, and I've been a waste of space the entire time. I need to get out of the house and touch grass. I need to see people."

I need to stop hiding away and licking my wounds.

Shell frowned. "Okay, that's not at all what I was going to say."

"Maybe not, but I'm sure you're thinking it."

"Wrong again." Shell had concern written all over her face. "I'm worried about you. That's all. I can tell you're processing something big, something upsetting, and that's fine. Take all the time you need to get your head on straight and be in a good place. You need time to process and maybe heal, which means something happened that you need to heal from. Something I don't know anything about. And that's fine. You are an adult who no longer needs to tell your mommy your problems, but I want to make sure you know that you can. You can always talk to me, no matter how old you get. You don't have to go through anything alone."

"Mom…" She blinked away moisture. How did she get so lucky to have the most incredible mother?

Shell stood. "That's all. I'm not here to pressure you into talking if you're not ready." She leaned down and kissed the top of Beth's head. "Just know I'm here if you need me. And I'm so happy you're home."

Her throat thickened, making it hard to swallow. "Thanks, Mom," she croaked. "I think I'm going to take a walk into town to try to drag myself out of this funk."

"Really?" Shell's forehead wrinkled. "It's about two and a half miles to town."

Perfect. A five-mile walk should help clear her head. It's exactly what she needed. Fresh mountain air, sunshine, and movement were better than growing stagnant in her parents' house.

After changing from sweatpants to shorts and an athletic tank, since Copper kept the house like a damn ice box, she headed out on her way. Once she got to town, she'd grab a bottle of water for the walk back. Hopefully, she wouldn't run into anyone she knew. Some friends from her childhood still lived in the area. They'd probably be pissed once they found out she came home and didn't make contact, but the truth was too awkward to share, and she didn't feel like lying to everyone.

Hey, Beth, it's so great to have you back. What made you decide to come home?

Oh, well, my abusive boyfriend was choking the life out of me, so I figured it was finally time to end things.

Not exactly how she wanted to jump back into the social scene around town, being the daughter of an outlaw biker meant she'd spent plenty of time as gossip in her younger years, but those were awed whispers and wild speculation about what went on in the club. This would be pity and cattiness disguised as sympathy.

No, thank you.

This walk was supposed to pull her from a negative headspace, and so far, despite the gorgeous blue sky and warm sun on her skin, she remained maudlin.

"Enough," she muttered aloud. "No more thinking about Jason and what happened in Texas for the rest of the walk."

She inhaled as deeply as possible, held it for a few seconds, and then let it out slowly. Something about the mountain air hit different. It had a freshness she'd missed living in Texas.

Slowly but surely, the tightness in her neck and shoulders began to unwind. Tension bled from the muscles as the sun warmed her skin, and her mind began to wander.

She'd need to get a job soon. Over the past few years, she'd fallen in love with her career at the pet grooming salon. Working with animals made her endlessly happy. One of her goals was to open her own salon one day. Saint mentioned they didn't have a good grooming salon in town. Apparently, Screw constantly complained about having to bring his dogs over forty minutes away for a quality groom.

And now she was thinking about Saint.

It irked her how he'd skipped out on the barbecue, leaving without so much as a see-ya-later. It also irked her how she hadn't heard a peep from him in the five days since she'd come home. Most of all, it irked her that it irked her.

"God, you're ridiculous."

Still, was what Gator told her true? Did he get all hot and bothered with her riding behind him? Did it get him so worked up that he passed on the barbecue to sleep with some random? And if so, why did it bother her? Saint was nothing more than a friend to her. Instead of being annoyed, she should be happy for him. The man gave up days of his life to drive halfway across the country and rescue her ass. The least he deserved out of the deal was a good orgasm.

Because you want to be the one to give it to him.

"No. No, I do not. And now I'm full-on talking to myself like a crazy person. Fantastic."

The rumble of a Harley, a sound she'd know anywhere, came from far up the road. Shielding her eyes, Beth squinted to bring the rider into view. He wore a cut, but his distance and helmet made it impossible to distinguish which of the Handlers rode toward her. Not that it mattered, she'd be happy to run into anyone in the MC.

As the rider drew closer, she stopped walking and lifted a

hand to wave hello. He slowed and, within seconds, came into full view.

"Oh shit," she muttered as they pulled off to the side of the road, then came to a complete stop next to her. He was *not* wearing a Handlers' cut. She frowned. He wasn't wearing a cut she recognized. Devil's Dominion? What the hell? Did he not realize they were in HHMC territory? "I'm so sorry," she said as the rider lifted his visor. "I thought you were someone else."

His dark, unfriendly eyes made a slow journey from her sneaker-covered feet to her face, pausing along the way to give her chest a longer leer. Her stomach turned, and she took a step back on instinct.

"Sorry again," she mumbled, then began walking.

"Wait." His arm shot out, and he grabbed her wrist. "Who'd you think I was?"

"Hey!" She tried wrenching out of his hold, but his grip was unbreakable. "Let me go."

All she could see were dark eyes beneath even darker eyebrows and tanned skin, framed by the full-face helmet. Amusement sparkled in his gaze.

"I said, let me go." Her heart kicked into overdrive, sending anxious chemicals zooming through her bloodstream as she tried to tug her arm free.

"One of those outlaw bikers?" he asked as he yanked her closer. "Hell's Handlers?"

Shit. She glanced around, but no one else was on the quiet mountain road, which was why she had taken this route in the first place, something she now regretted.

"What? No." She shook her head, keeping a steady pull on her wrist. I thought you were… a friend. Just a guy who rides a motorcycle."

"Hmm." He tilted his head, studying her, and though she couldn't see his mouth, it was easy to imagine a sinister smirk curving his lips. "You look familiar."

"No. We've never met." She'd have remembered those soulless eyes.

"Reddish hair," he said as he reached for her ponytail with the hand not holding her captive.

"Don't." She smacked his hand away, only thinking it might be a bad idea afterward, but he laughed as though finding her immensely amusing.

"Green eyes."

He yanked her so close she had to arch back to keep from smacking her head into his helmet as he inhaled. "Leather and motor oil. Smells like MC pussy to me."

"Let. Me. Go," she said through clenched teeth. She smelled like Bahama Breeze body wash, not the goddamn clubhouse.

The guy laughed. "Tell your father Demo says hello. And maybe he should be a little more accommodating to the newcomers in town. You know, roll out the red carpet a bit more. Everyone can use more friends, right? Better than having… *enemies*."

Fear fled, morphing into white-hot rage. *How dare he threaten her family?* The anger felt good, powerful after being on the wrong end of a man's anger for too long. In Texas, she'd been alone, no backup, no one to turn to when things with Jason went sour. But here in Tennessee, if someone messed with her, they paid a steep price. "I'm not telling anyone shit so that you can fuck right off."

His mood changed in an instant, going from playfully sinister to full-blown evil. The grip on her wrist tightened until his fingers dug into the delicate bones, making her whimper.

"I wouldn't be so fucking cocky if I were you, princess. Your club's been on top for too long in this town."

As she opened her mouth to blast him once again, the low purr of an engine, a car this time, not another motorcycle, had him releasing her with a harsh shove. She stumbled back, barely managing to keep herself from hitting the ground. Two blinks later, he was speeding away, leaving her trembling on the side of the road with a jackhammering heart.

"Shit. Shit. *Shit*." She dug her phone out as a cherry red sedan, whose driver had no clue he'd just saved her ass, whizzed by.

Two seconds later, her mom was answering on the first ring with a light laugh. "Told you that you wouldn't want to walk all the way to town."

"M-mom," she said, furious with the tremor in her voice.

All teasing disappeared. "What's wrong?"

"I need you to come get me," she said, before rattling off her location as she tried to control her breathing. "Some asshole in a cut I didn't recognize just stopped me on the side of the road and threatened the club."

"*What*?" Shell practically screamed into the phone. "Are you okay? Did he hurt you? Are you safe?"

"Yes. Yes, I'm fine. Just a little shaken."

"Okay, I'm already in the car on my way to you."

"Um, you should probably call Dad." Even though her surroundings were now quiet but for the chirping of birds and buzzing of cicadas, she glanced over her shoulder every few seconds. She could call her father herself, but wasn't in the headspace to deal with the level of freak out he'd have. At least her mom could talk him down before Beth had to deal with him.

"I will after I get to you. I want to stay on the line with you until I get there."

"T-thanks." She'd be forever grateful for a mom who knew and understood her so well. She knew how scared this made her daughter, and how Beth was too stubborn to admit it aloud. What could she say? Growing up around the club made her obstinate as hell.

She fidgeted and paced for the five minutes it took her mother to reach her. As soon as Shell's headlights rounded the corner, Beth took off in a run toward the car.

"Thank you," she said, breathless as she slipped into the passenger seat. Shell had pulled over and was already dialing Copper.

As soon as she shut the door, Beth hit the lock button.

"Copper, Beth, and I need to meet you at the clubhouse. She was walking into town and was stopped and threatened by a guy in a cut she didn't recognize. I'm assuming it's one of those bikers you guys have been tracking the past few weeks."

Shell paused for one second before saying the entire thing all over again. After a slow inhale, she nodded. "Yes. Yes, Copper, she's safe and not hurt, just freaked out. We'll be at the clubhouse soon. I love you." She nodded a few more times before saying goodbye, then turned to Beth. "Dad said you did well."

"Thanks." Despite the relative safety of the car, all she wanted was to be in the clubhouse, surrounded by people who had her back at all costs.

Shell reached across the console and took Beth's hand. They stayed quiet for the rest of the ride. Beth was lost in thought, wondering what came next and how she'd managed to stay away so long when all she wanted at the first sign of trouble was to be as close to her club family as possible.

"Honey."

Beth blinked.

"We're here."

"Shit. Sorry… totally zoned out there for a minute. Thanks for rushing right to me."

Shell snorted. "What else would I have done? Come on. Your dad should be here any second."

As she climbed out of the car, a motorcycle sped into the

parking lot way faster than a safe speed. They skidded to a hard stop, sending a cloud of gravel and dust into the air.

Saint.

He ripped his helmet off and seared her with an assessing stare so intense she felt like heat against her bare skin.

She shivered. Saint looked furious in the same way she'd seen right before he beat her ex-boyfriend to a bloody pulp. Before she had a chance to react outwardly, two more motorcycles pulled up beside Saint, parking with much less ferocity than he did.

Copper was off his bike in a flash, storming toward her. Were he any other six-foot-five tattooed man with such a scary expression, she'd have backed up, but for all his gruff demeanor, he'd never once frightened her.

He grabbed her and crushed her to him in a suffocating hug. "You okay?"

She nodded against his chest. "Yeah, Dad, I'm good."

"Okay," he said as he released her. "Let's get inside." As he turned, he kept his heavy arm around her shoulders and tugged Shell to him with his other hand. After kissing his ol' lady and whispering how much he loved her, he signaled to a prospect to tail her as she left. One of Beth's younger siblings had to be picked up from volleyball practice soon, so Shell couldn't stick around, but there was no way Copper would let her drive around unchaperoned right now.

The prospect jogged over from where he'd been standing. "On it, Prez," he called as he mounted his bike.

After hugging and thanking her mother again, Beth allowed Copper to lead her into the clubhouse.

Five minutes later, she found herself seated at a table with her father, Rocket, and Maverick, who'd placed an eleven a.m. glass of whiskey in front of her. Saint was the only one who'd separated himself from the group. He sat at the bar, facing her table, one hand wrapped around a glass he hadn't touched. His stare burned with barely leashed rage.

Never once did he look away.

She swore he didn't even blink.

A muscle in his jaw ticked with each breath.

Every so often, she snuck a glance his way to find him in the same position, burning her with an intensity she'd never experienced.

It was unnerving.

It was also hot. The man oozed sexiness from his pores, and with it channeled in her direction, she had a hard time keeping her cool. Though her father's presence sure killed any chance of returning the stare.

"You sure you're okay?" Copper asked for the fiftieth time.

"Yes. I was shaken at first, but I'm good now. Just pissed off by the situation."

"What did you say when he asked you to say hello to Copper and tell him we didn't want them as an enemy?"

Beth took a large sip of the whiskey. It was good quality, but still burned on the way down. She loved that fiery sensation, the way it woke her up from the inside. Loved the respect in the guys' eyes when she downed it with ease. Jason had hated it when she drank whiskey. Claimed she was trying to compete with the boys.

It was never a competition. She could drink his friends under the table. *God, she really was a biker princess.*

"I told him he could fuck right off. That I wouldn't tell anyone shit on his behalf."

Mav slapped a hand on the table. "That's our girl."

Copper whacked him on the back of his head as he said, "Christ, Beth." He pinched the bridge of his nose. "If you're ever in a situation like that, you don't fucking antagonize the asshole. Who knows what he would have done if a car hadn't driven by?"

A week ago, she'd tried that. She'd been docile, she'd done

what she was told, she'd tried her hardest not to antagonize, and what happened? She still ended up slammed against a wall with a man choking her.

Fuck being docile.

"I'm done taking shit like that from men."

The mood changed so fast that her stomach flipped. *Shit.* She'd said too much. *He'd know.* Her father would know something had happened with a man.

Guess she was lucky he had more pressing issues to deal with.

Risking a quick peek at Saint, Beth found him practically vibrating with restrained fury. He held a glass with white knuckles. Hopefully, the cup wouldn't shatter in his hand. All of a sudden, the overwhelming urge to go to him and rub her finger over his ticking jaw washed over her. Of course, she'd resist. Her father would go berserk, and Saint himself would probably reject the touch, but the impulse remained.

"Saint," Copper barked, jerking them both from their secret stare-off.

"Yeah, Prez."

"Can you take Beth home for me? Maybe stick around until Shell or I get back."

Her stomach fluttered—another ride on the back of Saint's bike.

"You okay with that, Beth?"

"Um, yeah. Of course, but I don't need a babysitter."

Copper just shot her a look that asked if she was crazy.

"All right. All right." She raised her hands in surrender. "I had to try. Should we go now?" she asked, turning toward Saint.

He nodded once.

Okay, guess we're not chatting today.

His stoic attitude did nothing to stem the buzz of excitement now coursing through her veins. She rose and rounded the table, hugging her father from behind. "Love you, Dad."

He turned his head to kiss her cheek, and she almost giggled as she used to as a child when he'd tickle her face with his beard.

"Love you too, kiddo." He pointed to Saint. "Keep her safe. You're carrying precious cargo."

"Understood."

She said goodbye, exchanging hugs with the others before heading toward the exit. Saint met her there and held the door open. As she walked through, he placed his hand on her lower back, guiding her outside without a word. It remained there warm and strong until they reached his bike. He didn't speak but radiated tension, and by the time they reached his motorcycle, Beth couldn't take it anymore.

She turned and stopped him with her hands on his upper stomach. "Are you okay?"

He wouldn't meet her eyes. "Get on the bike, Beth."

"Saint." Frowning, she increased the pressure on his stomach. "*Saint.*"

Finally, he sighed. "I can't right now, Beth. Please… get on the bike."

As much as it sounded like a frustrated dismissal, it didn't feel that way. It felt deeper, like he was struggling with something he couldn't voice. Like he really needed her to get on the motorcycle. So instead of pushing back as her instincts told her to, she nodded.

And she climbed on the bike.

Chapter Nine

He wanted to crawl out of his skin.

Actually, he wanted to go hunting through town until he found the fuckhead who threatened Beth and make sure he spent the very short rest of his life in excruciating pain.

"Are you pissed at me?" she asked after sitting that pert ass on his motorcycle. The one he'd spent the last few days trying not to think about.

He breathed, rolling his shoulders back. *Was he pissed?* Fuck yes. At her? A little.

"No."

Beth grunted in the same way Copper did when in disbelief. "You're acting like you're pissed at me."

"Beth." He pinched the bridge of his nose.

"What is your problem?" She huffed and threw her hands in the air. His eyes immediately went to the strip of stomach showing as her tight tank top shifted with the movement. "I'm sorry that you got stuck babysitting me this afternoon. I certainly didn't ask for this. You're more than welcome to drop me off at home and go do whatever the hell you have to do."

Fire shot from her eyes. Part of him felt a surge of pride.

Just last week, she'd been injured and threatened by a man, and instead of cowering, she'd stood up to a damn outlaw today. The other part of him wanted to throttle her for her carelessness and stupidity.

He leaned down until their noses nearly brushed.

Beth sucked in a breath and stopped hollering.

"You told a wannabe gangster to fuck off. So, yeah, I'm fucking pissed. Today could have ended very differently for you. We could be scraping you off the side of the goddamn highway, or your fucking family could be searching for you while some psycho holds you in his basement."

Christ, his heart was racing as horrifying images ran through his mind.

"So what the hell should I have done, huh? Cowered and let him see how terrified I was? Fuck no," she spat out with a harsh swipe of her arm. "I lived that for too long. Never again. I refuse to cower to any man."

She proved her point, yelling at him in front of the clubhouse without apprehension. Him, a man who could snap her in half with ease. Equal parts brave and stupid.

But still, her courage and conviction took the wind out of his sails. He exhaled a long pent-up breath as he nodded. "Okay."

Frowning, she blinked. "Okay?"

"Yes." It would take a few minutes for his rage to cool to a simmer, but the ride to Beth's house should help. "I get it. I respect it." She had no idea how much. "Sometimes, I get a little… intense about the safety of people I ca… know."

She huffed a breath. "Ya think?"

He responded with a smirk.

After a hefty inhale, Beth sighed. "I get it. I didn't know anything about him, his intentions, or how dangerous he was. Antagonizing him might have been… less than smart."

Saint grunted. That was one way of putting it.

"It's just... after what happened with Jason and the way I did nothing for so long, another man using his size and strength to overpower me made me so angry. All I could think about was how I refused to let it happen again."

Before his brain clocked his intentions, he lifted his hand to cup her cheek. No woman deserved to be intimidated by a man, and he couldn't fault her for fighting back the best way she knew how. Thankfully, before he crossed the line and touched her, his good sense kicked back online, and he reached for his spare helmet instead. "Let's get you home, killer."

Beth snorted and rolled her eyes as he plopped the helmet on her head. Once he had it in place and buckled, she smiled at him, making his damn cock twitch. She looked hot as hell astride his bike with her green eyes sparkling at him. She still wore a light layer of makeup to hide the fading bruises, but they'd mostly disappeared, giving her a fresh, bright appearance. If she were any other single woman, he'd lean in to steal a kiss. But this was Beth, and if he did that, it'd likely be the last thing he ever did.

Her effortlessly sexy smile was making it difficult to care about the consequences.

"Let's roll," she said.

Saint forced himself to turn away and climb on the bike. As soon as his ass hit the seat, her hands settled on his sides like two brands searing him through his clothes. It'd take nothing for her to slide them forward and cup his dick, which was growing more interested by the second.

"Fuck my life," he muttered as he fired up the bike.

"What was that?" Beth yelled in his ear.

He shook his head. "Nothing, just thinking out loud."

They took off, heading for Copper and Shell's house, where Beth had been staying since she came home. Did she enjoy it there? It had to be nice to spend time with her parents and younger siblings, but after years on her own, moving back in with them couldn't have been easy.

About five minutes into his ride, the Bluetooth on his helmet made an announcement. "You have one new message. Play message from Stillman?" the robotic feminine voice spoke in his ear.

The old friend he'd told Copper he'd contact for information about the mystery bikers in town. And that was before one of them approached Beth. Now, he didn't just want to speak to Stillman, he *needed* to talk to the guy. Getting information had gone from helpful to necessary in less than an hour.

"Yes, play message," he replied.

"Playing one new message from Stillman. Yo, Lee, long time. I'll be out at The Barn for another twenty minutes. Get there before I leave if you want to chat."

Shit.

He immediately pulled over to the side of the road so he could safely answer the message.

"What's wrong?" Beth asked as he slowed the bike.

"Have to answer a text."

"Oh, okay."

He stared down at his phone. Twenty minutes was not enough time to drop Beth off at home and get out to The Barn, as they used to call their old hangout. Back in his late teen years and early twenties, Saint spent many nights out at the abandoned barn getting high with that crowd. Looked like not much had changed for Stillman. Even if he headed straight there, he'd be cutting it close.

"Fuck," he muttered as he tried to puzzle through a plan.

"What's wrong?"

He glanced over his shoulder to find her watching him with concerned eyes. "Nothing. I have to meet someone to get some information about these bikers, and I don't have enough time to drop you off before he leaves where he's at."

"Oh." She shrugged. "Easy, just bring me. I don't have anything going on."

"Hell no." Over his dead body would he bring her around that crowd. They were unpredictable at best and extremely violent at worst. "It's not safe."

Her arms came around his waist in a hug as she settled her chin on his shoulder. "You're being stubborn."

"Trust me, this is not a place you want to be. Copper would peel my balls if I took you along. It's not even a place I want to be."

"Sure, but it doesn't sound like you have any other options."

"I'll figure something out." He stared down at his phone, but nothing came to him. He could call Gator to pick up Beth, but it'd take too long, same with returning her to the clubhouse.

"You're wasting time," she sing-songed with a smug hint in her voice. "Don't think Copper will be too happy if you let this opportunity pass by."

"Fuck." Saint grunted. "You're a little shit, you know that?" He was truly wedged between a rock and an incredibly hard place.

Beth squealed and wiggled behind him. She knew she had him backed into a corner. This was an opportunity he couldn't pass up. When he'd texted Stillman earlier, he'd never expected to receive a response. At least not for a few days. He tended to go off the grid and spend days at a time in a drug-induced stupor. If he didn't make it to The Barn in time, who the hell knew when Saint would get another opportunity to pump him for information? And as of now, Saint's former friend might be their only potential lead.

"Fine," he said over his shoulder. "You're coming, but I swear to God, Beth, if you don't glue yourself to my side while we're there, I'll spank your ass, fuck what Copper thinks."

She stilled behind him, and he groaned. *God, how stupid could he be?* Her boyfriend had just hit her, and he'd threatened to put his hands on her. Not that he ever would. It was just talk, but still.

Fucking idiot.

"Sorry," he said quickly. "I'd never lay a hand on you in anger, Beth. I hope you know that."

She cleared her throat. "Um... yeah... of course I know that. You were mouthing off. No big deal." Her voice dropped an octave, sounding huskier than usual.

It almost sounded turned on. *But there was no way, right?* She'd just gotten out of an abusive relationship. The last thing she needed was another man's hands on her, even if those hands would worship rather than wound. Christ, that would be a complication neither of them needed. Hiding his attraction to her was one thing, but knowing she wanted him as well would make it nearly impossible to stay away.

Her weight disappeared from his back as she straightened, but kept her hands resting on his hips enough to stay safe behind him.

He hit the throttle and sped off, faster than the law would like, but time was not on his side. Mountain views zoomed by, something he'd usually appreciate, but today he had a single-minded focus—get to The Barn before Stillman left, and his chance to help his club went up in smoke.

They rolled to a stop in front of the dilapidated barn with five minutes to spare.

Behind him, Beth tensed, which he took as a good sign. She should be tense. This place was a shithole, crawling with people who'd slit her throat to get at five dollars in her wallet.

The place hadn't changed much in the decade since he'd hung out here. It was as advertised, a faded red barn with a crumbling ceiling and rotting wood planks. Old tires, broken-down cars, and piles of garbage littered what was once a grassy area surrounding the barn. The inside, if he remembered correctly, was always a hazy, smoke-filled cesspool where addicts and dealers passed out on random couches and futons, salvaged from the side of the road God knew how many years ago.

He'd rather lick a toilet seat than sit any part of his body on one of those couches.

"Wow," Beth whispered as he killed the engine. "Who exactly are you meeting here?"

"An old friend."

"Did you…"

He could imagine her wrinkling her nose as she took in the sight.

"Have you been here before?"

He grunted. "Unfortunately, I went through a bit of fucked-up stage after we left the cult."

She stayed quiet but squeezed his waist once before releasing him to undo her helmet.

"If I can't touch you, you're too far away. Got it?" Saint asked as he dismounted the bike.

"Uh, yeah. Don't worry. I'm not exactly eager to explore this place."

As soon as her feet hit the ground, Saint palmed the back of her neck and pulled her close. She gasped at the possessive move, then squeaked when his lips met her ear. "As far as they are concerned, you're *mine*."

"Oh," she whispered on an exhale. Her breath wafted across his neck, raising goose bumps along his skin. He fought to keep from letting a punch of lust distract him from his task as he scanned their surroundings.

"It's the only way to keep you safe in here," he whispered. Movement from the crumbling barn caught his attention.

Someone, a woman who looked as though she'd not eaten in weeks, stumbled outside on unsteady legs. Her eyes had that high-as-a-kite glaze he'd seen too many times. She wobbled off to the side of the building, hiked her dirty sundress over her hips, and squatted to piss right there out in the wild.

Lovely.

Saint tightened his hold on Beth. "Try not to tense up if I get handsy. We've got to sell it. One whiff that you're not protected, and every fucker here will be looking to take advantage."

She nodded, making the shell of her ear brush against his lips. Fuck, how he wanted to retrace the path with his tongue, maybe nip her earlobe just to feel her shiver against him.

But this was not the time or the place.

And as much as she turned him on, she was not the woman.

"Whatever you need, Saint."

If only.

"Okay." He straightened and tucked her against his side with an arm around her shoulders. Of course, her skin had to be smooth and warm, enticing him to run his fingertips up and down her arm. If it weren't for the need to stay as alert as possible, he'd have struggled to resist the urge.

"Is that woman peeing?" Beth asked as he steered her toward the shitty red building. A woman squatted right on the grass for all to see. "Gross."

"We'll be damn lucky if that's the grossest thing we see while we're here."

"Awesome," she muttered. "You have no idea how hard I'm trying not to ask you hundreds of questions about your past."

He grunted. "It was fucked up."

"Yeah." She slid her arm around his waist, anchoring them even closer. "I gathered that much."

As they reached the open entrance, a man at least five inches shorter than Saint stepped in their path. He wore jeans and a dirty wife-beater showing off his track-mark-riddled arms. His greasy hair and unkempt beard spoke to his poor hygiene as much as the decaying teeth spoke to his drug habit.

"The fuck are you?" he asked, eyes narrowed as he took in Saint's cut. "We ain't got no trouble with the MC."

"Not yet, you don't. I'm looking for Stillman."

He raised an eyebrow. "He want you to find him?"

Saint nodded. "Yeah. He told me to meet him here."

The guy's cloudy gaze shifted to Beth, who stiffened under his blatant perusal. Saint could practically feel the effort it took her to keep from snapping at him, but thankfully, she squashed her instincts. Any other time, he'd have loved to watch her verbally eviscerate this piece of shit, but they'd be leaving with nothing if she did that now.

"He's in there. I can get him for you, but it's gonna cost ya." He grinned, revealing the yellowed nubs of what was once a complete set of teeth. "Seems like you brought the perfect payment."

He reached for Beth, who sucked in a harsh breath, but before his hand got anywhere near her, Saint captured his wrist in a punishing grip.

"Unless you want your insides ripped out through your asshole by your own hand, I suggest you do not touch what's *mine*."

"Fuck you, dickhead. Now I ain't telling Stillman shit."

Saint gripped him harder. The guy's fragile wrist bones shifted beneath Saint's squeezing fingers.

"Fuck. Fine!" he shouted as he arched his back, trying to relieve the pain. "Jesus, he's in there. Go ahead."

Saint shook his head once. "Get him. We're not setting foot inside that cesspool."

"Fuck y… okay! I'll get him. Christ."

He finally released the writhing guy, who turned and wandered into the dark, putrid barn.

"Didn't want sloppy biker seconds anyway," he muttered as he stumbled away, rubbing his wrist.

"You good?"

Beth nodded, but a wrinkle had formed between her eyes. One he wanted to smooth away with his thumb, or better yet, his lips. "This place is just fucking depressing."

She didn't know the half of it.

Less than a minute later, Stillman wandered out, and Saint was greeted with the stark reminder of what his life would have been without the MC. Of the drain he'd been circling and the soul-sucking pit he'd been so close to drowning in.

His stomach turned, not from disgust, but from recognition.

"Lee, shit, man, it's been a fucking minute."

"Yeah, a few years at least." And in those years, Stillman had gone from a twitchy, frequent drug user to an absolute shell of a human. He'd lost so much weight he looked as though a sneeze would take him out. His once-full cheeks with the dimples that scored him more women than anyone in their group had sunken in, giving him a skeletal appearance. A wide grin revealed missing teeth. Weeping sores that had to be painful covered his face and arms.

"We need to hang more, brother. I got some great shit. New shit, man. Like you've never fucking had before. I can give you a taste for free, for old times' sake."

Beth went rigid beside him, and he couldn't help but stroke his thumb over her shoulder, trying to let her know he'd never do that with her present. Hell, he didn't mess with that shit in general anymore, but he'd rather die than be incapacitated when her safety rested in his hands.

"Thanks, man. I'm gonna pass for today. I'm more

interested in the source than the product."

Stillman's grin disappeared, and his eyes went cold in an instant. Nothing would piss him off more than the thought of his drug supply getting interrupted. "Why?"

Saint shrugged, trying to keep his stance casual. "Curious. You know how it is. We like to keep tabs on all the players in town."

"We? The MC?"

Saint held his gaze but didn't respond.

"No. Fuck that. You assholes don't own this town."

Oh, but we do.

"You ain't gonna fuck this up for me. They got some Grade-A product and at good- fucking-prices." Stillman shook his head. "I ain't telling you shit. You'll have to deal with the competition."

"Not competition. You know the MC doesn't push that shit. But we know who does, and there seems to be some new kids in town who don't want to play by the rules."

"No." Stillman set his jaw as he shook his head. The jaw that would probably shatter with a half-power slap. "I ain't telling you shit."

Saint cocked his head. "You owe me, Stillman."

"Oh, come on, man." He groaned and stared up at the clear blue sky, so in contrast to the murky brown of his gaze. "That's not fucking fair."

"Was it fucking fair when I took a knife to the side, saving your ass from that fucking psycho whose girl you were fucking?"

Beth gasped and glanced up at him. He squeezed her shoulder in response.

"You're an asshole, you know that?"

Saint shrugged.

Stillman lifted a thumb to his mouth, where he chewed the already destroyed nail for a moment before spitting on the ground. His agitation grew by the second until his eyes shot fire and his twitching became almost violent jerks. "Fuck!" He glanced over his shoulder into the hazy barn. "They're gonna… *fuck*. After this, we're even, and you stay the hell away from me."

Saint snorted. "Trust me, Stillman, I have no plans to visit this petri dish ever again."

"You're not who you were. You used to be fucking fun. The bikers turned you into a pussy bitch."

He gave Stillman the glare he used even more often than his fists as an enforcer. Zach claimed it was his greatest weapon, one that could make a man shit himself. Stillman wasn't too far gone to realize the shit pile he'd stepped in. His face paled to a sickly gray, and he sighed.

"This is gonna fuck me so hard," he whispered, shaking his head. "The only name I have is Silas Crow. Don't know if it's real or not. Don't give a shit. Heard he's up from Memphis. That's all I fucking know."

"How do you contact him?"

"Saint…" he groaned. "Don't fucking do this." His gaze shifted to Beth. "If I tell you—"

"Don't fucking finish that sentence, Stillman. As of now, I'm planning to leave you breathing with your dick still attached to your body. That can change."

His jaw twitched. His eyes darted in every direction, never landing on anything fixed for more than one second. For a heartbeat, Saint worried Stillman would run. Then he'd be faced with the choice to let go of Beth and give chase or let him get away.

And with Beth to protect, there really wasn't any decision to make.

"I'm getting impatient. You've got ten seconds, Stillman."

A low growl came from his former friend before he shook his head and spat on the ground again. "Fucking fine. You go to that new laundromat in town. Jesus," he muttered. "They're gonna kick my ass."

"Yeah, but I'll kill you."

"Fuck you." Stillman must have believed him because he sighed. "Go to the laundromat. Ask for machine thirteen. There ain't no fucking thirteen. They'll give you a number to text. It's different every fucking time. Text it, and they text you back a location. That's all. Now will you please get the fuck out of here before someone realizes what I told you."

The distinct clicking of a shotgun being primed had Saint's spine snapping straight.

"S-Saint..." Beth's eyes widened as she tried to find the source of the familiar sound. Most likely, someone hiding in the shadows in the barn got tired of their presence.

"Unless you want the entire MC tearing this place apart, you'd better call off your guard dog, Stillman."

The scrawny guy lifted a hand. "Let them leave," he shouted. Surprising as it was, given his physical appearance, Stillman seemed to be in charge, or at least had a lot of sway. "Go. Next time you show up here, we'll shoot on sight."

"I'll shoot myself before I come back here. Take care of yourself, Stillman, maybe buy a fucking toothbrush." With that parting shot, he guided Beth back to the bike at a rapid clip, feeling the sight of the shotgun on his ass the entire time.

She didn't need any instructions. She immediately climbed on the bike and jammed the helmet on her head. As he settled in front of her, she gripped his hips tighter than usual and rested her helmet against his back. "That was intense," she whispered. "But we got what we came for."

"You did good, Beth. You're a good-fucking-wing woman."

Though impossible, he swore he could feel her smile as he sped off, leaving his past where it belonged, firmly in his rearview.

Chapter Ten

Some people could tie a cherry stem with their tongue, wiggle their ears, or bend their thumb back so far it touched their forearm. Beth had her own party trick. One she'd never bothered to mention to anyone but had honed to perfection over the years. With a quick inhale, she could almost, to the brand, tell what someone was smoking. The easy ones were cigarettes, cigars, and weed. She'd grown up smelling all three regularly. Over the years, she'd noticed subtle differences in types and brands, leading up to today, where she stood in the clubhouse, detecting the rich and bold notes of Jigsaw's favorite Padrón cigars.

She inhaled deeply, holding the comforting aroma of easier times in her lungs. It'd been too long since she had been surrounded by anything other than the stale ashtray odor of Jason's Pall Malls.

"You know, you don't have to suck in second-hand smoke to get your fix. Jig will be more than happy to share his cigars."

Beth turned her head to find Lindsey sliding onto a barstool next to her. Her friend practically yelled to be heard over the ear-splitting rock music.

"I'm good," she said with a chuckle as her face heated. "Just being a weirdo and sucking in the scents of my childhood."

Lindsey tilted her head and studied her with a scrunched look of confusion.

"Jig started smoking those specific cigars when I was twelve or so." She shrugged. "Smells like my childhood."

"That's sweet. My childhood smelled like desperation and poverty." Lindsey winced. "Wow, I made that dark. Ignore me. I'm in a strange mood."

Beth tilted the neck of her beer bottle Lindsey's way. "Cheers to that. I've been in a strange mood since I came home."

Smiling, Lindsey tapped her glass to the bottle. "To pulling our heads out of our asses."

"I'll drink to that." They sipped their drinks, then Beth leaned in. "You look hot tonight. Trying to impress anyone?"

Dressed in a leather miniskirt, leopard print halter top that showed a generous amount of cleavage, and cowgirl boots, Lindsey looked like she'd come ready for the hunt.

"Nah," she said with a shake of her head. "No one in particular, though I'm hoping someone will give me an orgasm or two tonight." She sighed. "It's been way too long, and while I love my vibrator, I started talking to it last week. I figure that means it's been too long since I've had a human man in my bed."

Beth burst out laughing. "It's only concerning if the vibrator talks back."

"Oh shit. It hasn't gotten that bad yet." They laughed together, clinking their drinks again.

The MC party had been in full swing for the past few hours. All around her, men and women drank, danced, smoked, and hooked up. Her parents sat at a table in the corner with some of the others who'd been around for decades, while the younger patched members danced and worked to reel in their nightly conquest.

Civilians, or those not raised in MC culture, might find the scene weird or inappropriate, but to Beth, it represented home. The loud music, the testosterone-fueled atmosphere, the free-flowing booze, and even blatant public displays of affection were all so familiar that something inside her ached while at the same time tension uncoiled. This was where she and everyone in her club family could be their authentic selves without judgment, and she hadn't realized the hole leaving home left in her life.

But she was back now, and with each passing day, she thought she might stay for good.

"Hey, I'm gonna go chat with Rizz. Wanna come?"

Beth glanced over to where a beautiful man she'd only met for the first time a few days ago was standing by himself, staring across the room at Lindsey. He was trim and tall, with a blond goatee and glacier-blue eyes. "Um, hell no. He looks like he wants to rip all your clothes off. No way am I interfering with that. Go get your ho on, girl."

Gaze glittering, Lindsey raised an eyebrow. "You sure? I don't want to leave you all alone over here."

Beth shook her head. "I'm gonna mingle, I promise. Just wanna finish this beer and get another."

"All right." Lindsey stood and leaned forward to kiss Beth's cheek. "Love you, cuz. So glad you're home." Then she winked. "Don't wait up."

Laughing, Beth gave her friend a gentle shove. "Don't do anything I wouldn't do."

Lindsey waved over her shoulder as she let out a throaty laugh, already in seductress mode. Beth watched for a few moments as Lindsey made her way to Rizz. When she reached him, she plucked the beer out of his hand and brought the bottle to her glossy lips, tipping her head back for a long sip. Rizz's eyes darkened as he watched Lindsey's throat work. Before she lowered the bottle, he had his arm around her waist and was whispering something in her ear that had her giggling.

Beth chuckled as she lifted her own bottle. "Get it, girl," she whispered with a grin.

As she turned back toward the bar to ask the prospect for a second beer, her breath hitched. Seated on a couch against the wall was Saint. She hadn't seen him come in and assumed he'd bailed on this party as he did the one the night they returned home. But no, there he sat, wearing a serious expression while he chatted with Zach.

And holy shit did he look good. He hadn't bothered shaving since she'd last seen him yesterday, and a dark, scruffy stubble coated his cheeks, giving him an air of danger. Or maybe it was the intense expression in his dark eyes. Or the bulge of his muscles beneath the tight sleeves of his T-shirt. Whatever it was, her heart thumped, and she squirmed on her stool as her pussy tingled.

She hadn't been able to stop thinking about him since their little field trip to crack house central yesterday. He'd handled the precarious situation with a calm, impressive competence. Despite their creepy surroundings, she'd felt safe with him the entire time. He'd made her safety his number one priority, keeping her close and pretending she was his.

And she'd liked it.

A little too much.

The feel of his hands on her skin, his lips whispering next to her ear, and his firm body pressed all along hers had made it difficult to concentrate and nearly impossible to feel fear. On the way home, she'd had to fight to keep from rubbing up against his back and humping him like a horny dog.

Now, watching him have what was obviously a serious conversation with Zach, all those feelings came rushing back with a vengeance. She wanted him more than she'd wanted any man in a long time, maybe ever, and that was a big problem.

After a few moments, Zach slapped Saint's knee and stood. They bumped knuckles, then Zach took off toward his ol' lady, Toni, who danced with Stephanie and Chloe.

Beth shifted her gaze from the women she considered aunts to Saint, who was staring at her with raw intensity, electricity shooting down her spine. Their gazes locked, heated and powerful. She might as well have been naked. It felt as though he could see beneath every layer of her clothes and every wall she'd ever put up to guard her vulnerable center.

An invisible force wrapped around her, creating a strong pull in his direction, a near compulsion to go to him, and just as she was about to give in to the extremely foolish urge, a woman cut through her line of sight.

Melody.

She waited tables at Toni's diner and had served Beth and Shell the other morning when they popped in for breakfast, though she sure looked different tonight. The long, dark, curly hair she typically pulled back tumbled down her back in a gorgeous waterfall tonight. Dressed in ass-revealing denim shorts and what had to be a fucking bikini top, Melody planted herself next to Saint on the couch.

Right next to him.

Practically in his lap.

A sickening twist curdled the beer in Beth's stomach as Saint shifted his attention from her to Melody, who planted a hand on his chest and basically drooled on him. She hiked up a leg and rested it on his thigh. If she shifted it a few inches, she'd be straddling him.

Saint didn't smile at her, but he didn't shove her away either. He placed a hand on her side, just above her hip.

Anchoring her to him or preventing her from ending up fully straddled across his lap?

They spoke back and forth a few times before Melody threw her head back and laughed as though Saint was the funniest man in the world.

Beth's eyes narrowed. If this went on much longer, she'd be tempted to march over there and rip Melody off him by her cheap hair extensions.

Saint nodded at something Melody said, which seemed to embolden her even further. She walked her red-tipped nails up his chest. When she could go no further, she grasped his chin and turned his head slightly, planting a long kiss on his cheek.

Beth's grip on her bottle tightened. Was he enjoying this? Did he like Melody's bony fingers on his skin and her overfilled lips on his face?

Why do you care?

Shit. Why did she care?

Saint was not the man for her. He wasn't even *a* man for her. He was one hundred percent off-limits due to his position in the club. Copper would lose his mind. Hell, Saint most likely didn't see her as anything more than his president's daughter, and there she was, losing her mind with jealousy over a man who'd never want her. She could be as attracted to him as she wanted, but that's where it had to end.

God, why did he have to be so attractive?

And protective?

And good?

Why did he make her feel safe and empowered at the same time?

"Ugh." She polished off the last sip of her beer, then set the empty bottle on the bar without asking for another, as initially planned. Time to go. If she sat there much longer, mooning over an untouchable man, she'd hit an unacceptable level of pathetic.

After a quick goodbye to her parents, she'd head home.

She weaved her way through the crowded clubhouse to where her parents sat laughing and drinking with their chosen family.

"Hey, sweetie, having fun?" Shell asked as she reached their table.

"You bet," she lied with a smile that probably fooled no one.

"P-cess!" Gator seemed to materialize from nowhere. "Where you been all night?" He wrapped an arm around her shoulders and yanked her close, planting a long, sloppy kiss on her cheek.

"You've got one second to get your filthy lips off my daughter before I slice them off and turn them into earrings." Copper's voice boomed over the music. His narrowed eyes burned with outrage.

Gator immediately released her, stepping away as he raised his hands in the air. "Sorry, Prez. Meant no disrespect."

"Seriously?" Beth shook her head.

"Dead serious." Copper folded his massive arms across his chest in a move meant to intimidate Gator, but it only pissed Beth off. For fuck's sake, she wasn't a child and didn't have a lick of interest in Gator.

"Dad, it's no different than you kissing Aunt Steph on the cheek or vice versa, and you guys do that shit all the time."

"It's *very* different. Gator is a stupid shit who only thinks with his dick."

She scoffed, and Gator, proving he was in fact a stupid shit, said, "He has a point."

"Really?" She stared at him, incredulous. "Not gonna help me out at all?"

He shrugged. "Just trying to get back on my prez's good side." He spoke out of the corner of his mouth as though

Copper wouldn't hear him somehow.

Maybe if she hadn't been lusting after one of her father's men just two minutes ago, this wouldn't be an issue. Perhaps if she hadn't left a horrible relationship less than two weeks ago, she'd have been less sensitive, but her father's lack of faith in her ability to choose her own partner got under her skin in a way it never had before.

"Are you done?" she asked Copper before he could bark another order. She tried to keep her temper in check, but her hands curled at her sides, clenched with annoyance. "Because if you're finished threatening my friend over a kiss on my cheek, I'd like to say something."

Shell's eyes widened, and for a moment Beth worried her mom was about to step in and try to diffuse the situation, but instead her lips curled. More than one set of eyes watched her, people she'd known and loved all her life, but she didn't care.

She hadn't stood up for herself in so long, a surge of power kept her mouth moving. If she was overreacting, it didn't matter. She needed this. Needed to speak her mind in a situation where she'd be safe no matter what she said.

Her dad's jaw tightened. "Gator crossed a line."

"No." She shook her head. "You did, Dad." Her heart pounded so hard it felt like it'd burst right through her chest, but she didn't back down. "He kissed my cheek. Like family. Like someone who knows me and respects me, and you threatened him like I'm some piece of property you need to guard."

Someone whistled, and Maverick, snarky as ever, yelled, "You tell him, girl."

"Hey, p-cess, it's really okay," Gator whispered from beside her. "I shoulda kept my lips to myself."

"No. It's really *not* okay." She turned back to her Dad. "I'm an adult. I have been for a while. Hell, Mom already had a toddler at my age. I want to stay. I want to be back here in Tennessee, home with my family permanently, but when you act like this, you're telling me you don't trust me. And if my own father can't trust me, or the men he calls family, then why would I stay here?"

Copper reared back with a flabbergasted expression, as though she'd smacked him.

Shell put her hand over his, linking their fingers as she looked between her husband and daughter with heartbreak on her face.

Shit.

She stepped back, her chest heaving. *What had she done?* That was too much, too over the top. She knew how Copper was. She knew he loved her and only wanted to protect her body and heart. She hadn't meant to spew all her pent-up feelings at him, but that's precisely what they were—emotions that had been building over weeks and months, festering in silence while Jason chipped away at her piece by piece. They'd finally exploded from her mouth at the man who'd shown her unconditional love her whole life.

The wrong man.

The safe man.

"I'm sorry." She shook her head, walking backward. Luckily, people moved out of her way, allowing her escape.

"Beth…" Copper called after her.

"No." Tears burned behind her eyes, threatening to spill, and she refused to cry in front of the club on top of her emotional vomiting. "Not tonight. I… I need to go."

She turned and rushed through the parting crowd with her face burning. At least the music still played. If not, the place would probably be as quiet as a cemetery at midnight. As quiet and as depressing.

Shame washed over her, hot and suffocating, as she walked out into the warm, peaceful night. All that was missing from her epic tantrum was a foot stomp and an eyeroll.

God, she was a mess. A complete fucking disaster.

"Dammit," she muttered, jamming her hands on her hips. She tipped her head back and stared at the stars, blinking hard against the sting in her eyes. The night air cooled her flushed cheeks, but nothing could cool the sick churning in her gut. She'd just publicly dressed down the man who'd taught her to ride a bike, who'd held her when she cried, who'd probably stayed awake countless nights worrying about her while she was with Jason.

And she'd done it because she was jealous of a woman touching a man she had no right to want.

Pathetic.

The door opened behind her, and her stomach dropped. Probably her dad. She exhaled slowly, trying to prepare herself for his outrage or his pain. She wasn't sure which would be worse.

But it wasn't Copper.

Saint stood a few feet away, looking fierce and sexy, and something inside her cracked open with relief. He'd come after her. Not her dad, not her mom, not Lindsey—*him*. The man she had no business wanting had followed her out into the night.

"Come on." His voice was low, steady. "Let's go for a ride."

Her breath caught. "Where's Melody?" She didn't bother to keep the snark from her question.

Saint's lips quirked as he shrugged. "Fuck if I know."

Well then…

He started toward his bike with long, sure strides. "You coming?"

Her gaze fell to his ass, where it filled out those jeans in a way that made her groan. This was a terrible idea. If she had any brain in her head, she'd turn back, go inside, and apologize to her father.

"Yeah." She hurried after him. "I'm coming."

Chapter Eleven

The second Melody touched him, Saint knew tonight was the night he'd fuck up in a colossal way. But not in a way that had anything to do with the woman hanging all over him.

Beth's gaze had stayed on him while Melody tried her hardest to seduce him, morphing from hot and needy to something darker, laced with jealousy and possession.

He liked it. That angry fire in her eyes, the quick hint of potential violence and hatred as she'd watched Melody practically sit in his lap. He liked thinking Beth was imagining ripping Melody off him and taking her place, sliding one of those toned legs across his lap, and settling her pert ass on his thighs while forgetting Melody existed.

Yes, he was fucked up. His view on love and relationships bordered on obsessive, but he'd come to grips with that part of himself long ago. It was others who might not accept his intense need, but maybe Beth could.

Unfortunately, she was the one woman completely off-limits, as her father made extra clear tonight. Still, Saint found himself compelled to follow her outside and offer her a reprieve after Copper pissed her off.

They rode for about forty-five minutes before he pulled

over at one of his favorite scenic overlooks. The off-the-beaten-path location was a favorite of the locals but not well known to tourists. That tended to mean peace and quiet rather than wide-eyed visitors taking pictures of every mountain peak and every tree leaf in sight.

Being summer, the day had reached scorching temperatures, but now that the sun had set hours ago, the air held a slight chill. Beth must have been cold, dressed only in shorts and a fitted tank top. She snuggled up against his back the entire ride, and while he probably should have pulled over long ago, he didn't want to break the comfortable spell that riding wove over them, and she hadn't asked him to stop.

As soon as he killed the engine, she released him, straightening away from his back. He immediately missed her soft weight and the way she wrapped her arms around his waist.

"Oh, I love this spot. God, I haven't been here in years." She inhaled the fresh mountain air, and he caught her unrestrained grin as he dismounted the bike. Beth stayed astride his motorcycle, watching as he climbed off. "Thank you. I needed this." Her gaze drifted to the gorgeous moonlit mountain view before returning to him. "How pissed do you think my dad is?"

He shrugged. Copper loved her unconditionally. She and Shell were the only two who could get away with putting the MC president in his place without worry of repercussions. "Babe, you could probably commit murder in front of Copper, and he'll still think you can do no wrong."

Her soft huff of laughter felt weighted with sadness. "Well, I fucked up, unloading on him like that. It wasn't even about him getting on Gator for kissing my cheek. Well, not just that. With everything that's happened over the past few weeks, I haven't really had a… release. Tonight, I let the stress get the better of me, and I snapped at my dad over something stupid." She shook her head as she sighed. "I'll apologize to him in the morning. Anyway, thanks for whisking me away on your chrome steed."

He chuckled and offered her a hand to help her off the bike.

"Oh. Thanks." Her cheeks flushed as she grabbed his hand and came to stand beside him.

He refused to acknowledge how nice her smaller, softer hand felt in his. Or how he couldn't think of anything but how it would feel wrapped around his cock, stroking him.

"Cold?" he asked as she rubbed her arms.

"Actually, I am a little. Suppose I should have thought of that before hopping on the back of your bike."

"Nah, my fault. Shoulda grabbed a jacket for you before we left. Come here." He tugged her close, settling her back against his front as he wrapped his arms around her and tried to share as much of his body heat as he could. Her denim-covered ass settled against his thighs, and she sank against him, soaking up the warmth he offered.

"T-thanks," she said, slightly breathless. "That's better."

It was. So much better. *Too much better.* His cock certainly thought so, thickening in his jeans. He tried to adjust his hips so she couldn't feel the hardness against her back, but squirming only made it worse. Even thinking of the murderous way Copper looked at Gator for a simple brotherly cheek kiss didn't deflate his desire. Being close to her felt that damn good.

He was fucked.

They stood that way, locked together, taking in the scenery for a while before his mouth acted of its own volition. "So… no release, huh?"

"Oh my God." She laughed and shook her head against his chest. "I did say that, didn't I?"

"Yep."

"I meant… emotional release. You know, like I haven't let my stress out in a healthy way, so I flipped on my poor dad." She chuckled. "Not the other type of release. I've got that covered." She gasped. "I mean…"

He laughed. "Do you, now?"

"Oh, fuck off, you know what I mean."

"Got someone helping you out since you've been home, Beth?" He asked the question in a teasing tone, keeping in line with the mood, but the thought of her getting off with some guy had ice sliding through his veins.

"What?" She half huffed, half snorted. "No! I'm perfectly capable of taking care of myself, thank you very much."

Shit. The image of her lying on a bed, legs spread, while she worked herself over with a toy exploded through his mind.

"Well… that's a hot thought," he managed in a strained voice.

"I mean… shit, why am I even explaining myself to you?" She laughed again, but this time it sounded strained, breathy.

"I imagine it's hard to go from a live-in boyfriend to minimal privacy at your parents' house."

"Oh, yeah, because Jason and I had such an amazing sex life." If that wasn't heavy sarcasm, he didn't think he knew the definition of the word.

"No?" Fuck, why couldn't he shut his mouth? This road led nowhere but to extreme disaster.

"Ah, no. It was very… let's say… one-sided."

"He didn't make you come?"

"Jesus, Saint, why are we talking about this?"

Because I need to know.

"Answer the question."

Beth sighed. For a moment, he thought she'd tell him to fuck himself, but then she said, "Not very often, okay? Jason was a selfish asshole who only cared about one person, and that wasn't me. Happy?"

"How long?"

"What?"

He grabbed her chin and turned her head so she was looking up at him. Wary desire swirled in her gorgeous green eyes. "How long has it been since a man made you come?"

Her eyes flared, and she sucked in a breath. "Saint…"

"How fucking long?"

"Um…" Her cheeks flushed, and she tried to avert her gaze, but he held her in place. "Maybe like a year. Things were bad with Jason for a while. It wasn't all his fault. I should have left. When things got bad, I wasn't attracted to him anymore, so it was hard to relax with him and let it happen. I, uh, faked it for a while, but when it seemed like he didn't care if I got there or not, I just… didn't bother anymore. God, Saint, this is so embarrassing."

"Beth, it's one hundred percent all that motherfucker's fault. The second you felt uncomfortable, it became *his* fault. Your man's job is to make you feel loved, cherished, protected, and like a goddamn-fucking-queen. You spend one second feeling anything other than those things, then he failed you."

"Saint…"

He no longer bothered trying to conceal his erection from her, letting it press into her back. Her breathing picked up, and she stared at his mouth as she licked her lips.

Unconscious? Or was she telling him she wanted him as much as he wanted her?

With each passing second, his desire to kiss her, to touch her, to give her the pleasure she'd been denied, and take some for himself grew exponentially. Crossing that line would have life-altering repercussions for him more than her, and there, with the mountains in the backdrop and the moon lighting their way, he found himself not caring.

He wanted a taste.

Needed a taste of Beth.

Fuck it. He'd never been the type of man to play it safe. If he hadn't broken the rules, he'd still be living a life of misery serving a psychotic cult leader. He leaned in, bringing their lips a breath away.

"Don't," she whispered, pleading in her voice. "This is a terrible idea."

"But you want it?"

"Saint… we can't."

"But…"

Her breath drifted across his lips, sweet and soft. "Fuck. I can't do this to you. You—"

"I'm a big boy, Beth. My eyes are wide open. I wanted this from the moment I beat the fuck outta that piece of shit in your apartment. Tell me you don't want it too."

"I can't." She swallowed, and he nearly licked up her throat.

"Yes or no?" he whispered, lips brushing hers.

"Shit." Her eyes fluttered closed. "Yes. Yes, Saint… fuck, the answer is yes."

He barely waited for the words to finish falling from her mouth before he crushed their mouths together.

Beth whimpered, and he swallowed the delicious sound of submission as her lips parted, allowing him entry. He slipped his tongue into her mouth, tangling with hers as the warm, intoxicating flavor of Beth hit his senses with a brutal punch. His cock throbbed painfully against his zipper, desperate to be buried inside her.

She groaned and tried to turn into him, but he held her against him with a hand splayed across her lower belly as he continued to ravage her mouth. He could feel the heat of her skin through the thin fabric of her tank top and her nipples hardening against his forearm. The slight sound of frustration she made only fueled the fire in his blood. After a few seconds, she gave in and melted against him, grabbing onto the arm that held her chin with one hand as though afraid he'd release her.

Not a chance in hell.

Who knew how long he stood there in the moonlight, mapping every corner of her mouth and growing impossibly hard against her. Every time she shifted, her ass rubbed against his aching cock, and he had to grit his teeth to keep from grinding into her like a desperate teenager. Eventually, he gave her a moment to breathe, pulling back only far enough to see the dazed look in her eyes and admire her kiss-swollen lips.

She was disheveled and wide-eyed as she gulped air, so sexy he could barely think.

Too bad sexy-woman-induced insanity wouldn't fly as a defense with Copper.

Beth blinked and seemed to come back to earth. "Saint, that was…" She shook her head. "Touch me," she whispered. "Give me more."

He released her chin, sliding his hand to her neck, where he rested it without squeezing. Beth stared at him with absolute trust, and after what she'd been through recently, he didn't take that lightly. It made him feel like a king whose throne rested atop the highest mountain.

"Beth, if we do this, there's no going back."

The cat already clawed its way out of the bag, so no point in trying to wrangle it back in now.

"I know. I… I still want it. I want you, Saint."

That's all he needed to know. He kissed her again as his hands went to the button on her jean shorts. Pausing, he nipped her lip then waited for her breathless, "Yes. Please, yes, Saint," before flicking the button open and lowering the zipper.

He flexed his erection into her back while sliding his hand into her panties, where he found her soaked. She immediately flexed her hips, increasing the contact. "Damn," he whispered against her mouth. "Feeling needy, baby?"

"Guess you were right. He didn't give me what I needed."

Something dark and primal twisted in him. "Don't mention that motherfucker again, especially not when my hand is in your fucking pants." He punctuated the hardened command by brushing his thumb over her clit. "He doesn't belong anywhere near us."

Beth gasped as she shivered. "I won't."

He circled her opening, dipping his fingertip in, then swirling around again, loving the way she jerked and whimpered. "You wanna come?" he asked before nipping her lower lip.

"Yes."

"Out here? Where anyone could drive by?" He stilled his hand, and she groaned. "Or should we head back to my place for some privacy?"

"No." She shook her head and gyrated her hips. "Too far. I can't wait. Please, Saint."

"Please what, gorgeous?"

"Please make me come."

"Such a good girl, asking so nicely," he said as he slid one long finger inside her tight, wet pussy.

"Oh God." Her walls clamped around him immediately, silky and scorching hot, gripping him like she never wanted to let go. He groaned against her temple as he drew out slowly, his finger glistening in the moonlight, before pushing back in.

"Good?" It was so hot and slick inside her, he couldn't think of anything but how amazing the same grip would feel strangling his cock. He'd last about thirty seconds if he ever got inside her.

"S-so good. More. Please, more."

He kissed her as he slid a second finger inside her, stretching her, and she moaned into his mouth, a broken, desperate sound that went straight to his dick. He was so hard it hurt, his cock leaking in his jeans, but he didn't care. All that mattered was the wet heat clenching around his fingers and the way she rocked against his hand, fucking herself on him.

"That's it," he growled against her lips. "Take what you need, baby. Use me."

She whimpered and moved faster, her hips rolling in a rhythm that made him want to bend her over his bike and bury himself inside her until neither of them could walk. He curled his fingers, searching for that spot, and when he found it, she cried out so loud it echoed off the mountains.

"Saint!" she shouted into the quiet night, her head falling back against his shoulder.

He latched onto her exposed throat, sucking hard enough to leave a mark—a brand that said she'd been his tonight, even if only for these stolen minutes. His hand was fucking soaked, her arousal running down his wrist, and the obscene wet sounds of his fingers pumping in and out of her filled the night air.

"So fucking pretty," he rasped against her skin, kissing his way up her neck to her jaw. "So wet for me. You have any idea how bad I want to drop to my knees and lick this pussy until you scream?"

She grabbed his forearm with both hands, digging her nails into the tattooed skin hard enough to sting as she used him for leverage. "I'm close," she gasped. "God, Saint, I'm so close. Don't stop. Please don't stop."

A low, possessive rumble left his chest. "Come for me, Beth. Let me feel this pretty pussy squeeze my fingers. Show me what I do to you."

He captured her mouth as he rubbed tight, fast circles over her swollen clit with his thumb. Her whole body went rigid, her back arching, and then she shattered, clenching around his fingers in rhythmic pulses as she screamed into his mouth. Her knees gave out completely, and he caught her weight easily, holding her up as wave after wave crashed through her.

She trembled for long seconds while he worked her through the powerful orgasm. Kissing became impossible as she lost coordination and focus. Instead, he kept his forehead pressed to hers, sharing the air.

After a few moments, the quakes slowed, and she blinked with heavy lids. "H-holy shit," she whispered with a light chuckle. "That was… God, Saint, that was intense."

He watched her as he slowly removed his hand from her pants, his fingers coated and shining. Her slightly disappointed grumble brought a smile to his face. She was beautiful like this—soft, sated, and staring at him like he hung the damn moon.

He lifted his hand, wet with her arousal, and held her gaze as he brought his fingers to his mouth, sucking them clean one by one. Her lips parted, her breath catching, as she watched him taste her.

"Fuck," he groaned. She was sweet, musky, and absolutely addicting. He could eat her for hours.

Before she could speak, he ran his thumb across her lower lip, leaving a trace of her own arousal behind. Her eyes widened, but he didn't give her time to react. He leaned in and sucked her lower lip into his mouth, chasing her flavor.

"Delicious," he whispered when he released her. "Can't wait to bury my tongue in your pussy and make you come on my face."

Next time? Fuck, you did not say that.

"N-next time?"

He'd said it. It was a promise he couldn't make. Shouldn't make. Tonight had been charged with a host of emotions. In the light of day, when they realized how far they'd jumped over the line, he'd bet she wouldn't want a repeat. And he'd force himself to forget her sweet scent or the way her flavor was more potent than any drug he'd sampled. This was a one-shot moment of insanity. He'd got to see her come, to make her come, and now it was over.

And if his president found out, he'd skin Saint alive.

Fuck, what had he done?

He cleared his throat. "I should get you back," he said as he released her.

Beth blinked and stepped back. Her hands went to her shorts, fastening them immediately. "Shit, uh, yeah. We've probably been here longer than we realized." A strained laugh bubbled out of her, full of tension they hadn't experienced before. "What about... um..." Her cheeks flushed, and she gestured toward the bulge in his jeans. The one that wouldn't go anywhere until he got home and took himself in hand. "What about you?"

"Not sure you wanna get caught out here with my dick in your hand. Who knows who might drive by?"

If she found his sudden change in attitude hurtful, she didn't let on. "Right," she said with an awkward huff. "Good point. So, I guess, you can drop me off at my parents', if that's okay."

He nodded. "Sure."

Without another word, she walked to his bike and climbed on. When he sat himself in front of her, she settled her hands on his side with the lightest, most impersonal grip she could manage, basically holding the sides of his coat but not him. Even the night he'd found her in Texas, she'd sat closer and held him tighter. Now she seemed to want anything but to be near him.

That was probably for the best.

He kicked the bike into action and pulled out onto the windy mountain roads.

As they drew closer to his president's house, the fact that he had made a huge-fucking-mistake slammed into him like a sledgehammer. No matter how loudly he told himself this was one and done, now that he'd had his hands and mouth on Beth, he didn't think he could resist another chance to touch her if the opportunity presented itself, which meant he'd have to keep his distance.

Chapter Twelve

Despite not falling asleep until sometime after two in the morning, Beth woke with the sun. A mess of emotions swirled in her head, heart, and stomach before she even opened her eyes. Regret and shame for yelling at her father, annoyance at him for his rigidity and refusal to see her as an adult, frustration with her seeming limbo in life, and shock over the lines she crossed with Saint.

Of course, part of her still buzzed with lingering pleasure left behind by his talented hands and hungry mouth. Her inner thighs ached from how hard she'd clenched them together as she came, and every time she shifted, she felt the phantom press of his fingers inside her, the ghost of his breath hot against her neck. She was still slick between her legs, her body refusing to forget what her mind kept trying to file away as a one-time mistake.

God, what a mistake. Not because it was bad. No, no, no. The mistake came from the fact that she'd be thinking about him all day, every day, for the foreseeable future, and wishing she could go back for seconds.

And thirds.

Maybe even a fourth helping of Saint.

She pressed her thighs together and bit back a groan. At this rate, she'd need a cold shower before she could face her family.

But she couldn't indulge again. They couldn't, no matter how good it had been. She'd have to get that cold, hard fact through her stubborn skull.

With a sigh, she forced herself to roll over and sit up on the edge of the queen-size bed she'd had since she turned fifteen. The walls no longer held One Direction and *Supernatural* posters, and the photos of her friend were replaced by tasteful artwork and framed family photos, but everyone still called it her room all these years later.

The clock read seven a.m. By now, her mom would have driven her youngest sibling to swim practice, and the older one would have driven herself to the diner where they bussed tables, following in Shell and Beth's footsteps.

Copper should be home, though, and she owed him some face time.

After brushing her teeth, she padded out to the kitchen in her sleep shorts, tank, and the fuzzy slippers she kept here at her parents' house. After filling her favorite coffee mug, a large one that read *World's Okayest Adult*, she glanced out the French doors to find her dad sitting on the rocking bench he'd gifted Shell five years ago.

Beth grinned at the way his enormous form took up more than his half of the bench. Her mom loved it, claiming it meant mandatory cuddles when they sat out there taking in the mountain view, which they did often at the end of the day with a glass of whiskey.

He, too, had an oversized mug of coffee wrapped in his oversized hands. As soon as she stepped outside, he glanced her way. "Hey, kiddo." If he was smiling, it was hidden behind the coppery beard that earned him his name.

Already, the day had warmed to where she was

comfortable in her sleep clothes.

"Everyone else up and out already?"

He nodded. "You gonna come sit with the grumpy old man?"

Rolling her eyes, she sat next to him. "You're not old."

His grunt was so familiar and comforting that it sent her back ten years to when she was a kid, unloading her problems on her superhero father. "But I am grumpy?"

She shrugged. "There have been some rumors."

"Smartass. Just like your mama."

Beth lifted her mug to hide her smile. They sat in silence, absorbing the peaceful view for only a few seconds before she felt compelled to speak. "I'm so sorry, Dad. I was out of line last night. I'm so sorry I yelled at you like that, and at the clubhouse…" She shook her head. "I'm surprised you're even talking to me this morning."

"Since when am I one to give the silent treatment?"

She snorted a half-laugh. "Never. You're more of a holler-and-beat-your-chest type."

"Exactly." He fell silent, sipped his coffee, then said, "Suppose I was a little over the top going after Gator like that."

Raising an eyebrow, she looked up at the man who raised her as though he'd made her. "A little."

"I don't want you with one of my guys, Beth. That's a hard line for me."

Guilt twisted in her, sharp and hot. He had no idea what she'd gotten up to last night, and he never would, but it was still a betrayal. She could still feel the imprint of Saint's mouth on her throat, could still hear the filthy words he'd growled against her skin as he made her come harder than she had in years. Her father sat inches away, oblivious to the fact that his daughter had screamed one of his men's names into the mountain air just hours ago. Saint was right to call it off when he did, even if it dented her ego.

"I know, Dad. But Gator is nothing more than a friend. It's like Mav kissing mom on the cheek."

His face screwed up, making her chuckle. "Ugh, he is a little like Maverick, isn't he?"

"A bit. Though I think he's crazier if that's even possible."

Copper laughed, which made her smile. How had she not realized how much she missed her family? "I think you're right on that one. I'll… uh, I'll try not to be such an asshole about you being friends with my guys. As long as you leave it at friendship."

There was that clench of unease again. "I know. And thanks, Dad." And that was that. It had always been that way between them, open communication and little bullshit or emotional outbursts, save for last night. They'd always been able to talk through issues and move on with ease, something she greatly appreciated about Copper.

She brought a leg up, bending her knee and resting her foot on the cushion as she leaned her head against her father's bulky shoulder.

"So," he said just as she'd gotten comfortable. "You ready to tell me what the fuck was going on in Texas?"

Her eyes flared as she stiffened. *Shit, he'd notice her reaction for sure.* "I…"

"Beth," he said, his voice heavy with suspicion.

She didn't even need to say anything for him to know she was full of shit. Never had she been able to lie to him. Anytime she'd tried to pull one over on him as a kid, he'd known. He'd see through her, and she'd crumbled, not able to spew untruths to the man she respected above all. Of course, he'd known there was more to her ridiculous story about being overworked and stressed in Texas. This was why she worried so much about hooking up with Saint. As long as he didn't sniff something suspicious and ask her, they'd be fine, but if he suspected and confronted her, she'd be screwed.

Lifting off his shoulder, she turned on the bench to face him, resting her back against the wooden armrest.

"Can you promise me you won't lose your shit if I tell you?"

"No." Not a flicker of a smile or twinkle in his eyes. He was dead-fucking-serious.

"Dad."

"Christ, kiddo." He rubbed his beard the way she'd seen him do a million times over the years. How could she feel so nostalgic, yet so annoyed and so anxious at the same time? "You know I'm unreasonable when it comes to you, your mom, and your siblings. I won't apologize for it, and it's not going to change. So no, I will *not* promise to keep my fucking wits about me when you no doubt tell me something I'm going to fucking hate."

"All right. Okay." She sighed and stared at a hawk circling high above their house. It was time to let her family in on the deep, dark secret she'd been keeping for way too long. Facing him again, she found his green eyes, the same as hers, full of concern.

And love.

What a bitch she was to feel frustrated at being loved so deeply.

She averted her gaze once again, unable to look him in the eye as she unloaded the truth. "Jason turned out to be a... less-than-stellar boyfriend. I lost myself a little there in the end and needed to get away."

Wow, cop-out much?

Copper's jaw ticked. "Less-than-stellar?"

"Uh-huh."

He didn't need more details than that, right?

"Beth, I'm going to give you exactly five seconds to elaborate before I lose my fucking shit."

Okay, so maybe he did want details.

"He, um, got a little rough with me."

"Got a little rough with you." The deep timbre of his voice turned lethal. "So, he… hurt you?"

Instant tears sprang to her eyes, and she blinked as rapidly as possible to keep them from falling. Tears were kindling to Copper's burning fire. "He did."

"Hit you?" The malice in his voice made her shiver. Not with fear. Never once had she feared him, but for anyone who crossed him.

"Yes," she whispered.

"Worse?"

She nodded. "Yes."

"And Saint?"

Her stomach bottomed out. "W-what about Saint?"

"Is he aware of this?"

"Uh…"

Her dad pinched the bridge of his nose as he nearly growled. "Swear to Christ, Beth, this is not the time to try and feed me a line of horseshit. *Is. Saint. Aware*?"

Fuck. Fuck. Fuck.

"I asked him, forced him really, to keep quiet."

Copper was going to crack a tooth at this rate. She pulled his arm down so she could see his face, and the fury in her eyes had her wishing she hadn't. "Please be mad at me. Not him. He only agreed to keep my secret because I promised to eventually tell you. I just needed some time."

"So tell me, Beth. Tell me now and tell me everything."

Oh, this was going to go over about as well as that time she and her friends decided to try riding his motorcycle when they were fifteen. They tipped it and scratched the hell out of it before they made it out of the driveway. Copper nearly had a massive coronary event, or maybe she'd had the heart attack while waiting for him to wake up and discover what she'd done.

She glanced down at her chewed and ragged nails. They'd taken quite a beating over the past few weeks. "Yes, Jason was abusive. Saint…" She swallowed and blinked away new moisture in her eyes. "Well, there's a good chance he saved my life. Jason attacked me that night in a way he hadn't before. H-he had his hand around my throat and was choking me. Saint happened to arrive at that moment and heard a commotion. It was dumb luck. He kicked in my door and pulled Jason off me. I-I thought Saint was going to kill Jason," she whispered.

"He fucking should have." The way Copper's nostrils flared and clenched his fists left no doubt in her mind he'd have done just that. "Why the fuck didn't he?"

"No." She shook her head. "I couldn't have that on my conscience. He came close. Jason was in bad shape when Saint got through with him, but I… I couldn't have lived with the guilt of him killing someone because of me."

"This is one of the main reasons I don't want you to tangle up with my men. It fucks with their heads."

"There's no tangling." At least at the time, there hadn't been tangling. "I barely know him. He's someone I've seen a handful of times over the years. And I was supposed to be okay with him killing someone on my behalf? Killing someone for some woman who might as well be a stranger?"

"You're his fucking president's daughter, Beth. It's his job, his club duty to keep you safe." His thunderous expression matched the rise in volume as he shouted.

"And *he did*," she yelled right back. "I'm the one who begged him to stop. I'm the one who fucked up," she said, slapping her own chest. "I stayed with a piece of shit who hurt me. The mistakes were *mine*. I'm so fucking ashamed of it. How could I live with myself if one of your men had to take a life because of my fuckup?" The sob she'd been trying to suppress burst forward.

Copper's fury turned to horror one second before he hauled her to him, wrapping his arms around her in a crushing bear hug. "Christ, Beth, you didn't fuck up. None of this is your fault."

Everything she'd held in over the past few weeks, hell, the last year, burst from her in a torrent of hot tears that drenched her father's shirt. In the safety and comfort of his arms, she wept for long minutes until there couldn't have been a drop of liquid left in her body. All the while, he rocked her back and forth, murmuring about how she hadn't done anything wrong and had nothing to feel bad about.

Eventually, she calmed. Copper rubbed her back as he rested his furred chin on her head. "Better?"

She let out a weak laugh. "Yeah," she said as she pulled out of his embrace. "Sorry about that," she said with a wince as she wiped his tear-soaked shirt as though she could brush away the wetness.

"Not the first time you've sobbed all over me."

"Yeah, guess that's what you get for being a girl-dad."

He chuckled, then grew serious. "Listen to me, Beth," he said, holding her shoulders so she had no choice but to face him. "There is only one person to blame here, and that's the ball-barnacle who pretends he's a man."

Her lips twitched. "Ball-barnacle?"

But Copper wasn't in the mood to laugh. "Yes. He's a fucking two-pump tragedy and not worth the paper I wipe my ass with. No one can call themselves a man if they do not treat their woman like a fucking queen."

"I know." She lowered her eyes, staring at the tear spot on his olive T-shirt. "I know that. I've seen it my whole life. I've seen nothing but the best examples of relationships. It's why I'm so ashamed of staying so long."

"Beth…" He lifted her chin. "You know our sister chapter

runs a women's shelter down in Florida. Hell, you've been there."

"Yes."

"Do you think any of those women should be ashamed of the situations they've found themselves in? Of how long they stayed with someone who abused them?"

"No, of course not. I'd never think that. There's so much nuance, manipulation, and fear. The only feeling I have toward them is admiration for leaving, no matter how long it took."

"So why can't you show yourself the same grace and understanding?"

Good question. Why couldn't she?

"Um… I think it's almost easier to blame myself than feel like a victim. That's fucked up, right?"

He tilted his head, studying her. "Well, how about you start thinking of yourself as a survivor instead? Surviving isn't a weakness. It's proof you've been tested, hurt, and still refused to disappear."

Surviving meant strength. It meant courage. It meant clawing her way out of the dark, even when life tried to swallow her whole. It meant breathing through the pain, choosing to stand when it would have been easier to stay down.

She swallowed a lump in her throat, refusing to cry again. "Yeah. I think I can do that."

"Good." He released her shoulders and grabbed his mug again. "Thank you for telling me, Beth. And thank you for coming home."

"Please don't lose your shit on Saint. He did what you asked. He rescued me, protected me, and brought me home."

Copper pressed his lips together until they flattened into an unimpressed line. "He also withheld information."

"Because *I* begged him to. He also told me he wouldn't

flat-out lie. That if you asked him straight, he'd have no choice but to tell you. *Please*."

"I can't let it slide, Beth."

Okay, she got that. Kind of. She nodded. "Just… please remember I'm the one who put him in a horrible position."

Sighing, he looked out at the calming scenery. "I know, kiddo. I'll try not to make him cry."

She huffed a laugh despite the anxiety now swirling in her. Whatever consequences Saint suffered to keep her secret would plague her for a long time.

"Fuck," Copper muttered, looking at his watch. "I have a dentist appointment in half an hour."

That had a real laugh bubbling from her. "Even big bad bikers have to take care of their teeth, huh?"

"Such a smartass."

She grinned, the first genuine smile of the day, and it did wonders to lift her mood.

Copper kissed her head before he stood. "I'm gonna go get ready. You good?"

"I am." She looked up at him, towering over her. "Thanks, Dad."

"Your mom and I are so glad you're home, kiddo."

"Me too." And it was the truth.

He left her to her coffee and scenery, but she didn't plan to sit idle for long. Now that she'd gotten one difficult conversation out of the way, she had to dive straight into another. Saint deserved to know Copper would be coming for him.

Her pulse quickened at the thought of seeing him again. Of being alone with him. Would he look at her the way he had last night, like he wanted to devour her? Would those talented hands find their way back to her skin?

She squeezed her thighs together and cursed under her breath.

This was a warning, not a booty call.

She needed to keep her head on straight and her panties firmly in place.

Easier said than done when it came to Saint.

Chapter Thirteen

Copper: Eleven a.m. Clubhouse.

That's it. Short and sweet text command from Copper, which stuck to the president's style, but something about the summons had Saint on high alert.

Maybe because you had your hands all over and in Beth last night.

Had Copper found out? Did someone drive by and spot them when he'd been too lust drunk to notice? Or was his guilty conscience playing tricks on him?

Fuck, he'd messed up royally last night.

He'd wanted her with a force that shook him to his core, and when it became clear she'd wanted him, too, he'd taken it. Instead of getting it out of his system, the feel and taste of her only made his craving worse. Maybe it was because he hadn't come, at least not by her hand. He'd jerked off furiously the second he got home, but his gut told him it wouldn't matter. If she got her hands or mouth on him, he'd become addicted.

Obsessed.

Even more than he already was, which felt impossible.

"You're a fucking idiot," he muttered as he stared at his

phone.

Saint: I'll be there.

He set the phone face down on the counter and reached for his protein shake. Two swallows in, his doorbell rang.

Saint frowned. He lived in a small two-bedroom cabin slightly off the beaten path. One of the best things about his place was the lack of solicitors or guests popping by for no reason. Even his sister knew to inform him before she showed up.

Could it be Copper? Was his president so fucking furious that he'd decided not to wait until eleven to castrate him?

"Fucking great," he muttered as he walked to the door barefoot and dressed only in a pair of lightweight gray sweats. If he were going to die, it might as well be in a comfortable outfit in his own home. "Coming!" he hollered after the bell rang again.

He yanked the door open and lost his breath as his gaze fell on the woman he'd spent all night thinking about. "Beth."

Her eyes darkened as her attention went straight to his bare chest. Jesus, if she gaped at him like that for more than two seconds, he'd be hard as a fucking spike and his pants couldn't hide a cotton ball, let alone a raging boner.

"Hey. Um…" She licked her lips, and he nearly groaned.

"What are you doing here?"

His tone came out harsher than he'd meant, causing her to blink and jerk her focus to his face. "Sorry. I should have called."

Sighing, he leaned against the door frame while folding his arms across his chest. "This have anything to do with the text I got from Copper demanding I meet him at the clubhouse at eleven?"

Beth grimaced. "Shit. I was hoping I'd beat him to it."

He stepped back, making room for her. "Come on in."

"Thanks. And I'm sorry for dropping by unannounced. I

hate that shit. In my defense, I wasn't thinking."

He chuckled as he pointed toward the small, plush couch in his den. "That's your defense?"

She shrugged. "Didn't say it was a good defense."

Her cutting wit had him smiling more than usual, even during these tense interactions. "Have a seat. Want some coffee or, I don't know, a shot of tequila?"

Her laugh ran over his bare skin, making goose bumps rise. "Nah, think I'll hold off the booze. Not much of an early morning drinker. And I've already had three cups of coffee. Better not have any more unless you want me to vibrate out of here." She sat, bouncing a little as though testing the comfort of his couch. "Um, take your time. I can wait while you get dressed or whatever."

So, she found his half-naked state distracting, did she? He raised an eyebrow.

"Or not. It's your house. Of course. You can do whatever you'd like." Beth let out a tense laugh, then rolled her eyes. "Oh my God, I'm rambling. Sorry. I just… I kinda didn't expect to see you again so soon after last night."

Her cheeks turned pink.

"And then this morning happened and…"

"And Copper found out we fucked around last night?"

Her eyes nearly fell from their sockets. "What? No! No, no, no. God no. I'm pretty sure I would have had to knock him over the head with a frying pan to beat him here if that were the case."

He'd be lying if he said he wasn't relieved as hell. "So then what's all this about?"

Beth cleared her throat and angled so she could see him where he sat on the opposite end of the couch. "I told him about Jason. The *whole* story about Jason."

"Ahh. And now, Pres knows I kept it from him."

Biting her lower lip, she nodded. "I'm so sorry, Saint. I

made sure he knew I basically forced you to go along with my plan."

"You didn't need to do that, Beth. I made my choice, and I stand by it. Copper was always going to find out, and my actions were always going to bite my ass. But I don't regret it."

She groaned. "Saint…"

"No, babe, stop feeling guilty. You must feel better now that it's out there."

She thought about it for a second, then nodded. "I do, for the most part. Still have to talk to my mom about it, but Copper and I had a good chat. It helped."

"I'm glad. I'm also relieved as fuck he didn't find out about last night."

"Ha. Yeah." Her weak laugh sounded through the quiet room right before his attention went back to his bare chest. He could feel her gaze like a caress, tracing all the tattoos he'd collected over the years. As he sat there under her intense perusal, growing harder by the second, he could only think one thing.

Why the fuck didn't I put a shirt on while I had the chance?

***

THE MAN WAS sexier than any one man had the right to be, and he wasn't even trying. He didn't have to do a damn thing but sit there shirtless for her body to react. Like last night, her nipples tightened to stiff peaks, and the lace of her bra was suddenly unbearable against the sensitive tips. Heat pooled low in her belly, and she had to fight the urge to press her thighs together as her pussy clenched around nothing, remembering the talented way his fingers had filled her. Her palms tingled with curiosity over the way his smooth, warm skin would feel as she ran them all over his body. Even breathing became difficult. She had to fight to keep her inhales and exhales steady instead of panting over the sight of his naked chest.

Beth had obviously been turned on before. She'd slept with a handful of men over the years, some of them great experiences, some mediocre, and in the last year, quite dreadful, but she'd never experienced this soul-rattling level of raw desire. The longing felt more like an unrelenting prickle expanding beneath her skin. The kind that couldn't be ignored without going mad. If he didn't touch her to appease that itch, she'd go out of her mind with need.

Which meant she might end up in a padded room because nothing could happen. They could not cross that line again, not after her conversation with Copper this morning. Saint's involvement with her already jeopardized his standing in the club. They could not make it worse.

And yet, the need persisted. Hell, it grew with every second in his presence.

She blew out a slow breath as she fought to come up with something to break the awkward silence. "I like your ink."

Great, Beth, point out how you're staring at his delectable chest.

He glanced down at his torso. "Thanks. Izzy did ninety percent of it." As he spoke, he rubbed a hand over the muscular plane of his chest where multiple tattoos resided. The temperature in his house spiked at least fifteen degrees.

"And the last ten?"

His expression could only be described as a half smirk, half cringe. "My buddy did them from his garage when we were eighteen and high."

She snickered as she winced. "Ah, back when you were making really good choices."

That had him laughing out loud. "You have no idea how good." He scratched his left pec where an inked bird, she didn't know what kind, soared. It seemed to be a bird of prey of some sort, but she knew shit about birds beyond the fact that his tattoo mesmerized her. Izzy did outstanding work, and when he moved in the right way, the bird seemed to flap its wings. "Maybe one day I'll show you the ones my buddy did. They're not available to just anyone." He winked.

Fucking winked.

Christ.

She fanned herself as sweat broke out across her hairline. "Is your air conditioning broken or something?" The temperature in the house felt near boiling.

"Nah, fully functional."

Of course. Maybe he didn't turn it on. Something was making the house unbearably warm.

Or maybe you're a horny bitch who can't walk away from the one man you can't have.

Okay, she could do this. She could be a mature adult, stand up, and leave Saint's damn house without giving in to her baser urges.

Every second of the night before had played through her mind countless times since she'd left him, with each memory being better than the last except for one very significant fact.

She hadn't gotten to touch him.

To taste him.

To hear his moans.

To see him come.

And suddenly, it felt so wrong that it overwhelmed her.

But Saint had been the one to come to his senses last night, so she had to try today at least.

She stood. "Well, I'm gonna head out. I'll—"

"Come here." The command snapped out like the crack of a whip in the quiet house.

She stopped breathing.

Go to him.

Walk out the door.

The internal battle raged loudly and fiercely inside her head.

"Beth..." His voice beckoned her. A sensual promise for a repeat of last night. More forbidden pleasure no one would know about. No one could know about.

Instead of saying goodbye and running out the door as she should, since she'd already fucked up his life enough, she stepped toward him, drawn by Saint's magnetic pull.

His gaze darkened and heated until she could feel the warmth on her skin. His attention locked onto her, following every move she made. When she was close, he widened his legs and glanced down between them before looking back up at her. A non-verbal command she followed at once, stepping between his muscular thighs.

"Saint," she whispered. "We can't..."

"What do you want? Fuck everything else, fuck everyone else. What do you want right here and right now?"

Time slowed as they stared at each other. Her heartbeat thudded slowly and steadily, pulsing in her ears. She swallowed.

"I want to make you feel as good right now as you made me feel last night."

His eyes widened, and he sucked in a breath.

No doubt he thought she'd say she wanted his hands on her again, and she did, but first she wanted a turn at driving him out of his mind.

"Fuck." His head fell back on the couch as he swore. When he raised back up, the primal desire staring back at her stole her breath. He lifted his hips, hooked his thumbs in the sides of his sweats, and shoved them down, kicking them off in one fluid move.

And there he was gloriously and unapologetically naked.

Her gaze dropped to his cock, thick and flushed dark with arousal, already leaking at the tip as it curved up toward his abs like it was begging for her attention. *God, he was big*. Her inner walls clenched at the thought of taking all of him.

"Have at it."

Her mouth watered. It had been a long time since she wanted to give a man head. She wanted to lick and suck while feeling the weight of a cock in her mouth. But she wanted it now more than anything.

"You're sure?" she asked in a moment of sanity. "Be sure, Saint, because this is such a bad idea."

"I'm fucking sure, Beth. I want your mouth, I want your hands, and I want your pussy."

Her eyes widened, and her sex clenched.

"Fuck everything else."

"Fuck everything else," she whispered. There were only so many ways she could make sure he understood the gravity of the situation. They wanted each other, both fully aware of the consequences. And though they'd protect this in secret as much as they could, should the worst happen before it burned itself out and someone discovered them, she'd do her damnedest to shield him from Copper's wrath.

He winked, and the simple, playful action sealed the deal for good.

She sank to her knees on his plush carpet, giving him a wicked grin.

"Look at you on your knees for me." His voice dipped, rough and hungry. "You gonna let me fill that pretty mouth, Beth? Let me feel that throat swallow around my cock?"

"I am." She glided her hands up his inked, lightly furred thighs as she inched closer on her knees. "And I'm going to make you lose your mind."

His smirk did something to her insides, twisted them all

up in a tangle of knots. She ignored it. This was nothing more than a physical release, so that's where his focus would lie.

She wrapped her hand around his erection, loving the immediate hiss that left his lips. He was long, thick, and so hot against her palm, and hell, he'd feel good inside her.

Maintaining eye contact, she lowered her head and licked around the crown of his dick, tasting the salty bead of precum that had gathered there. His eyelids grew heavy, forcing him to watch her through slits. His grunt and a few whispered curses spurred her on. She drew the head between her lips, sucking as she teased the sensitive underside with her tongue.

"Christ, your mouth is so fucking hot."

She smiled around his cock and then set about shattering him. She took him to the back of her throat, fighting the reflexive urge to gag, and his whole body jerked in response. His abs contracted, thighs tensing beneath her palms, and the groan that tore from his chest sounded like it was ripped from somewhere deep inside him.

His hands flew to her hair, gripping but not controlling, letting her set the pace. "Fuck, that's it. God, Beth, this mouth is fucking sinful."

Yes. Tell me how much you love it.

This was what she craved. The words. Hearing how much Saint enjoyed everything she was doing to him. He seemed to understand what she wanted instinctually, or maybe they were just that damn compatible.

She worked up to a furious rhythm, bobbing on his cock as she'd never experienced anything better. He hit the back of her throat again and again, and while in the past she might have backed off or tried to end it quickly, his constant stream of mindless chatter and praise made her want to spend the next hour right there swallowing his cock.

"More, Beth. More, more, more. Baby, it's so fucking good.

You're so good."

After being with someone who put her down for so long, Saint's admiration drove her wild. Maybe she'd developed a praise kink after being with a jerk for almost two years. She kept at him, adding her hands to the mix, raking her nails up his thighs. His back arched as he groaned.

"So beautiful," he managed between rapid breaths. "So beautiful with that mouth stretched wide around my cock."

She hummed around him, letting the vibration travel through his shaft, and he cried out a raw, broken sound that made her pussy clench. His grip tightened in her hair, fingers flexing against her scalp, but still letting her have control.

"Fuck, I felt that all the way in my balls. You like that, huh? Like it when I tell you how good you suck me? How it's the best mouth I've ever felt?"

She moaned, squeezing her eyes shut as a wave of intense lust crashed over her. She was drenched, her pussy throbbing in time with each stroke of her mouth. The ache between her thighs had become almost unbearable. She was tempted to shove her pants down and ride her own fingers to take the edge off. Instead, she focused her efforts on Saint, doubling down until he began to tremble, and the skin beneath her palms grew slick with sweat.

"Fuck, Beth, I'm close." His voice had gone ragged, wrecked. "Get ready, baby. I'm about to fill that pretty throat."

She whimpered and took him deep one more time, swallowing around him as his cock pulsed against her tongue. He came with a guttural shout, his entire body bowing forward as he spilled hot and thick down her throat.

"Fuck!" The word tore out of him, raw and desperate, as she swallowed every drop, milking him through the aftershocks until he collapsed back against the couch, chest heaving.

He softened between her lips while his body settled from the powerful contractions. She let him slip from her lips, lifting to meet his sated gaze. Thank God she couldn't see herself reflected in his eyes. She must look like a damn mess with rumpled hair, swollen lips, and saliva on her chin.

As she opened her mouth to say who knew what, Saint surged forward and grabbed her under her arms. In one world-tilting move, he had her on her back on the couch while he jerked her pants and panties off together. Then he bent her knees, shoving them wide.

Oh God, was he going to return the favor? "Wha—"

"Yes or no?"

Her eyes widened, and she nodded her head so fast the room spun. "Yes. Yes, yes, yes."

He gave her the most roguish grin imaginable right before he lowered his head and dragged his tongue through her folds in one long, devastating stroke. She cried out and arched her hips, but he grabbed them and anchored her to the couch before devouring her like a man starved.

"Oh my God," she shouted. It was so intense, so good, the way he tongued and sucked at her clit. She was already so turned on that, at this rate, she was going to come in three seconds flat.

Her neck arched, and she tried to thrust against his talented tongue, but he held her trapped in the most erotic prison.

"I'm not going to last." She threw an arm over her eyes. "Oh, God, Saint, I'm not going to last."

She swore she could feel his lips curl into a smile against her sex. "You loved sucking my cock that much, huh?" He shoved his tongue inside her, fucking her with it, and the world whited out.

She screamed as the orgasm slammed into her. Suddenly and devastatingly, pleasure ripped through her in violent waves. Her back arched off the couch, thighs clamping around his head as she shattered, coming so hard she couldn't breathe, couldn't think, and could only shake beneath his relentless mouth.

After, she melted into the couch, exhausted and shaken from the power of the swift and brutal orgasm.

"Damn, I am good. What was that, fifteen seconds?"

She lifted her head and flipped him off as she laughed, finding him crawling up her body, still gloriously naked and smirking.

Ice flooded her veins. No. Oh no, he could not make her laugh. Getting each other off was one thing, but teasing and laughing? That was dangerous. He either needed to shut up or say something obnoxious before she started drifting toward hazardous thoughts, such as she might actually like this guy.

Saint sighed and let his forehead fall to her chest. "Fuck. I have to get to the clubhouse," he muttered against her shirt.

To meet with your father.

Welp, that did the trick.

She wasn't laughing anymore.

Chapter Fourteen

Saint strode into the clubhouse with his usual outward confidence—easy gait, loose shoulders—but anxiety churned beneath the surface. Letting Copper down sucked. Worse, he'd done it knowing his president would eventually learn the truth about Jason's treatment of Beth. Knowing Copper would view it as a betrayal of trust.

And still he'd done it. Like he'd done other things with Beth that Copper would hate even more, but one sin at a time.

"Hey, brother," Zach said, looking up from the bar. Maverick and Jigsaw were there, too, as was Rocket.

Saint slowed.

Well, fuck. Had the club's entire executive board gathered to kick his ass? Or strip his patch? Maybe they'd be merciful and only demote him from Baby Enforcer to plain old club member. The thought twisted something sharp and dug in his chest. He'd worked hard for his position. And he valued it, knowing one day he'd fully take the role over from Zach.

Knowing he fucked with their ability to trust him would hurt almost as much as exile. "What's going on?" he asked as he came to a stop in the middle of the space.

Copper strode out of his office. He didn't rush. Didn't scowl. Just watched Saint with flat, unreadable eyes, his expression hidden beneath his auburn beard.

"Everyone, head out," Copper said calmly. "I need five minutes with Saint."

Here it comes.

Zach glanced between them, curiosity blatant in his raised eyebrow, but he kept his questions to himself. "Sure thing, Prez."

The room emptied fast. The door shut behind them with a soft click that sounded louder than it ever had.

"I had a long talk with Beth this morning," Copper said, folding his arms across his massive chest.

Saint kept his face neutral. Copper didn't know Beth had come to him first. He didn't know what she'd divulged. Nor did he know she sucked his brain out through his dick less than an hour ago.

Thank fuck.

They stood twenty feet apart. Far enough that Copper couldn't reach him if he decided to throw a punch. Close enough that Saint felt every ounce of his president's scrutiny.

"Okay…"

"If you'd gotten to her ten minutes later…"

"But I didn't."

Copper sighed, rubbing a hand over his beard. "Yeah." He studied Saint for a long moment. "What did you do with Jason?"

Since Beth had told him the entire ugly truth about her abusive piece of shit ex, Saint had no reason to keep anything from his president. At least not regarding why he pulled Beth's ass out of Texas.

"Beat him fucking bloody with my bare hands right there on the floor of Beth's apartment."

Copper nodded once.

"I would've killed him if it went on much longer, but..." He shrugged.

"Yeah. Beth told me." His jaw tightened. "What did you do with him after?"

"Dumped him in a fucking field somewhere in bumfuck, Texas, after a heart-to-heart about what would happen to him if he came within a hundred miles of Beth."

"Think he'll be a problem in the future?"

Saint pursed his lips. "He's a pussy. The kind of guy who thinks he's tough because he roughs up women. He couldn't take one fucking punch. My money is on him being too chicken shit to do anything."

"Okay. I still want eyes on him. For a bit."

"Done."

Copper looked up at the ceiling like he was searching for patience. "I'm fucking torn about how to handle this shit, Saint. The club's never had a problem with you before. I don't fucking like it."

"I know."

"I hate being kept in the dark."

Saint straightened, meeting Copper's gaze head-on. "I get it. And I'm not trying to give you a line of bullshit excuses. When I agreed to keep quiet, I knew I was risking your fury. I knew it wasn't acceptable to you or the club, but Beth needed space. She planned to tell you once she processed. I made sure of that. Everything happened fast. She was reeling. Keeping my mouth shut gave her the dignity to share painful information on her own terms."

He didn't look away. Didn't hedge.

"I fucked up with you, Prez. I own that. But if I'm being totally honest, I'd do it the same way again. I think I made the best decision at the time, given what I had to work with."

"You're protective," Copper said with a solemn expression. "It's one of the reasons I knew my daughter would be safe with you."

For fuck's sake.

He nodded, fighting to keep his expression neutral while the taste of Beth still lingered on his tongue. An hour ago, he'd had his face buried between her thighs, making her scream his name, and now he stood here pretending to be the loyal soldier Copper believed him to be.

"I want to rip your head off..." Copper muttered, "... but I also understand. And I need to respect my daughter's autonomy and right to privacy, or some shit. At least that's what Shell said," he muttered.

Saint pressed his lips together to keep from smirking. It seemed the wisest idea.

"Just don't forget..." Copper added, "... your first obligation is to this club."

"I won't." It wasn't a lie. He hadn't forgotten his club. He'd made a choice.

A few choices.

Keep Beth's secret.

Let her suck him off.

Make her come on his tongue.

"So now you owe me. You're going to make it up to me by heading to the laundromat and getting that number so we can find out who the fuckers are dicking around in our town.

"Now?" Saint blinked.

"Right fucking now."

He cleared his throat. "You got it, Prez." It looked like he had about five minutes to get in the headspace to fuck with some drug dealers. Not what he had planned for the day, but he sure as hell wasn't going to argue with Copper.

"Good. Zach, Mav, and I will ride along but stay out of sight unless it goes tits up."

"Okay." Already, he'd begun the shift into enforcer mode, pushing everything out of his mind except his duty to his club family.

"Let's roll." Copper strode toward him, slapping his shoulder as he passed. His expression softened to the mildly murderous appearance he usually wore as opposed to the violent visage he'd had when Saint first walked in.

He followed his president outside to find Zach and Mav already on their bikes and primed to go.

"All right," Zach said from astride his motorcycle. "We'll be near if there's trouble, Saint. Go in, get the number, and get out. Leave your cut off and fingers crossed that whoever is working doesn't recognize you as one of us."

He grunted. Fat chance of that happening. Almost everyone in their small town knew the Handlers. Half the town feared them as villains, while the others saw them as vigilante saviors. Reality lay somewhere in between. They wanted to live their lives their way, and sometimes that didn't always follow the letter of the law.

"Easy enough," Saint said as he grabbed his helmet.

Mav snorted. "Let's fucking hope." Then he fired up his bike and gestured for Saint to head out. "After you," he shouted.

Their crew of four took off, flying through the mountains into town. The ten-minute trip gave Saint the time to get in the zone.

When he made the left into the parking lot of the small shopping center housing the laundromat, an antique store, and a dental office, the rest of his brothers kept riding. They'd circle back and park in the far end of the lot, but wanted anyone watching out the window to think they rode on.

Saint parked his bike in front of the antique store sandwiched between the laundromat and dental office, removed his cut, and stowed it in his saddlebags before striding toward his mark. A large sign on the door read *No Loitering*, and beneath it, an ever-popular *No Shoes, No Shirt,*

No Service sign hung crooked in the front window.

The bell over the laundromat door jangled too cheerfully as Saint stepped inside. Overfilled washers rattled with angry metal clangs like they were seconds from tearing themselves apart. Fluorescent lights buzzed overhead, harsh and unforgiving. They blasted him with light brighter than the midday summer sun.

Two customers occupied the laundromat.

They clocked him instantly.

One, a twenty-something woman folded towels on top of a dryer, while an older gentleman sat on a bench near the front window, waiting for his cycle to finish. He went back to scrolling his phone after a quick, wary glance Saint's way.

Saint crossed to the counter slowly and deliberately.

"Can I help you?" the attendant asked without looking up from a decade-old, crinkled muscle car magazine.

The guy had shaggy, light brown hair with a matching mustache and was thin enough to be blown over by a gentle breeze. His plain white T-shirt had orange dust speckled across it. An empty Cheetos bag rested next to his open magazine.

"I want to use machine thirteen."

The guy froze mid-page turn. The room didn't go quiet, but something shifted.

The attendant lifted his head in a slow pan up Saint's body. His eyes widened as round as the porthole on his washers. Yeah, cut or no cut, this guy knew exactly who stood in front of him.

"Uh, sorry, man. No, thirteen," he said too fast. "Boss is super, uh, super… whatever that word is. Don't like the number thirteen."

"Superstitious."

"Yeah. That's it. Twelve and fourteen are open."

Saint placed his palms flat on the counter and leaned

forward, looming over the attendant. "I want thirteen."

The guy's pointy Adam's apple bobbed as he swallowed hard. "Right. Uh…" He wiped orange fingers on his T-shirt as he reached beneath the counter.

Going for a gun?

Saint's pulse jumped. He immediately reached for the piece on his belt, but before he had a chance to grab it, the guy's hand returned, empty. "Okay, here you go." He grabbed a pencil and a scrap of paper, scrawled a ten-digit number, then shoved the paper across the counter like it was hot to the touch.

As he reached for the paper, the door jangled, announcing a new arrival. From the corner of his eye, Saint caught both customers glance up from their seats. The woman gasped and paled while the man mouthed a curse. She abandoned her folding and scurried toward a back exit. Two seconds after she ran past him, the older man left as well.

Their sudden departure was enough to have the back of Saint's neck prickling with unease. "What did you do?" he asked the attendant, who looked everywhere but at Saint.

Slowly, so as not to startle whoever had entered, Saint turned around to find a large man blocking the exit. Jet-black hair, black jeans, and a black T-shirt, combined with a scowl and a jagged scar crossing his left jaw, gave the newcomer a menacing look. Thick gold rings that would hurt like hell if they smashed into Saint's face rested on at least five of his fingers. He didn't bother to conceal the knife hanging from his belt, but at least he didn't have a gun unless it was hidden.

"You called in the muscle," Saint said with a sigh. He must have a panic button under the counter. He glanced over his shoulder. "What'd you go and do that for? I followed the protocol."

The attendant stood there, eyes bugging and mouth

flapping like a suffocating fish.

"Time to go," the guy said in a deep, reverberating voice that matched his size and stature.

"Works for me. I got what I came for." He fanned himself with the scrap of paper containing the phone number. Lord knew if the attendant gave him the real contact information.

"Leave the number."

Of course, this wasn't going to go down easily.

"Really?" he asked, tilting his head. "Your boss doesn't like to make money? What's his name? Silas Crow?"

In his peripheral vision, Saint caught sight of Zach and Maverick on foot, inching closer to the laundromat. Backup had arrived. Knowing they were close and ready to jump in to kick ass lowered Saint's blood pressure.

The guy's eyes narrowed upon hearing the name. "Not from you. We know your club. You have no interest in using that number." The guy narrowed his eyes and stared with what he probably assumed was a menacing glare, but this fucker had no idea who raised Saint. Deadlier men than him tried to destroy Saint from infancy, and if they hadn't succeeded, this loser sure wouldn't.

"Well, sure." He shrugged. "We don't need it for… business purposes." Neither of them was willing to say the word drugs out loud. The last thing he needed was this guy or the laundromat attendant getting a video of him saying he wanted to buy or sell drugs. Clearly, the newcomer wasn't an idiot if he monitored his words as well. "But if you know our club, as you claim, you know we love a good party."

"Find a new way to get your… party favors."

"Nah, I don't think so. This seems really convenient." He glanced at the paper, then back to his new friend with a smirk. "Yeah, I think I'll give them a call as soon as I leave here. Unless you wanna pass a message along for me."

The guy took three menacing steps toward Saint, who held

his ground without flinching or reaching for his gun as instinct demanded.

The man came close enough that Saint noticed the scar transecting his jaw was part of a larger network of wounds. It was the darkest while smaller, web-like lines crisscrossed his cheek. Whatever he'd been through left a permanent reminder.

The guy's hand went to the hilt of his hunting knife. "Think I'd rather send you back to your club with a message from my boss."

"Oh yeah, what's that? You're coming for us? You wanna run our town? You think your band of cute little wannabe outlaws is going to take territory the Handlers have held for decades?" He laughed, making sure it sounded as mocking as possible. Taunting this asshole was a bad idea. He didn't want a bloody brawl in the middle of the laundromat that would alert the local cops. Sure, the club had some in their pocket, but there were still many in the police force who hated them and would love to toss their ass in jail. "You have no idea what you're up against."

The guy's hand closed over his knife handle as his face darkened. "Fuck y—"

The door jangled, and Maverick strode in, followed by Zach and Louie, the trusty Louisville Slugger he'd had for years. That bat had busted countless kneecaps and deserved its own cut. Louie was a tried-and-true member of the HHMC.

"Maintenance," Maverick announced. He clapped his hands together once, then rubbed them back and forth as though eager for fun to start. "We heard machine thirteen is out of order."

"Oh fuck," the attendant squeaked out. "C-can you guys take this outside? I can't have blood in here."

"No worries, buddy," Mav said with his customary don't-give-a-fuck attitude. "We ain't gonna shed any blood. We're just gonna have a friendly chat with our new friend here." He walked over to the outnumbered guy and gripped his shoulder. "Right, friend?"

The guy looked like he could have murdered Mav with his bare hands right there in the laundromat, but he also knew he'd be dead before Mav took his last breath.

"I said, right, friend?" Mav shook him a little with a mischievous gleam in his eye.

"Right," the guy managed through his tightly clenched teeth. Saint could almost see his blood boiling beneath his skin.

"All right. Good answer. So, Saint, my brother, what did you want to say to my new friend?" He squeezed the guy's shoulder as he spoke.

Fucking Maverick.

Zach stayed off to the side, letting Saint run the show as he'd done increasingly often lately. He leaned against a non-running washing machine, resting Louie across the top, a gentle reminder of his power and authority.

And willingness to cause pain.

Saint stepped forward, getting in the guy's space. He lifted the paper with the number to eye level. "My president wants to talk to your boss. When we call, and we'll fucking call, someone better fucking answer. And they better be able to get us to your boss. This is our town, as it always has been. One of your shit stains fucked with my president's daughter."

The guy's eyes flared as a small smirk quirked his lips up on one side.

Saint let the fury he'd felt when one of these guys approached Beth resurface. "It pissed our president off."

And it pissed Saint off. *So. Fucking. Much.*

"Was it you? You Demo?"

The guy waggled his eyebrows, and Saint nearly attacked.

Only the need to impress his club superiors kept him from launching himself at the man.

"Our president is not someone you want on your bad side. So now he wants to chat. Understand?"

Tension in the room ratcheted to near bursting as Demo's jaw worked back and forth. No doubt he was struggling to rein in the temper that wanted to burst forth. As the four of them stared in silence, Saint readied his muscles for an attack. He wiggled his fingertips ever so slightly, prepared to curl his hands into fists the second the situation went south.

A loud washing machine buzzer went off, making all of them jolt as though electrocuted.

The attendant made a choking sound.

Mav squeezed their new friend's shoulder. "Fucking hell," he muttered, then laughed. "That'll wake you up. So whatcha say, pal? You gonna pass along the message, or we all gotta pull out our dicks and start measuring?" He cupped a hand around his mouth, jerked his other thumb in Saint's direction, and said in the loudest whisper possible, "I've heard this guy here has a monster in those jeans. I wouldn't test it."

"Mav, shut the fuck up." Zach's scold lost its effect as soon as Saint saw the way he failed to keep from laughing.

"Fine," Demo spat out, literally hocking on the floor as he spoke. "I'll pass it on, but I fucking promise we're not going anywhere. My boss doesn't scare easily, and he likes it here. I'd plan on getting used to us."

"Keep telling yourself that, man," Mav said, slapping his shoulder. "Gentlemen, our work here is done. Let's fucking get the hell outta this shithole. Smells like musty clothes." He leaned to see around Saint. "Might wanna check some of those washers for mold, buddy," he called to the attendant.

Zach rolled his eyes as he rested Louie on his shoulder and strode toward Maverick. "You're such a fucking troublemaker."

Saint followed without another glance at the guy. Just as Mav reached the door, the guy called out. "And say hi to Copper's daughter for me. I enjoyed our time the other day."

Saint froze.

The world narrowed to a single point—*that smug fucker's face*. Heat flooded his chest, spreading outward until his skin felt too tight to contain the violence churning beneath it. His hands curled into fists so tight his knuckles ached.

Zach whipped around and grabbed him by the sleeve before he had a chance to whirl on this piece of shit and snuff the life out of him.

"Don't," Zach muttered.

Saint couldn't hear him.

Beth's face flashed in his mind.

"I said, *don't*." Zach hauled him outside.

The fucking bell chimed gleefully overhead.

"He's fucking with you, and you know it. Beth didn't go looking for him, and he didn't do anything more than grab her arm."

Yeah, because some random car drove by and interrupted whatever the fuck he had planned.

Saint shook off Zach's hold and stormed across the parking lot toward his bike. This fucker signed his death warrant the second Beth's name fell from his lips. Saint didn't care what it cost him. His patch, his standing, his fucking life. Anyone who threatened her would bleed.

"Fill me in," Copper said as soon as they approached.

Zach did, thankfully, because Saint was seething too hard to recount it without losing his shit. Copper's frown deepened as he processed Zach's tale.

"I want to set up a meet with whoever is at the top of their food chain," Zach said. "This guy wasn't low-level, but he doesn't have any decision-making power. So…"

"He threatened Beth."

Copper's attention whipped to Saint. "What?"

He was so tense he could have snapped in two. "He was the fucker who stopped Beth on the road the other day. Demo."

Copper straightened to his full height. "And he's still breathing?"

"All right, hold the fuck on." Zach put his hands on Copper's chest, keeping him from advancing. "This is not the place. I saw Garner's car parked ten seconds up the road when we came in. Last thing we need is that particular cop showing up here."

Garner was new to the police force with a chip on his shoulder and a something-to-prove attitude. He hated the MC and salivated over the thought of locking any of them away in jail.

"Let's get out of here and talk somewhere else."

"Fine." Copper rolled his shoulders. "I wanna grab Beth first. She's at lunch with Lindsey."

That got Zach's attention. "Yeah, let's pick 'em up and escort them to the clubhouse."

"Mav, I know you gotta get to work. Saint, if you're not busy this afternoon, I want you with us."

He nodded, rolling his shoulders to ease the tension. "Whatever you need, Prez."

Plus, even though he knew Beth was safe, now that her name had been thrown into the mix, his agitation wouldn't settle until he saw her with his own two eyes. Until he could put his hands on her and feel for himself that she was whole and unharmed.

And maybe that need should have scared him.

How quickly she'd become essential.

But all he felt was the hollow ache of wanting what he couldn't have.

Chapter Fifteen

"What are you doing right now?" Lindsey asked before Beth had a chance to answer her phone with a hello.

"Uh, trying to decide if I want to eat leftover lasagna or an entire tub of fudge brownie ice cream."

And trying not to think of a certain sexy biker I'm not allowed to touch, again.

"Well, shit, that sounds dark. It's a good thing I called. Come meet me for lunch."

Beth shut the freezer. "At the diner?"

"Nope. Someone is serving me lunch today. Meet me at Laurel and Spoon? I'm about five minutes out."

Beth grinned. This was precisely what she needed. Get out of the house, hang with her girlfriend, eat some yummy food, and not think about Saint. "That sounds amazing. I'm leaving now."

"Yay! See you soon."

Beth shoved her feet into her ballet flats, grabbed her purse, and dashed out the door. Ten minutes later, she walked into the moderately crowded restaurant.

"Hi! Welcome to Laurel and Spoon. Table for one?"

She quickly glanced into the dining room to see Lindsey

waving at her. "No, thank you. I see my friend I'm meeting."

"Perfect, go right on in," the perky, young hostess said with a wide grin.

"Thank you." Beth wove her way through the busy dining room toward her friend. The ambience could only be described as southern charm with white-washed brick walls, reclaimed wood tables, and soft, natural lighting. Drinks came in mason jars, and the cloth napkins looked like they'd been embroidered by a southern grandma. About halfway to the table, she slowed her gait. Someone else sat with Lindsey. Someone with dark curly hair, Beth would recognize anywhere.

Melody.

Her stomach dipped.

What had she gotten herself into?

"Hey, sweetie," Lindsey said as she approached the four-person table. Melody and Lindsey sat across from each other, so she had no choice but to sit adjacent to each of them.

"Hi, Linds. Hi, Mel. Thanks for the invite."

"Glad you could make it, Beth. I'm looking forward to getting to know you." Melody's welcome smile seemed sincere, and Beth experienced a twinge of guilt for the negative thoughts she'd allowed at the last Handlers' party. The woman was gorgeous, whether dressed for a night out or, as she was today, in a simple magenta maxi dress. She'd toned down the makeup compared to what she'd worn at the party, and while Beth preferred this version of Melody, she had to admit the woman pulled off both looks flawlessly.

"Same, Mel. I feel like I've run into you a ton since I've been home, but I don't really know you at all. So what's good here?"

Lindsey groaned. "Everything, but my absolute favorite is the Pimento cheese melt on sourdough."

"Oh, that sounds amazing."

"It is," Melody said. "I'd eat it every day if I could get away with it."

Beth studied the menu for a few minutes, but when their server arrived, she went with her friends' recommendation. In fact, all three of them ordered the same meal.

"So..." Lindsey said after the waitstaff walked off with their orders. "I have to admit we had a bit of an ulterior motive in asking you to lunch today."

"Okay..." She straightened and glanced between the two of them, immediately on high alert.

Melody shot her a sheepish grin.

"Mel has the world's biggest crush on Saint." *Oh dear God.* "And I thought we could put our heads together and figure out a way to get her a date with him."

Lindsey's words hit like a slap across the face. White-hot jealousy coiled in her chest, burning like a hot poker shoved beneath her skin. Her stomach lurched, and she had to grip the edge of the table to keep from visibly reacting.

If they brought her a meal now, Beth wouldn't be able to choke down a single bite.

Could they tell? Could they see it on her face? She felt a spotlight shine on her, a neon sign flashing above her head, revealing her secret encounters with Saint.

She had to say something. They stared at her, expecting an appropriate reaction.

"Wow," she croaked, throat dry as a dusty desert road. "Um, I kinda suck at relationships, so I don't know what you think I can contribute."

She unrolled her silverware from the napkin, laying it over her lap to give herself something to do besides reach over and yank Melody by her hair.

"Well, you've spent some time with Saint recently, so we thought you could help." Lindsey grinned all giddy like a kid on Christmas while Melody stared at her with pleading in her gaze. *Oh God, she really did like him.*

"Exactly," Melody said. "He's so hard to read, and he barely talks to anyone. He's like a sealed vault, and I can't find the combination to save my life. I'm getting desperate."

Beth frowned. She wouldn't describe Saint in that way at all. Sure, he didn't reveal much about himself, but he talked to her, and she knew enough about Makenna's past to know Saint's was traumatic as well. Who could blame him for taking a slow approach when opening up?

"Um, I don't know how much help I'll be."

Lindsey waved away her concern. "You guys have hung out a lot. You know him better than both of us, that's for sure."

Nodding, Melody chuckled. "Seriously, if it weren't for the fact that everyone knows your dad won't let any of the MC guys near you, I'd be worried you wanted him for yourself." Her tone had a strange underlying bite that felt almost like a warning.

Or maybe she was paranoid.

Keeping secrets could do that to a person.

"Oh." Beth laughed weakly. "You have nothing to worry about there." She grabbed her water glass and gulped. Maybe she'd get lucky, and one of the waitstaff had poisoned it. She could drop dead before she had to help another woman snag the man who'd given her an orgasm a few hours ago.

"Of course I don't." Melody's smile seemed less friendly and more condescending now.

What did that mean? Did she think Beth wasn't pretty enough or good enough for Saint?

Lindsey snorted. "Can you imagine Copper's reaction if you guys had something going?"

At least she could respond with the truth. "I'd rather not think about it."

She was going to throw up. Her skin prickled with

discomfort. Good thing the napkins were fabric, or she'd have torn hers to shreds by now.

"Anyway, I've been a little aggressive with my flirting, and I'm starting to think that might be the wrong approach for a guy like him. What do you think? Do I need to be more subtle and coy? Or maybe I should be straight up, tell him I want him, and ask him on a date outright."

"No!"

Melody jumped while Lindsey pressed a hand to her chest.

Beth grimaced. "Sorry. That was loud. I don't think that's the best way."

Oh, you little liar. You're going straight to hell.

"Really? This is good?" Mel bounced in her seat, sending a wave of guilt over Beth. "Why do you say that?"

"Yeah, I mean. It's just… you know? I think he's the type of guy who'd rather ask you out than have you ask him." Beth cleared her throat.

Lindsey frowned.

Oh God, was she onto Beth's bullcrap?

"Okay, so maybe a more subtle approach. I can do that, I think." Mel sighed and leaned in closer. "Look, I'm trying to play it cool since I barely know you, but I've been working on Saint a long time. I'm getting to the point where I'm ready to do anything to make him mine. I won't let any of the bitches who hang around the club get close to him. Promise you that."

"Whoa, intense there, Mel," Lindsey said with a chuckle.

"Maybe." Mel shrugged and tossed her luscious hair over her shoulder. "But I'm done playing nice. I *want* that man, and I'm willing to play as dirty as necessary to get him in my bed. I've put a lot of time and energy into the MC. I deserve to be an ol' lady. It *will* happen."

Yikes, intense was right.

Lindsey pressed her lips together.

"Here we go, ladies." Their server delivered their meals with a flourish. The smell of melted cheese and salty French fries would have had Beth salivating on a typical day. Now she wasn't confident she could stomach a bite.

"So here's what I'm thinking," Melody said after consuming a crispy French fry. "You invite Saint to hang out. Maybe meet you at the clubhouse for a drink. Tell him you need a break from living with mommy and daddy again."

Her chuckle had Beth frowning, as did the cunning gleam in her eye. Gone was the friendly woman she'd met on arrival, and in her place was the woman who wouldn't hesitate to shove her down a flight of stairs to get at Saint.

Beth cleared her throat. "I'm in transition."

"Of course." Lindsey covered Beth's hand with hers as she shot Mel a warning look.

"Sure, whatever." She waved a hand, clearly not concerned with Beth's feelings. "Anyway, when he gets there, you find some reason to leave. Linds can text you with an emergency. I'll happen to be there, and, voila, I'll keep poor abandoned Saint company. All. Night. Long."

Beth's phone chimed. "Um," she said as she checked the screen. She'd tried not to think about the meeting between her father and Saint. *Would Saint even tell her what her father said?*

Copper: Where are you?

"I don't know, Mel. I'm pretty sure Saint is not a game player, and he wouldn't appreciate those kinds of tricks."

Beth: Lunch with Linds at Laurel and Spoon.

"Well, he won't know it's a trick, will he?"

Copper: On my way.

She frowned. Did her dad's text have to do with Saint? Was he on his way to tell her he'd stripped Saint's patch?

No. He wouldn't.

Copper: Zach too. Don't leave.

What the hell?

"Hello? Are you even listening? You're not texting Saint, are you?" Mel's voice dropped low and accusatory. She craned her neck, trying to get a peek at Beth's phone.

Beth blinked as she flipped the screen face down on the table. "What? No. It was my dad." She shifted her gaze to Lindsey. "He and Zach are coming here. They said not to leave."

"Shit." Lindsey set her sandwich down, looking at Beth with concern. "That doesn't sound good."

"No. It doesn't."

"Maybe Saint is with them."

Lindsey scoffed. "Even if he is, something isn't right. This won't be the time for flirting, Mel."

Shrugging, Melody sipped her iced tea. "I'm sure I'll make it work."

Okay, she could leave any time now. Too bad Beth wasn't mean enough to ask her to go.

They ate in silence for the next few minutes. She and Lindsey exchanged troubled glances every few seconds, while Melody probably fantasized about Saint's dick.

Which Beth could attest was a very nice dick.

Not the time.

About five minutes later, the atmosphere in the restaurant changed. Customer chatter fell to whispers and murmurs, punctuated by pointing and wide-eyed stares.

The Handlers had arrived.

Beth glanced right to find Zach and *well, shit*—Saint striding their way. Her breath caught. He moved through the restaurant like he owned every inch of it, all that barely-leashed power on display, and her body responded before her brain caught up. Heat pooled low in her belly. Her worry abated, but her heart kept racing for an entirely different reason.

Melody gasped. "Called it." She sat straighter, pouting her lips.

Saint looked incredible, navigating through the restaurant, not giving a shit about the stares and comments. Tall, strong, tattooed, and oozing confidence and capability from every pore. His fierce expression matched the rumors about him being tough, ruthless, and brutal. But Beth knew there were layers to the man. He was protective to the extreme, without smothering her or making her feel overshadowed. And when he touched her with those hands that were skilled at violence and destruction, he did so with nothing but the intent to bring extreme pleasure.

Zach went straight to Lindsey while Saint came to stand behind Beth's chair, sending a thrill down her spine.

"Where's my dad?" she asked, peering up at him.

"Hey, Saint, you're looking good," Mel cooed.

Beth could have smacked her.

He rested his hands on Beth's shoulders, giving a reassuring squeeze, or maybe holding her back. To anyone else, it would look like a friendly gesture, but he circled his thumb along the back of her shoulder, out of sight of the others. The subtle caress had her fighting a shiver.

"Hey, Mel." Then he looked down. "He's outside on the phone with Shell."

Beth studied his troubled expression. "Is everything okay? You look tense."

His hands were warm and huge, cupping her entire shoulder joint. She wanted them everywhere. Wanted them to slide down her chest and cup her breasts right here in the middle of this restaurant. Wanted him to pinch and play with her nipples until she begged him for more, consequences be damned.

Shit, she really had it bad for this guy.

Even when she'd met Jason, whom at one stupid point she

thought she'd marry, she hadn't wanted him this badly. She hadn't felt his hands on her skin even when he was across town. She hadn't craved his kiss or thought about his lips the way she couldn't stop doing with Saint.

Goose bumps erupted under his thumb, still making circles behind her shoulder. She was helpless to think of anything but the way that same thumb stroked over her clit the other night.

Maybe she needed to fuck him for real to get him out of her system. One good fuck, no one would ever find out about, then she could go about her life and move on.

Keep telling yourself that, girl.

"Some drama," he said in a low voice while Zach spoke to Lindsey in the same tone.

Mel frowned. "Uh, anyone want to clue me in?" When Zach looked her way, she batted her lashes. Somehow, her chest seemed larger than it did five seconds ago. Was she arching her back?

Breathe. He's not yours.

Not hers either.

Beth hid a smile at her internal bitchiness.

"Sorry, Mel," Zach said. "No can do. Club business."

Her expression darkened to a menacing scowl.

Is this what she wanted? To be on the inside? Did she even have feelings for Saint, or was her mission strictly to become an ol' lady to gain deeper access to the club?

Saint shrugged. "You know how it goes. Sorry to do this, but we gotta steal Lindsey and Beth from you."

Mel pouted, full-on, toddler-style pouted with her lip sticking out and her doe eyes blinking at Saint.

"Hey, Saint, why don't you follow Mel home just to be extra cautious?" Zach said. "Copper and I will head to the clubhouse, and you can meet us there."

Now Beth had the urge to pout, but she squashed it. She

was a damn adult, after all.

The way she lit up, someone would have thought Zach offered her a million dollars.

Saint's fingers flexed against Beth's shoulders, pressing in just slightly before he released her. A wordless message she felt all the way to her bones. "Sure, I can do that." His voice was flat. Unreadable. But his hands had said what his mouth couldn't.

Mel had a victorious smile as if she'd just beaten Beth in a boxing match. Or maybe that was Beth projecting how she'd feel in Mel's place.

Ugh.

He's. Not. Yours.

If she thought it enough, maybe it would penetrate her thick skull.

"I'm done eating anyway," Melody said as she stood. She came over and wrapped herself around Saint's arm like a koala.

Beth clenched her teeth so hard her jaw popped, and Lindsey side-eyed her.

"I'll go take care of the bill," Zach said. "Meet you two outside." He wandered over to the hostess stand to pay their check.

Beth pushed her chair back and stood. "Let's go."

"Really?" Lindsey gaped up at her. "You don't want to finish?"

She'd only eaten half her food but couldn't stand to look at it any longer, even though it was delicious. "No, I wanna know what's going on."

"Okay. Yeah, good point." She placed her napkin on the table and stood. "Let's go."

Irrational anger swirled deep inside Beth. All she wanted was to get the hell away from Melody as fast as possible, but that meant the woman would be leaving with Saint. He'd be following her to her house, where they'd be alone. And Melody was a damn octopus, hands flying all over Saint like she was marking her territory. Beth's nails bit into her palms. She couldn't make eye contact with him. If she did, he'd see everything, the jealousy, the possessiveness, the irrational fury at watching another woman touch what her body had already decided was hers.

Zach waited for them by the exit and escorted the group outside, where Copper stood near their three bikes.

"Good to go?" her father asked. One look at his face told Beth that everything wasn't okay, and whatever reason they'd come for her and Lindsey, it wasn't a good one.

"Yeah."

"Okay, see you at the clubhouse. I'll be right behind you," Copper said. She wanted to ask him to explain what the hell happened between this morning and now, but he'd never talk club business in a public parking lot and especially not in front of Mel.

Speaking of the interloper, Melody had practically glued herself to Saint's side. If someone didn't unstick them soon, he'd be riding home with Melody dangling off the side of his bike.

"Hope you guys don't need this stud back right away." She giggled and snuggled even closer. "I might keep him busy for a while." She winked.

Beth swallowed what felt like a mouthful of bees. How many tugs would it take to rip off Melody's fake eyelashes? Would they come off with one yank, or would she really need to give it a few solid pulls?

Instead of giving in to that delicious urge, she merely smiled and murmured, "Try not to send him back to us with something we'll all catch."

The words were spoken too low for her father to hear, but Melody caught them. She gasped, and her jaw dropped. She turned to Saint, clearly waiting for him to jump to her defense, but his eyes sparkled, and he did a terrible job at concealing his smirk.

She shouldn't take so much pleasure in getting under Melody's skin, but after the mild ambush of a lunch, she couldn't help but feel a little better after the cheap shot.

Score one point for the petty woman you are, Beth.

Now, if only she didn't have to wonder what would happen when Saint got to Melody's house.

Chapter Sixteen

The last place Saint wanted to be was riding behind Melody's Chevy Spark on the way to her house. He'd never been there and had a feeling simply watching her walk inside and waving goodbye wouldn't satisfy her.

If he had his choice, he'd be at his house in bed with Beth, but that pipe dream wouldn't come to fruition any time soon. At least he'd see her back at the clubhouse once he extricated himself from Melody's clutches, although he loathed the idea of not being there when Copper filled Beth in on what went down at the laundromat.

She'd hate finding out they'd encountered the guy who hassled her on the side of the road, and she'd hate knowing he could come for her again.

Over my dead body.

If Copper wanted someone tailing Beth for the foreseeable future, he'd make damn sure he covered most of those shifts himself, even if it was typically a job for prospects or newer club members. It'd be the perfect way to stay close to her while keeping her safe and flying under the radar.

The trip to Melody's place took about fifteen minutes. She lived in a newer townhouse development in eastern

Townsend. While she drove her car into the attached garage, Saint pulled to a stop in front of the townhouse. He didn't kill the engine, staying astride the bike to see her safely inside.

After exiting her car, Melody came straight to him, all swaying hips and sultry eyes. Maybe her tricks would have worked in the past. She was a beautiful woman after all, but Saint's mind was already back at the clubhouse.

With Beth.

Melody stopped a few feet from his bike, standing on her small lawn. Keys dangled from her right hand. The same hand she propped on her hip as she smiled at him. "Thanks for the escort. Maybe I can return the favor and escort you inside." Her voice dropped to a low, seductive tone that left little ambiguity to her statement. She wanted to go inside and fuck.

"I need to get back to the clubhouse."

She pouted. "Oh, come on. You can spare a few minutes so I can properly show you my gratitude. Promise I'll make it worth your while." She winked.

Saint sighed internally. He hated this shit, the hunt and the games. When he wanted to fuck, he went out, found someone willing, and made his intentions clear. Mutual physical satisfaction and nothing more. When it was over, he went home. He'd never, not once been tempted to stick around for a repeat, a morning-after conversation, or even a real date.

He knew himself that he had a bit of an obsessive personality. It served him well over the years in meeting his goals and advancing in the club. But when it came to women, that same level of energy could be intense. Most people didn't want the kind of codependent, all-consuming possessiveness he'd give and demand. He wasn't a dick and didn't want to control someone, but if he ever got seriously involved with a woman, he wanted their relationship to be the type where they wove every single aspect of their lives together. The kind where they couldn't breathe without each other, not because one person demanded or forced it, but because they both wanted and needed it.

He'd mentioned this to Makenna once, years ago. She'd laughed and told him to get therapy. By now, she'd probably forgotten the conversation or maybe thought he'd outgrown the thoughts he'd had in his twenties, but they'd never gone away. If and when he fell for someone, it would consume him.

Unfortunately, he could feel himself inching toward those feelings when he thought of Beth. Leave it to him to finally be interested in the one woman he could not have.

"Look at me," he said, as gently as possible. "We've been at this dance for a while now."

She raised an eyebrow. "We have. So, how about we stop circling each other and head inside."

"I don't want to sound like a dick, but I'm gonna be straight with you."

Her smile wilted.

"It's not gonna happen, Mel."

"Excuse me?"

"This…" he waved a hand back and forth between them, "… us. It's *not* going to happen."

She laughed, but not the flirty giggle he'd grown accustomed to. This laugh had a harsh edge. "You're kidding me, right?"

He shook his head.

She scoffed as she threw her hands in the air. "It's her, isn't it?"

Saint stiffened. "What?"

"Beth."

"You're crazy."

Melody's mouth twisted into a sinister smile. "Holy shit. That's it. You've got a hard-on for the club princess. This is the best thing I've ever heard."

"Mel," he said, voice full of warning. "*Stop*."

"No," she said with a tinkering laugh. "I don't think I will stop. What the fuck do you see in that mousy little bitch?" She grabbed her tits over her long dress. "Look at all you're passing up. I got tits, ass, and I know how to use my pussy. Trust me, a man like you will not be satisfied with anything less."

"That's enough, Mel."

She arched one perfectly plucked eyebrow. "Imagine how her daddy will react if he finds out his future enforcer gets hard for the princess?"

"Mel—"

"He'll lose his mind," she continued. "Probably take your patch."

Her voice grated on his nerves like three-inch nails on a chalkboard.

"Doesn't seem worth it when she's probably a dead fish in bed anyway. I heard she had to come home because she couldn't keep her boyfriend satisfied."

"*Enough*!" Saint shouted. Never in his life had he been tempted to strike a woman, but if Melody didn't shut her mouth, he might do just that.

Her eyes widened as she jumped. "Saint, I—"

"Shut your *fucking* mouth, Melody."

"How dare y—" Her jaw snapped closed, probably due to the homicidal gleam in his eye. But it didn't last long. "I've been hanging around the club for years… *years*. I deserve to be an ol' lady."

He didn't give a fuck what she thought she deserved. There was no way in hell this woman would get within one inch of spreading gossip that would harm Beth. "If you want the slightest chance of staying close to the club, here's what's going to happen."

She looked stunned, and any other time, he might have felt sympathy for her, but she'd destroyed any of that with her catty bullshit.

"You will stay the fuck away from Beth. No more lunches. No hangouts. Don't let me catch you fucking looking at her. You wanna get fucked? There are plenty of single dipshits who'll fuck you no questions asked. I am *not* one of them."

"Saint…"

"And if you ever, *ever* threaten to go to my president with whatever horseshit you've drummed up in your head, I will personally make sure you can *never* show your face at our clubhouse again. You're not ol' lady material, Melody. An ol' lady would never threaten someone in the club."

Melody had been coming around the club since before he was a prospect. They were around the same age, and he knew she had no blood family. The Handlers were important to her. She'd worked at the diner for years, and her entire friend group revolved around his club. Her long-standing connection to the MC was the only reason he didn't ban her from the clubhouse for life, but he wouldn't hesitate if she didn't back off.

"You wouldn't," she said with less bravado than she'd had before.

"You have no idea what I'd do to protect my family." He practically snarled the words, imagining just how far he'd go to keep Beth safe. No mountain was too high, no river too wide, and no man too unkillable. "Do *not* fucking test me."

He must have expressed himself with enough conviction because Melody's shoulders drooped, and she took a step back. "Well… I guess that's that."

He nodded. Perhaps she wanted an apology, but he had no intention of giving her the power in this situation. Melody would run with it and view it as a victory over him.

"Thank you for following me home."

"Happy to do it. And I'm happy to stay your friend, Mel."

"You can fuck right off with that, Saint," she said, finding her voice again. "You don't want me, you don't get any part of me. I'll find someone else to help me out next time. I'm done with you."

He wished he could say he was sorry, but her dismissal was for the best. At least she wouldn't be clinging to him at parties anymore. Most likely, she'd be moving on to another of his brothers within the week, and he'd be off the hook and forgotten.

Maybe Gator was looking for a new conquest.

Shit, he couldn't do that to his friend now that he knew Mel had a vindictive side.

She turned with a huff and stomped to her front door, where she yanked it open and flipped him the bird before flouncing inside. Well, she'd made it home, safe and sound. His work here was done, lovely as it had been.

As soon as her door shut, he got the hell out of there. Before he made it to the clubhouse, Zach called with a few favors and errands he needed completed for the club. Zach's tasks kept Saint busy for the next few hours, and by the time he finally made it to the clubhouse, it was early evening. He'd long moved past antsy and into straight-up agitated with the need to see Beth.

After all that had gone down earlier, he'd expected chaos and commotion at the clubhouse, but enough time must have passed, and the place was calm and quiet.

"Hey, man," Gator said as Saint reached the bar. "Drink?"

"Hell yes. Whiskey. Lots of it."

"You got it. Yo! Prospect!" Gator shouted, though he stood behind the bar. "Saint wants some whiskey. Get your ass over here." He winked at Saint.

"Seriously? The bottle is right in front of you, and he's all the way across the room."

Gator shrugged. "It builds character."

The new prospect, Frisco, because he'd hailed from Northern California, hustled over. "What can I do for you, sir?" he asked Gator, making Saint raise an eyebrow.

Sir? He mouthed.

"Whiskey for my brother here," he said, pushing the bottle Gator's way. "One for me too. Don't be skimpy."

"You got it." Frisco rushed around the bar, grabbed the bottle, and then turned away to get glasses.

"You're fucking unbelievable."

Gator merely grinned, the psycho.

"So what'd I miss while I was out collecting loan payments?" All in all, it had been an easy afternoon. Everyone he visited paid their loans on time, so no one needed their asses kicked. Normally, Saint would consider that a good day, but he had a restless energy buzzing under his skin that would have gotten worked out if he'd gotten the opportunity to beat the shit out of someone.

"Not much. Prez filled everyone in and warned Beth to be extra vigilant. He mentioned he was thinking of having someone tail her for a bit." He snorted. "She did not like that, but you know, Prez. He's feral when it comes to his girls."

Saint grunted. Of course, she didn't want a babysitter, but fuck that. He was with Copper on this one. Whatever it took to keep her safe. If it were his choice, he'd keep her hidden away until they were sure this jackass posed no threat. Hidden away in his bed, preferably.

"Copper drive her home?"

"Nope." Gator shook his head with a smirk as Frisco returned with the whiskeys.

"Thanks, man," Saint said.

The prospect grinned so wide as he handed Gator his drink. Saint couldn't keep his laugh at bay. Poor guy wanted in this club so bad he was willing to kiss Gator's crazy ass.

"Get lost," Gator said, shooing the prospect with a hand wave.

"Copper didn't take Beth home?"

Gator shook his head as he tossed back his entire drink in two swallows. "Nah," he said when he'd finished. "Beth told him she wanted to crash here for a night or two. Said she needed a little break from being at their house." Gator grabbed the bottle Frisco abandoned and refilled his glass. "Copper nearly blew his top at first, but Shell talked him down as she always does. She reminded him that Beth was used to being on her own and needed some space. Shell told him this way Beth could have fun, have a few drinks, and not worry about driving home."

"Huh." So she was somewhere in the clubhouse, planning to spend the night.

Interesting.

His cock sure liked the new knowledge.

"Think she claimed the last room on the left."

Saint raised an eyebrow. "And you're telling me because…"

Gator shrugged. "Because you get hard every time she's around. So does she. Figured you might want to bang it out already."

Saint nearly choked on his whiskey. "Uh, no, she doesn't. Pretty sure she doesn't have a dick, Gator."

"You'd know, wouldn't you?" Gator asked, waggling his light eyebrows.

Saint reached across the bar and shoved his idiot friend back with a hand on his face. The move sent Gator into a fit of wild laughter.

"All right. We need drinks, and we need them now," Lindsey announced as she walked from the back hallway of the clubhouse arm in arm with Beth, whose gaze shuttered when she noticed Saint at the bar.

What the hell was that about?

Twenty minutes later, Saint found himself seated in an Adirondack chair out behind the clubhouse with Lindsey, Gator, and Beth. It was too early, too bright, and too hot to start a fire, so they sat around the remnants of last night's bonfire. Lindsey angled her chair so she could prop her bare feet in Gator's lap while her sandals lay on the ground beneath her chair. Beth sat next to Saint in her own chair across from the other two, holding the bottle of whiskey Gator had snagged before they came outside.

She was quieter than usual and stiff. Maybe tense was a better word.

"You okay?" Saint leaned over to ask in a low voice.

"Sure." She took a swallow directly from the bottle as his eyebrow arched.

"Gimme, Bethy," Lindsey ordered. She leaned forward, motioning for the bottle, which Beth handed over. "So I think I owe you an apology. Saint too."

He frowned as he looked between Beth's troubled expression and Lindsey's sheepish one. "What do you mean?" *What the hell?* Had she done something to Beth?

"Easy there, Rambo," Gator muttered with a chuckle. "Your face is getting all murder-looking."

Saint flipped Gator off.

Lindsey took a swig from the bottle before passing it off to Gator. "I invited Beth to lunch today with Melody and me because I thought she might have some insight into, well, you."

He motioned for the bottle from Gator. "What are you talking about?" The whiskey had a pleasant burn as it traveled down his throat.

"I knew Mel was into you, and she suggested Beth might have some tips on how to snag you since you guys have spent time together recently. I didn't realize Mel was so...

aggressive in her interest in you, and that you didn't return it."

"How do you know he doesn't want Mel?" Gator lifted the bottle to his smirking lips. "He disappeared for a while after taking her home. Maybe they spent the afternoon rattling her headboard."

"The fuck?" Saint straightened. He could feel waves of tension and discomfort coming off Beth, who had yet to say a word since they sat outside.

"Stop being a shit-stirrer," Lindsey said, whacking Gator's arm. Of course, all that did was make him snort out a laugh.

"I'm kidding. I'm kidding. Don't worry, Beth, he was doing shit for Zach all afternoon."

Beth blinked, but Saint swore she relaxed a fraction of a percent. "What? Why would I care? Saint can… rattle whatever headboard he wants. Not my business."

Gator snorted, and Lindsey tilted her head. "Sure, sweetie," she said in a placating tone. "Keep telling yourself that."

"Wha—"

"We're losing the plot here, people. Bottom line… I'm sorry for the ambush. I did not think Mel would go that hard. She seems to have a fixation on becoming an ol' lady." She ripped the bottle out of Gator's hands and tilted her head back for a long gulp of whiskey.

"Watching you drink that gets me so fucking hard," Gator said, and Saint had no doubt he meant it.

Lindsey choked. She lowered the bottle, coughing, and her eyes watering. "Jesus, Gator," she said when she regained control of her airway. "That's supposed to be some kind of compliment? Everything gets you hard."

He shrugged completely unashamed. "True, but watching you swallow gets me extra fucking hard."

Lindsey rolled her eyes. "You're a pig."

As the two of them bantered back and forth, Saint turned to Beth to find her watching him with a host of questions swirling in her green eyes. At some point, she'd pulled her hair into a high ponytail that gave him a view of her entire face.

"So, Zach kept you busy this afternoon?"

"He did. Had a whole bunch of bullshit for me to take care of."

"Mel must have been disappointed you couldn't stick around."

He grunted. "Not sure, disappointed is the right word. More like rabid."

"Hmm."

"But that had nothing to do with Zach. I shut her down before he ever called me."

"Oh... really?"

He nodded. "I'm not interested in Melody. Never was."

She blinked. Her gaze softened, melting to hot liquid jade he could lose himself in for the rest of the night. For the rest of his life, if she'd let him.

Whoa, that was a thought.

"It'd be safer if you were," she whispered. "Easier."

"Maybe," he whispered back so only Beth could hear. "But I've never played it safe a day in my life."

A loud throat cleared, startling them both. Their heads whipped forward simultaneously. Sure enough, Lindsey and Gator gawked at them with twin shit-eating grins like two goons.

"Whatcha talking about?" Gator sing-songed.

Saint and Beth flipped him off at the same time, which made Lindsey burst out laughing. Gator followed, and in seconds, all four of them were laughing like they didn't have a care in the world. It seemed the whiskey had kicked in.

They stayed out there for hours, laughing, chatting, and

enjoying the gorgeous summer night. Now that they'd cleared the air about his afternoon activities, Beth relaxed and joined in their nonsensical conversations. Saint listened more than he talked, which was typical for him, but this time it stemmed from his inability to do anything but watch Beth.

Everything she did drew him to her, from the animated way she told stories to her teasing to the secret smiles she gifted him every so often. He wanted to take her back to her room and spend the rest of the night making her beg and scream his name. He wanted to consume her, to absorb her into himself so he could ensure her safety and happiness always.

Eventually, when the sun had set and the whiskey had long run out, the back door opened, and Zach popped his head out. "Lindsey, you out there?"

"Yep. What's up?"

"I'm heading out. You need a ride home?"

"Uh, yeah, please. I drank more than I planned."

Zach laughed. "Sounds good. Meet you out front."

"Well, guess that's it for me, folks." Lindsey stood, wobbled a bit, then laughed. "Shit. I'm drunk."

Snorting, Gator stood as well. "I'll help you out front." He swung an arm around Lindsey's shoulders, making them both stumble.

Beth laughed. "Pretty sure you'll only make it worse, Gator."

Truer words had never been spoken.

"Nah, we're all good. Right, babe?"

Lindsey leaned into him and blinked heavy-lidded eyes. "Huh?"

Saint rolled his eyes while Beth laughed.

After saying their goodbyes, Gator and Lindsey somehow made it into the clubhouse without falling flat on their faces, leaving him and Beth alone outside.

"This was fun," she said. "I, uh, I should probably turn in." She stood and faced him. "I'm gonna crash here tonight."

"I heard."

Her cheeks flushed, and she glanced at the clubhouse before looking back at him while she wrung her hands near her waist. "Okay. Well, I'm in the last room on the left, down the main hall." She paused, and the air between them thickened. "Just… so you know." She shifted, bit her lip, and his gaze dropped before he could stop it. Beneath her thin tank top, he could see the faint peaks of her hardened nipples pressing against the fabric.

God, she was turned on, aroused, and offering him her room number like a key.

His dick thickened in his jeans, filling so fast it bordered on painful.

"Now I know." His voice came out rougher than intended.

She nodded once, then headed toward the clubhouse.

Saint forced his gaze to stay straight and not drift down to her round ass as she walked away. If he was going to walk into the clubhouse after hanging out with her, he needed to do it without a visible boner tenting his jeans.

The heavy door creaked open, then closed with a thud as Beth disappeared into the clubhouse.

Saint breathed out slowly, letting his head fall back against the chair. One hundred seconds. That's how long he'd give himself before he followed her inside, found that last room on the left, and did what they'd both been dying to do since the moment she came home.

He began to count down from one hundred.

Chapter Seventeen

Beth sat on the edge of the queen-size bed with fresh sheets and blankets, staring at the white ceiling above her. "Why do you do this shit?" she muttered. When no voice from above answered, she stood and paced the length of the small, minimalistic clubhouse room. Back in the day, they had one bunk room with ten or so beds. As the club expanded, opening a chapter in Florida, Copper renovated the clubhouse, adding six private rooms, each with a small, attached bathroom for guests who might require more privacy. Currently, club members and prospects occupied three of them and would continue to do so until they found a more permanent living situation.

The rooms weren't luxurious by any means, but they were clean, had a bed, a small dresser, and an easy chair. A few black-and-white pictures hung on the wall, Smoky Mountain scenery, and motorcycles, all shot by a local photographer.

She'd planned on having a quiet, family-free night to herself, where she could stew and stress about what Saint got up to all afternoon, but then he showed up.

And they hung out the entire evening into the night. Beth learned something during that time, and now she felt as if the ground beneath her had fractured, and if she didn't watch her step, she'd fall through a crack into a deep crevasse.

She liked Saint.

A lot.

Liked the way his mind worked. Liked his dry wit. Liked his intensity, especially when he stared at her as though he could see every one of her thoughts. Sure, she'd been attracted to him all along. He was a gorgeous man, tall with tattoos and muscles for days. He had dark eyes she easily lost herself in, and the perfect length of hair to tangle her fingers in.

But tonight, she realized her attraction went deeper than his very appealing physical attributes. She wanted to know him. To crack him open and have him tell her everything he'd kept hidden from others.

He wasn't nearly as talkative as the rest of them, but she found that charming as well. He didn't need to fill every second with conversation and seemed totally at ease just being in a space.

Had she ruined the fragile bond they'd forged by hinting he should join her in this room? Or maybe she hadn't hinted well enough, and he didn't get it. For all she knew, he'd gone straight to his bike and ridden home while she, an anxious mess, waited to see if he'd show up.

That'd be humiliating.

The light knock on the door jolted her so hard she whacked her hip on the dresser.

He'd come.

That was him, right?

She stood frozen, heart hammering, staring at the door when another knock sounded, louder than the first. The sound propelled her into action. She hurried across the room, unlocked, and opened the door to find Saint, arms up and propped against the doorframe.

"Hey," she whispered.

God, he looked so good, tall, dark, and dangerous in his jeans and T-shirt that stretched across his chest and thick arms. Heat and desire reflected in his eyes, warming her from head to toe. He represented everything she wanted, but she should shut the door on him.

Bad decisions and ecstasy rolled into one tempting package.

Unfortunately, they'd already crossed the line, so she knew what waited for her on the other side. And she wanted it more than anything in the world.

"Gonna let me in?"

She blinked out of her Saint-induced trance. "Yes. Of course. Sorry. Come on in." She stepped to the side, giving him plenty of space, yet he still chose to brush against her as he strode into the room like a sleek, prowling animal.

She shut the door behind him, then locked it. The click reverberated through the room like a gunshot. Guess she'd just made her intentions known. Why lock the door if she planned to say goodnight and send him on his way?

"Are there a lot of people out there?" she asked as she suddenly had no idea what to do with her hands.

Saint didn't seem to suffer from the same affliction. He leaned against the wall, folding his arms across his firm chest. The one she'd imagined falling asleep on more than once. "Some. Not many. No one paid any attention to me, though. Most are wasted by now, and Rizz is too busy trying to get in some chick's pants to notice anything else."

Beth chuckled. "I'm sure he'll succeed. They don't call him Rizz for nothing."

His eyebrows shot into his forehead. "Got a thing for Rizz, do you?"

"Uh, no." She shuddered. "I'm pretty sure he's slept with six different women, including Lindsey, since I've been back.

He's probably a walking petri dish."

"You might be right."

Neither spoke for the next few moments. Beth couldn't take her eyes off him, though. She wanted him. Not a quick blowjob or grope session. She wanted to peel every stitch of clothing off him and have him do the same to her. Then she wanted to spend the rest of the night horizontal in that bed, exploring the fascinating man before her.

But her feet stuck. She couldn't make the first move. "Um…"

Saint arched off her wall. He dropped his arms and walked toward her in what felt like a slow-motion clip. His eyes blazed with so much heat that a bead of sweat trickled down the center of her back.

When he reached her, he grabbed the back of her neck, drawing her to him in a move she'd come to crave. Saint slid his arm around her waist, anchoring her against him. There was no hiding the erection that nestled against her stomach.

"Saint," she whispered.

His lips hovered inches from hers. The whiskey on his breath intoxicated her more than anything she'd consumed earlier. Though she hadn't taken a drink in hours, she no longer felt the effects of the alcohol.

"This is such a bad idea."

He nodded. "It is. But I'm willing to risk it."

"If the club finds out, you'll…"

"I know, Beth. And I don't give a fuck."

He kissed her with a hunger she'd never experienced. A claiming kiss that made her knees weak and had her clinging to him to keep from melting into a puddle on the floor. One hand stayed at the back of her head and neck, controlling the kiss, while the other went to her ass. He squeezed and rocked her against him, making her moan into his mouth.

His tongue stole into her mouth, demanding attention she

happily gave it. He tasted of the whiskey and a hint of mint, but mostly Saint. Something about his flavor tempted her more than the sweetest treat, and she was helpless to resist.

After long minutes, he broke from the kiss. Beth tried to follow his mouth as it moved to her neck, sucking and biting. She whimpered and let her head fall back, giving him more surface area to attack. The way his stubble scraped skin and the suction of his lips had her rocking against him. He slipped a leg between hers, and she immediately took advantage, grinding against him for the friction she desperately needed.

"I know the risks," he whispered after trailing his lips to her ear. He grazed her jaw with his teeth, then her earlobe before sucking it.

"Ah, Saint..."

"And I still want you."

"Please..."

"Please, what?"

She was completely shameless in her need for him, head back, body arched, and hips fucking humping his leg. Anything he wanted, she'd give him, including begging. "Please touch me. Touch me, fuck me. Saint, I want it all."

"Yeah?" His dark gaze studied her eyes as though searching for the truth in her words.

"Yes. So much." She smiled. "You have full consent."

"If that changes..."

"It won't." Her heart surged at the care in his words. "But I know." She pushed onto her tiptoes, kissing him again. This time, she slid her hands under his shirt, getting a feel of all that warm skin hiding beneath his tee.

Saint stepped back, crossed his arms by his waist, and pulled the shirt over his head in one swift move. Before he'd had the chance to discard it, Beth smoothed her palms up his flat stomach. She stepped close and kissed the center of his chest.

He grunted, pushing his erection into her as he grabbed the hem of her shirt and began to work it up and off her body. Beth raised her arms, allowing him to remove the garment and deposit it wherever he pleased.

She'd worn a simple, pale pink cotton bra, not anticipating where the day would end up when she'd dressed that morning. Saint sure didn't seem to have a problem with it. He shoved her pants over her hips, revealing her matching light pink bikini panties. At least she'd gone as far as to wear a matching set.

"Beth," he whispered, staring at her as though she were the most beautiful woman he'd ever seen. "You're fucking stunning."

Fucking stunning. What a statement. And the reverence in his voice matched the words. Her insides melted. Unfortunately for her, this was never going to be just sex. Chances were high she'd be left with a broken and battered heart, but she could worry about that when it happened.

She kicked the pants away, having removed her shoes when she'd arrived. Saint kissed her shoulder, then her neck, as he reached around and unclasped her bra with ease, dropping it to the floor. Then he stepped back, taking her in.

Her nipples pebbled under his awed scrutiny. She couldn't wait to have his hands and mouth on them. Before she knew what was happening, he grabbed the backs of her thighs and hoisted her off her feet into his strong arms.

She squeaked, then took advantage of being mouth-to-mouth and kissed him. As they made out, the room spun, the world flipped, and she landed on her back on a surprisingly comfortable mattress. Not once did their mouths break contact, and as soon as they were on the bed, Saint's weight pressed down on her.

Her eyes rolled back behind her closed lids. Was there

anything better than the heavy feel of a sexy man along her entire body?

Nope. Not a thing.

The next time they came up for air, Saint cradled her face between his big hands. He stroked his thumbs across her cheeks and merely watched her. The moment felt charged with more than just physical need.

And it scared the hell out of her even as she wanted more of it.

"You're so beautiful," Saint whispered. "So beautiful. And you're strong, intelligent, captivating."

Her breath caught. "Saint…" It was too much. Too many strong emotions. Too many complications, and yet so perfect.

His lips quirked, and he glanced down their bodies. "And these tits…"

That had her laughing, and the heavy emotional charge shifted back to the physical.

Easy and safe territory.

"Help yourself," she said with a flirty smirk.

Saint's grin turned lascivious. "Don't mind if I do." He kissed his way from her mouth, down her throat, to her chest, where he cupped her left breast, plumping it.

She arched with a gasp from the simple feel of him holding her. And then came his mouth, and she nearly lost her mind. He licked across her nipple, drawing a harsh gasp from her, then pulled it into his hot mouth with strong suction.

"Oh God." Her head pushed into the pillow as she arched into him for more. She wrapped her ankles around his back and pressed her pelvis against his as her hands went to his hair. The soft strands tickled her fingers. Incredible sensations came at her from all angles, overwhelming her senses and stealing all rational thought.

He sucked hard, sending sharp pleasure from her nipple to her clit. Beth gripped his hair for dear life, oblivious to whether it hurt, but he didn't complain. When he had her squirming and panting, he kissed across her chest to the other breast, treating it to the same voracious treatment. This time, as he sucked, licked, and nipped, he pulled her panties down. They got trapped around her calves, but she widened her knees to make room for him.

Without releasing her tit, he slid two fingers inside her, immediately curling them to find the spot that had driven her wild the other night. Beth bucked and shouted.

A dark chuckle rumbled in Saint's chest as he clamped a hand over her mouth. "Shh," he soothed around her breast.

"Sorry," she mumbled against his palm. "It's just so go… oh shit."

He gently raked his teeth over her nipple as he finger-fucked her, making her see stars.

"Sadist," she managed, panting.

Saint sent another evil laugh floating into the room.

"Saint…" She couldn't think beyond the waves of pleasure originating beneath his hands and mouth. "Please… *now*."

He lifted his head, fingers still working inside her, and the white-hot yearning nearly had her coming right then. "I don't know if you're ready for my cock yet?"

"What?" she scowled at him. "I'm ready."

His lips curved while he pressed his thumb to her clit.

Beth flopped back on the pillow, breathless. "Now you're just being mean."

He kissed her quickly, once. Then again, longer and sweeter, slowing his hand inside her. "I like you like this," he whispered. "Hungry, desperate for me."

"Yes." She craned her neck, chasing his lips for another kiss, which he granted. She felt drugged, out of her mind. He overwhelmed all her senses until nothing existed but Saint.

His intoxicating taste.

His spicy, leather scent.

The whispered murmurs and curses.

His gorgeous face and body.

And the way his hands and mouth brought her more pleasure than she'd ever experienced with a man.

This time, when he broke the kiss, she whimpered.

"I'll only be gone a minute," he whispered as he rose on his knees. The hand inside her disappeared, only to end up on his zipper.

Beth pushed up onto her elbows. No way was she willing to miss a second of the show. Their gazes met as he flicked the button open, then lowered the zipper. One of his dark eyebrows arched as if to say, *'keep going?'*

Beth nodded, licking her lips. She'd had that cock in her mouth and still ached to see the reveal.

He backed up until he could step off the bed, then, slowly, to torture her, of course, lowered the jeans and his boxer briefs while watching for her reaction the entire time. She almost forgot to look down, lost in a sea of rippling abs and gorgeous inked artwork. But as she followed the roots of a tree down his side and over his hip, her attention went to his rigid cock where it jutted from his body. Long, thick, and reddened with need. A bead of precum dotted the tip, and had her licking her lips.

The crinkle of a condom wrapper snapped her attention upward. Her pussy clenched as he tore it open. Only a few more seconds and he'd be inside her.

As he rolled the condom down his length, Beth stared. She drew her heels up, bending and widening her knees.

"Fuck yes," he whispered. "So fucking sexy."

He pounced forward, crawling up her body until his hips nestled between hers. She tilted her pelvis as she reached between their bodies. "Allow me. You're taking too long."

He leaned over until their lips were an inch apart. "Knock yourself out. It's your dick now."

Her heart skipped a fucking beat. *Did he mean he wanted more than sex?* No, of course not. It'd never work. He just meant for the night.

So she'd better make the most of her time.

As he kissed her, she guided his cock to her entrance. Saint needed no instruction. He thrust forward into her with slow but steady pressure. Her body yielded to him at once as though he belonged there, as though they'd done this a hundred times.

He ripped his mouth away, then rested his forehead against hers. "Jesus-fucking-Christ, you're tight. I can barely breathe. Good?"

"Yes. So good. It feels…" *Right*. So incredibly right.

"Full?"

"Fuck yes. You fill me perfectly."

His eyes flared, and he groaned. "Fucking perfect." Then he kicked into gear, drawing his hips back and snapping forward again. Beth locked her ankles at the base of his spine and wrapped her arms around his upper back, clinging to him as he fucked her with powerful rolls of his hips.

Every thrust hurtled her closer to an explosive finish, rushing at her way too quickly. She wanted to stay here, suspended in this high for as long as possible, where nothing mattered but her and Saint.

But he apparently had other ideas.

"I want to be deeper," he ground out, voice deep and sensual. He slipped an arm under her thigh, hiking her leg onto his shoulder. The new position spread her impossibly wide and allowed him to get closer, deeper. So deep she could practically feel him in on a cellular level.

"Saint…" She whined and gasped, trying to stay in the moment when her mind felt fuzzy with pleasure.

"That's it, baby. Fuck, can you feel how deep I am?" He pressed a hand to her lower belly as he fucked her like a man possessed.

"Yes, yes. It's never been like this." She gripped the sheets for dear life, feeling like she'd fly straight to heaven without the anchor.

"Jesus, you take me so good. This pussy was made for me, Beth. Made for fucking me."

"Yes!"

"You're fucking *mine* now, Beth. Your tits, your pussy, your gorgeous body. It's all fucking *mine*."

God, she wanted that so much. To belong to him. To be owned by him. He'd never take advantage. Never make her feel afraid or constrained.

He stared down at her as he fucked her, muscles bulging with effort. Sweat trickled over his pecs and stomach. His dark hair flopped in front of his eyes, and his mouth twisted in a sexy snarl.

The raunchy, possessive words combined with the intense visuals and extreme pleasure was too much. The orgasm rushed at her like a charging bull. "Oh God," she cried, arching her back. "I'm gonna come. Saint, I'm gonna come."

"Give it to me."

"Kiss me. Kiss me while I come."

He growled, actually fucking growled as he bent forward, sealing his lips to hers. His knee was at her ear, with her legs stretched so far apart she'd probably be sore later, but now she felt nothing but joy.

He plunged his tongue into her mouth at the same time he thrust his hips. The new position had his pelvis grinding against her clit.

The orgasm slammed into her with supersonic force. She threw her arms around his back and slammed her eyes shut, holding on for dear life when wave after wave of pleasure undulated through her. Two seconds later, Saint shouted against her mouth as he stiffened in her arms.

Their hearts slammed against each other as they trembled through their climaxes.

She clung to him, riding the delicious sensations until their bodies calmed.

"Holy fuck," Saint eventually whispered. He shifted his arm, and her leg flopped onto the bed.

Her muscles protested, drawing a groan from her.

Saint's head popped up. He kissed her quickly, then asked, "You okay?" Before she had the chance to answer, he began massaging the crease between her leg and her pelvis, where she'd been stretched to capacity. "Was I too rough?"

Why was he being so tender? The concern in his gaze and the gentle way he kneaded her leg set off a swell of intense emotion in her core. Men didn't do this. They took what they wanted and rolled over. They didn't check in, didn't massage away the ache they'd caused. Her eyes began to prickle, and she blinked hard.

Crying was not an option.

"I'm wonderful. You were perfect."

There was that word again, small and powerful, but she couldn't deny its veracity.

Oh shit.

Had she really begged him to kiss her while she came like some love-struck fairy-tale character?

How humiliating.

Lucky for her, the afterglow was strong enough to overpower the embarrassment over her neediness.

Later, though, she'd want to crawl into a hole.

Chapter Eighteen

Christ, Saint hadn't fucked like that in, well, maybe ever, with such a frenzied need to consume his partner. He'd have absorbed Beth into his body if he could. He'd also stay there, buried deep inside her for the rest of the night if he could. Unfortunately, he had to deal with the condom. And she probably wanted to take a deep breath without a two-hundred-plus-pound male crushing her into the mattress.

With a grunt of effort to help his sated muscles work, he pushed up off her. As he lifted, his dick slipped from her warmth.

Beth whimpered from the loss, as though she hated to sever the connection.

Me, too, baby. Me too.

Sleepy, satisfied eyes stared up at him with a hint of wariness. Made sense. He'd made some fairly strong, possessive statements while fucking her. Statements he fully meant and didn't regret, but could understand how they might be too much for her at that moment.

"Be right back," he whispered before kissing her swollen lips.

"Okay."

He rushed to the bathroom, dealt with the condom, then gave his hands a quick wash. When he returned to the bedroom, he found Beth lying on her side, facing the bathroom. She watched him with unabashed interest, which he fucking loved.

"You going?" she asked, doing a shitty job of hiding the vulnerability in her voice.

"You want me to go?"

She worked her lower lip between her teeth. "No."

"What do you want?"

Her cheeks turned pink, and she shrugged. "You first."

"I want to crawl back into the bed, wrap my arms around you, and fall asleep. Then later I want to wake you up with my hands all over you and fuck you back to sleep."

He thought for sure she'd tell him it was a terrible idea and send him on his way, so when she scooted over and said, "Yes. Please," his heart went wild, and his spent dick tried to rally.

He slipped into the bed, beneath the covers she held open for him. As soon as he settled on his side, facing her, she snuggled up against him, all warm and soft.

This is where she belonged, right there in his arms, safe, happy, and protected.

He hiked a leg over her hip, trapping her against him. She didn't seem to mind if her hum of satisfaction was any indication.

"This is nice," she whispered, breath tickling his chest.

Nice didn't begin to describe it. Her arms went around his back, then he felt her lips press a kiss to his chest. Then another.

His dick grew half hard at the contact. He gripped the back of her head, tilting her mouth up to meet his. After a long, drawn-out, drugging kiss, he released her. Her eyes had a renewed lust, and he really wanted back inside her, but after the way he went at her earlier, she was probably a little sore.

"The way you kiss…" She shivered. "It takes over my entire body and short-circuits my brain."

"Is that a good thing?"

"Oh yeah. It's the best."

Smiling, he tucked her head against his chest and shut his eyes, enjoying the peace and calm. Beth ran her hands over his back, pausing to explore every time she found a random scar. After a few moments, she focused only on the scars. He could practically hear the wheels turning in her head. The questions she wanted to ask but wasn't sure how to voice. The answers were ones he never gave. Those physical scars were the reason he had tattoos. Ink hid the worst. The mental scars, of course, were easier to hide, but far more damaging. His past was the biggest trigger. Even Makenna didn't broach the topic with him, and she'd lived through it. Well, they'd lived parallel lives during that time, each enduring a unique hell until they finally escaped.

But for the first time in his life, he wanted someone to ask. Wanted her to ask. It was the only way she'd know him, and while his baggage was heavy as fuck, some instinctive part of him understood Beth was strong enough to help him carry it.

"Go ahead," he whispered when'd she'd fondled a particularly long scar for a while. "Ask."

She lifted her head from his chest, staring up at him. "From where were you raised? In the… cult. I guess. Is that the right word?"

He nodded. "Yes. It's what Mak and I use. And yeah. They're all from that time. Well, I have one on my side from when Gator tried to fuck some dude's girlfriend, and I stepped in to help him. And another on my shoulder from when Gator was drunk as fuck and accidentally sliced me with his belt buckle."

She blinked, then laughed. "What? How does that even

happen?"

God, that had been an insane night. "It happens when you're Gator, and you drink a damn bottle of tequila then decide to use your belt as a lasso."

"Wow. Maybe you should steer clear of him when he's drinking."

"Yeah, the other scars don't have such funny stories."

Her fierce frown made something in his stomach quiver. It felt like she was furious on his behalf, hating the very idea that someone would hurt him. "Who gave you these? Your father?"

"Some of them. But not most. Mak and I lived very different lives in that compound. Her life's mission was to get married off to some old fucker who'd keep her knocked up for the rest of her days while he collected a harem of wives. My job was to become a weapon. A good little child soldier ready for the end of the world or an attack on our compound, whichever came first. My entire life was spent on manual labor, prepping for the coming apocalypse, farming the fields, and training to fight whatever threat came our way, real or perceived."

He said it in a manner one would if they were reading from a boring book—flat, monotone, detached. In reality, he felt anything but those emotions. They were the mask he'd constructed over his entire life. Thinking about that time brought a galloping heart, nausea, and horrific memories. Speaking about it made his skin prickle with a burning itch as though thousands of fire ants went to town on his flesh.

As though sensing his mounting distress, Beth ran her fingers over his back in random soothing patterns. "I'm sorry you lived that life. No child should ever live that way."

Her eyes held no judgment, which he didn't know how to handle. She should judge him. Anyone would. Hell, she should probably fear him on some level. By the time he was five, he knew twenty ways to kill a grown man. By the time he escaped the cult? Well, he'd been more feral than human, tamed only by the need to protect his siblings.

"It's still in there," he said. God, he couldn't believe the words coming out of his mouth. His chest felt cracked open, exposed. What a perfect example of self-sabotage. Beth would run screaming by the time he finished vomiting his feelings. Any sane woman would. But now that he'd started, the dam broke, and he couldn't shut his mouth. "Those experiences, they're always there. They…"

How on earth did he describe this to someone with such a vastly different upbringing?

"They shaped you."

Yes, but he hated the truth in those words.

"They fucked me up."

She gave him a sweet smile tinged with sadness. For him? Or because of him?

"Maybe, but you escaped, and you turned yourself into someone amazing. You got all your siblings out. You helped give them a sense of normalcy and a healthy childhood. You have a family, both blood and chosen, who love you. You're good, Saint, and kind, and…"

"Beth."

She shook her head as she kissed the underside of his chin, then placed a hand over his mouth. "No. You're gonna hear me out."

He growled and nipped her palm, making her giggle.

"You, Lee, are an incredible man. Of course, you have a mountain of baggage. Your childhood was as traumatic as it gets, and I'm guessing you haven't had much professional help to deal with it. But you don't scare me. I'm onto you. You're trying to warn me away, but it won't work. I know shitty men. I lived with one for almost two years. You're not that. You're a good man, Lee, really fucking good."

Lee. She hadn't used his real name since he'd told her his club handle in her Texas apartment. But hearing it now somehow made her words that much more meaningful, and he didn't have a clue how to process that.

"You don't scare me, Lee," she whispered again. "You've seen me at my lowest point. Hell, you rescued me from my lowest point and never once judged me for staying with Jason or for how I handled the situation. You deserve the same grace. I will never make you feel bad for surviving hell and becoming the man you are today. *Never.*"

She spoke the words with such sincerity that if he didn't have proof otherwise, he'd start to believe her.

"You make me feel safe. I'd gotten to the point where I didn't recognize how constantly tense and on edge I was around Jason. I never felt safe, and not just from the outside world, but from him. No matter what you've done or who you worry you are, the fact that I feel safer with you than any other man says it all."

The way she talked made it sound like they were more than a few secret hookups. Wild thoughts, but maybe they could find a way to try for something more.

Though if Copper killed him, it would put a damper on the plan.

"You're thinking hard."

He grunted. "I guess."

Beth rested her head back on his chest as she squeezed him to her. "Come on. It's late. Let's get some sleep."

"Beth, I can't stay all night. Or more accurately, I can't wake up in here tomorrow morning."

Her sigh punched him in the chest. "I know. Can you stay for a bit?"

No. Of course, he couldn't. That would only make him want her more. "Yeah. I can do that." He tugged her hair, tilting her chin up for a soft kiss before tucking her back against his chest.

Her breathing evened out almost instantly, and the arms that had been squeezing him slackened but didn't fall away. Warm, sexually satisfied, and comfortable, Saint couldn't resist the lull of sleep for more than a few moments. He shut his eyes and drifted off, promising himself he'd only take a short nap.

The next thing he knew, someone pounded on the door like a damn SWAT officer. He didn't have time to register the feel of Beth sprawled all over him before she shot up. The blanket slipped down, baring her tits. It did nothing to erase Saint's morning wood.

"Oh my God," she whispered, frantic. She brushed her hair out of her face. "It's morning, and you're still here."

Another loud knock sounded, followed by Gator's voice. "Sorry to wake you, Beth, but your dad is on his way here. Thought you might want to, uh, have breakfast with him."

Her eyes widened to the size of bike tires. "He knows," she whispered. "Oh my God, he knows you're here."

Christ, it was too early and too brutal a wakeup for so much drama. He smoothed a hand down Beth's silky back.

"Maybe, but he's trying to help us, so don't leave him hanging."

"Oh, uh, thank you, Gator. I'll be out in a few minutes." She drew up her knees, wrapped her arms around them, and dropped her head against them with a groan. "The loudest and most obnoxious club member knows you stayed here last night."

"Yes, but he's also a loyal motherfucker who loves both of us and saved our asses right now." Saint continued rubbing her back as she turned her cheek, resting it on her knee to watch him.

"That feels nice."

"For me too." On the outside, it seemed he touched her to

comfort her, but he did it for himself as much as for Beth. Touching her grounded him, as though some of her confidence in him transferred through the contact.

Her eyes fluttered shut as a happy hum left her. Saint couldn't resist leaning forward and stealing a kiss. She sighed against his lips, then wound an arm around his neck and shifted into his lap. The kiss, which started soft and sweet, turned ravenous within seconds. His dick, which softened the second Gator knocked, hardened once again. Beth rocked against him, whimpering before she tore her mouth away.

"Shit. We can't do that now."

He chuckled. "You started it."

"Uh, pretty sure you kissed me."

He gave her ass a light pinch. "Technicality." Her sassy eyeroll made him laugh. He loved how she could give him hell without fear of repercussions, the way she'd had to worry with her ex. "Get dressed and go out there. I'll slip out the window and wander in through the front in a few minutes."

She shook her head, whipping her hair around. "What? No, that's ridiculous. You can't go out the window like some naughty teenager caught sneaking into his girlfriend's room."

"You got a better idea? You want me to waltz out from back here while everyone is hanging out in the room?"

"Shit." Her head fell back on a groan, exposing her throat.

Not the time, buddy.

"Ugh, I'm so sorry. This is ridiculous."

He kissed her quickly, then smirked. "Better get moving."

"Yeah, yeah, yeah." Beth climbed off him and disappeared into the bathroom. Of course, he stared at her ass the whole way. They'd have to pluck his eyes out to keep them from zeroing in on her naked ass.

He had to resist the urge to join her in there. Even something as simple as brushing teeth would turn into a temptation.

Less than two minutes later, she returned dressed in a T-shirt and jean shorts. "Had these in my car," she explained as she pulled her hair into a high ponytail. "Okay. I'm heading out. See you in a few?"

"Yep."

Her gaze went to the window, then she frowned.

"I'm good, babe."

She huffed and rolled her eyes, but walked to him. "Kiss?"

"Of course." He gripped the front of her T-shirt and yanked her to him. They shared a short but brutal kiss that had his dick twitching with anticipation.

And then she left, leaving him to flop back on the bed with a heavy sigh. After rubbing a hand over his face, his gaze went to the window. The small-fucking-window.

"Fantastic," he muttered. "Fucking teenager is the only one who could fit through that thing without injury."

Still, he'd rather scrape the shit out of his arms, climbing through the window and spend the entire night wrapped around Beth, than be wound-free but have slept alone in his bed. Hell, the thought of turning in without her tonight held no appeal, and he'd only had a few hours of sleeping next to her.

He forced himself to sit up. The small window loomed a mere six feet away, mocking him with its stream of sunshine pouring into the room. *How the fuck was he supposed to stuff his full-grown man ass through that small window?*

Guess he was about to find out.

What a fucking disaster.

Chapter Nineteen

Fucking Gator.

He sat across from Beth with the biggest, most self-satisfied smirk she'd ever seen. She glared daggers at him, but, of course, it only made him laugh and wink. Not only did her dad show up five seconds after she walked out of the room, but her mom and basically every other club member arrived for what Shell called 'family breakfast.' She claimed the fanfare was a frequent ordeal Beth would know about if she 'bothered to come home more than once a year.'

Point taken.

When she offered to help with the food, her mom steered her out of the kitchen. "Thanks, honey, but I've seen your cooking skills," she'd said, which was how Beth found herself sitting across from Gator, cutting fruit at the table, and stressing over whether Saint was wedged in the window.

"Hey, Rizz," Gator called to his club brother across the room. "Have you seen Saint this morning? Thought he'd be here by now."

Beth narrowed her eyes at the shit-stirrer. She pointed her knife at him and mouthed, *Your dick is next,* before hacking it through the strawberry with brutal force.

Gator paled and moved his hands below the table to cover his junk.

Beth gave him a sweet smile and resumed her task.

"You're fucking evil," Gator muttered.

The door opened, and before anyone greeted the newcomer, the back of Beth's neck tingled.

Saint had arrived.

Her hands stopped moving, and she forgot what the hell she was doing until Gator grabbed a strawberry chunk from her bowl and threw it at her forehead. It bounced off, landing right back in the bowl.

"Score," he cried out, raising his arms in victory.

Beth blinked. Okay, she could do this. She could act normal around the man she'd slept with. The one who would cause out-of-control drama in the club if anyone found out. Well, anyone but Gator, apparently.

"Ew," she said as she wiped her head with the back of her hand. "That's your piece. You'd better eat it without touching another strawberry."

Rolling his eyes, Gator grabbed the hunk of chopped strawberry and popped it into his mouth. "Yummy." He waggled his eyebrows.

And then Saint was there, standing behind her, and she could barely breathe as her body went on high alert. Now that he'd seen and touched all of her, now that he'd been inside her, she seemed to be aware of him on a visceral level. Her skin prickled with heat. Her breath came shorter. Every nerve ending was tuned to his presence like a compass finding north.

"Good morning," Saint said as he took the seat beside her.

"What's up, brother?" Gator asked, holding out a fist, which Saint bumped.

Beth risked a sideways glance his way. Thank God he wasn't wearing the same thing he'd had on last night. She might expire on the spot if she had to sit there and listen to the guys grill him about who he'd been with the night before.

"Hey," she said in a breathless, high-pitched voice that sounded nothing like her usual self.

Wow, Gator mouthed because she was looking across the table at him instead of at Saint. "You suck at this."

Pull yourself together.

If she didn't figure out a way to act normal, she'd be the one to give the entire thing away. Copper was no one's fool. If she acted like a lovesick teenager, he'd pick up on it right away. Maybe she should feign a stomachache and go home before she fucked the entire thing up.

Saint faced her with a raised eyebrow. "Want some help with that?"

"Nope. I'm good." So good, in fact, he should go somewhere else before she did something stupid like climb in his lap and kiss the hell out of him. How did he look so good early in the morning after climbing out of a damn window? She needed a gallon of coffee, under-eye patches, and more coffee to feel halfway human, and here he was looking like a damn snack after performing high-level evasive maneuvers.

At least no one saw him.

Wait, no one saw him, right?

Her heart kicked into gear, slamming against her rib cage. For all she knew, one of Saint's brothers saw him sneaking out of the room, and they now had to trust he could keep this massive secret, which would never happen because who'd keep secrets from their president?

Gator. Gator would keep the secret, and that meant he'd be in a horrible position if anyone found that out. This was so bad. *Why had she slept with Saint?*

The worst part of it all was how she couldn't regret it. If she had to go back in time, she'd probably do it again. She liked him. Liked him in a way she hadn't experienced in a long time. And that was an enormous problem. What the hell was she supposed to do about these feelings? How could they ever try for something more with a Copper-sized obstacle directly in their path?

Her stomach flipped. She wouldn't be able to eat a bite of breakfast at this point.

A knee pressed against hers. Instead of jolting, her heart rate immediately settled.

Saint.

After a glance around, revealing no one paid their trio any attention, Beth turned to look at him.

He sat with as relaxed a posture as he could, resting back in his chair and looking mouth-watering in his customary T-shirt, jeans, and HHMC cut. *Breathe,* he mouthed. "No one suspects. I got you."

Strong, solid, protective as hell, Saint.

She did as he asked, taking a cleansing breath before turning back to finish cutting a hundred strawberries. Across from her, Gator stared with a shrewd expression. His smile changed from the roguish one he typically sported to one of surprise and even acceptance.

"Oh," he muttered.

"Gator…" Saint's tone left no room for misinterpretation. If Gator didn't shut up, Saint would knock him out.

Gator lifted his hands in surrender. "So that's how it is."

Saint flipped him off before Beth could respond, and at that exact moment, her father walked in from his office.

Instead of yanking his knee away, Saint kept it pressed against hers under the table. Of course, her father had no idea, but it was still a risk. Still, she didn't freak out again. Something about him, his touch, helped even her out. *Did she do the same for him?*

God, she hoped so.

"Morning, kiddo," Copper said as he strode over.

"Hey, Dad. You and Mom have a good night?"

He nodded as he dropped into the empty chair beside Gator. "We did. Watched that new comedy your mom's been wanting to see."

Beth grinned. She loved how, despite Copper being a huge, tough-as-nails MC president, he'd bend over backward to make his wife happy, including spending his night watching a rom-com, which he hated. But Shell loved them, and what Shell wanted, Copper delivered.

"What's your plan for the day?"

She shot her dad a suspicious glance as she set the knife down. "Why? Are you planning on having someone follow me everywhere I go?"

He shrugged. "Haven't decided yet."

"Well, let me make the decision for you. That's a big, fat *no way*."

"Beth…" She shook her head at her father.

Saint frowned. "Beth…"

"Nope." She pointed back and forth between the two of them. "You are not ganging up on me about this. Not happening. I have a job interview with a grooming salon in town, and I will *not* have one of you guys sitting outside the shop, intimidating the hell out of some poor salon owner."

"Beth, they'll be discreet," Copper said. "This isn't our first rodeo."

"No."

"You're not interviewing at The Barking Beautician, are you?" Gator asked without any comment about her safety. Beside her, Saint practically vibrated with what she assumed was the need to shove her in a locked box and throw away the key.

She cringed. "Yes. That name is awful, but they're the only game in town. They're new, and they're hiring."

"Huh. Heard they kinda suck."

"Jesus, Gator," Saint muttered. "Way to be supportive."

"No, it's okay. I've heard the same thing, but I need a job."

"No, you don't." Copper stroked his beard. "We said you could stay at home for as long as you like. There's no rush."

Well, I'm sleeping with one of your enforcers, and I sure can't do that at your house, so there kinda is a rush.

"Dad, I'm used to my own place. I miss the independence," she said instead. "I miss working too. You know I enjoyed my job."

"I know. I just like having you at home," he muttered, face reddening.

She grinned. "Me too." Nothing but a big old sap, her dad was.

"Wow, this is really touching." Gator sighed and rested his chin on his hand as he fluttered his lashes.

Copper smacked him on the back of the head.

"Ow! What the hell? It was a compliment."

"Look, Beth, after yesterday, I'm concerned," Copper said without acknowledging Gator further. "These motherfuckers have already messed with you once. Until we know more, I'm not taking any chances."

She sighed and looked at Saint, who stared at her with hot eyes. Hot eyes that dared her to deny protection again. "Fine." Saint seemed to relax visibly. She wanted to reach over and squeeze his hand, but curled her fingers into her palm instead. "But they stay out of my way."

Copper nodded. "Promise."

Sure, he did. It was an easy promise to make but a much harder one to keep.

Her mom blew into the clubhouse wearing an apron and barking orders like a breakfast drill sergeant. Everyone, all these big, potentially violent bikers jumped into action following her every command without question. The way they all loved and respected her mother made Beth's heart happy, but she couldn't help but laugh. Tiny Shell wielded a ton of influence around here.

Within five minutes, they'd set the table, delivered the food from the kitchen, and had everyone seated at various tables. Kids ran around causing the usual ruckus, teenagers sat together, staring at their phones with sullen expressions, and loud laughter rang out through the building.

Beth ended up sitting with her parents, Zach, Toni, Lindsey, Maverick, and Stephanie. A few regulars were notably absent, Screw being the one whose presence she missed the most. He never failed to have her cracking up with wild stories from his misspent youth. The only cloud on an otherwise sunny experience was Saint ending up on the opposite side of the room.

It had to be that way, of course. She couldn't exactly demand he sit at her table without garnering a few unanswerable questions.

Well, she could answer them, but she wasn't in the mood for a fireworks show right then. So she spent the meal chatting with her loved ones, embracing the mushy feelings of being home with family, enjoying delicious food, and trying not to glance over at Saint every two seconds.

One of those things didn't happen as planned.

Once the group had consumed every ounce of food—these guys had some serious appetites—Beth stood to help start the cleanup. Before she had a chance to grab a platter, the door flew open, and Screw blew in like a hurricane.

"Beth!" he screamed, whipping his head around as he searched for her. His hair, longer than she'd ever seen it, was pulled back in a man bun, but whisps flew around his face as though he'd been messing with it. His eyes had a wild, panicked gleam. "Where the fuck is Beth?"

She stepped forward. "I'm right here. What's wrong?"

"Oh my God, there you are."

Screw darted toward her.

Saint shot up, gaze sharp, and muscles primed to dive between them if he found Screw a threat, which was absurd. She gave him a firm headshake.

When he reached her, Screw grabbed her shoulders—*Saint must have loved that*—and sighed as though a hundred-pound anvil sat on his chest. "You won't believe what they did to her. It's so bad. Beth, it's horrible."

She blinked at the insane man before her. "What the hell are you talking about?"

He huffed. "I'm talking about what they did to my baby. It's goddamn criminal."

"Jazz had a baby?" No, that couldn't be right. The throuple of Screw, Gumby, and Jazz had decided to remain kid-free, last she heard.

"What? No. Fuck no. I'm talking about… you know what, fuck it." He bent forward and gently drove his shoulder into Beth's stomach as he wrapped a hand around the back of her thighs. She yelped as she folded in half and was hoisted off the ground in a fireman's carry.

"Screw!" she shouted as laughter bubbled out of her. "What is wrong with you?"

"You just have to see it," he said as he marched toward the door with her hanging down his back like a sack of potatoes.

Beth laughed until her stomach cramped, and tears dripped down her forehead. But then she caught a glimpse of Saint's thunderous expression.

Yikes. That was one unhappy man. Screw's days might be numbered, and he didn't even know it. *Could it be jealousy?* A thrill ran through her at the idea, which was probably not what she should be feeling, but the thought of him, possessive and feral, turned her on like nothing else. Jason's jealousy had been a cage, suffocating, punishing, and designed to control, but Saint's felt like a claim, like being wanted so fiercely it bordered on desperation. He'd never hurt her or take his frustration out on her, and that gave her the freedom and safety to enjoy the intensity with which he wanted her.

Screw ripped the door open and stormed outside. Hot air and sunshine chased away the air-conditioned chill within five seconds.

"Oh, for fuck's sake," Gumby's voice rang out from somewhere nearby.

"Screw! Put her down. Oh my God, you're making way too big a deal of this." Jazz had laughter in her voice.

"Can someone please tell me what's going on?" A sharp yip had her trying to peer around the side of Screw. "Did you get another dog?"

"She's a foster. We picked her up last night," Jazz said as Screw finally set her down.

She grabbed his arm for stability until the world stopped wobbling, then set her gaze on the small white terrier practically bouncing around Gumby's feet.

Beth crouched down, and the dog bounded toward her. "Oh my gosh," she gushed as she held her arms out. "What a cut! Holy shit, what the hell happened to her?"

"See," Screw said to Gumby. "I told you it's fucking criminal."

The dog wriggled all around as Beth stroked her horribly cut hair. The poor girl looked like someone hacked at her fur with a machete while blindfolded. The uneven tufts stuck out in all directions. "What happened?"

Screw threw his hands in the air and practically shouted, "She was butchered. That's what happened."

"Okay, baby." Jazz walked over to him and rubbed his back as she kissed his cheek. Her eyes sparkled with laughter, but she wisely appeased her husband. Well, one of her husbands. The other rolled his eyes. "This is Mary Lou. We picked her up from the shelter last night. She was filthy, so Screw took her to the Barking Beautician this morning..."

"And that evil woman destroyed her," Screw said with a growl.

Beth cringed. This didn't bode well for her interview later today. Did she really want to work for someone who did such shoddy work?

"Pretty sure she did it on purpose too," Screw muttered.

Beth blinked up at him. "Really?" Being shitty at her job was one thing, but if the woman were malicious, Beth would cancel the interview in a heartbeat. "Why do you think that?"

The dog rolled to its back, soaking up belly rubs with an adorable wiggle.

"Because when I walked in, she started preaching to me about the family unit and how disgusting it was for me to be with a man *and* a woman. She got pissed when I told her to shove her opinions up her ass.

Her jaw dropped. Well, that sealed the deal. No way could she work with or for someone who thought that way. Screw, Jazz, and Gumby had one of her favorite relationships on the planet. The three were so over the top in love with each other, even after a decade and a half of being together.

Now what the hell was she supposed to do for work?

"Can you fix her?" Screw asked, sounding near desperate.

"Yes. She won't be perfect, but I can even her out. It'll be too short, but at least it will grow in properly, and she won't look like a gremlin anymore."

"Thank fuck," Screw said. He seemed to lose fifty pounds of tension as he put his arm around Jazz's shoulder and tucked her into his side.

The dog scampered back over to Gumby, so Beth stood. "I'm glad you came by. I was supposed to interview there today."

"Oh no, I'm so sorry, Beth." Jazz looked gorgeous in a hunter green V-cut tank top and white denim shorts. A litany of scars covered her arms and chest from a past trauma. Back in the day, Jazz would wear full-length sleeves no matter the temperature or time of year. Having two men worship her for the goddess she was helped her overcome any insecurities she had regarding her appearance, and now she wore whatever the fuck she wanted, and she looked fantastic.

"No. God, don't apologize. I'd much rather know she's an evil bitch now."

"Tell you what," Screw said. "You should open your own salon. Put that monster out of business. There's a need for it. She has a terrible reputation, but is the only game in town. She's only been open a few weeks too. Before that, we had to drive almost an hour for a good groomer."

"Yeah, I'd love to have my own place." She shrugged. "Maybe someday. I don't have the capital for that right now." Her parents had offered to help, of course, but she wanted to do it without their assistance.

"Huh." Screw rubbed at the stubble on his chin.

A grin broke out across Gumby's face. "Uh-oh, you've got him thinking, Beth."

"What do you mean?"

"He's been talking about investing in a local business for months, but hasn't found one that speaks to him," Jazz said with a smile. "You might have just given him the perfect idea."

Her heart skipped a beat. "Wait, really?"

"Want to talk about going into business together, Beth?"

"For real?" *Holy shit. Was he serious? Could this possibly be real?* She'd kill to own a salon and to be in business with one of her favorite people.

Hell yes.

He nodded. "Yeah, I think this would be perfect. Let's get

together this week and talk details."

Fuck the details. Where did she sign?

She squealed and threw herself at Screw, who managed to unwind his arm from Jazz in time to catch her. "Thank you!" she whispered as she hugged him tightly.

He squeezed her until she worried she'd pop. "I'm as excited as you are."

Over his shoulder, she caught sight of Saint leaning against the clubhouse with his arms folded over his chest and a scowl on his face. He watched her every move with hawk-like intensity.

"I'll come by this afternoon to fix up Miss Mary Lou, that work?" she asked as she released him.

"Perfect." Screw hugged her one last time. "Love you, kiddo."

Saint's eye twitched.

Rolling her eyes, Beth moved to hug Jazz next. "Long time since I've been a kiddo."

That had Jazz laughing. "You could be fifty, and he'll still call you that," she said as she and Beth embraced. "Better tell your guard dog to be careful," she whispered in Beth's ear. "He's shit at masking his feelings."

"I don't… I mean…"

"I fully approve," Jazz whispered. "And I'm here if you need me."

She nearly cried right there on the spot. What had she done to deserve such incredible women in her life?

As they drew back from the hug, Jazz winked. "Love you."

"Love you too."

She bid goodbye to Mary Lou and Gumby as well. The trio took off. Screw stuck Mary Lou in a doggie backpack for the bike trip while Jazz climbed on behind Gumby.

As soon as they left, she turned and walked toward Saint, whose irked expression hadn't changed. "He's like an uncle," she said, rolling her eyes.

"I know."

"And yet you have a problem with him hugging me?"

"I have a problem with anyone touching you who isn't me."

His gruff voice sent a shiver down her spine. "I probably shouldn't like that so much, but I do. It makes me want to get back in bed with you so you can show me just how much you hated him hugging me."

"Fuck." His eyes flared with instant lust. After a glance left and right, he grabbed the back of her neck and yanked her in for a bruising kiss that weakened her knees instantly.

It ended before it started, but was no less brutally core-shaking.

"You'll make an incredible business owner," he whispered as she tried to find her footing.

"Oh, thank you." Excitement surged. "I can't believe Screw wants to open a grooming salon with me."

Saint tilted his head, studying her. "I can. You're fucking amazing. I'll follow you to his place later so you can fix that rat dog."

"Hey! Be nice. She's a sweetie."

He leaned in and whispered in her ear, "Then afterward, maybe we can go back to my place, and I'll show you what happens when you let another man touch you, platonic or not."

Her knees wobbled. Her thighs clenched.

He kissed the side of her head, then strode away as though he hadn't lit a fire between her legs.

They had to talk.

Really talk about what the hell they were doing, but for now, she preferred to bask in the glow of all the good fortune finally coming her way.

Chapter Twenty

"Two weeks." Zach dropped into a seat across the booth from Saint with a disgusted huff. "Two fucking weeks and not a goddamn thing to show for it." He set a burner phone on the table, then flicked it across the surface, away from himself. "Someone else needs to take this before I lose my mind and Toni has to have me committed."

Two weeks ago, Zach texted the phone number the laundromat attendant gave them from this burner phone. He'd made it clear who they were in a slick way and demanded a meeting with whoever ran the drug operation happening under their noses.

And it had been crickets since. No text. No sightings of the bikers. No reports of increased drug trafficking in the area.

One would think Zach would be relieved, but he was a suspicious fucker who wouldn't be satisfied without absolute closure, and that would come in the form of someone's head on a spike.

"I'll take it," Saint said, scooping up the phone. "Maybe they left town. It really could be as simple as that, Zach. If they're small-time, they can't risk taking us on. The easiest thing to do is pack up shop and find a new home."

Zach shook his head. "I know. And you're right. The simplest solution is usually the right one, but I can't fucking shake this feeling in the back of my mind that they're playing a long game."

Saint lifted his hands. "Hey, I didn't say I believed they'd gone. Just floating it as an idea."

Toni wandered over with a full coffee pot. "Hey, guys. I'm guessing you need some caffeine.

"Always." Saint pushed his mug her way.

"Hey, baby." Zach stood and quickly kissed his ol' lady. Toni stepped back from the day-to-day operations of the diner, but she enjoyed hanging out with customers and mingling occasionally. She could usually be found assisting the servers once or twice per week.

Saint had only agreed to meet Zach here because Melody didn't work on Tuesdays. He'd been avoiding her and the diner like the plague since the scene in front of her house.

"You guys hungry?" Toni asked.

"I'm good with coffee," Saint said, lifting his mug to his lips.

"Same, baby."

She looked between them with concerned eyes. "Okay. I'll let you talk business. Holler if you need me."

As soon as she reached another table, Zach said, "So you think it's bullshit too?"

Saint considered before answering, "Yes. Probably. Maybe I'm reading into shit, but I keep thinking if it were me, I wouldn't be so quick to back off."

Zach grunted. "This is why we work so well together. We think the same way."

"So, what's the plan? I hate sitting around waiting to be caught with our hands on our dicks." After a week of silence, Copper deemed it safe for Beth to no longer take someone with her everywhere. Well, after a week, Beth demanded

Copper call off the babysitter. She and Saint were able to sneak time for each other much more easily when they weren't worried about whoever had been assigned to tail her that day. Saint signed up for as many of those shifts as he could without raising suspicion, but it wasn't enough. Since Copper called off the watch team, they'd taken advantage of her newfound freedom, fucking on every surface of his house and anytime they could slip away for some privacy.

Even though no one had seen or heard from Demo or any of his cronies, Saint, like Zach, apparently couldn't shake the feeling that they hadn't seen the last of the assholes. But they were stuck, powerless to do anything if they couldn't even find the fuckers, and he hated that feeling. Especially when he felt an overwhelming need to keep Beth safe.

"I don't fucking know," Zach said, strumming his fingers on the tabletop. He downed his coffee in three gulps and set the mug down with a hard clunk. "I'm gonna go talk to Copper. We need a more proactive approach. I want to start with a thorough search outside of town. I need to do something to set my fucking mind at ease."

Mine too.

"I went back to the laundromat three days ago."

Zach's eyes narrowed. "By your fucking self?"

Shrugging, Saint nodded. "Yeah…. just listen. The same guy sat at the counter, still nervous as fuck, but he pretended he had no fucking idea who I was. I asked for machine thirteen, and he said they didn't have one. Stuck to that story no matter what I said. Been keeping my eye on the place too. Haven't seen anyone suspicious come and go."

"Fuck, I'm afraid to hope it was this easy to get them to fuck off."

"It's never this easy," Saint said with a snort.

"Exactly. Fuck. All right, lemme go talk to Cop. You coming to the clubhouse?"

"Not yet. I gotta swing by my house for a bit, but I'll meet you at the clubhouse later."

Zach cocked his head. "You doing some work on the place or something? Rocket didn't mention anything."

Rocket had owned a contractor company for almost two decades. No one in the club would dare use anyone else for their construction projects.

"What? No. Why?"

Zach shrugged as he stood. "You keep having to rush home for shit lately."

"Oh."

Well, Z, I'm fucking Beth so…

"Just family shit."

"Your siblings good?"

"Yeah. There's just a million of 'em, so someone always has some drama going on."

"Good luck with that, brother," Zach said with a laugh. He clapped Saint's shoulder as he passed by. "I'll find you later."

"Yeah. Later."

Thank God Zach bought the lie. Well, it wasn't a lie, one of his siblings was always in some state of crisis, but it sure as fuck wasn't why he'd been rushing home lately. That was all Beth.

He stayed for a few minutes, finishing his coffee. Around him, the diner bustled with activity as it always did. Waitstaff rushed from table to table, delivering food, clearing plates, and seating newcomers. They stopped serving at two in the afternoon, but most of the time, customers lingered past three.

Beth was due at his house around two. She and Screw spent the morning with their corporate realtor scouting locations for the grooming salon. Over the past two weeks, they'd developed a comprehensive business plan and were moving full steam ahead.

Pride welled in him. It turned out, Beth worked her ass off once she set her sights on something. She was a force to be reckoned with and had flourished with her newfound purpose.

It was a beautiful thing to watch.

Each time she came to his house, he found it harder to watch her leave. More than once, he'd had to resist the strong temptation to tie her to his bed and demand she remain there for the rest of her life. Last night, he'd fantasized about slashing her tires to keep her from leaving.

He was sick in the head, but he didn't act on the impulses, which had to count for something. Beth made him want to be better. To be the man she saw when she looked at him with those trusting eyes.

Right?

Really, they needed to have a serious discussion. He was ready to claim Beth, to put a label on it, lock her down, and call her his. Fuck the obstacles in their path. He didn't give a shit about their age difference, and worry about the club faded with each passing day. Copper had to relent once he realized his daughter was respected, treated like a queen, and would be taken care of no matter what.

Keep telling yourself that.

His constant hard-on appeared to have siphoned so much blood from his cranium that he'd suffered brain damage and was experiencing delusions. He drained his mug, dug out a twenty, and dropped it on the table. Toni wouldn't keep it. She'd split it between her hard-working staff.

"Have a good one, Saint," Toni called as he made his way to the exit.

"Bye, Tone. See ya, Lindsey."

"Oh! Bye, Saint. Sorry, I didn't have time to chat. It's nuts today." Lindsey rushed around the counter to give him a quick kiss on the cheek.

"No worries. I'll catch you later." He was a few years older than Lindsey, but not many. They'd been close for almost a decade, with a relationship more like cousins than mere friends. She'd played a massive part in helping him pull his head out of his ass in his early twenties when he was angry, bitter, and high more often than not. Who knew where he'd be without her slapping him upside the head and telling him to stop being a fucking idiot and prospect with the club.

Beth's car was already parked in his garage when he arrived home. Instantly, everything faded but the anticipation of seeing her, holding her, touching her. After parking his motorcycle next to her car and closing the garage so no one would discover their secret, he went inside through the interior garage door.

The second his foot hit the tile floor, a soft weight slammed into him.

"Saint!" Beth shrieked as she jumped into his arms.

Somehow, he managed to catch her with two hands on her ass. She wrapped her legs around his waist and kissed him like they hadn't been together in months. He pressed her against the wall and ground his instantly rock-hard dick against her as he devoured her.

The scent, taste, and feel of her went straight to his head, stealing all rational thought. Nothing mattered but getting inside her as soon as possible.

"Christ," he said as he nipped her lower lip.

"Fuck me. Fuck me *right now*." She'd worn a short skirt, and he could already feel the heat of her pussy through his jeans.

His hands trembled with need as he held her with one arm and ripped his jeans open with the other. She had her arms wrapped around his neck and continued to attack his mouth as he somehow managed to free his cock and shove his jeans below his ass.

Their mouths met again in a feral kiss. She tugged at his hair, nearly possessed as their tongues battled for control.

"I want you so badly," she said with a whimper against his mouth. "It's all I can think about. *You*… all damn day."

Did she have any idea what those words did to him? How did they make him want to possess every inch of her? "Fuck, you're never leaving my house," he rumbled as he placed hard kisses down the column of her throat. "I'm gonna fucking keep you. Own you, Beth. You'll never remember life before I got inside you."

Her head hit the wall as she gave him more room to work. "Yes, I want that."

He stared her in the eye. "No more fucking condoms. Not a goddamn thing between us." They'd already discussed and decided, shared test results, and she had an IUD. "Every time I fuck you, I will fill you with my cum from now on."

They weren't necessary or wanted.

"Please. God, that's so hot."

He hooked two fingers in the triangle of her tiny fucking panties and yanked. The material tore with ease. Beth's eyes flared molten with desire before slamming closed.

No way. An out-of-control need to embed himself in every cell of her body tore through him. When he was through with her, he'd be imprinted on her very existence, and she wouldn't be able to breathe without thinking of him.

He sank a hand into her hair. "Look at me when I fuck you."

Her eyelids fluttered, and then those gorgeous green eyes stared into his soul.

He grabbed his dick, running the tip through the wetness at her entrance. Beth gasped and bit her lower lip. The move was so sexy his hips acted of their own accord, propelling him into her with a powerful thrust.

She clutched his shoulders. If it weren't for his leather cut, he'd have nails cutting into his skin and leaving marks for days. Maybe he should burn the damn garment.

The scorching, wet clasp of her pussy brought such a violent surge of carnal bliss that it took him out of his body and to another plane of existence. He slapped his hand on the wall next to her head, using his other arm to hold her up as he fucked her like it would be the last time.

Beth cried out, he bottomed out over and over. She rode him, hips working furiously to bring them the most pleasure possible.

"Saint…" She whimpered and whipped her head back and forth against the wall. "It's so good."

"Keep looking at me, baby," he said, voice deeper than usual. "Wanna see my favorite eyes when you go over the edge."

Her gaze softened, mixing affection and care with the lust. "Everything about you makes you my favorite," she whispered.

He rolled his hips into her, pressing deep and holding there. They stared at each other for a moment, breathing heavy. A vortex of emotions he'd never had to define before swirled in him, expanding his chest until it threatened to burst. He peeled his hand off the wall and smoothed his thumb over her swollen lips before cupping the back of her neck.

"We'll make it work," he whispered.

She blinked rapidly. "H-how?"

Since he didn't have an answer, he kissed her, tasting the desperation and worry on her tongue. He might not have a solution yet, but he would.

Nothing and no one would keep him from Beth.

Not jealous women he had no interest in.

Not drug dealers.

Not even an MC president.

As much as it would kill him to walk away from the club, he'd do it for her.

Copper might not like that, but he had to understand. He'd made impossible choices to protect Shell. Choices that changed their entire lives.

With their lips sealed together, the tone of their fucking changed to a more sensual, emotional coupling. Slower. Deeper. The frantic edge smoothed into something that felt dangerously like making love.

Feeling connected to her on every level, knowing she wanted more, changed fucking everything.

Repeatedly sliding into her tight heat had his balls drawing up within minutes. His lower stomach clenched with each jerk of his hips. Before long, his movements grew uncoordinated, and his muscles spasmed.

Saint ripped his mouth from Beth's. "Eyes on me."

She nodded, mouth open and panting. "Fuck," she whispered. Her back arched off the wall, and she shouted his name as she came. Her eyes darkened and glazed over, giving him a view straight to her heart and soul.

At the first rhythmic clench of her channel, he lost the last threat of sanity and came, flooding deep inside her. Their gazes held as he gently fucked her through the orgasm. When her legs went slack, he stopped moving.

Beth tilted her head and gifted him a beaming smile. "We signed a lease," she said, joy radiating from her.

Saint burst out laughing. "That why you attacked me the second I walked in the door? Lease signing gets you all hot and bothered?"

Her cheeks flushed pink. "No," she said, slapping his shoulder, then she pursed her lips. "Well, maybe a little."

"Congrats, baby." He leaned in and kissed her. "That's fantastic news."

"It is!" She did a happy little wiggle, which had intense

sensation shooting through his oversensitive cock, making him gasp. "Oh, sorry!" Her laugh negated the apology.

"Sure you are." Gently as could be, he slipped free of her warmth and lowered her legs to the floor.

Beth frowned. "I liked it better up there in your arms."

God, she was too damn sweet. "Me too."

"I should get cleaned up." She pointed toward the bathroom. "And find some underwear you haven't shredded."

He chuckled at that. "If you left any here, I can't make any promise that I didn't tear them up."

"Perv," she said, laughing as she strode past him toward the bathroom.

Fifteen minutes later, wearing sweatpants she'd left at his place, Beth sat next to him on the couch. He immediately lifted her legs into his lap, turning her to face him, then took her hand and interlaced their fingers. Hers was so much smaller, yet fit like they'd been cut to interlock perfectly.

Beth stared at their joined hands with intense concentration.

"Hey," he said in a low voice.

She glanced up, and the shimmer in her eyes hit worse than the most brutal gut punch.

"No, baby, don't…" Fuck, the thought of her crying over him, over them, crushed him.

She blinked and forced a weak laugh. "I'm just being stupid."

"You aren't. You couldn't be stupid if you tried."

"Ha. You forget how you found me a month ago."

"Beth, that wasn't stupidity. That was fucking survival."

She shrugged. "Yeah, well…"

He tucked a lock of hair behind her ear with his free hand, then smoothed his thumb over her cheek. "I want this, Beth. I want you. For real. Not just quick, secret fucks or dinners hiding in my house. I want dates. I want to dance with you at club parties. I want you in my lap, wrapped in my arms, when we sit around the bonfire with our family. I want entire nights to explore you. I want to wake up, slide inside you, and hear you moan my name first thing in the morning. I fucking want you in every aspect of my life."

A tear rolled down her cheek, breaking his heart. He swiped it away with a gentle brush of his thumb. "Saint," she whispered as she nuzzled into his palm. "I want that too. So much that I can barely breathe because of it. Every time I leave you here by yourself, it feels like a limb is being torn from my body. I ache for you, lying alone in my bed at night. But I don't know how to move forward without causing chaos."

"We'll make it work. We will find a way. Beth, I'm a stubborn motherfucker when I want something. If I have to, I'll leav—"

"No!" She pressed her fingertips to his lips, squashing the life-changing words he'd have spoken. "I will not let you do that. I can't be the reason you lose your family, Lee. That would destroy me. We'll find another way. Promise me you won't do that." Her voice trembled with near panic.

He kissed her fingertips, then gently pulled them from his lips. The words scraped like glass coming out. "All right. I promise." He'd have done it. In a fucking heartbeat, he'd have walked away from everything for her. But he swallowed that truth and gave her the lie she needed.

He might not have a choice anyway. Once Copper found out, he might be cast out of the family, no matter what he promised Beth. He just hoped they'd let him live.

"Okay. Good. Thank you." She shifted until she straddled him. After a sweet, desperate kiss, she wrapped her arms around him and lay her head on his chest, clinging to him like a monkey. Saint slipped a hand under her shirt, stroking up and down her back as he stared off into space.

They stayed that way for a long time, taking comfort from touch and enjoying the peace of each other's presence.

This was worth fighting for.

This was everything, and no matter what happened, he'd find a way to keep Beth by his side.

Chapter Twenty-One

Beth brushed a sweaty strand of hair off her forehead with the back of her arm. Her gloved hands were covered in bleach and aching from hours of scrubbing the inside of her new grooming salon. The place had sat vacant for almost a year, and before that, it had been a nail salon. Thick dust had accumulated over the months, and at some point, someone had been squatting there, as food wrappers littered the floor. She cleaned those up quickly with a push broom, but she'd wanted to give the entire space a proper scrub down before equipment began arriving next week.

Excitement zinged through her as she gazed around the large, empty salon. She had big plans for the place, including setting up a small shop featuring locally sourced items. Last Saturday, she visited a farmers' market where she met a vendor who made pet-safe shampoo and another who designed collars and harnesses. After exchanging contact information, they planned to meet to discuss her salon hosting their items.

"Okay," she said over the sound of Olivia Rodrigo belting out from her phone. "That's enough for today." She'd spent the past six hours cleaning on her hands and knees, and every part of her body ached. She needed a bath, a glass of wine, and Saint's magic hands rubbing her, well, anywhere.

As she peeled off her purple rubber gloves, she scanned the street through the front window. The location couldn't be better. In the center of town, near many other shops, and only ten minutes from Saint's house. She'd been shocked to find the place available. Every so often, someone would walk by and peer through the window. Screw helped her hang a coming-soon sign with the name and slogan they'd decided on.

Hell's Hounds Clubhouse

Handling your best friend with the best care.

It was never too early to advertise. She hoped to have a full house at their grand opening in a few months, once they had all the proper permits and renovations completed.

As she was about to turn and grab the bucket of sudsy water to dispose of it, she caught sight of a couple strolling up the sidewalk. They were arm in arm, deep in conversation. A pang of longing speared through her chest. What she'd give to cling to Saint that way in public, to show the world he belonged to her and how proud she was of that fact.

"Someday," she muttered. They just had to figure out how.

She took a few steps back from the window so she could watch them walk by without making her snooping so obvious. As soon as they walked in front of her window, she froze.

The woman stood closest to her shop, but her head was turned toward the man, so Beth could see only the back of her hair. Still, Beth would know those curls.

"Melody," she whispered, taking another step back. The last thing she needed was to be accused of spying on the woman who already hated her. She shifted her gaze to Melody's partner.

They locked eyes.

Beth gasped.

Demo appeared to be engaged in conversation with Melody, but he stared straight at her, his fiendish smirk sending a chill down her spine.

He was back in town.

Or maybe he'd never left.

What the fuck was he doing with Melody?

Did he know who she was? Was she a friend of the club? That she had a huge thing for Saint? Could that be why he'd sought her out, or was it all a huge coincidence? Melody probably had no idea the danger she was in, being caught in the middle between the MC and the dealers.

Demo pushed Melody's back against the front window of the salon and kissed her.

Beth stood frozen, unable to move, as though doing so would make everything worse. He kept making out with Melody, but his eyes stayed open and on Beth the entire time. Her stomach swooped as a cold sweat broke out along her forehead.

This was bad.

Really-fucking-bad.

After a few moments, Demo ended the kiss. They spoke for a second, then separated. Demo walked back the way they'd come, while Melody continued up the street, though a little less steady than before, like a woman who'd been kissed well and good.

"Shit," Beth muttered. "What do I do? What do I do?"

She crept toward the door and pulled it open as quietly as possible. As she poked her head out an inch, she caught sight of Demo turning down the nearest side street, out of sight. She whipped her head around the other way, where Melody continued walking, maybe floating, up the sidewalk.

Without giving herself time to think, Beth rushed out the door and jogged up the street. "Mel," she called as she got closer. "Melody, wait up! Oh fuck." She tripped over an uneven crack in the road and stumbled. She windmilled her arms as she kept moving forward, trying not to hit the ground.

She plowed into Melody, catching her to stabilize herself.

"What the fuck, Beth?" Melody shook her off and stepped away with an expression of disbelief.

"Sorry." Beth panted and raised her hands. "I tripped." Her chest heaved, and her heart galloped like a greyhound as she tried to catch her breath. "I need to work out more."

"What do you want?" Melody stepped back, putting distance between them as she crossed her arms. She looked beautiful as usual in a short, fitted athletic dress that clung to her every curve.

"Um…" *Maybe she should have thought this through.*

"If you're here to yell at me about Saint, you can save it. Nothing fucking happened. He was the perfect little Saint when he dropped me off at my house, and I haven't talked to him since."

"No." Beth waved away the statement. "That's not… shit, this is kinda awkward. Um, okay, that guy you were just with? That was Demo, right?"

Melody gasped. "Are you fucking spying on me?"

"What?" Her eyes bugged. "No. No, definitely not. You walked past my… I mean, I leased…" She shook her head. "That doesn't matter. I'm not spying, I just happened to see you with that guy."

"And? What, you want him too?"

"No. *No.*" This was not going well. "That's not what I'm saying. Melody, he's not a good guy. I don't know what he's told you about himself, but he's dangerous."

"Oh, come on. Seriously? You do know who your father is, right? And the guy you're fucking? You know his role in the club, right?" She laughed, a nasty sound of suspicion.

"What? I'm not..." Beth blinked and jerked back as though slapped. Then she took a cleansing breath.

Melody didn't know anything about her and Saint. She was trying to get under Beth's skin. That's all. "None of that is the point. That guy is causing a lot of trouble for the club. Mel, I'm worried he sought you out on purpose. I'm worried you're not safe."

"Wow, you really are a piece of work. What's the matter? Is Saint not interested in you, so you're gonna go after another man I want? Princess Beth can't be happy unless all the men want her?"

"What? No, that's absurd. I'm literally telling you I'm worried for your safety."

"It's pathetic, really."

Beth threw her hands in the air and huffed in exasperation. "Will you just listen to me? I'm trying to help you."

"Fuck you. I don't need your help." Melody lunged closer, practically snarling.

For a moment, Beth wondered if she was about to get into her first physical fight right there on the sidewalk in the middle of town.

"Don't mess with me, Beth. I know everyone in the club thinks the sun shines out of your ass, but not me. I'm on to you. You're nothing but a conniving bitch with daddy issues who wants to fuck as many men as you can under his nose."

Beth's jaw dropped as she staggered back a step. Melody might as well have slapped her across the face with the vitriol she spewed. The words burrowed under her skin like parasites.

Daddy issues. Conniving bitch.

Did others see her the same way? Would they think that she was using Saint to rebel? That she was playing games to mess with her father? *No.* That was absurd.

She'd never worried about such a thing before and

wouldn't start now. It was merely Melody grasping at straws and trying to stir up drama.

"That's not…" She shook her head. "I…" How did she respond to that?

Melody's lips curved in a victorious smile. "Wonder what will happen if Daddy finds out what his precious princess is really like. I think he'll be very interested to know you've been fucking Saint for the past month."

She wouldn't. Beth fought to keep her face neutral. For all she knew, Melody was fishing. No way could she know for sure Beth had been seeing Saint. Still, Beth's stomach soured.

"Yeah, that's what I thought," Melody said when Beth didn't respond. "Stay the fuck away from me, and if I see you anywhere near my man, I'll rip your fucking hair out." Mel turned and strutted up the sidewalk, tossing her hair over her shoulder as she went.

Beth sagged as she let out a long breath. That did not go as planned. Not that she'd formulated a plan. She tore out of her salon without a damn thought.

"Fuck," she whispered. Now she'd have to tell Saint and probably others in the club about Melody's connection to Demo. She'd be banned from coming around, and as much as Beth disliked Melody, she knew how important the club was to the other woman.

"Fuck, fuck, fuck."

She walked back to the soon-to-be salon with a pit in her stomach. How could she handle this in the best way? If she told her father and he confronted Melody, would Melody spill her suspicions about Beth and Saint? She probably wouldn't be receptive to talking to Saint either. *Maybe Gator could talk some sense into her.*

A bit of tension eased in her stomach. That could work. Gator could give it a day or two, then claim he saw Melody with Demo and had concerns about her safety. As soon as she got to the clubhouse, she'd run the idea by him.

After returning to the salon, she emptied the bucket of soapy water, took a final inventory of what still needed cleaning, and locked up.

Twenty minutes later, she parked at the clubhouse and pulled out her phone to text Saint.

Beth: At the clubhouse. U here?

Saint: 10 minutes out. Missed you today.

She grinned. They hadn't had much time to text throughout the day. Hearing that he'd thought about her made her giddy. She bounced in her driver's seat with a happy squeal. If only she could grab him and kiss the hell out of him when he arrived. Hopefully, they could sneak away for a few minutes alone in one of the bunk rooms.

But first, she had to tell him about Melody.

As she walked into the clubhouse, she glanced around. It was still early, so the place wasn't overly crowded. Rizz chatted up a woman Beth didn't recognize at the bar. Jigsaw and Rocket played a game of pool while their ol' ladies sat nearby, laughing and drinking margaritas. Others played darts, some danced, and one of the newer guys, Beth didn't know well, practically ate the face off some woman in a teeny-tiny minidress.

Just a typical chaotic night at the clubhouse, and she loved it.

She spotted Gator coming out of the kitchen and headed his way. As she reached him, she noticed her dad sitting in his usual spot at a table in the back of the room. What stopped Beth dead in her tracks was the sight of Melody sitting at the table with him. She wore a fake-fucking-expression of extreme sorrow, like someone who had terrible news to unload but knew it must be shared.

"Hey, p-cess," Gator said. He smacked a kiss on her cheek. "How's it hang… whoa, Beth, you okay? You just got really fucking pale."

"H-how long has Melody been here?" If she hopped right in her car and came to the clubhouse, she had about a twenty-minute headstart on Beth.

" 'Bout ten minutes. She got here same time I did. Why, what's up?"

An icy wave of dread washed over her. "I saw her earlier. She was making out with Demo."

"The fuck…"

Beth faced him. "Demo saw me. Looked straight at me and winked while his damn tongue was halfway down her throat."

He gripped his hair where it spilled out over his red bandana. "Fuck, this is not good."

"No, it's not. I was worried he knew she had a connection to the club, so when they went their separate ways, I ran after her to warn her."

Gator raised an eyebrow. "And?"

"And she accused me of trying to steal him. Said if I came near her again, she'd tell Copper I was sleeping with Saint." She lowered her voice. "How does she know?" Beth whispered.

Gator ran a hand over his face. "Jesus Christ."

"What do I do?" Beth grabbed his arm. "Is that why she's here? Is she telling him? Should I go over there?"

"Give me a second to fucking think, Beth," he snapped.

She winced. "Sorry."

"No. No." He pulled her into a one-armed hug. "I shouldn'ta barked at you. We gotta warn Saint. She could be running her big mouth right now. Oh, fuck."

"What?" She whipped around, spotting her father across the room. He wore a stony mask of fury so intense that even Melody looked apprehensive. Beth's heart sank to the floor. "She told him," she whispered.

"Beth, maybe you should go," Gator said in a tone more serious than she'd ever heard from the man. "You don't want to get into this here."

Copper rose, appearing to grow ten times his usual size. Fury radiated from the tense set of his shoulders to his narrowed eyes to his curled fists. Around him, people began to notice the angry giant whose presence grew by the second.

He scanned the room until his laser gaze found her.

Beth swallowed. "Too late," she whispered.

Copper only stomped three steps toward her, but his long stride ate up too much distance between them. Anxiety popped and fizzled across her skin, making her tremble. Not with fear. Copper wouldn't hurt her in a billion years, but worry for Saint had her heart pumping triple time. In no universe would this conversation end well, and Saint would take the brunt no matter what she said to her father now. In his mind, Saint had committed a grave sin. Hell, her dad probably saw her as a victim. She'd do everything in her power to prove that wasn't true.

"Wish me luck," she muttered as she took a step toward Copper, who stopped dead in his tracks, eyes fixed toward the door.

A sick feeling washed over her.

Gator grabbed her arm and yanked her back. "Fuck," he said. "Shit's about to get messy."

"Wha..." She followed Gator and her dad's gaze to the door where Saint stood, scanning the room.

Looking for her.

"No," she whispered. Her knees buckled, and if it weren't for Gator's hold on her, she'd have collapsed to the floor. "Not like this."

Gator stared down at her. "Oh, shit. This is real, isn't it, p-cess? You and him? It ain't just fuckin'."

"It's real."

After that, things seemed to happen in slow motion and hyper speed simultaneously. Copper's heavy boots hit the wooden floor with a shotgun crack, then he charged toward Saint.

Beth gently shoved Gator toward the kitchen. "Find my mom," she shouted before racing away.

Saint stood still, gaping at Copper, horror on his face. His gaze flicked to her, and something passed between them—understanding, acceptance, an unspoken vow that whatever happened, they were in this together. *I've got you,* his eyes said. *I'm not going anywhere.* Somehow, even with her world crashing down, she believed him. He relaxed his posture. He wasn't going to run or fight back. He'd take whatever came his way from his president. A ghost of a smile crossed his lips, gone so fast she could have imagined it. But she didn't. It was his way of reassuring her when it seemed hope was lost.

In her mind's eye, all she saw was Copper's fist slamming into Saint's face, and she nearly threw up. Pulse pounding in her ears, she skidded to a stop in the space between Copper and Saint. She threw her arms wide. "*Stop*!" she screamed.

Copper immediately halted.

So did everyone else.

Someone killed the music, and all chatter disappeared at once. Every eye in the place turned to the spectacle. Then the murmurs started. Whispered questions of "what the fuck" and "what's wrong with Copper?" came from all around.

"Everybody get the fuck out." Copper's booming command left no room for argument as it shook the clubhouse walls.

The entire place sprang into action, weaving around them to reach the exit as quickly as possible. Beth didn't see Melody anywhere. The bitch must have slipped out after dropping her bomb in Copper's lap.

Shell burst through the kitchen door, eyes wild, and Gator

hot on her heels. Within thirty seconds, the clubhouse had cleared out, leaving only five of them remaining.

"Gator!" Copper roared.

"Yep, on my way out, Prez." He hustled toward the door. Beth could hear him patting Saint on the shoulder as he left.

"Shell," Copper said in a quieter yet no less serious tone.

"Don't even think about it, big guy," she said, folding her arms across her chest. She didn't go to her husband but leaned against the bar, watching.

Any other time, Beth would have laughed. No one, no one told Copper what to do. Except for Shell. She had that man wrapped around her pinky finger for so long that he wouldn't know how to breathe without her. But tonight was no time for laughter.

"Beth, you need to move out of the way," Copper said. "This is club business."

She snorted. "The fuck it is."

Shell snickered as Copper's eyes widened. But Beth wasn't done.

"Baby, it's okay," Saint said. "I—"

"The fuck did you just call her?" Copper thundered.

For fuck's sake.

"Dad!" she snapped, bringing Copper's attention back to her. "I will drop my arms and move, but only if you promise you will not hurt him."

He narrowed his eyes. "He doesn't need your protection, Beth. He's a goddamn enforcer."

Two could play the narrowed eye game. "I'm aware of that. But I know him, and he won't fight back. He'll let you beat the shit out of him because of some misplaced sense of guilt. So until you promise me, your daughter, that you will not hurt him, I will *not* move."

Copper rolled his shoulders. He blew out a breath, shaking his head as he seemed to think. Beth risked a glance at her mom, who gave her a sad smile. She had to be as shocked as Copper, but she'd always had a more reasonable head on her shoulders.

"Fine," Copper said. "I won't fucking touch him."

A massive amount of pressure eased from her chest. "Thank you." She dropped her arms, then turned and walked to Saint. Copper growled like a damn lion ready to pounce. Beth took Saint's hand. Maybe the move was akin to throwing gasoline on a fire, but she had to make her father understand how important Saint was to her.

Saint stood steady. Only the tight grip on her hand betrayed his confidence.

"I trusted you," Copper said, jabbing a finger at Saint. "I sent you across the country to bring my daughter home because I trusted she'd be safe with you."

She opened her mouth to blast her father, but Saint gave her hand a quick squeeze. It was important to him to have this conversation with Copper.

"You did, Prez. And I kept her safe. She's always safe with me."

"But not from you."

She clenched her teeth to keep from shouting.

"I sent you to help her, and you took advantage of her. I trusted you to help her, and you fucked her."

"Dad! Jesus."

"Copper!" Shell snapped.

Beth's face heated to a million degrees.

"That isn't what happened," Saint said. How he managed to keep his cool while Copper spewed such hatred at him, Beth would never know. But she appreciated it more than she could say. Saint losing his mind right now and attacking back would make everything worse.

"There is one rule regarding Beth."

Okay, enough was enough. "Um… I'm right here, and I'm

a fucking adult who can make her own choices. I don't need you to give your club rules about me like I'm some unstable person who can't be trusted to make a good decision for myself."

Copper stared at her hard, probably thinking of the horrible choice she made in choosing Jason, but thankfully didn't say it.

"I've never done anything to harm this club, Copper," Saint said, solemn as could be. "And I never would. I do not believe my relationship with Beth causes any problem for the club."

Copper laughed, but it sounded ugly and mocking. "Relationship."

"Yes. I am deadly serious about Beth. About us. I won't walk away from her."

Beth stared up at him in awe as realization crashed over her like a wave she never saw coming. She loved him. *She loved him.* Not just wanted him, not just needed him, but loved this man who'd risk his entire life to be with her. Who'd stand in front of her father, knowing Copper held so much power over him, and say he wasn't leaving as if it were the simplest truth in the world. Her throat tightened, and she blinked back tears.

Copper scoffed. "You're what? Fucking twelve or thirteen years older than she is?"

Shell coughed.

Beth gawked at her father. "Seriously?" The man had sixteen years on his wife, whom he worshiped to this day. Who the hell was he to judge?

"You fucked your position in this club, Saint. No matter what happens right now, you've destroyed the trust of every fucking brother."

"No, he didn't," Beth said, exasperated beyond belief. "That's insane."

"It ends now. Maybe you can salvage something if you cut it off now."

"Dad!"

"I'm sorry, Copper. I can't do that. I won't do that."

Relief made her knees wobble.

"Then get the fuck out of my clubhouse. The club will vote because that's how we do it, but you're done. You fucking betrayed me."

And there it was.

She wanted to scream. To beg her father to change his mind, but the stern set of his jaw and the flat look in his eyes told her it'd be a waste of breath. Copper had made up his mind.

"I'll go too," Beth whispered. "If you make him leave, I'm going with him."

An expression of pain she'd never seen before crossed Copper's face. "I wish you wouldn't," he whispered in a resigned voice because he knew.

She'd made up her mind.

Beth looked to her mother, who also had tears rolling down her cheeks. Shell nodded and mouthed, *I love you*. At least they had the support of one of her parents.

Still holding her hand, Saint turned, and together they walked out of the clubhouse. The pain was excruciating. It felt like a death. She'd have to grieve the part of her life she'd just gotten back and realized how much she loved.

As soon as the door slammed shut behind them, closing them off to their entire world, Beth's knees crumbled. If Saint hadn't caught her, pulling her against his chest, she'd have collapsed on the concrete.

"We'll be okay, Beth," he whispered as she buried her face against his chest and wept. "I fucking promise we'll find a way to make it okay."

Chapter Twenty-Two

Beth didn't say much on the ride to his house. Saint tucked her into her car's passenger seat and texted Gator to pick up his motorcycle later. Gator agreed to deliver it to the house in a few hours, with Rizz's help. Beth was too distraught to ride home on the back of his bike safely.

He held her chilled hand and didn't try to make conversation as she stared out the window, lost in thought. She needed this time to absorb everything that happened tonight.

Copper's face, when Saint strode into the clubhouse, would stay with him for a long time. Shock, betrayal, and hatred. A man he'd respected and admired since the first time they met stared at Saint as though he were no better than a deranged serial killer.

That fucking hurt.

But it had to be agony for Beth.

How had Copper found out? There's no way Beth told him. At the very least, she'd have mentioned it so they could run through the pros and cons. Plus, she'd seemed as stunned as Saint by the course of events. He refused to believe Gator spilled the beans. As mouthy and unpredictable as that crazy man was, he'd never out Saint that way. *So who?* Did someone see them together? It didn't seem possible. They were beyond careful, spending all their time behind closed doors.

He sighed. It was a question for later. Now he had to figure out how to comfort Beth.

When they arrived at his house, she broke contact and left the car without a word. He followed up to his front door, then inside, all without talking.

"I'm going to take a shower," she said, finally breaking her silence. She spoke in a flat, lifeless tone and carried herself as though beaten down and exhausted. After her announcement, she walked straight into the primary bathroom.

Ten minutes. He'd give her ten minutes before barging in and demanding she tell him what was happening in her head.

As he listened to the shower turn on, he went to his bar cart and poured himself a healthy shot of tequila. After downing it, he poured another, this time a double. They both needed something to dull the edges of pain and shock.

After another minute, his phone chimed with a text from Gator.

Gator: It was Melody.

Christ, Melody was the one to tell Copper. Of course, she fucking ratted them out.

But why? What the fuck did she gain by blowing up so many lives?

What a shit show.

He pinched the bridge of his nose and breathed in and out, trying to calm the raging storm in his bloodstream. The first order of business was to console Beth. They could worry about Melody's motivation and how to fix this catastrophe later. He set his phone on the back of the couch and stripped his clothes off right there in the den, leaving a pile for later. Then he grabbed the glass of tequila and walked naked toward his en suite bathroom.

Beth had shut the door, which she didn't usually do. More often than not, they showered together, but even when they cleaned up separately, she left the door open. He loved watching while she was in his shower. Light and steam came from the bottom of the door, while the sound of rushing water called to him. He reached out and twisted the doorknob. It turned with ease. *At least she hadn't locked him out.*

"Thank fuck." He'd tear it off the hinges if he needed to, but it wasn't his preference.

Warm steam engulfed him as he entered the space. He fanned it away with a few swipes of his hand. As the room cleared, the sight before him cracked his heart in two. Beth stood in the center of the shower, her back to the spray and her face buried in her hands. Her shoulders shook with the force of her sobs.

Fuck no. This was unacceptable.

Saint opened the walk-in shower door and stepped into the warm stall with Beth. She didn't so much as glance up when he moved in front of her, showing how lost she was in the sorrow.

Fuck, he hoped he never had to hear the gut-wrenching sound of her crying again.

"Baby…" he said, in a low tone so as not to startle her.

She dropped her hands and peered up at him with her gorgeous, red-rimmed eyes filled with gallons of sadness and pain.

He couldn't keep from touching her a second longer. He set his drink on the built-in ledge, then wrapped his arms around her and cradled her against him as she wept. Her body jerked every few seconds as her breath hitched from the force of her sobs.

"I'm so sorry," she eventually whispered, voice agonized.

What? She was *sorry?*

"Christ, Beth, what the fuck are you apologizing for?" he asked as he gently moved her a step back. He smoothed wet strands of hair off her forehead and handed her the glass of tequila. "Drink this."

She swallowed half in one gulp, eyes locked with his. His dick stirred when her lips hit the glass, then thickened as her throat swallowed the liquid. "Your turn." She handed him the glass.

"I already had some. That's for you."

"Please," she said, still offering it to him. Her eyes darkened with need. "I want to taste it on you."

His gut clenched, and his cock went from semi to rock-hard. An army of soldiers couldn't keep him from fulfilling that request. He brought the glass to his lips and poured the rest of the tequila down his throat, staring at her as he swallowed. Then he set the empty glass back on the shelf next to his shampoo.

Beth raised on her tiptoes, and he grabbed the back of her head, pressing his mouth to hers. He immediately plunged his tongue inside, giving her a taste of the tequila on him and tasting it on her as well.

She moaned and hooked her leg around his thigh, rocking her pelvis into his. He kissed her until his lips felt bruised and his head dizzy from the heat and lack of oxygen.

As soon as their lips separated, she spoke again, "I'm sorry," she whispered. "I'm so fucking sorry."

Every word was a goddamn dagger to his chest.

He kissed her again. First, her lips, then each cheek, her eyelids, and back to her addicting mouth. "Stop," he whispered against her lips. "Do not fucking apologize to me, Beth. For fuck's sake, I should be apologizing to you for fucking up your family."

She dropped her head to his chest as she shook it back and forth, mumbling something he couldn't make out.

"What's that, baby?" he asked as he dug his thumbs into the tense muscles in her neck.

"I don't think I'm worth it."

He stilled as fury crawled across his skin. Not at her, *ever*, but at every fucking person and circumstance that made her believe something so goddamn wrong. "*What*?"

"You've lost so much tonight. As angry as Copper is, tomorrow I'll still have my family. But you're losing everything, Saint. *Everything*. I can't possibly be worth that. If you walk away now, you can still have the club. I'm just one person. I'm not worth losing all of your brothers."

He cupped the back of her head as he stared down at her. "I want you to listen to every fucking word out of my mouth, Beth. Listen and hear it. The entire world could crumble to dust, and as long as you're still here, I'll be a happy man. You are worth every goddamn thing. There is nothing I would not do, nothing I would not leave behind for you."

She blinked. "For *us*."

Hell yes. That's what he wanted. Having a passel of siblings meant he'd never be alone in life, but having a front row seat to Makenna falling in love made him realize he'd been missing something even more important. A person who was his. Just his.

"That's fucking right. I love you, Beth. Nothing that happened tonight or will happen tomorrow changes that. You are who I want."

Her eyes widened, and for the first time tonight, she smiled. It lit her green eyes until they glowed. "I love you too."

"Fuck." He cupped her face and kissed her again, hard, but briefly.

"What do we do now?" She ran her hands over his back down to his ass. "What do we do, Saint?"

"We show 'em. We show them it's real. We're not leaving, we're not hiding. We show them this is as real as any of their relationships. I've found my ol' lady, and you've found your ol' man. Simple as that."

A mild lie, of course, but they both knew getting the club on board wouldn't be simple and were willing to pretend for a while.

He slid his hands down to her ass, kneading the globes as she pressed into him. The water warmed her slick skin. He could do nothing more than touch her like this for the rest of the night and be in heaven.

"Okay, we show them. I guess that's our only move right now. I'm not ready to talk to my dad yet. Maybe in a few days, after we've had time for our emotions to simmer."

"Hmm, a few days with you all to myself?" He nuzzled her neck, licking the drops of water that cascaded across her skin. "I can try to suffer through that, I suppose."

She chuckled and playfully shoved his hip. It wasn't her usual happy laugh, but tonight he'd take what he could get. Any emotion other than sadness counted as a win right now.

Beth ran her hands up his chest, stopping to flick his nipples, sending a zing straight to his cock. "I don't want to talk or think about this for the rest of the night. I just want to think about you and me and how good your cock feels inside me."

He still had questions, mainly why the fuck Melody chose tonight to ruin their lives. Waiting until the morning to find out wouldn't change anything. "Sounds like a perfect-fucking-plan to me. But first..." He grabbed the expensive shampoo she kept in his shower and squeezed a dollop of the citrus-scented gel into his hand. "Turn around."

Beth complied, and he set about washing her hair, taking

much longer than was necessary to massage her head. She rested against him, groaning with pleasure as he kneaded her scalp.

They could have stayed in that shower all night, and he wouldn't have known. Time didn't matter, nor did the outside world. They spent long minutes soaping each other, touching until they were both trembling on the brink of climax, then backing off only to start again.

"No more." Beth gasped as he had her back plastered to his front, two fingers buried in her pussy, and a hand on her tit. "I can't take it anymore. If you don't get your dick in me in the next thirty seconds, I'm going to hurt you."

He chuckled against her neck where he'd sucked a purple brand of ownership. Cat was out of the bag now. Any motherfucker interested in her could see that a man already had a claim to her.

"On the bed," he whispered.

Beth groaned. "It's too far away. "

"Promise I'll make the wait worth it."

She groaned again as he reached beyond her and shut off the cooling water. Then he kissed her neck, jaw, and cheek. "Don't move," he said before catching her earlobe between his teeth.

"Hurry."

Saint left the shower to grab a fluffy towel from the rack. When he stepped back in, he wrapped Beth in it, drying her.

She gazed at him with lust-filled eyes and so much trust the entire time. The way she let him maneuver her, wash her, dry her, and touch her showed her trust, and that fucking slayed him.

"I love you," she whispered as he swiped the towel down her hair, squeezing to wring the strands dry.

"I love you too, baby." He did a quick, dirty dry-off with the damp towel, then hung it back on the rack. "After you," he said, gesturing toward the open door to the bedroom.

Beth grinned and then walked ahead of him. "A free towel dry, and impeccable manners. Such a gentleman."

He snorted. Nothing gentlemanly about the way he stared at her round ass while she walked. "On your stomach."

Beth stopped at the foot of the bed and peered over her shoulder at him with a hungry gaze. "Yes, sir." She winked and crawled up onto the bed, grabbing a pillow as she lay herself down, propped on her elbows. Her spine sloped to a dip at her lower back, then came the tempting swell of her ass. The time spent touching and teasing in the shower had him hard, but when combined with this visual, his cock leaked precum like a sieve.

He crawled up onto the bed and over Beth's prone form. When he reached her ass, he nipped the firm globe, drawing a yip and a laugh from her. Then he kissed his way up her spine, paying attention to each vertebra.

"Saint." She breathed heavily as he reached her neck and latched on with strong suction. "Please don't make me wait any longer."

He rocked back, grabbing her hips along the way and pulling her onto all fours. Once he maneuvered himself between her spread legs, she turned her head, watching him with heavy-lidded, glassy eyes.

"So pretty," he said, running a hand up her spine.

"So horny."

He laughed. "I caught that."

"So do something."

"How about this?" He gripped his dick, placing it at her soaked opening, then thrust forward, not stopping until he bottomed out.

"Yesss." Beth hissed. Her head dropped down as though too heavy to hold up. "I love it this way," she whispered. "So deep."

He gripped her hips as he pumped in and out of her. As always, the pleasure took his breath away and made him see stars, but tonight he needed more than release. He needed closeness. He needed even more connection than being inside her. He covered her body with his, wrapping an arm around her chest and kissing everywhere he could reach. Across her shoulders, her neck, her cheek.

Beth whimpered and pushed back on him every time his hips punched forward. Her breasts swayed as he fucked her with increasing force.

Once he had a solid hold on her, he reared back onto his knees, taking Beth with him. She gasped as the change of position drove him even deeper. "Oh God," she said. He gripped the arm holding her up and wrapped her other arm around his neck. They moved as one, no longer furiously slamming together but rolling their hips.

She turned her head, offering her mouth, which he gladly took. Their lips met in a sloppy, unrefined kiss, more a desperate joining. Saint kept one hand banded across her chest, cupping her breast so he could play with her nipple. He used his other hand to reach for her clit, stroking with purpose.

Beth bucked in his arms, crying out into his mouth. Her pussy clamped down, milking him with strong pulses. He kissed her harder, worked her clit faster, and pinched her nipple until she tore her mouth away from his and let out a high-pitched moan as she came. Her body jerked and spasmed against him, clenching his dick in a rhythmic pattern. Whenever he saw or felt her come, he was helpless to last another second himself. He pressed his dick deep inside her and sucked on her neck as he filled her with his cum.

His body quivered, out of his control for long seconds, until he blinked and found Beth's head resting back on his shoulder as she watched him with sleepy eyes.

He cupped her chin and kissed her. The angle was still awkward, but who gave a fuck? All he wanted was more. He kissed her once, then again. "I love you," he said before kissing her again. "I love you." Another kiss. "I fucking love you." One more kiss. "You understand what that means?"

Dazed, she nodded. "It means I'm never getting away from you, and that makes me the luckiest woman in the world."

He kissed her once more for good measure, and this time it turned into a languid makeout session and eventually another round of sex that left them sated, exhausted, and happy.

Tomorrow, the world would come crashing back.

But tonight, they had this.

Chapter Twenty-Three

Shell stared at her husband through the kitchen window with her heart in her throat. She'd woken at three, alone in bed, and knew exactly where she'd find him. Shell couldn't remember a time she wasn't head over heels in love with the man, but that didn't mean she was blind to his flaws. Copper was far from perfect and usually the first to admit it.

He'd fucked up tonight, and if she knew him, which she did better than anyone on the planet, she knew he was out there berating himself worse than anyone else could. Her chest ached as it did any time they had strife in their family.

Copper loved his family more than any man she knew. He'd slice his veins and spill his blood if he thought it would increase their happiness even a fraction of a percent. He was protective as hell of all of them, but Beth had always brought out the extra fierce defender in him.

Shell knew why, and she loved him for it, even if he did take it too far as he did tonight.

Many years ago, Copper had a brother, Rusty. Shell shuddered. It had been a long time since she'd allowed herself to think about Rusty. The memories were too painful, too traumatizing to do anything but shove them to the back of her mind. Rusty was Beth's biological father. He'd raped Shell, resulting in the pregnancy.

For years, she hid the secret, petrified of what it would do to Copper and how it would make him see her. She'd loved Copper with every fiber of her being and feared she'd lose even his friendship if he learned about what Rusty had done. When the truth finally came to light, Shell and Beth's lives took a dramatic turn, but Copper never wavered in his love for them. He adopted Beth after marrying Shell, and they'd been family ever since.

But learning what happened changed something in Copper. How could it not? He'd always been extra protective of Beth as though feeling he owed it to her, as though trying to make up for the circumstances that brought her into this world. Circumstances he'd had no control over. His crazy rule about no one in the club being allowed near her came from a deep-seated fear of history somehow repeating itself. Copper might not have voiced it, but his greatest fear was someone violating Beth the way they had Shell.

But Beth was a grown woman who'd chosen a man for herself. A really great man Shell respected. Copper did too. He was too deep in his shock and anger to admit it now, but he loved Saint. He trusted Saint and counted on him to help the club run smoothly.

Shell grabbed a bottle of whiskey and poured too much into a glass, but she intended to share it with her husband. Then she opened the French doors and stepped outside onto their back deck.

Copper sat on the steps leading down their yard, staring at the scenery they'd spent so many hours admiring while wrapped in each other's arms. He had his elbows propped on his knees and his head in his hands.

Barefoot, Shell padded over to him. She kneeled behind him, rested her chin on his broad shoulder, and draped her arms around him, offering the whiskey.

Copper lifted his head and took the glass. After two long gulps, he handed it back. Shell sipped, letting the burn of Copper's favorite whiskey warm her throat.

"How badly did I fuck up tonight?" he croaked in a ragged voice.

Her lips twitched. Shell kissed his shoulder, then set her chin back on it. "Pretty badly. You were quite the asshole."

He grunted. "Has there ever been a time when I was an asshole that you didn't call me out on it?"

"Hmm…" Shell pretended to think. "Probably not. I love you too much to let you fuck things up by acting like a jerk."

She felt his heavy sigh deep in her heart.

"It's Beth…"

"It is. But she's an adult, Cop. You can't control who she dates. You can't control any of her choices anymore."

"The last guy hurt her."

She nodded, rubbing her chin along his shoulder. "He did. And he paid the price for that. Saint made sure of it. And Beth is home, safe and sound. She's strong and independent, and she grew from that awful situation. The man she picked now is a damn good one who'd die before hurting her."

"We know what can happen, Shell. We've seen and experienced so much. She can be hurt so badly…"

God, how she loved the way this man loved his family. "She can also be happy. She can also have what we have, Copper. Don't you want that for her?"

"Why does it have to be with one of my guys?" he grumbled.

Shell smiled. "To be honest, I'm surprised this is the first time she's broken that rule of yours."

He groaned. "Don't put that idea in my head."

She kissed the curve of his ear. "What happened to me is not going to happen to her," she whispered. Her eyes watered, and she blinked to keep from crying. "Her last relationship is not your fault. What happened to me so many years ago is not your fault."

"I know," he rasped, emotion clogging his throat. "The age she's at is bringing that time back for me. She's around the age you were when I found out about—"

"I know, love." She didn't want to hear him say Rusty's name.

He took the glass, swallowed the rest of the whiskey, then set the glass on the deck. "Come around," he said, tugging her hand. "I want to hold you."

Shell maneuvered around until she was in his lap, straddling him. His thick arms closed around her, and he buried his head against her chest. She wrapped her arms and legs around him in kind, holding him as close as possible. She'd worn nothing but a thin, low-cut tank top to sleep, and his breath and beard tickled her cleavage.

"Give yourself some time to think and process, then you need to do some serious damage control."

He grunted. "I know."

"If you want, I'll go with you when you talk to them." She stroked the back of his hair while he began to place light kisses across the top of her chest. Her body reacted immediately as it always did when her husband touched her, even after so many years together. "Copper…" She shivered when he sucked on her skin.

"I always want you with me, baby. But I'm definitely going to need you for this one, right next to me, ready to slap my mouth when I say something stupid."

She grasped the sides of his face and pulled his head back so she could see the green eyes he shared with Beth. "I look forward to the task."

Copper squeezed her side, making her squirm and giggle. "Brat."

That had her laughing harder.

He grew serious again. "Don't ever leave me, Shell. I'd be so fucking lost."

Her grin fell. "I hope that's never something you worry about, not for one millisecond of your whole life. The devil himself couldn't drag me away from you. You hear me?"

"I hear you, baby. I hear you, and I love you."

"I love you too, Copper."

She kissed him with a heart that felt pounds lighter than it had earlier in the night.

Everything would work out, and her family would be back on track in no time.

Chapter Twenty-Four

"Hold up," Saint said as he rolled to a stop in front of Hell's Hounds Clubhouse. "I'll come around."

Beth pressed her lips together to keep from grinning too widely. She didn't often ride in Saint's repo truck. The Ford F550 was a monster of a vehicle. A workhorse that could do everything short of towing a semi-truck. The cab was so high off the ground that she felt like she needed to pole vault to get into it. That or find herself a sexy man to boost her in and out of the truck.

Saint strode around the driver's side with sure, efficient steps. When he reached her door, he opened it, reached in for her waist, and plucked her from the truck as if she weighed no more than a doll.

Well, look at that, a sexy man to help her out. Just as ordered.

"Thank you," she said as her feet hit the ground. She didn't move away. Instead, she wrapped her arms around Saint's waist and breathed him in, storing his scent for later when she needed a hit.

"I feel like shit for bailing on you today," he said, rubbing a hand over his scruff. Usually, he shaved every morning, but today she'd convinced him to hold off. His stubble felt incredible, scraping across her skin, and she had plans that included that very sensation later.

"How many times do I have to tell you, you're not bailing on me?" She rolled her eyes. "You'd be stupid to turn down this job."

Saint had planned to join her at the salon for what she hoped would be the final day of cleaning. Tomorrow, the first delivery of equipment will arrive, so she has no choice but to finish preparations today.

A last-minute, high-paying repo job came through early this morning. Saint would be a fool to turn down the money for what seemed like a reasonably easy job. Some big-shot tech guy drove his mistress to Dollywood for a scandalous weekend rendezvous. It turned out the guy had a mountain of gambling debt that caused him to default on multiple vehicle loans. While he and his *girlfriend* were enjoying Dollywood, Saint would be scooping up his Lamborghini for a pretty penny.

Money and a way to fuck with a cheater. *Who could resist?* Beth's only frustration was not being able to ride along on this task. She'd love to see the asshole's face when he realized his precious seven-hundred-thousand-dollar Lambo Revuelto had disappeared from the parking lot while he was screwing someone who wasn't his wife of twenty years.

"Besides, Screw will be here in a few hours to help."

He frowned, unconvinced.

"Lee, I'll be fine. Go have fun in Pigeon Forge. Maybe ride some rollercoasters while you're there. Or catch a country music show." She smirked.

He grunted. "Do I seem like the banjo music type?"

That had her giggling. She slid her hands down to his ass. "No. You're all rock and roll, baby," she said before squeezing his firm cheeks.

"Smartass," he replied with a growl, attacking her neck

with kisses.

Beth laughed. Two days ago, she'd been convinced her world was ending. But the sun rose as usual, and the mountains surrounding them looked as beautiful as ever. Her heart carried a heaviness she didn't know how to name, but Saint promised her repeatedly that they would get past this monumental hurdle with her father. Because she trusted Saint with everything in her, she tried to push aside the worry and despondency in favor of hope.

She'd texted back and forth with her mom a few times over the last couple of days, and they had Shell's full support. Still, both thought it best to let Copper have some time to process and pull his head out of his ass before trying to have a productive conversation with the bullheaded MC president.

"All right." Saint straightened. "Get inside before I fuck you against my truck in the middle of Main Street."

Now there was an idea. Maybe not in the center of town, but against his big work truck had some potential.

"Stop it," he said with a growl, making her burst out laughing. "Such a troublemaker."

"I didn't say anything." She blinked at him innocently.

"Your eyes are begging me to fuck you." He adjusted his crotch. "So much fucking trouble. Now go." He nudged her toward the building, slapping her ass as she walked by.

Beth yelped then wiggled her butt for good measure, smiling at Saint's groan.

As she reached the door, he called out. "Hold up," then grabbed her hand and yanked her back to him. "You forgot something." It was all the warning she got before he tipped her backwards and kissed the ever-loving hell out of her. By the time he righted her, her head was spinning, her pulse raced beneath her skin, and she throbbed between her legs.

"Um…" She staggered back when he released her, pressing a hand to her pounding chest. "Wow. Okay." Her back hit the glass door. "That was mean."

Saint laughed. "See you later, baby," he said with a perky wave and a lascivious wink.

"Yeah. Bye." Her brain hadn't come back online yet. It was still stuck in that hot-as-hell kiss.

How the hell was she supposed to concentrate on anything now that he'd fried her brain?

Saint watched from his truck until she was safely behind the closed door. She waved, but he pointed to the door handle with a frown and mouthed, *Lock it.*

Rolling her eyes, she did as he demanded. Knowing him, he'd stress about her all day if she didn't turn the lock in front of him. They'd had this discussion at least a dozen times so far. Once the shop opened, there were times, many times, she'd be in there alone during the day, and the door would be unlocked. How the hell did he expect her customers to come and go if she kept the place boarded up?

He informed her that cameras and a top-of-the-line alarm system would be installed as soon as the equipment arrived. Part of her wanted to argue that she wouldn't need such an elaborate system, but she'd learned over the years that the MC went overboard with security. She'd never win the argument, so she decided to pick her battles. There were sure to be others who needed her attention more.

Once the door was locked, Saint winked from his truck. She blew him a kiss, waved, and then he drove off. Alone with a mountain of cleaning, Beth popped in her ear buds, blasted her favorite playlist, and got to work.

Several hours later, she set her mop aside. The whole place smelled lemony-fresh and gleamed as though brand new.

Over the past few days, she'd cleaned and sanitized every nook and cranny. The space looked wonderful and ready for the tubs to be installed. Her knees ached and her back twinged from kneeling and crouching half the morning, but the result was worth it. When equipment began arriving, it would slot perfectly into the pristine building.

She had about twenty minutes until Screw showed up, and she deserved an iced coffee for all her hard work. Lucky for her, a new café opened a few months ago, two shops over. She'd yet to try it but had heard great things from Lindsey.

"Fuck, this is heavy," she said with a groan as she lifted the bucket full of filthy mop water. She hefted it toward the back door, muscles straining, but somehow managed not to spill any dirty water on her freshly scrubbed floors. She planned to dump the bucket in the drain out in the alley behind the salon as she'd done several times already.

Using her ass to operate the push bar, Beth shoved the heavy door open. Stifling hot air accosted her sweaty skin the second she stepped outside. "Ugh, I must smell fantastic," she muttered as she flipped the door's kickstand down. It'd be a miracle if the café let her in like this. She'd probably drive away half their business with her sweaty clothes and stench.

After emptying the bucket down the storm drain, she set it beside the door to dry in the sun. As she turned back to reenter her shop, she froze.

Two feet stuck out from behind a large blue dumpster about twenty-five feet away.

Her pulse skipped once.

Then again.

They were small feet with pink, polished toes, encased in feminine sandals that looked way too expensive for someone who might be unhoused and searching for a shaded place to rest. A ripple of unease slid down her spine. Saint would lose his shit if he knew what she was about to do, but she couldn't leave someone out there when it was almost a hundred degrees. What if they'd already passed out from heat stroke?

"Hello?" she called as she cautiously approached the

dumpster.

One foot twitched.

"Are you okay?"

A thin, pain-filled whine answered her.

The hair on the back of her neck stood on end. Her instincts whispered something's wrong, and her stomach clenched tight. She slowed her steps, every sense sharpening as she approached.

"I just want to check on you," she announced, forcing her voice to stay light even as her heart began to thud harder. "Would you like some water?"

She reached the end of the dumpster and released a breath she didn't realize she'd been holding before peering around.

"Oh my God, Melody."

Beth rushed forward and dropped into a crouch beside the woman whose curls gave her away every time. The sight of her hit Beth like a punch to the chest.

Someone had beaten Melody until her face was nearly unrecognizable. Her eyes were swollen almost shut, her cheeks grotesquely puffy, and her lips split and crusted with blood. A dark stream ran from her nose down her chin to her white T-shirt, staining it red. Some had even splattered onto her denim shorts.

Beth's hands trembled. "Jesus, what happened?" Panic surged, fast and sharp. "I'm calling for help."

She reached for her pocket.

Nothing.

"Fuck. My phone's inside." Her breath came quicker now, uneven and wheezy. "Okay. Okay." She swallowed hard. "Let me help you. We should get you out of the heat, then I can call for an ambulance. Can you stand?"

Melody tried to speak, but the sound barely made it past her lips. She clutched her ribs, breathing in shallow, broken breaths.

"What?" Beth leaned down until her ear hovered just above Melody's mouth. "Say it again."

"You… were… right…"

Beth's blood turned to ice. The only thing she could be referring to was the warning about Demo.

"Demo did this to you?" The words tasted rancid on her tongue. *Was he still in the area?* Fear spiked, icy and sharp. "We have to go. You need EMS, and I have to call S… my dad." This involved the club, and as much as it gutted her, calling Saint wouldn't get her to the MC right now. She'd call him directly after her father. And if they both showed up, well, she'd cross that bridge when she came to it. Now she needed to make sure Melody wouldn't die.

"I'm sorry," she said shakily, slipping an arm behind Melody's back. "This is going to hurt. On three. One…"

Melody pushed a weak hand against Beth's shoulder. "No."

"What?" Beth leaned in again, confusion tangling with fear. "We can't stay here."

"S-sorry."

Beth shook her head. "Shh, we'll deal with that later. Right now, we need to move."

Melody shook her head again, making Beth sigh in exasperation.

"Mel, we need to move."

She said something.

"What? Red?" She leaned in. "Is that what you said?"

"R-run."

The word hit her like a gunshot.

"Run?" Beth's stomach dropped. "Fuck, is he here? Melody, is he still around? We need to move fast."

Melody shook her head but whispered it again with what seemed to be her last speck of strength. *"Run."*

"I can't leave you here," Beth whisper-yelled. "You're hurt.

I—"

Pain exploded across her scalp.

A rough hand tangled in her hair, wrenching her head back. Beth cried out, instinctively clawing at him as she was yanked away from Melody and hauled to her feet.

"Get the fuck off me." Tears burned her eyes as her scalp screamed.

A male laugh rang out above her.

Her heart slammed against her ribs. She knew that voice. Panic flooded her system, fast and blinding in its strength. Her legs trembled, and her chest heaved as she struggled to think. The world narrowed, sounds muffled by the rush of blood in her ears.

Stay calm. Breathe. Don't panic.

The hand left her hair, but relief only lasted two seconds. Demo twisted her arm behind her back and jerked it upward. White-hot pain shot through her shoulder, forcing her onto her toes.

"You're not exactly in the position to make demands, princess."

If she never heard that fucking nickname again, it'd be too damn soon.

"What the fuck do you want?" She gasped as he jerked her, sending another burst of pain screeching across her shoulder.

"Just a little chat."

"Yeah? Sounds good. How about we head to our clubhouse? We can chat there all you want."

He laughed. "Shit, princess, you're funny. I think I like you. That's too bad."

A large white van backed into the alleyway.

Fear slammed into her, cold and absolute.

Don't get in the car.

Don't ever let them get you in the car.

That was 'How Not to Die 101.'

"But I think we'll have a better time at my place."

"Fuck no." She fought him with everything she had, kicking, thrashing, and screaming, pain be dammed. Her heel connected with something solid, and he cursed, loosening his grip just enough.

She broke free and managed two frantic steps before he tackled her from behind, sending her crashing to the ground.

Gravel tore into her palms and knees. She barely felt it over the adrenaline surging through her veins.

"That was fucking stupid," he snarled. His hot breath wafted across her face, stale and acrid. "I don't think I like you anymore."

The second his heavy weight moved off her, Beth pushed herself up, breath ragged and vision swimming. She would not stop. She would not—

His palm cracked across her face.

Stars burst behind her eyes. Her ears rang as her head snapped to the side.

A thick arm locked around her throat.

"No!" She croaked as her air supply disappeared in a brutal burst of pain. She attacked him, scratching mindlessly and kicking with weak jerks, but her strength drained fast.

Black crept in at the edges of her vision.

Saint was going to freak out.

If only she could have told him she loved him one more time.

As shadows engulfed her, she conjured the image of Saint's face to keep her company in the darkness.

Chapter Twenty-Five

High-paying jobs like today's almost made Saint feel guilty for accepting the hefty payout.

Almost.

Then he remembered countless jobs he'd completed for peanuts and how he'd been spat on, screamed at, chased by dogs, and once had to flee an axe-wielding grandma in her bathrobe and curlers. For every clean recovery he completed, he suffered through a half dozen miserable ones, so he'd take the fat paycheck and sleep well tonight.

Once he dropped the Lambo at the impound lot, he headed straight home to file the recovery report. If he'd remembered to bring his laptop, he could have finished the report at Beth's salon, but he'd been too distracted by her ass in the tiny denim shorts she loved to remember a damn thing.

His house already bore many signs of Beth's influence on his life. Her favorite blanket, one she'd received as a Christmas gift a few years ago, sat folded on the back of the couch because she consistently complained that he kept his house colder than the refrigerator. Her toothbrush and skincare products littered his bathroom counter, and the mug she loved sat in his sink, ready to be cleaned and used for tomorrow's morning coffee.

Fuck, he was turning into a goddamn sap because he loved seeing the signs of Beth all over his space.

Hopefully, one day soon, they would officially call it their space.

He shot off a quick text to Beth, letting her know he'd be back at the salon after he finished this report. She didn't respond, but he didn't expect her to. By now, she probably had her gloved hands elbow deep in a bucket of sudsy water.

Fifteen minutes later, he'd filed the report. By morning, there'd be a fresh four thousand dollars in his account. Not bad for a few hours of work. Tomorrow, he had three repo jobs lined up, but the rest of the day, he planned to spend helping Beth and Screw with whatever they needed. Beth had spoken to Screw multiple times since the incident with Copper at the clubhouse, but Saint had not. No one would ever describe Screw as judgmental about relationships. Hell, the guy had been in a throuple for more than a decade, but that didn't mean he wasn't on Copper's side when it came to Beth's relationships.

She'd assured him they had nothing to worry about when it came to Screw, Gumby, or Jazz, but Saint wouldn't be able to relax until he verified for himself.

His phone rang as he shut his laptop.

Screw. Guess he was about to find out how the man felt.

"Hey, bro… hey, man." Did he still have the right to call Screw brother? It hurt even more than he'd thought to think he lost that.

"Hey…"

Shit. Screw's voice sounded off, which didn't bode well for him.

He grabbed his bike keys and started for the door. "What's up?"

"Is Beth with you?"

Saint froze. His blood went cold, then hot, then cold again. "What do you mean? I dropped her off at the salon hours ago. She's been cleaning there all morning."

"Brother, don't lose your shit, but she isn't here. And her phone is."

"Okay…" He forced the panic away. He needed logic now, not a fucking freak out. "The coffee shop. She said she wanted to try that café a few stores over." As he talked, he ran out to his bike.

"Checked there. They haven't seen her. Saint, there's more." Screw's voice went full-on worried.

"What the fuck do you mean, there's more?"

"The door to the back alley was open. I checked around and…"

Saint gripped the phone so hard it should have shattered. "And the fuck what?"

"There's some blood on the ground. It's fresh."

"Oh fuck." He doubled over, gut clenching so hard he nearly vomited. "Oh, fucking fuck. It's gotta be Demo. Fuck, Screw, did he fucking take Beth?"

"I don't know, brother, but we'll find out."

"I'm on my way."

"No. Go to the clubhouse. There's nothing for you to do here. A few of the stores have cameras in the back alley. I'm going to see if there's footage. I'll call you as soon as I find anything."

Saint's hands shook with a combination of rage and fear. Demo would die today. Saint had killed before and made peace with it.

Self-defense—justified.

This would be different.

This would be fucking pleasure.

He'd watch the light drain from Demo's eyes and enjoy every damn second.

"Saint!" Screw snapped. "Keep your shit tight. Okay? Beth needs you."

He rolled his shoulders, trying to dislodge the murderous desires, but they remained. At least he was able to answer Screw. "I'm good. Just find some fucking useful footage."

"Will do."

Screw disconnected, and Saint mounted his bike. He peeled out of the driveway and shot down the road, engine roaring and tires squealing. In record time, he haphazardly parked in front of the clubhouse and rushed for the entrance. Before he got off the bike, Screw called.

"You were right. It was Demo," he rushed to say before Saint had the opportunity to speak. "He beat the fuck out of Melody and left her lying in the alley. Beth found her and tried to help. Demo showed up and tossed them both in the back of a van. I got the plate number. Maverick is running it now. I'm on my way to the clubhouse." He hung up before Saint responded, but that was fine. He'd heard everything and didn't have time for chitchat.

Blood boiling, he sprinted toward the clubhouse.

Saint didn't bother knocking, even though he no longer belonged.

The clubhouse door swung open hard enough to rattle the frame, and every head inside snapped toward him. All conversations died mid-sentence. Chairs scraped across the floor. Hands stilled on beers and cue sticks, and a few went to their knives on belts or guns in holsters.

Copper stood near the bar, broad shoulders rigid beneath his cut. His green eyes went flinty the second he saw who dared to enter in such a dramatic way.

Saint walked straight to Copper.

No cut. No patch. Just denim, boots, and the weight of everything he'd lost sitting heavy in his chest.

"You have some fucking nerve," Copper said, his voice

calm in the way that meant violence was already decided.

Saint stopped an arm's length away. He lifted his chin and stared his president in the eye. "Beth's gone," he croaked, voice breaking.

The room went silent as a graveyard at midnight.

Copper's jaw flexed. "What did you say?"

"She's missing." Saint didn't look away. Didn't soften the blow. "She was at the salon while I had a repo job. Screw went to meet her. Her phone was there, but she was not. There's some blood in the alley out back and tire tracks." His voice wavered. "She... she didn't walk away on her own."

A ripple went through the room, anger, alarm, and fear sharp as broken glass.

"I know I lost the right to be here. I'm not here to argue that, but there's no fucking way I'm walking out that door and letting you find Beth without me. You can throw me out on my ass, and I'll come right back in. You can beat me bloody, and I'll fucking crawl back in. Short of killing me, there isn't a goddamn thing you can do that will keep me from being here to find her."

That gave Copper pause. His eyes narrowed, and then he nodded once. He might be a pigheaded MC president, but he'd take every hand offered to search for Beth.

"What do we know so far?" he said, shifting into crisis management mode.

"Demo has her."

"Fuck." Copper interlaced his fingers at the top of his head. He strode five steps away before coming back. "What else?"

"He beat the shit out of Melody. Dumped her in the alley behind the salon. Sounds like Beth found her and tried to help."

"Of course she fucking did," Copper muttered. "Damn sweet woman."

Saint's lips twitched despite the horror of the situation

because Copper was right. Of course, Beth tried to help the woman who'd set out to destroy her.

"What happened next?"

"Demo appeared. He drove off with Beth and Melody in a van. Screw gave Mav plate numbers to run."

Screw hadn't mentioned whether Beth was hurt, and that was for the best. Saint managed to hold it together so far, but if he found out Beth was injured, he'd burn the entire town to ash.

His hands trembled at his sides, so he shoved them in his pockets.

Copper stared at him with cold, hard, calculating eyes. For a moment, Saint feared the prez was about to thank him for the information and kick him the fuck out. Then Copper turned away, dragging a hand through his beard as he spat a series of curses. When he faced Saint again, the fury still burned, but it was aimed inward now too.

"You're in. We find Beth. Then we'll talk."

Saint sagged just a fraction. The relief nearly knocked him to his knees.

"Thank you," he said quietly. He'd humble himself anyway necessary to be involved.

Copper nodded. "Let's bring her home." He turned to face the rest of the men who didn't bother to pretend they weren't hanging on every word of that conversation. "You all heard. We're done dicking around. I want no stone unturned. Call every damn contact you have, every person who might know where Demo and his crew hole up. Use every ounce of force and every threat in your arsenal to get me information as fast as possible. Beth is depending on us."

Christ. Saint's throat nearly closed at the thought of her hurt, scared, and alone. Bleeding. Crying out for him when he wasn't there.

"My daughter is tough."

Saint turned Copper's way to find the president openly watching him.

"I know. She'll give them hell for sure."

Copper huffed a humorless laugh.

"Still, the thought of them… I can't fucking take it."

Copper nodded. "Feels like you're torn apart from the inside. Worst kind of pain imaginable."

Saint met his gaze. "Yes."

Copper looked at him with what almost looked like respect, but that couldn't be, could it?

"Then let's get her back home where she belongs as fast as possible."

Saint's phone rang, making them both jump. He yanked it out of his pocket so fast he bobbled, almost dropping it in the flood.

After a quick frown at the screen, he had at his ear. "Stillman?" he said, heart stuttering. He walked away to hear better.

"Fuck, I shouldn't be calling you." Fear bled through Stillman's whispered words. "Never mind. Sorry."

"Stillman, don't you fucking dare hang up."

Silence.

"You know something."

"They have your girl," Stillman whispered rapidly. "The one with you when you came to the barn."

Yes. Fucking yes. A goddamn lead. "Where? Where do they have her?"

Stillman groaned. "They'll kill me if they find out I talked."

"I'll kill you if you don't. Swear to Christ, Stillman, there's nowhere on earth you'll be able to hide if they hurt my woman and you could have prevented it."

Another groan. "I shouldn't have called."

"But you did. It's too fucking late to pussy out now."

"I ain't a pussy."

Saint knew that would get to him.

"You have five seconds before I hang up this phone and track you down. Trust me, you don't want that to happen."

Silence.

"Four… three… two… on—"

"Fine! Fucking fine." He lowered his voice so Saint had to strain to hear him. "That old sawmill. You know the one."

"The one that closed five years ago?"

"Yeah."

Fuck yes, they had a location. He waved Copper over. "Thank you, Stillman. Text me where you are, and I'll send someone to bring you to the clubhouse for safety."

"Saint?"

"What?"

"She doesn't look too good. Busted lip. Maybe worse. She got a mouth on her, man, and Demo don't like that."

Saint's vision went red at the edges. In no reality would Beth sit back quietly while someone kidnapped her. Of course, she was fucking with them. Hell, knowing her, she'd probably try to protect Melody as well.

Pride surged, mixed with terror and dread.

When he got her back, he'd tie her to the bed for the rest of her life.

"I owe you, Stillman," he said as Copper reached him.

"Nah, Demo's a real shit heel. Deserves whatever's coming to him. Don't let him kill me, and we'll be even."

The line went dead.

Saint was already sprinting for the door. "She's at the old sawmill."

"For fuck's sake, Saint. Hold the fuck up."

He reached the door. "All due respect, Copper, I'm not fucking waiting."

"We need a battle plan."

Saint slipped out the door. The last thing he heard before it closed was Copper's pounding boots and shouted, "Mount up!"

He threw a leg up and sailed onto his bike like a trick horse rider. Two seconds later, he peeled out of the lot while the rest of his club raced to their bikes, and Copper cursed him to hell and back.

Riding a motorcycle on mountain switchbacks was a skill he'd mastered after so many years of living in the Smoky Mountains. Saint took the sharp turns at a harrowing clip, burning rubber and sending a trail of smoke behind him.

His own safety never crossed his mind. All he could hear was Stillman's warning echoing. *'She doesn't look too good.'*

Every slam of his heart against his ribcage was a command.

Faster. Faster. Faster.

He obeyed, pushing the throttle to its limit.

Finally, he parked about half a mile away from the Sawmill, laying his bike down in the brush off the road so no one would see or hear him coming. Then he set off on foot, running as fast as he could in fucking jeans and boots in the middle of the summer.

After thirty seconds, sweat poured down his face, soaking into his T-shirt. The salt burned his eyes, but he didn't give a fuck. All he could think of was getting to Beth and murdering Demo.

He slowed as he approached, moving off the road into the woods for the final trek in case they'd installed cameras at the old sawmill.

Each step brought him closer to Beth. Closer to wrapping his hands around Demo's throat and feeling the cartilage crush beneath his fingers.

Someone latched onto the back of his T-shirt and yanked… *hard*.

"The fuck?" He whirled around, fists curled and up,

blocking his face for the incoming attack. "Thunder? How the fuck are you here?"

Thunder smirked and wiggled his phone in Saint's face. "Copper texted. Told me you went half-cocked. You know Mak and I live about a mile from here."

Right. He hadn't been thinking of anything but getting there.

"Whatever. I'm going in to get Beth."

His brother-in-law's smirk disappeared. "No, the fuck you're not. Not until backup arrives. They're about two minutes out on foot, like you."

"I'm not waiting." He gestured toward the sawmill. "Beth is in there, and I don't know what they're doing to her."

Thunder grabbed his shoulders. "Look at me." He shook Saint hard. "Look at me, asshole."

He met Thunder's gaze. "Mak was right. You love her, don't you?"

"Yes." He'd never hit his brother-in-law, but there was a first time for everything, and if he didn't get the fuck out of Saint's way, he'd take a punch to the face in the next ten seconds.

Thunder's expression was dead serious. "Then wait *two fucking minutes* to give her the best chance to get out of there. You know going in alone is stupid."

"Fuck." Goddammit, Thunder was right.

Saint rubbed his arm. He wasn't itchy or cold, but every nerve felt raw and on fire. "I'm crawling out of my skin, man. Never felt like this before."

Thunder nodded. "Hope you never have to feel it again." Thunder knew what it was to worry for his woman's life. Years ago, Makenna almost died at the hands of their psychotic father. No doubt, Thunder would never forget the stark fear in the moments before he had Mak back in his arms.

The crunching of leaves had them both looking in the direction Saint came from.

"Cavalry has arrived," Thunder said, slapping Saint's back. "Let's get your ol' lady back."

Ol' lady.

Fuck, that sounded good.

Chapter Twenty-Six

Beth's skull cracked against the van's metal wall for the third time, and she tasted blood. No seat belt. No seat. No way to brace herself as every turn catapulted her across the cargo hold like a rag doll. After slamming into the side of the van three times, she managed to brace herself, propping her back against the wall and using her feet to push against a ridge in the floor. Not a great system, but it kept her from violently flinging back and forth across the van.

The other challenge, besides keeping calm, was helping Melody.

The other woman groaned in pain, cradling her ribs. Every bump and turn made her cry out. After a few moments, she started to sob.

The van rolled to a stop.

Beth straightened off the wall, straining to hear. When the driver's door didn't open, she scrambled across the vehicle toward Melody, who lay sprawled in the center of the van. They'd either stopped at a light or hit some traffic.

"Come on, Mel," she said as she slid her hands beneath Melody's shoulders. "Let's get you secured somehow."

Beth's abraded knees screamed as she kneeled on the

unforgiving floor, tugging Melody toward a wall. It took more strength than she had, but inch by inch, she managed. Melody tried to help, bending her knees and pushing off the floor, but every movement made her cry harder.

Beth's back hit the van wall just as it began moving again.

"Okay." She breathed in heavy gulps of air. Her shredded palms felt on fire after dragging Melody across the floor. "Almost there. I know it hurts, Mel, but help me one more time. Then you can rest."

Melody must have heard her through the sobs. She dug her heels in and pushed once more. Beth's ass dropped to the floor, and she was able to pull Melody's head onto her lap. Then just as the van took a turn, she braced her feet against the ridge in the floor once again. They jostled through the turn but stayed where they were instead of mimicking a pinball machine.

Melody groaned, but her crying lessened with the more stable position. "T-thank you," she managed between sobs.

Beth nodded. Melody probably couldn't see her through those swollen eyes. "We'll be okay. The club will come for us." She glanced down at the battered woman with a wince. Melody's hair stuck to wet cheeks. Mascara mixed with the bruising under her eyes gave her a grotesque horror movie victim appearance. Gently as possible so as not to add to the pain, Beth brushed the hair back from Melody's face.

"Why are you being nice to me?" Melody mumbled.

Beth sighed. "If you haven't noticed, we're kinda all we got right now."

Melody made a noise Beth chose to take as an acknowledgment.

"If it makes you feel better, I'll call you a bitch and a bunch of other names after we get out of here."

"I'll be ready."

"I've thought a lot about slapping you, but someone

obviously beat me to it."

Melody surprised the hell out of her with a bark of laughter that turned into an agonized groan.

Gallows humor. Who didn't love it?

They spent the next stretch in silence, save for Melody's labored breathing and occasional whimpers. Beth closed her eyes and tried to figure out where they were by feel. All she could determine was they'd hit a section of switchbacks, but that could be any hundred roads in these mountains.

Where are they taking us? What do they want? How long until the club realizes I'm gone?

They turned left, and the road changed, becoming consistently bumpy and jarring the van so much her teeth rattled. Her ass bounced on the hard floor, sending jolts of discomfort shooting up her spine. It had to be torture for Melody.

And then, without warning, the van stopped.

The engine cut.

Beth's heart slammed against her ribs.

This is it.

"We're not moving," Melody mumbled. "The van isn't vibrating."

"No." She straightened and stared toward the back doors. "I think we've reached our destination."

The doors opened, sending in a flood of sunlight. Beth squinted against the searing brightness. A large man she didn't recognize filled the doorway, blocking out the sun. She couldn't see his face, just his silhouette, massive shoulders, arms like tree trunks, and legs as wide as her hips. He radiated the kind of confidence that came from knowing no one could stop him from doing whatever he wanted.

He grabbed Melody's ankle and yanked.

Melody screamed.

"Hey!" Beth scrambled after her. "Be careful. She's

injured."

The guy grunted. When he got Melody to the edge of the van, he pulled her up and out, setting her on her feet. Beth winced as Melody cried and tried to find her footing.

"Let me help her." She jumped out of the van and moved to put her arm around Melody, only to be hauled away by a rough hand gripping her bicep.

Demo.

He started walking, dragging her with him. His strides were so long, and his grip was practically lifting her off the ground. She had to run on her tiptoes to keep up.

"Slow the fuck down," she demanded, looking over her shoulder. "Where are you taking Melody?"

Demo laughed. "I'd be a little more worried about where we're taking *you* if I were in your shoes."

Ice slid down her spine. She knew exactly what men like him did to women they had power over.

She'd survived one monster.

She could survive another.

She had to.

Unable to do anything for the other woman, Beth shifted her attention from Melody and onto her surroundings. If she could learn as much as possible about where she was, maybe she could find a way to escape.

She blinked as she glanced around. "The sawmill?" When she was a kid, this place ran a thriving business. She'd never forget trips here with Copper to pick up lumber. He and Rocket built her a playhouse in the backyard when she was six. Together they'd made trips here, and Copper would let her ride on the flatbed cart. She'd sit on a pile of lumber and direct him where to go. The place closed a handful of years ago as the area's lumber industry declined.

Demo didn't respond, just yanked open a heavy door and shoved her into the building.

From darkness to bright light to dark again. Beth blinked, trying to get her eyes to adjust faster. The place was mostly empty. Some ancient, dust-covered pieces of equipment were bolted to the floor in various locations around the large warehouse. A fluorescent light flickered overhead with an insistent hum that would drive her crazy any other time. Today, she had bigger problems.

The air still smelled of sawdust and something else, something chemical and sharp that burned her nostrils.

About a dozen men sat at folding tables, weighing and packaging white powder while others supervised. A few looked up when she entered. Their eyes tracked her body with the casual assessment of men who'd done terrible things and would do them again.

Beth's skin crawled.

"Why am I here?"

Demo towed her over to a chair, shoving her to sit. "My boss wants to talk to your father."

She laughed out loud. "What? You do know they've wanted to meet with him for a while now, right? You could have just answered the text instead of all this drama."

"We don't operate on Copper's terms."

"Let me guess… you operate on your boss's terms. Must be nice, being somebody's errand boy."

Something flickered in Demo's expression. Just for a second, there was a tightening around his jaw, a flash in those dead eyes. *She'd hit a nerve.*

"I'm not anybody's errand boy, princess." He leaned down, close enough she could see the thin white scar running along his hairline. "I'm the guy who does the things even the boss doesn't want to think about. The guy who makes problems disappear. Your daddy's club has been a problem for a long time." He straightened. "But I'm patient. Grew up with nothing, learned how to wait. Your old man's had his kingdom for thirty years. I can wait another thirty to take it."

Beth snorted. "So… what? This is some kind of dick-measuring contest? Your boss thinks snatching me shows he's king of the Smoky Mountains? *Please*. The Handlers have ruled this area for decades. You're—"

She never saw the slap coming.

The world tilted, and she was on the floor before she registered the blow, the crack of his palm against her cheekbone, the explosion of pain, the way her vision went white, then black, then spotted. Fire bloomed across the left side of her face. Her ear screamed with a high-pitched ring that swallowed every other sound.

Get up. Get up. Don't let him see you broken.

Her arms wouldn't cooperate. She lay there, gasping, hip throbbing from where it had slammed against the concrete.

Somewhere in the room, a man chuckled.

Fucker.

Beth cradled her cheek as she stared up at Demo.

The man who'd pulled Melody out of the van came over and whispered something to Demo.

Where the hell had he stashed Melody?

"Why the fuck is he here?" Demo asked with a hard head shake. "He's a low-level dealer. Tell him to get the fuck out of here if he still wants a job."

The guy nodded and jogged back outside.

Beth began to stand only to have a boot slam into her chest, driving her flat onto the concrete. Demo loomed over her, all his weight pressing down through that single point of contact.

She couldn't breathe. Couldn't move. Her ribs groaned under the pressure, and she clawed at his boot with fingers that felt like they belonged to someone else. Black spots danced at the edges of her vision.

I'm going to die here. On a filthy warehouse floor. Before I fixed things between Saint and his family.

One more ounce of pressure and her sternum would crack like kindling.

"I don't give a fuck how much power your daddy thinks he has. We have his princess. He'll come running when we contact him."

Beth wheezed. "It's funny you think that's how this is gonna go down." She managed to squeeze the sentence out in one shallow breath.

Demo chuckled, but there was something almost like respect in it. "A bitch 'til the end, huh? You know what I like about you, princess? You remind me of my sister." His boot pressed harder for one agonizing second. "She had a mouth on her too. Never knew when to shut up." The pressure eased just enough for her to gasp. "Didn't end well for her either."

His boot disappeared off her chest, and she sucked in an enormous greedy breath only to have it whooshed back out when he kicked her in the side with his steel toe.

She curled into a ball, coughing and dry heaving. Demo strode away, but two sets of hands yanked her up and dropped her on the chair. She still gasped for air as her diaphragm spasmed. Someone jerked her arms behind her back, securing them with a zip tie, while another goon tied her legs to the chair.

Then they walked away, leaving her alone, struggling to breathe.

She coughed and spat blood onto the concrete. The red splatter against the gray floor was almost fascinating in a detached, shock-induced way.

Internal bleeding. That's internal bleeding.

Her head dropped forward. For a long moment, the only thing she could do was focus on the simple act of breathing.

In. Out. In. Don't pass out. Don't give them the satisfaction.

Demo had to know she wouldn't be of much use to him if

she died.

Maybe she should stop antagonizing him and let him think he'd won.

Beth closed her eyes and let the fear wash over her. Thirty seconds. She'd give herself thirty seconds to fall apart.

Her hands shook. Her breath came in shallow gasps that made her damaged ribs scream. Tears leaked from beneath her closed lids, hot, shameful, and unstoppable. She thought of her dad. Of her mom. But mostly of Saint's face when he'd said he loved her. Would she ever see any of them again?

Twenty-eight. Twenty-nine. Thirty.

Beth opened her eyes. It worked. Thirty seconds to freak out, and now she was angry.

Incensed.

Fuck fear. When she left Jason, she promised herself she'd never cower before another man, and she didn't plan to start now.

Fuck Demo and fuck these other assholes.

The Handlers would come for her, and they'd rain down hell on these assholes.

BACK PROPPED AGAINST a huge oak tree, Saint stared at the sawmill through the woods. His assault rifle hung from a strap across his chest, ready to mow down anyone who tried to keep him from Beth. He bounced his heel and tapped a thumb against his leg to try to expel some anxious energy.

It didn't work

If Copper didn't give him the go-ahead to charge in the next two minutes, he was going in anyway. Fuck waiting and fuck the plan.

Zach strode over. He and Copper had taken point. They'd distributed weapons and were deciding where everyone would go. When Saint protested, Zach squeezed his shoulder and told him he was too close to the situation and too volatile to be in charge.

There was also the small matter of Copper kicking him out of the club.

"This shouldn't be hard," Zach said. He rested his palm on the tree near Saint's head.

Saint nodded, not taking his eyes off the sawmill.

"They're fucking amateurs. No cameras. No guards. Easy as fuck."

"Maybe they're just that cocky."

Zach shrugged. "Either way, good for us."

Saint nodded.

"Hey."

He turned in Zach's direction.

"Happy for you, brother." Zach slapped his shoulder.

Saint arched an eyebrow.

"You and Beth. That's a damn good fit."

His system couldn't handle another shock. At least this was a positive one. Saint cast a glance at Copper, then focused back on Zach, who chuckled.

"Give him time. He already feels like shit about what happened the other night. There are a lot of fucked-up thoughts tangled in his head. He's never gotten over the guilt for what his brother did to Shell. It's always made him unreasonably protective of those two. He sees you're good for her. He just needs to admit it."

Saint grunted.

"Bring it in," Copper called, waving everyone his way. The fifteen or so of them who'd come to help gathered close. "We go in loud, and we go in aggressive. Get everyone on the floor, face down. We'll tie 'em up and leave 'em for the cops to deal with. Only shoot to kill if you got no choice. We don't need the heat right now."

Murmurs of agreement went around his brothers.

"Okay, let's roll," Copper announced.

Fucking finally.

Saint kicked straight into action. He secured the butt of his rifle against his shoulder and marched forward alongside the other MC members. Zach stood at his left, Maverick at his right. Sweeping right and left, he scanned the distance between the woods and the sawmill.

Nothing.

No cameras, no one monitoring the building's exterior.

Easy as fuck, like Zach said.

Saint reached the door first. He grabbed the handle and whispered, "Three… two… one." Then he yanked it open and burst through. "Everyone on the fucking floor! Now!"

Chaos erupted. Workers scrambled from the tables, white powder scattering like snow. One guy reached for his waistband, and Maverick put him down hard, boot to the back of the knee, face to the concrete.

A gun went off somewhere to Saint's left. Someone screamed. He didn't stop. Couldn't stop. Beth was in here somewhere, and nothing else mattered.

The rest of his brothers fanned out, taking guys to the ground while Saint's gaze swept the warehouse.

Saint turned right, rifle at the ready, and stopped dead in his tracks. Beth sat, tied to a chair, tears in her eyes, staring at him. He dropped the gun and rushed to her, falling to his knees beside the chair.

"Baby," he whispered, cupping her bruised face between his hands. He wanted to crush her to him in a fierce hug, but couldn't stand the thought of hurting her.

"I'm okay," she whispered, but there was a wheeze quality to her voice.

She was most definitely *not* okay.

He was most definitely *not* okay.

He leaned in and brushed the gentlest of kisses across her swollen lips before resting his forehead on hers.

"Told them they were a bunch of stupid fuckers for thinking this plan would ever work," she said with a weak chuckle.

"Jesus, Beth." That explained the bruises. Demo sure as fuck wouldn't have appreciated that.

"Sorry," she said. Her laugh turned slightly hysterical. She was probably in shock. "You're not in love with a delicate flower."

"Fuck no, I'm not. I'm in love with a badass."

She kissed him this time, wincing as she pressed her sore lips against his.

"Can… can you please cut me out of this chair?"

"Fuck yes." He released her and grabbed his knife from its holster, slicing through the zip tie on her hands first. It was so goddamn tight, she hissed in pain as he tugged on the plastic. "Sorry, baby. Those fuckers put it too goddamn tight."

"It's okay. Just get it off."

As soon as he freed her hands, he helped her bring her arms to the front of her body. Beth did a good job hiding her pain. Someone who didn't know her inside and out might buy her tough-as-nails routine, but Saint knew she was hurting. He kissed her fingertips, afraid to touch the raw and bloody circle around her wrists or the ruined skin on her palms.

"Someone needs to find Melody," Beth said as he cut the ties on her legs. "She was with me on the way here, but I don't know what they did with her."

"Okay, we're on it."

"Saint, she's pretty fucked up. They beat her badly. I'm worried about her."

Of course, she was. Beth was too fucking good. Too good for him, but she was stuck with him now.

"One of the guys will get her. I want you out of here… *now*." He scooped her into his arms.

"Saint! I can walk," Beth said as he started for the exit.

"Don't care." Maybe she could walk, but her breathing sounded off, and he wasn't taking any chances.

She sighed and relaxed into his hold, resting her head on his chest. "What about Demo? I thought for sure you'd come charging in here on a mission to kill him."

"I did." He'd had every intention of killing that fucker. Still did, given the chance.

"So why didn't you go after him?"

"Because you're a million times more important." One look at Beth and he knew where his priority lay. "I'll get my chance with him." He had no doubt one of his brothers would keep Demo on ice just for Saint. Unless, of course, he wasn't allowed near the club.

Saint strode outside with Beth in his arms. She closed her eyes against the harsh sun. As he strode toward a truck one of the prospects drove over, his gaze met Copper's.

The president's gaze landed on his daughter's swollen face, the blood on her lips, the way she curled into Saint as if she might shatter. His expression shifted from fury to something colder. Something lethal.

Demo was a dead man.

The only question was how slowly Copper would make it happen. And that was okay with Saint. As long as the man couldn't go after Beth again, he'd accept the outcome, even if he couldn't make the kill.

As he approached the truck, the prospect rushed to the passenger-side door to open it, and Saint tucked her into the seat.

"Hey, prospect." He dug in his pocket for his keys. "My bike is with the others about half a mile away. See that it gets back to the clubhouse in one piece, or you'll never fucking patch."

The guy's eyes widened. He took the keys, nodding like a

bobblehead doll. "You got it, Saint. I'll treat it better than I treat my own."

He chuckled. "You'd better. It's a hundred times nicer than your piece of shit."

When he looked back at Beth, she was shaking her head at him with a weak grin.

Saint grew serious. "Tell me how you're really feeling."

"Pretty shitty. Um… he, Demo, knocked me on the floor and kicked me with his boots a few times."

Saint's jaw ticked. "Then we're definitely going to the ER."

"I don't think I need that."

He seared her with a look that scared men twice her size. "It's non-negotiable."

Beth rolled her eyes, then she frowned and grabbed the front of his shirt. "I was scared," she whispered.

He leaned in, cupping her hips. "I was fucking terrified."

"Thank you for saving me."

"Any fucking time, baby. Though, please never again."

She chuckled, but it turned into a groan. "Don't make me laugh. It hurts."

Yeah, first stop, emergency room.

"I fucking love you, Beth."

"I love you too," she whispered.

Saint kissed her forehead, then backed away. After he buckled her in, he shut the door and started for the driver's side, where the prospect left the keys in the ignition. As he turned, he found Copper watching them with a pensive stare.

Instead of barging over, chasing Saint away, or demanding to talk to his daughter, he gave Saint a single nod.

Saint returned the gesture.

Approval?

Maybe not, but it was a first step.

Chapter Twenty-Seven

"Saint, I'm fine," Beth said for the thousandth time.

"Shh, hold up. Don't move," Saint said as he patted her thigh while staring at the monitor above her hospital bed.

Beth rolled her eyes. Since Demo kicked her in the torso and she'd complained of difficulty breathing, the ER doctor ordered her to be placed on supplemental oxygen and a telemetry monitor. It kept constant tabs on her heart function and oxygen saturation, plus checked her blood pressure every thirty minutes, which it was currently doing.

Saint couldn't tear his attention away from that damn monitor. Every time he heard the whir of the filling blood pressure cuff, he shushed her and demanded she lie still for an accurate reading. He focused on that screen as though it were the only thing keeping her alive.

"One ten over seventy. Oxygen is ninety-eight percent," he said with a nod. "Good."

God, she loved this man, even if she wanted to wrap the EKG leads around his neck and choke him.

"Saint."

"Huh?" He made the noise without glancing away from the screen.

"Saint, look at me."

He seemed reluctant to turn away from the screen but did as she asked. Worry etched lines into his forehead. Beth reached out and smoothed a finger over the grooves before cupping his cheek.

"Really look at me. I'm okay. They x-rayed my face and ribs. Nothing is broken. You know that. I don't have any internal bleeding. I spat blood earlier because I have a pulmonary contusion and lots of deep bruising. And yes, it hurts like a son of a bitch, but it's not serious. The only reason they haven't discharged me yet is that they want to make sure I don't have any more trouble breathing because of the lung contusion. But as you said, my oxygen level looks great."

The intensity in his gaze would have made her uncomfortable if he were any other man. It felt as though he were trying to crack her open and see straight into her soul. To see every part of her, even those she'd never let anyone else have. But she wanted it with him. She wanted to grow so close to him that it felt like they were one.

"I'm okay," she whispered, sweeping a thumb across his lower lip. "You can relax."

He leaned in, resting their foreheads together. "Baby…" The agony in his voice slayed her.

"I know," she whispered.

He shook his head against her. "You can't. You can't possibly know."

She stroked his hair, sifting her fingers through the soft strands. "So tell me."

He pulled back so they could see each other better. Then he took her hand, his big one swallowing hers like he was afraid she might vanish if he let go. He swallowed hard, jaw working. His eyes were red-rimmed, bloodshot, not from tears, but from hours of refusing to let them fall.

"When Screw called and told me you were missing…" His breath hitched, sharp and distressed. "It felt like someone took a crowbar to my chest and kept prying until they cracked it wide open. I couldn't fucking breathe. The world tilted the wrong way, and I was suddenly facing the possibility of standing in it without you."

His grip intensified. Protective. Desperate.

Beth's throat closed completely. Her eyes burned. She couldn't have spoken if her life depended on it, so she just held on tighter, letting him know she was here, she was listening, and she wasn't going anywhere.

"I was terrified," he admitted. The word dragged out of him as though it hurt to say. "Not scared. Not worried. Fucking terrified. I've only been that terrified one other time in my life. The night Makenna and I took our siblings and ran from the cult."

Oh God.

"I know what kind of monsters lurk out there, and the thought of one of them putting a hand on you…" His voice broke. He looked away, jaw clenching so hard she could see the muscle jump. When he looked back, his eyes were wet. "It broke something in me, Beth. Something I didn't know could break."

He leaned in, dropping his forehead to her shoulder. She rubbed his back and kissed his temple, the only thing she could think to soothe him.

"I was so fucking, angry, Beth. I've been angry before, but this, this was different. This was clean, pure, and murderous. There wasn't anything in me except the need to find you. To get to you. To end anyone who stood between you and me."

His voice dropped to a whisper, thick with promise and pain.

"I didn't care about the consequences. I didn't care about blood. I didn't care if I came back. The only thing that mattered was you, *is* you. I was ready to tear the world apart piece by piece if that's what it took."

He lifted his head. His eyes were wet now, and he didn't try to hide it.

"My brothers kept me from spiraling out of control. They brought me back to earth and helped me get to you. And when I saw you…" His voice cracked before he pressed his lips together, fighting for control. "Bruised, hurt, tied to that fucking chair, and still so fucking brave." A sound came out of him, not quite a laugh, not quite a sob. "Relief hit me so hard my knees almost gave out." His thumb brushed her skin in a reverent sweep.

"There is nothing… *nothing*… I wouldn't do to keep you safe. No line I wouldn't cross. No darkness I wouldn't run into. You are it for me, Beth. You're my anchor, my reason, and losing you…" His voice cracked. His face crumpled for just a second before he caught it, and that single moment of almost-breaking undid her completely.

"I'm here," she said quickly, cupping his face, pulling him close. "I'm here, I'm alive, and I'm going to walk out of here hand in hand with you. And I'm going to go home with you. And get into bed with you."

He nodded. "Christ, Beth, I saw a version of myself I always suspected existed but never had to meet. I now know what I'm capable of, and there is no limit when it comes to you."

"Does it give you any second thoughts? About me? Or us?"

"Fuck no." He kissed her, hard. "Never. You hear me? Not for a fraction of a second. I fucking love you, and there isn't anything that can change that."

Beth smiled. Despite her discomfort, it felt like she was glowing from the inside out. "Just checking."

Saint grunted a laugh. The feral intensity faded from his

expression as he narrowed his eyes. "Don't ask me that shit again," he said with a playful growl as he lifted their joined hands to his lips and nipped her knuckles.

"Kiss me," she said, leaning in. "Give me something to hold me over until we get home."

"I like to hear you call my place home."

Just as she grinned, he leaned in and kissed the smile off her lips. She sighed a soft, happy sound, which he took advantage of, sliding his tongue into her mouth. A nurse would probably come in before she knew it, but Beth still took the opportunity to deepen the kiss.

She could spend the rest of her life kissing him and never want for anything.

A deep throat cleared from the doorway.

Beth jerked back, face heating. Saint didn't release her hand as they both turned to see which doctor had come by to assess her.

But it wasn't a doctor who stood, watching them.

It was Copper, hand in hand with Shell.

Beth tensed. Saint must have felt it, and his eyes went straight to that stupid monitor. To keep him from having a damn heart attack, she breathed as deeply as her sore chest allowed to calm her nerves, most of which were for him.

The last person Saint would want to see after slicing his heart open and bleeding all over Beth's hospital bed was the man who hated him and banished him from their family.

He shifted a respectful distance from Beth, but didn't release her hand. She wouldn't have let him if he tried.

How long had her parents been eavesdropping? Had they overheard Saint bare his entire soul to her?

Shell had tears streaming down her cheeks, one hand pressed to her heart like she was trying to hold it together. Copper's expression was unreadable, but his eyes were suspiciously bright, and he kept swallowing like he had something stuck in his throat.

Yeah. They'd heard everything.

"Hey," Beth said as she rested against the raised bed.

"How are you, honey?" Shell tugged Copper into the room where they stood at the foot of the bed.

"I'm doing all right. Sore, but all things considered, it's not bad."

"They gave you pain medicine?" Shell asked.

Beside her, Saint snorted, making her chuckle. "All I took was Motrin. I didn't want anything stronger."

"Well, that's stupid," Copper finally spoke. "Why didn't you take something stronger?"

"Thank you," Saint grumbled, glaring at her. "That's what I said."

Oh my God. Beth met her mother's amused gaze.

How had she not realized these men were cut from the exact same damn cloth?

Shell pressed her lips together, but her eyes sparkled with mirth.

Yeah, laugh it up, Mom.

"Because, as I've told Saint countless times, the pain is not that bad. Plus, I don't want to be all loopy or tired. So you all can stop fussing like a bunch of mother hens."

A heavy blanket of silence fell over the room. Beth shifted, gritting her teeth so she didn't wince. They'd be all over her if she let slip how much moving hurt. *God, this was worse than awkward.* The last time they'd all been together, Copper screamed, shouted, and threw Saint out of the clubhouse. Where did they go from here? Would they leave now that they saw she wasn't badly hurt?

Copper sighed. He rubbed his beard while clearing his throat. When she was a kid, she used to put braids in his beard with sparkly clips. He'd hated every second of it but never refused when she wanted to 'play beauty salon.' He'd smile and praise her as she yanked his beard, probably pulling out a handful of hair. Without a doubt, Copper was the best damn father around. It truly hurt to cause him so much distress.

"Well, this is some bullshit, huh?" he finally said.

Shell rolled her eyes and hip-checked him. "Really, that's how you want to start?"

The big man shrugged. "Never felt like I didn't know how to talk to my daughter. It sucks."

Her heart clenched, and she squeezed Saint's hand.

"I can go if you three want some time?"

"No." Copper shook his head. "Stay, uh, please."

Saint nodded, watching Copper with wary eyes. "I wasn't gonna leave anyway," he mumbled, making Beth swallow a chuckle.

"Sounds about right," Copper muttered back.

Shell elbowed him.

After another sigh, Copper continued, "The other night, I was…"

Wrong?

Reactive?

Insensitive?

"A fucking asshole."

That worked too.

Saint's grip eased a fraction, as though some of the tension he carried evaporated.

"I've always been overprotective of Beth. After what happened to Sh—" His voice gave out. He pressed his lips together hard, staring at the ceiling, blinking rapidly.

Beth had never seen her father fight tears before. *Never.* Not once in her entire life.

Shell leaned into him, and he pulled her close, burying his face in her hair for just a moment before straightening.

"After what happened to Shell…" he continued, voice

rough, "… I've been so fucking determined I wouldn't let something like that happen to you. I think I wanted to make up for, uh… the way and the person who conceived you."

"Dad…" Beth's heart thudded hard against her ribcage.

Despite how he acted the other night, Copper was typically a reasonable man. He didn't like to be wrong or fuck up, but owned it when he did. Still, he rarely let anyone view this side of him. Not only was he letting her see his vulnerable side, but he was also giving Saint a glimpse too.

And that was the best apology she could ask for.

"Let me get this shit out, Beth," he continued with a huff.

Her lips quirked.

Copper's focus went to Saint. "I said some real fucked-up shit to you, Saint. Called you a predator. Said you were taking advantage of my daughter." He shook his head, disgust clear on his face, disgust aimed at himself. "That was bullshit, and I knew it even when I was saying it. You're a damn good man, which I've known for a long damn time. Witnessing you suffer today when Beth went missing and hearing what you just said to her, I didn't need that to know you love my daughter. I already knew. I was just too stubborn and scared to admit it. I'm fucking sorry, man." He extended his hand. "I'm proud to call you brother, and maybe one day I'll call you son." He winked at Beth.

"For fuck's sake, Dad. Pressure much?" Wasn't getting kidnapped stressful enough? Now her dad had to hint about marriage.

Saint stood and grasped Copper's hand. "Forgiven and forgotten, Prez."

Copper seemed to lose a hundred pounds of weight from his shoulders. He straightened, and his eyes lit. He tugged, bringing Saint in for a back-slapping hug.

"Oh!" Shell reached into her tote bag. "Think it's about time you put this back on." She handed Saint's cut over to him.

"Thank you." He slipped the cut back on. Beth's heart fluttered. He looked so damn hot in that HHMC cut.

"Beth? You okay?" Copper asked, frowning at the telemetry screen. "Your heart rate just jumped."

Saint whipped around. "Fuck, it did?"

"Oh God, there are two of them."

Shell laughed and placed a hand on her husband's arm. "Honey, I think she just got… excited seeing Saint back in his cut."

Copper's face screwed up. "I don't want to know that shit."

Chuckling, Saint came back to his seat and took her hand once again.

At some point in the near future, she needed to sit down with her dad for an in-depth heart-to-heart. Never once had she felt he owed her anything to make up for her birth father being a rapist piece of shit. It shocked her that he even felt that way. She never gave her birth father any thought. Copper was her dad in every way that counted. He'd given her a wonderful childhood and treated her mother like the queen she was. *What more could she ask for?*

She'd make sure he understood that and never stressed over it again.

"How's Melody?" Beth asked. "Have you heard anything?"

Copper frowned. By now, someone must have filled him in on the reason Melody was taken and the drama surrounding her, spilling the news of Beth and Saint. He couldn't be feeling too positive about her at the moment.

"Five broken ribs, a broken eye socket, and a broken nose. She's in surgery for the facial injuries now."

Beth winced. "Jesus." She sighed. "She apologized to me. I have pretty complicated feelings about her right now, but no one deserves what she went through."

Nodding, Shell said, "She'll need support when she gets out of here. She has family in Virginia. I assume she'll go there."

"That's good."

The room got quiet again, all lost in their heavy thoughts.

"Demo?" Saint asked in a low voice, after a few moments.

Copper's eyes sparked with delight. "We got him."

Beth sucked in a breath.

Oh shit.

FUCK YES.

Saint's insides lit up at that news.

He knew he could count on his brothers to jump in where he couldn't. He'd needed to be with Beth and trusted they'd capture Demo alive.

For now.

"W-what's going to happen to him?" Beth asked.

Saint squeezed her hand. He didn't relish telling her he planned to kill the motherfucker slowly and painfully, but he refused to lie to her.

"Beth, that's club business," Copper said, voice final.

She snorted. "So you're going to kill him?"

Shell sighed, but Copper stared Beth straight in the eye, not giving anything away. She turned to face Saint. "You're going to do it, aren't you?" she asked.

"Beth…" Copper stopped speaking when Shell squeezed his arm.

Saint didn't say anything, but let her search out the truth in his gaze. He wouldn't be responsible for giving her that information. Information that could be used against her in the future should the worst happen, and he be arrested. But she was smart enough to read him. And she knew this life. She hadn't wanted him to kill Jason on her behalf, but this was different. This was club business. Demo would die today regardless, and Saint deserved the kill.

"Be careful," Beth whispered.

"I'm always careful." He gave her a tense smile. Careful was his middle name. This would be the easiest job in the world. Easiest and most satisfying. His brothers were serving Demo to him on a silver platter. "You don't need to worry about me."

"He might be a little dinged up by the time you get to him, brother," Copper broke in before they could spend the next hour going back and forth about her not needing to worry about him.

"What do you mean?"

"He fired on Zach. Grazed his shoulder. Zach's fucking pissed. He wanted a little alone time with your guest before we let you at him."

"Oh my God," Beth whispered. "Is Zach okay?"

Copper nodded. "Yeah, really was just a graze. Got himself a Bluey Band-Aid and a kiss from Tori. He's good. Just pissed."

Saint didn't laugh with the rest of them. They'd come close to losing so much today. Too close. He'd be hearing Screw tell him Beth was missing in his nightmares for years to come. So much could have gone wrong, and while he should focus on how Beth was next to him and safe, he couldn't stop thinking about how close he'd come to losing her.

"Hey," Beth said, cutting through his darkening thoughts. "You okay?" Beth asked, searching his gaze.

He kissed her knuckles. "I'm perfect, baby." The last thing she needed was to be worrying about his headspace.

Shell cleared her throat. "We'll give you two some space. Beth, please call us if you need anything. Otherwise, we can come back when you're being discharged."

Beth blinked. "Oh, right." She chuckled. "I'm living at your house."

Sure, maybe on paper she was residing with her parents, but he'd be damned if she went there over Saint's house when they released her. He raised an eyebrow, silently asking her to come home with him. Her cheeks turned pink as she nodded.

"I got it, Shell. Beth's going to come stay with me when she's discharged."

Copper narrowed his eyes, earning a backhand to the stomach from his wife.

"Perfect," Shell said with a wide smile. "I was hoping you'd say that."

"What?" Copper scowled at her.

"We're going now." She blew them kisses. "Love you both."

"Shell…"

"Come on, big guy. They don't want us hanging around anymore." She somehow muscled her much larger husband out the door without much effort, waving as she left.

Copper muttered his displeasure the whole time. Saint was pretty sure he caught something about 'living in sin,' which made him snort with laughter.

As soon as they left, Beth sagged against the mattress. "What a mindfuck this day has been. My head is spinning in a million directions." She yawned as her blinks grew longer. "I'm exhausted."

"Sleep, baby." Saint stroked a hand over her hair. "I'll be right here when you wake up."

"Will you lie with me?"

"Babe…"

"Please. Just for a little while. I…" The tears came out of nowhere. One second, she was fine, and the next, her whole body was shaking, sobs tearing out of her chest despite the pain it caused. All the terror she'd shoved down in that warehouse, all the fear she'd counted to thirty and locked away, it came flooding back at once, drowning her.

"S-sorry," she choked out between sobs. "I don't… I can't —"

She couldn't even finish a sentence.

Couldn't stop shaking.

Couldn't do anything but cry.

"Fuck it." Saint climbed in beside her as she slowly scooted to the side. He pretended not to notice her grimace of pain. If he brought it up again, she'd only get more upset. Gently as possible, he tucked her against him, kissing the top of her head. "I've got you, Beth."

"I don't know why I'm crying," she whispered into his chest.

He grunted. "Because on top of being kidnapped and assaulted, today has been one huge mindfuck."

"It has. I'm sorry for what you went through today," she said.

Fuck, this woman. Lying in a hospital bed but thinking of him. "All I care about is that you are okay. Fuck everything else."

"Was I hallucinating, or did my dad apologize to us?" Her voice grew heavy, almost slurred with fatigue.

Saint chuckled. "He did. It was a good apology too. Sincere."

"Mmm, good. Everything is how it should be."

Almost. He smiled. "Just one more thing."

"What's that?" she asked in a sleepy voice.

"Now that I'm back in the club, will you officially be my ol' lady?"

Beth's heart stuttered. Through everything today, the kidnapping, the violence, the terror, this was the moment that made her cry a torrent of fresh tears. Happy ones this time.

"Fuck yes, I will." She kissed him, soft and sweet. "I love

you, Saint. I'm yours."

"And I'm yours," he murmured against her lips. "Forever." Beth needed sleep, not her ol' man riling her up.

They fell asleep in minutes, wrapped in each other on that tiny hospital bed, and Saint didn't wake until Beth's stern evening nurse stood at the foot of the bed, glaring at them like they were caught making out when no parents were home.

He held a finger to his lips. Whatever she had to do could wait. Beth needed sleep.

The nurse rolled her eyes as she jabbed her finger in the direction of the uncomfortable chair next to the bed.

Lifting a hand in surrender, Saint eased away from Beth and off the bed. She didn't so much as shift, so deep in sleep he could have jumped on the bed, and she wouldn't notice.

Good.

As soon as his ass hit the seat, the nurse gave him a thumbs-up. "Thank you," she whispered before leaving. Thankfully, she shut the door behind her.

Saint propped his feet on the edge of the bed, crossed his arms over his chest, and set about watching over his ol' lady as she slept.

A privilege he planned to enjoy for the rest of his life.

Epilogue

Three months ago, Saint had stood in a warehouse doorway, rifle in hand, heart in his throat, terrified he'd find Beth's limp body. Instead, he found her brave, bloodied, beautiful face staring back at him. Three months ago, he'd been cast out of his club and thought he'd lost everything.

Now he stood at the entrance of her new grooming salon, watching his ol' lady live her dream, and he'd never felt more grateful to be alive.

The shine hadn't faded one iota on his relationship with Beth. She moved in straight after being released from the hospital three months ago, and every morning he woke beside her, feeling like the luckiest bastard on the planet.

And now, standing near the entrance of her new grooming salon, watching people stream through the front doors, he'd never felt prouder of anyone.

Beth was in her element. Balloons danced in the breeze outside the salon, attached to a cheerful sign announcing the grand opening event. For opening day, she decided to offer a free mini groom for prospective clients. A brushing, nail clipping, festive bandana, and, of course, plenty of treats for anyone who stopped by with their pet during the four-hour event.

And did people ever stop by.

Beth hadn't taken a break since she opened the door. Hell, there was a line of people waiting more than thirty minutes before she opened. Even still, with only five minutes left, the bell above the salon door jingled every few seconds as Saint opened the door to admit potential customers.

An older woman walked toward him, cradling a freshly fluffed terrier in a pastel pink bandana that matched the shop's pale yet colorful palette. Beth's touch was everywhere, warm, welcoming, and playful.

"You have a good evening, Mrs. Barnett," he said as he pulled the door open for the woman who worked at the local library.

"Hmph." She side-eyed him, shifting her dog to her other arm as though he'd rip it away from her and devour it.

Not everyone loved the fact that the new grooming salon had ties to the MC, but it hadn't deterred people. If they didn't want to drive an hour for decent pet grooming, they'd learn to deal.

Saint's gaze drifted unconsciously to the dog pendant hanging around Beth's neck. Embedded in the gold lies a tracking device, should the worst happen again. Combined with the absurd amount of cameras Maverick installed and the state-of-the-art security system, he felt confident in Beth's safety while working.

Demo died three months ago. That chapter closed in the most satisfying way, but the man above him, the one pulling the strings, had vanished. No body. No arrest. No contact. Only silence. They still didn't know his name. All they had was a fuzzy photo Zach took of a heavily tattooed man with large ear gauges and what looked like a missing finger, slipping out the back on the day they rescued Beth.

Saint wasn't convinced it was over. More likely, the fucker

lay in wait for the day the club got complacent. Then he'd come roaring back into town ready to rumble.

They weren't taking any chances.

The club beefed up security across the board, including homes, businesses, and the clubhouse. The Handlers were prepared for whatever came their way.

That delicate gold chain around Beth's pretty neck allowed him to sleep at night. It was pretty enough that no one questioned it, and smart enough to signal him if she needed help.

After the kidnapping, Beth went straight back to work as though nothing happened.

That was his ol' lady. Brave didn't begin to describe her. Neither did stubborn.

She stood near the counter, laughing, hands flying as she spoke to a family with three school-aged kids and a beautiful golden retriever. The afternoon sunlight caught in her strawberry hair, setting it ablaze. She looked so goddamn happy.

For a moment, Saint couldn't breathe.

He thought of that warehouse. The chair. The bruises. The blood on her lips. He thought of how close he'd come to never seeing Beth in her element, surrounded by people who adored her, doing exactly what she was born to do.

She was here alive and thriving.

And Christ, she was beautiful when she won.

The rest of the event passed in the blink of an eye. Before he knew it, he was ushering the final customer out the door. He joined Beth, Screw, Gumby, and Jazz to clean and lock up. The five of them got the job done in record time.

"Well, goddamn, that was better than we could have asked for!" Screw shouted as he gathered Beth in a crushing hug.

Saint clenched his teeth and plastered a smile on his face so Beth wouldn't see that, yes, it still fucking bothered him when another man touched her, no matter who it was or how platonic the touch. Every time, he had to resist the urge to break fingers and bust jaws.

"Should we celebrate?" Gumby asked as Screw set Beth down. "Dinner?"

Beth caught his gaze and winked. Maybe he wasn't as good at hiding his possessive side as he thought. "Yes!" she said, grinning. "But I need to go home and shower first. I'm covered in fur."

"Same," Jazz said with a laugh. "How about we text you guys in an hour, and we can figure out where to eat."

"Perfect."

As soon as the trio left, Saint went to Beth, gathered her in his arms, and kissed the hell out of her, driving his tongue between her lips until she was soft, pliant, and whimpering.

"Whoa," she said, blinking at him with dazed eyes. "What was that for? Not that I'm complaining." She pressed her palms to his chest. "In fact, do it again."

Chuckling, he kissed her quickly this time. "I'm so fucking proud of you, Beth."

Something flickered across her face, surprise, maybe, or wonder. Like she still couldn't quite believe someone could be proud of her just for being herself.

"Thank you," she whispered. "That means everything to me. I'm pretty proud of myself if I'm being honest."

"You should be." Her confidence was so damn sexy.

Her grin grew wicked as she slid a hand down his stomach straight to his dick. "You know, it seems like you might be up for a different kind of celebrating than Screw was referring to."

"Not sure. Knowing him, he might very well be on the same page as me." He mock scowled as he attacked her neck, making her laugh.

"Are you always going to get jealous when he hugs me?"

"Yes, and if any other man hugs you."

"And will you always take me home and show me who I belong to?" She tilted her head to the side, giving him full access to anything he wanted.

"You know it."

She turned her head, meeting his lips. "So maybe we blow off dinner and spend the night having a private celebration."

Fuck yes. "Now that sounds perfect. Let's get the fuck outta here."

The bell above the door jingled again, and they both turned. Saint immediately blocked Beth with his body, shielding her from whoever dared to enter after hours.

Melody stood in Beth's shop.

Saint went still.

Of all the things that have happened tonight, Melody showing up was not on his Bingo card.

"SAINT, WHO…" BETH peered around her giant boyfriend, currently protecting her from, holy shit. "Melody?" She couldn't have kept the shock from her face if she tried.

She stepped out from behind Saint, ignoring his growl of protest.

"Babe…"

"It's fine."

Melody approached slowly. She looked smaller. Not physically, but the self-assured, seductive edge she'd once worn like armor had vanished. Her eyes were softer too. They had a nervous glint. She held herself like someone who'd learned the hard way that pride could cost too much.

"I won't take much of your time," she said in a meek voice. Her gaze darted between them before settling on Beth—the safer choice. "I just… I owe you both an apology."

Saint didn't interrupt, but he did place his hand on the small of Beth's back.

"I was angry. And jealous." She tapped the side of her head. "There are some things I'm working on, uh… some past things that affected me more than I realized. Not that I'm trying to use that as an excuse or a justification for my behavior. The things I said and did…" She shook her head, face falling into a grimace. "I caused harm I can never undo. I know that." She swallowed hard, blinking as she averted her gaze to the floor.

"I'm sorry. Truly sorry. And I'm getting help, uh… getting over what happened with D-Demo, and… other things. I won't cause trouble for you or the MC again."

Beth never told anyone, but she'd imagined this moment many times. In her darker moments, she'd pictured herself unloading months of built-up anger, making Melody feel every ounce of pain she'd caused. But as she stared at the woman before her, smaller somehow, fragile, clearly fighting her own demons, all Beth felt was compassion.

She knew what it was like to survive something that broke you.

She knew what it took to rebuild.

Melody was trying, and that counted for something. Whatever drove Melody to act the way she did and make the choices that caused so much pain, it ran deep. And Melody hadn't come out unscathed. Physically, she suffered far worse than Beth, requiring surgery and a lengthy and painful recovery period.

So instead of letting this play out the way she'd fantasized, Beth spoke from her heart. "Thank you for saying that. I'm not going to pretend what you did didn't hurt, because it did. But holding onto anger will only hurt more." She took a breath. "I hope you find peace, Melody. No matter what happened between us, no one deserves what Demo did to you."

A tear tracked down Melody's makeup-free face. Then

another. She pressed a hand to her mouth, nodding, unable to speak. Had Beth ever seen the other woman without a full face of makeup? Melody nodded once as relief flickered across her face.

"Are you back in town permanently?" Beth asked.

"I'm not sure. Kinda taking it day by day." She shifted, wringing her hands. "Well, thank you for hearing me out. I'm gonna go."

In some ways, it broke Beth's heart to see the once-confident woman so subdued. She couldn't say she wished for the old Melody, but hopefully the woman would heal, come out stronger and kinder, and find happiness.

Melody turned and walked out the door, then down the sidewalk without looking back.

Saint exhaled slowly. "Didn't see that coming."

Beth shook her head. "Me neither." She was quiet for a moment, processing. "But I'm glad it did. I didn't realize how much I was still carrying until I let it go."

Saint pulled her close, pressing a kiss to her temple. "You're incredible, baby." He slid a hand along her spine. "Ready to go home?"

The mood wasn't erotically charged as before, but they'd be back there by the time they got home. Riding on his bike always amped her up.

"Home with you? Always."

The salon lights were dim when they finally locked the door.

Beth's feet ached, and her throat felt scratchy from hours of talking to customers, but her heart was full to bursting. This grand opening had been everything she'd hoped for and more. The upcoming weeks were packed with appointments and an inbox full of new client requests.

She took a moment to admire the storefront before turning to Saint, who waited for her with an outstretched hand.

"You feel safe here?" he asked as she took his hand.

"Very. There are about six hundred cameras on me all day, a crazy alarm system complete with a panic button in each room, and my necklace." She whispered the last word as though someone might overhear and snatch the tracking device. "Before I might have called it overkill, but now..." She shrugged.

"Yeah."

"I kinda like knowing you can see where I am at all times. That's probably not normal, is it? Maybe too codependent."

He smiled softly, the smile he only showed her. "Fuck normal."

She laughed, tears pricking her eyes. "Yeah, fuck normal. I'm happy, and that's all that matters."

"Happy looks good on you, baby."

"Looks good on you too. So does love."

He leaned down, kissed her lips, and whispered, "Good, because that's not going anywhere. I will love you for the rest of my fucking life."

Beth's eyes burned. "I will love you for the rest of my life," she whispered back. "You're my missing piece, Saint."

She'd heard people describe their hearts feeling full, but she'd never understood it until now. This wasn't just fullness, it was overflowing. Spilling out of her in the form of joyous tears she couldn't hold back.

Hand in hand, they strolled toward his bike, parked in a covered garage at the end of the street. The town had quieted as the sun began to set. Old-fashioned streetlamps lit their way. Beth felt something settle inside her.

As the daughter and now ol' lady of an outlaw biker, she'd never have a typical life. She'd always be surrounded by big, loud, wild, overprotective men, and the fierce women who loved them.

Once, she'd found it suffocating, and she'd run to Texas,

thinking distance would give her room to breathe. But she'd learned something in the months since coming home—she didn't need distance. She needed the right person standing beside her.

And she'd found him.

Whatever came next, she'd face it with her family by her side.

And her heart tucked securely in Saint's hands.

Thank you for reading LEGACY OF LEATHER AND LACE. If you enjoyed this book, please leave a review on Amazon or Goodreads.

Other Books by Lilly Atlas

M/F

No Prisoners MC

Hook: A No Prisoners Novella
Striker
Jester
Acer
Lucky
Snake

Trident Ink

Escapades

Hell's Handlers MC

Zach
Maverick
Jigsaw
Copper
Rocket
Little Jack
Joy
Screw
Viper
Thunder

* * *

Hell's Handlers Florida Chapter

Curly
Spec
Tracker
Frost
Jinx
Lock
Ty
Pulse

Hell's Handlers MC 2nd Generation

Legacy of Leather and Lace

Mayhem Makers Series

Solo Rider

Blue Collar Bensons

First Comes Loathe
Shock and Aww

M/M

The Duality of Swans

Bottle Service Boys

Shaken and Stirred
Heavy Pour

Audiobooks

Audio

* * *

Join Lilly's mailing list for a **FREE** No Prisoners short story.

www.lillyatlas.com

Facebook

Instagram

TikTok

Join my Facebook group, **Lilly's Ladies** for book previews, early cover reveals, contests and more!

About the Author

Lilly Atlas is an award-winning contemporary romance author. She's a proud Navy wife and mother of three spunky girls. Every time Lilly downloads a new eBook she expects her Kindle App to tell her it's exhausted and overworked, and to beg for some rest. Thankfully that hasn't happened yet so she can often be found absorbed in a good book.

www.ingramcontent.com/pod-product-compliance
Lightning Source LLC
LaVergne TN
LVHW020040110826
845155LV00029B/573

* 9 7 8 1 9 4 6 0 6 8 5 8 3 *